SKIRMISH:
A Major Event in Science Fiction!

"THE BIG FRONT YARD, THE THING IN THE STONE, AND DESERTION ALONE WOULD BE ENOUGH REASON TO BUY THE BOOK!"
(Analog)

"Ten stories from one of the most enduring science fiction authors. *Desertion* and *Huddling Place* are from Simak's renowned City Series, a doleful twilight-of-the-gods account of an earth inherited by sentient dogs. Also included are several stories nominated for SF awards, among them: *The Big Front Yard* about aliens who set up a galactic communications gateway in the frontyard of a Yankee trader and begin swapping ideas, and *All the Traps of Earth,* a typical Simak about a robot who acts as proxy for humanity struggling for the purpose of existence . . ."
(Advance *Booklist*)

"MIND-STRETCHING . . . ALWAYS IMAGINATIVE, AND HIGHLY PROFESSIONAL!"
(Anniston *Star*)

SKIRMISH

THE GREAT SHORT FICTION OF
CLIFFORD D. SIMAK

A BERKLEY BOOK
published by
BERKLEY PUBLISHING CORPORATION

Acknowledgements

Huddling Place, copyright © 1944, Street & Smith Publications Inc.; copyright renewed 1972 by Clifford D. Simak.

Desertion, copyright © 1944, Street & Smith Publications, Inc.; copyright renewed 1972 by Clifford D. Simak.

Skirmish, copyright © under title of "Bathe Your Bearings in Blood," 1950, Ziff-Davis Publishing Co.

Good Night, Mr. James, copyright © 1951, World Editions, Inc.

The Sitters, copyright © 1958, Galaxy Publishing Corporation.

The Big Front Yard, copyright © 1958, Street & Smith Publications, Inc.

All the Traps of Earth, copyright © 1960, Mercury Press, Inc.

The Thing in the Stone, copyright © 1970, Galaxy Publishing Corp.

The Autumn Land, copyright © 1971, Mercury Press, Inc.

The Ghost of a Model T, copyright © 1975, Robert Silverberg and Roger Elwood.

Contents

Foreword

The writing of the stories collected in this book was a fairly simple exercise. Now comes the hard part. To try to write about one's work, to make anything approaching an honest evaluation of it, is extremely difficult. No writer is a competent critic of his writing. He stands too close to it; he is not able to step back those necessary three paces to gain a proper perspective. In it he may see many nuances that he may think are there, but which no one else detects. Likewise he may be unable to see some facets of it that are plain to someone else.

If I were to attempt to say what kind of writer I have been, it might be simpler first to approach it by listing those elements of storytelling that I have not used extensively, if at all, in my tales.

I have not used the standard theme of alien invasion to any great extent. "Skirmish," one of the earlier tales included in this collection, is one of the few in which I did use the concept. The theme, in this instance, however, is somewhat off the beaten track usually followed by such stories. I console myself by pretending to believe that it may be a forerunner of another theme I developed slowly and cautiously through the years—the confrontation of machines and men.

My reluctance to use alien invasion is due to the feeling that we are not likely to be invaded and taken over. It would seem to me that by the time a race has achieved deep space capability it would have matured to a point where it would have no thought of dominating another intelligent species. Further than this, there should be no economic necessity of its doing so. By the time it was able to go into deep space, it must have arrived at an energy source which would not be based on planetary natural resources. It should also, by that time, have come to a management of population so that expanded living space would furnish no motive for the domination of other planets. By the same reasoning, it would not need the muscle power of enslaved planetary populations, but would have evolved machines that could perform all necessary work. Because of this thinking it seems to me that the whole idea of alien invasion is unrealistic.

I have used, however, time and time again, the concept of first contact between human and alien. To me this has always seemed an exciting prospect. I have often asked myself what I would do if a flying saucer, turning out to be a craft from outerspace, landed in my backyard and its occupants emerged. I think that I would go out to meet them, being very careful to make no move they could interpret as hostile, fairly confident that as two intelligent species we could find a common ground of acceptance.

Another concept I have never used, if I remember rightly, is space war, which seems even more unrealistic to me than alien invasion. Nor have I ventured into the so-called empire story, in which planetary dukedoms and imperial intrigues flourish. It has always seemed to me that this is no more than a transference of the costume novel into the future and I have no taste for it.

My concern has been with people, showing the impact made upon their lives by extraordinary situations or events. My physically courageous heroes have been few. Courage, if it is there, is more likely to be an intellectual courage. By and large, however, my people are quite ordinary folk, having in their makeups the same weaknesses and strengths as are found in most of us.

I remember an editor who, while he published the story, objected to one of my tales. "Cliff, the people in that story were losers," he said. "I like losers," I told him—and I do. I like them because they are much more interesting than winners. Like most people, I abhor the man who always wins; he makes the rest of us look so bad.

In my novel, *The Enchanted Pilgrimage,* the only out-and-out book-length fantasy I have written, I found myself recoiling from following the usual practice of using an iron-thewed, invincible swordsman as a protagonist. So I made my protagonist a mild-mannered, rather ineffectual scholar. To make up for it, I gave him a magic sword. Even so, he was fairly awkward in its handling. To me that ineffectual little scholar, having trouble getting his magic sword in and out of the scabbard, was much more believable and sympathetic, and thus easier to write about, than would have been the standard brawny-fisted swordsman, for whom I'd have felt slight empathy.

My writing has been largely colored by southwestern Wisconsin, a land of jumbled hills and deep ravines, where I spent my early years. Many of my tales have been placed in this locale, many of the kinds of people I knew there have been used as characters. I have felt slightly self-conscious at times for making such excessive use of the land I knew in boyhood, but to compensate, I have told myself that at least I stood on familiar ground. And very early in my writing efforts I learned that such pastoral scenes provided highly effective contrast to the alien beings and unearthly events I placed within the settings.

Also I must plead guilty to the excessive use of robots, not so much as robots, but as surrogate humans. Jenkins, in my *City* stories, is an extension of the human race, and what is more, of the more admirable characteristics of the race, the kind of being that a human should be, but very seldom is. The same is true of Richard Daniel, the robot who is the central character in "All The Traps of Earth," included in this collection.

So now, the hardest part: What is it I have done or tried to do? I find this a frustrating and somewhat embarrassing question to approach. I could do much better if I were writing of someone else's work; I can't trust my judgment on my own.

It seems to me that, overall, I have written in a quiet manner; there is little violence in my work. My focus has been on people, not on events. More often than not I have struck a hopeful note. I am much more concerned with the human heart and mind than I am in human accomplishment. I have, on occasions, tried to speak out for decency and compassion, for understanding, not only in the human, but in the cosmic sense. I have tried at times to place humans in perspective against the vastness of universal time and space. I have been concerned with where we, as a race, may be going, and what may be our purpose in the universal scheme—if we have a purpose. In general, I believe we do, and perhaps an important one.

This, then, by my own evaluation, must stand as my small contribution to science fiction. It is, of course, only a very small fraction of the whole. My fellow writers have made many larger and more significant contributions.

The collection stands as fairly representative of my work, showing in some degree the progression of my writing capability and my thinking. There are many other stories I would have liked to see included, but the sheer economics of book publishing has made this impossible. I am thankful that the publisher put no pressure on me to include, as well, some of the truly horrible examples of my earliest writing, tales I wrote while I was learning the craft.

"Desertion" and "Huddling Place" are from my *City* series. In my own mind I view this series as the watershed between my earlier apprentice writing and my emergence as a craftsman. From that time on, for the most part, I was in control of my writing efforts rather than floundering around, trying to find myself as a writer. There still was much that I had to learn about writing (and I suspect there still is) but by this time I had some sense of the direction I wanted to be headed and some idea of how to go about it.

"Skirmish" has a newspaperman as its protagonist. There was a time, being a newspaperman myself, when I tended to use newsmen as characters. In doing this, of course, I was still groping to find my proper role as a writer, trying to smooth the way by using central characters with whom I could feel some familiarity. I still use an occasional newsman as a character, but not as often nor for the same reason.

"The Big Front Yard" is a story of first contact with an alien race, perhaps the best example of this kind of story I have done. Placed against the background of a small town and its people, it employs the pastoral contrast I wrote of earlier in this foreword.

"All The Traps of Earth" has as its theme the struggle of a robot (an extension of humanity, of course) to find the true purpose of his existence. "Good Night, Mr. James" is a vicious story—so vicious that it is the only one of my stories adapted to television. It is so unlike anything I have ever written that at times I find myself wondering how I came to do it. Not that I am sorry I wrote it. I'm glad I did, but still I wonder how I came to.

The last four stories are the ones I really love, if a man can love his own work. In time, "The Sitters" precedes the other three. It is, I think, the most tender story I have ever written—and I feel no embarrassment at confessing its tenderness. It has within it that quality of compassion and of human need that I have often attempted but never made come off so well as I did in this case.

"The Thing in the Stone" is another alien contact story, placed in the depth of that Wisconsin hill country I knew as a boy. "The Ghost of a Model T" is fantasy, pure nostalgia dredged out of the early 1920s, based on my own remembrance of that fabulous era. I think that what I have to say in the story probably is closer to the spirit of the time than all the books that have been devoted to it.

"The Autumn Land" is one of the few stories I wrote on order. In 1971, when I was to be guest of honor at the 28th world science fiction convention in Boston, Edward Ferman asked me to write a story for *Fantasy* and *Science Fiction Magazine,* to be published in the issue concurrent with the convention. Ordinarily, a written-to-order story does not turn out well. The author is too conscious of time pressure and the particular needs of the magazine to do a decent job. This one, I think, did turn out well. The atmosphere of the tale is consistent with the theme, an accomplishment that at times is difficult to manage. No writer, of course, is ever completely satisfied with what he writes. He sees failures in it and often wishes he might have done it somewhat differently. But this, in my case, is less true of "The Autumn Land" than of any other tale I've written.

This is enough. Perhaps more than enough. I wondered, as I wrote it, if a foreword was needed. I suspect that only a few people read forewords or introductions. If you have, in fact, read this one, you now have more important things to read—the stories. I hope you find some liking for them. If you do, they have justified their writing.

Huddling Place

The drizzle sifted from the leaden skies, like smoke drifting through the bare-branched trees. It softened the hedges and hazed the outlines of the buildings and blotted out the distance. It glinted on the metallic skins of the silent robots and silvered the shoulders of the three humans listening to the intonations of the black-garbed man, who read from the book cupped between his hands.

"For I am the Resurrection and the Life—"

The moss-mellowed graven figure that reared above the door of the crypt seemed straining upward, every crystal of its yearning body reaching toward something that no one else could see. Straining as it had strained since that day of long ago when men had chipped it from the granite to adorn the family tomb with a symbolism that had pleased the first John J. Webster in the last years he held of life.

"And whosoever liveth and believeth in Me—"

Jerome A. Webster felt his son's fingers tighten on his arm, heard the muffled sobbing of his mother, saw the lines of robots standing rigid, heads bowed in respect to the master they had served. The master who now was going home—to the final home of all.

Numbly, Jerome A. Webster wondered if they understood—if they understood life and death—if they understood what it meant that Nelson F. Webster lay there in the casket, that a man with a book intoned words above him.

Nelson F. Webster, fourth of the line of Websters who had lived on these acres, had lived and died here, scarcely leaving, and now was going to his final rest in that place the first of them had prepared for the rest of them—for that long line of shadowy descendants who would live here and cherish the

1

things and the ways and the life that the first John J. Webster had established.

Jerome A. Webster felt his jaw muscles tighten, felt a little tremor run across his body. For a moment his eyes burned and the casket blurred in his sight and the words the man in black was saying were one with the wind that whispered in the pines standing sentinel for the dead. Within his brain remembrance marched—remembrance of a gray-haired man stalking the hills and fields, sniffing the breeze of an early morning, standing, legs braced, before the flaring fireplace with a glass of brandy in his hand.

Pride—the pride of land and life, and the humility and greatness that quiet living breeds within a man. Contentment of casual leisure and surety of purpose. Independence of assured security, comfort of familiar surroundings, freedom of broad acres.

Thomas Webster was joggling his elbow. "Father," he was whispering. "Father."

The service was over. The black-garbed man had closed his book. Six robots stepped forward, lifted the casket.

Slowly the three followed the casket into the crypt, stood silently as the robots slid it into its receptacle, closed the tiny door and affixed the plate that read:

NELSON F. WEBSTER
2034-2117

That was all. Just the name and dates. And that, Jerome A. Webster found himself thinking, was enough. There was nothing else that needed to be there. That was all those others had. The ones that called the family roll—starting with William Stevens, 1920–1999. Gramp Stevens, they had called him, Webster remembered. Father of the wife of that first John J. Webster, who was here himself—1951–2020. And after him his son, Charles F. Webster, 1980–2060. And his son, John J. II, 2004–2086. Webster could remember John J. II—a grandfather who had slept beside the fire with his pipe hanging from his mouth, eternally threatening to set his whiskers aflame.

Webster's eyes strayed to another plate. Mary Webster, the mother of the boy here at his side. And yet not a boy. He kept forgetting that Thomas was twenty now, in a week or so would be leaving for Mars, even as in his younger days he, too, had gone to Mars.

All here together, he told himself. The Websters and their wives and children. Here in death together as they had lived together, sleeping in the pride and security of bronze and the marble with the pines outside and the symbolic figure above the age-greened door.

The robots were waiting, standing silently, their task fulfilled.

His mother looked at him.

"You're head of the family now, my son," she told him.

He reached out and hugged her close against his side. Head of the family—what was left of it. Just the three of them now. His mother and his son. And his son would be leaving soon, going out to Mars. But he would come back. Come back with a wife, perhaps, and the family would go on. The family wouldn't stay at three. Most of the big house wouldn't stay closed off, as it now was closed off. There had been a time when it had rung with the life of a dozen units of the family, living in their separate apartments under one big roof. That time, he knew, would come again.

The three of them turned and left the crypt, took the path back to the house, looming like a huge gray shadow in the mist.

A fire blazed in the hearth and the book lay upon his desk. Jerome A. Webster reached out and picked it up, read the title once again:

"Martian Physiology, With Especial Reference to the Brain" by Jerome A. Webster, M.D.

Thick and authoritative—the work of a lifetime. Standing almost alone in its field. Based upon the data gathered during those five plague years on Mars—years when he had labored almost day and night with his fellow colleagues of the World Committee's medical commission, dispatched on an errand of mercy to the neighboring planet.

A tap sounded on the door.

"Come in," he called.

The door opened and a robot glided in.

"Your whiskey, sir."

"Thank you, Jenkins," Webster said.

"The minister, sir," said Jenkins, "has left."

"Oh, yes. I presume that you took care of him."

"I did, sir. Gave him the usual fee and offered him a drink. He refused the drink."

"That was a social error," Webster told him. "Ministers don't drink."

"I'm sorry, sir. I didn't know. He asked me to ask you to come to church sometime."

"Eh?"

"I told him, sir, that you never went anywhere."

"That was quite right, Jenkins," said Webster. "None of us ever go anywhere."

Jenkins headed for the door, stopped before he got there, turned around. "If I may say so, sir, that was a touching service at the crypt. Your father was a fine human, the finest ever was. The robots were saying the service was very fitting. Dignified like, sir. He would have liked it had he known."

"My father," said Webster, "would be even more pleased to hear you say that, Jenkins."

"Thank you, sir," said Jenkins, and went out.

Webster sat with the whiskey and the book and fire—felt the comfort of the well-known room close in about him, felt the refuge that was in it.

This was home. It had been home for the Websters since that day when the first John J. had come here and built the first unit of the sprawling house. John J. had chosen it because it had a trout stream, or so he always said. But it was something more than that. It must have been, Webster told himself, something more than that.

Or perhaps, at first, it had only been the trout stream. The trout stream and the trees and the meadows, the rocky ridge where the mist drifted in each morning from the river. Maybe the rest of it had grown, grown gradually through the years, through years of family association until the very soil was soaked with something that approached, but wasn't quite, tradition. Something that made each tree, each rock, each foot of soil a Webster tree or rock or clod of soil. It all belonged.

John J., the first John J., had come after the breakup of the cities, after men had forsaken, once and for all, the twentieth century huddling places, had broken free of the tribal instinct to stick together in one cave or in one clearing against a common foe or a common fear. An instinct that had become outmoded, for there were no fears or foes. Man revolting against the herd instinct economic and social conditions had impressed upon him in ages past. A new security and a new sufficiency had made it possible to break away.

The trend had started back in the twentieth century, more than two hundred years before, when men moved to country homes to get fresh air and elbow room and a graciousness in life that communal existence, in its strictest sense, never had given them.

And here was the end result. A quiet living. A peace that could only come with good things. The sort of life that men had yearned for years to have. A manorial existence, based on old family homes and leisurely acres, with atomics supplying power and robots in place of serfs.

Webster smiled at the fireplace with its blazing wood. That was an anachronism, but a good one—something that Man had brought forward from the caves. Useless, because atomic heating was better—but more pleasant. One couldn't sit and watch atomics and dream and build castles in the flames.

Even the crypt out there, where they had put his father that afternoon. That was family, too. All of a piece with the rest of it. The somber pride and leisured life and peace. In the old days the dead were buried in vast plots all together, stranger cheek by jowl with stranger—

He never goes anywhere.

That is what Jenkins had told the minister.

And that was right. For what need was there to go anywhere? It all was here. By simply twirling a dial one could talk face to face with anyone one wished, could go, by sense, if not in body, anywhere one wished. Could attend the theater or hear a concert or browse in a library halfway around the world. Could transact any business one might need to transact without rising from one's chair.

Webster drank the whiskey, then swung to the dialed machine beside his desk.

He spun dials from memory without resorting to the log. He knew where he was going.

His finger flipped a toggle and the room melted away—or seemed to melt. There was left the chair within which he sat, part of the desk, part of the machine itself and that was all.

The chair was on a hillside swept with golden grass and dotted with scraggly, wind-twisted trees, a hillside that straggled down to a lake nestling in the grip of purple mountain spurs. The spurs, darkened in long streaks with the bluish-green of distant pine, climbed in staggering stairs, melting into the blue-tinged snow-capped peaks that reared beyond and above them in jagged sawtoothed outline.

The wind talked harshly in the crouching trees and ripped the long grass in sudden gusts. The last rays of the sun struck fire from the distant peaks.

Solitude and grandeur, the long sweep of tumbled land, the cuddled lake, the knifelike shadows of the far-off ranges.

Webster sat easily in his chair, eyes squinting at the peaks.

A voice said almost at his shoulder: "May I come in?"

A soft, sibilant voice, wholly unhuman. But one that Webster knew.

He nodded his head. "By all means, Juwain."

He turned slightly and saw the elaborate crouching pedestal, the furry, soft-eyed figure of the Martian squatting on it. Other alien furniture loomed indistinctly beyond the pedestal, half guessed furniture from that dwelling out on Mars.

The Martian flipped a furry hand toward the mountain range.

"You love this," he said. "You can understand it. And I can understand how you understand it, but to me there is more terror than beauty in it. It is something we could never have on Mars."

Webster reached out a hand, but the Martian stopped him.

"Leave it on," he said. "I know why you came here. I would not have come at a time like this except I thought perhaps an old friend—"

"It is kind of you," said Webster. "I am glad that you have come."

"Your father," said Juwain, "was a great man. I remember how you used to talk to me of him, those years you spent on Mars. You said then you would come back sometime. Why is it you've never come?"

"Why," said Webster, "I just never—"

"Do not tell me," said the Martian. "I already know."

"My son," said Webster, "is going to Mars in a few days. I shall have him call on you."

"That would be a pleasure," said Juwain. "I shall be expecting him."

He stirred uneasily on the crouching pedestal. "Perhaps he carries on tradition."

"No," said Webster. "He is studying engineering. He never cared for surgery."

"He has a right," observed the Martian, "to follow the life that he has chosen. Still, one might be permitted to wish."

"One could," Webster agreed. "But that is over and done with. Perhaps he will be a great engineer. Space structure. Talks of ships out to the stars."

"Perhaps," suggested Juwain, "your family has done enough for medical science. You and your father—"

"And his father," said Webster, "before him."

"Your book," declared Juwain, "has put Mars in debt to you. It may focus more attention on Martian specialization. My people do not make good doctors. They have no background for it. Queer how the minds of races run. Queer that Mars never thought of medicine—literally never thought of it. Supplied the need with a cult of fatalism. While even in your early history, when men still lived in caves—"

"There are many things," said Webster, "that you thought of and we didn't. Things we wonder now how we ever missed. Abilities that you have developed and we do not have. Take your own specialty, philosophy. But different than ours. A science, while ours never was more than ordered fumbling. Yours an orderly, logical development of philosophy, workable, practical, applicable, an actual tool."

Juwain started to speak, hesitated, then went ahead. "I am near to something, something that may be new and startling. Something that will be a tool for you humans as well as for the Martians. I've worked on it for years, starting with certain mental concepts that first were suggested to me with arrival of the Earthmen. I have said nothing, for I could not be sure."

"And now," suggested Webster, "you are sure."

"Not quite," said Juwain. "Not positive. But almost."

They sat in silence, watching the mountains and the lake. A bird came and sat in one of the scraggly trees and sang.

Dark clouds piled up behind the mountain ranges and the snow-tipped peaks stood out like graven stone. The sun sank in a lake of crimson, hushed finally to the glow of a fire burned low.

A tap sounded from a door and Webster stirred in his chair, suddenly brought back to the reality of the study, of the chair beneath him.

Juwain was gone. The old philosopher had come and sat an hour of contemplation with his friend and then had quietly slipped away.

The rap came again.

Webster leaned forward, snapped the toggle and the mountains vanished; the room became a room again. Dusk filtered through the high windows and the fire was a rosy flicker in the ashes.

"Come in," said Webster.

Jenkins opened the door. "Dinner is served, sir," he said.

"Thank you," said Webster. He rose slowly from the chair.

"Your place, sir," said Jenkins, "is laid at the head of the table."

"Ah, yes," said Webster. "Thank you, Jenkins. Thank you very much, for reminding me."

Webster stood on the broad ramp of the space field and watched the shape that dwindled in the sky with faint flickering points of red lancing through the wintry sunlight.

For long minutes after the shape was gone he stood there, hands gripping the railing in front of him, eyes still staring up into the sky.

His lips moved and they said: "Good-by, son"; but there was no sound.

Slowly he came alive to his surroundings. Knew that people moved about the ramp, saw that the landing field seemed to stretch interminably to the far horizon, dotted here and there with hump-backed things that were waiting spaceships. Scooting tractors worked near one hangar, clearing away the last of the snowfall of the night before.

Webster shivered and thought that it was queer, for the noonday sun was warm. And shivered again.

Slowly he turned away from the railing and headed for the

administration building. And for one brain-wrenching moment he felt a sudden fear—an unreasonable and embarrassing fear of that stretch of concrete that formed the ramp. A fear that left him shaking mentally as he drove his feet toward the waiting door.

A man walked toward him, briefcase swinging in his hand and Webster, eyeing him, wished fervently that the man would not speak to him.

The man did not speak, passed him with scarcely a glance, and Webster felt relief.

If he were back home, Webster told himself, he would have finished lunch, would now be ready to lie down for his midday nap. The fire would be blazing on the hearth and the flicker of the flames would be reflected from the andirons. Jenkins would bring him a liqueur and would say a word or two—inconsequential conversation.

He hurried toward the door, quickening his step, anxious to get away from the bare-cold expanse of the massive ramp.

Funny how he had felt about Thomas. Natural, of course, that he should have hated to see him go. But entirely unnatural that he should, in those last few minutes, find such horror welling up within him. Horror of the trip through space, horror of the alien land of Mars—although Mars was scarcely alien any longer. For more than a century now Earthmen had known it, had fought it, lived with it; some of them had even grown to love it.

But it had only been utter will power that had prevented him, in those last few seconds before the ship had taken off, from running out into the field, shrieking for Thomas to come back, shrieking for him not to go.

And that, of course, never would have done. It would have been exhibitionism, disgraceful and humiliating—the sort of a thing a Webster could not do.

After all, he told himself, a trip to Mars was no great adventure, not any longer. There had been a day when it had been, but that day was gone forever. He, himself, in his earlier days had made a trip to Mars, had stayed there for five long years. That had been—he gasped when he thought of it—that had been almost thirty years ago.

The babble and hum of the lobby hit him in the face as the robot attendant opened the door for him, and in that babble ran a vein of something that was almost terror. For a moment he hesitated, then stepped inside. The door closed softly behind him.

He stayed close to the wall to keep out of people's way, headed for a chair in one corner. He sat down and huddled back, forcing his body deep into the cushions, watching the milling humanity that seethed out in the room.

Shrill people, hurrying people, people with strange, unneighborly faces. Strangers—every one of them. Not a face he knew. People going places. Heading out for the planets. Anxious to be off. Worried about last details. Rushing here and there.

Out of the crowd loomed a familiar face. Webster hunched forward.

"Jenkins!" he shouted, and then was sorry for the shout, although no one seemed to notice.

The robot moved toward him, stood before him.

"Tell Raymond," said Webster, "that I must return immediately. Tell him to bring the 'copter in front at once."

"I am sorry, sir," said Jenkins, "but we cannot leave at once. The mechanics found a flaw in the atomics chamber. They are installing a new one. It will take several hours."

"Surely," said Webster, impatiently, "that could wait until some other time."

"The mechanic said not, sir," Jenkins told him. "It might go at any minute. The entire charge of power—"

"Yes, yes," agreed Webster, "I suppose so."

He fidgeted with his hat. "I just remembered," he said, "something I must do. Something that must be done at once. I must get home. I can't wait several hours."

He hitched forward to the edge of the chair, eyes staring at the milling crowd.

Faces—faces—

"Perhaps you could televise," suggested Jenkins. "One of the robots might be able to do it. There is a booth—"

"Wait, Jenkins," said Webster. He hesitated a moment. "There is nothing to do back home. Nothing at all. But I must get there. I can't stay here. If I have to, I'll go crazy. I was frightened out there on the ramp. I'm bewildered and confused here. I have a feeling—a strange, terrible feeling. Jenkins, I—"

"I understand, sir," said Jenkins. "Your father had it, too."

Webster gasped. "My father?"

"Yes, sir, that is why he never went anywhere. He was about your age, sir, when he found it out. He tried to make a trip to Europe and he couldn't. He got halfway there and turned back. He had a name for it."

Webster sat in stricken silence.

"A name for it," he finally said. "Of course there's a name for it. My father had it. My grandfather—did he have it, too?"

"I wouldn't know that, sir," said Jenkins. "I wasn't created until after your grandfather was an elderly man. But he may have. He never went anywhere, either."

"You understand, then," said Webster. "You know how it is. I feel like I'm going to be sick—physically ill. See if you can charter a 'copter—anything, just so we get home."

"Yes, sir," said Jenkins.

He started off and Webster called him back.

"Jenkins, does anyone else know about this? Anyone—"

"No, sir," said Jenkins. "Your father never mentioned it and I felt, somehow, that he wouldn't wish me to."

"Thank you, Jenkins," said Webster.

Webster huddled back into his chair again, feeling desolate and alone and misplaced. Alone in a humming lobby that pulsed with life—a loneliness that tore at him, that left him limp and weak.

Homesickness. Downright, shameful homesickness, he told himself. Something that boys are supposed to feel when they first leave home, when they first go out to meet the world.

There was a fancy word for it—agoraphobia, the morbid dread of being in the midst of open spaces—from the Greek root for the fear—literally, of the market place.

If he crossed the room to the television booth, he could put in a call, talk with his mother or one of the robots—or, better yet, just sit and look at the place until Jenkins came for him.

He started to rise, then sank back in the chair again. It was no dice. Just talking to someone or looking in on the place wasn't being there. He couldn't smell the pines in the wintry air, or hear familiar snow crunch on the walk beneath his feet or reach out a hand and touch one of the massive oaks that grew along the path. He couldn't feel the heat of the fire or sense the sure, deft touch of belonging, of being one with a tract of ground and the things upon it.

And yet—perhaps it would help. Not much, maybe, but some. He started to rise from the chair again and froze. The few short steps to the booth held terror, a terrible, overwhelming terror. If he crossed them, he would have to run. Run to escape the watching eyes, the unfamiliar sounds, the agonizing nearness of strange faces.

Abruptly he sat down.

A woman's shrill voice cut across the lobby and he shrank away from it. He felt terrible. He felt like hell. He wished Jenkins would get a hustle on.

The first breath of spring came through the window, filling the study with the promise of melting snows, of coming leaves and flowers, of north-bound wedges of waterfowl streaming through the blue, of trout that lurked in pools waiting for the fly.

Webster lifted his eyes from the sheaf of papers on his desk, sniffed the breeze, felt the cool whisper of it on his cheek. His hand reached out for the brandy glass, found it empty, and put it back.

He bent back above the papers once again, picked up a pencil and crossed out a word.

Critically, he read the final paragraphs:

The fact that of the two hundred fifty men who were invited to visit me, presumably on missions of more than ordinary importance, only three were able to come, does not necessarily prove that all but those three are victims of agoraphobia. Some may have had legitimate reasons for being unable to accept my invitation. But it does indicate a growing unwillingness of men living under the mode of Earth existence set up following the breakup of the cities to move from familiar places, a deepening instinct to stay among the scenes and possessions which in their mind have become associated with contentment and graciousness of life.

What the result of such a trend will be, no one can clearly indicate since it applies to only a small portion of Earth's population. Among the larger families economic pressure forces some of the sons to seek their fortunes either in other parts of the Earth or on one of the other planets. Many others deliberately seek adventure and opportunity in space while still others become associated with professions or trades which make a sedentary existence impossible.

He flipped the page over, went on to the last one.

It was a good paper, he knew, but it could not be published, not just yet. Perhaps after he had died. No one, so far as he could determine, had ever so much as realized the trend, had taken as matter of course the fact that men seldom left their homes. Why, after all, should they leave their homes?

Certain dangers may be recognized in—

The televisor muttered at his elbow and he reached out to flip the toggle.

The room faded and he was face to face with a man who sat behind a desk, almost as if he sat on the opposite side of Webster's desk. A gray-haired man with sad eyes behind heavy lenses.

For a moment Webster stared, memory tugging at him.

"Could it be—" he asked and the man smiled gravely.

"I have changed," he said. "So have you. My name is Clayborne. Remember? The Martian medical commission—"

"Clayborne! I'd often thought of you. You stayed on Mars."

Clayborne nodded. "I've read your book, doctor. It is a real contribution. I've often thought one should be written, wanted to myself, but I didn't have the time. Just as well I didn't. You did a better job. Especially on the brain."

"The Martian brain," Webster told him, "always intrigued me. Certain peculiarities. I'm afraid I spent more of those five years taking notes on it than I should have. There was other work to do."

"A good thing you did," said Clayborne. "That's why I'm calling you now. I have a patient—a brain operation. Only you can handle it."

Webster gasped, his hands trembling. "You'll bring him here?"

Clayborne shook his head. "He cannot be moved. You know him, I believe. Juwain, the philosopher."

"Juwain!" said Webster. "He's one of my best friends. We talked together just a couple of days ago."

"The attack was sudden," said Clayborne. "He's been asking for you."

Webster was silent and cold—cold with a chill that crept upon him from some unguessed place. Cold that sent perspiration out upon his forehead, that knotted his fists.

"If you start immediately," said Clayborne, "you can be here on time. I've already arranged with the World Committee to have a ship at your disposal instantly. The utmost speed is necessary."

"But," said Webster, "but . . . I cannot come."

"You can't come!"

"It's impossible," said Webster. "I doubt in any case that I am needed. Surely, you yourself—"

"I can't," said Clayborne. "No one can but you. No one else has the knowledge. You hold Juwain's life in your hands. If you come, he lives. If you don't, he dies."

"I can't go into space," said Webster.

"Anyone can go into space," snapped Clayborne. "It's not like it used to be. Conditioning of any sort desired is available."

"But you don't understand," pleaded Webster. "You—"

"No, I don't," said Clayborne. "Frankly, I don't. That anyone should refuse to save the life of his friend—"

The two men stared at one another for a long moment, neither speaking.

"I shall tell the committee to send the ship straight to your home," said Clayborne finally. "I hope by that time you will see your way clear to come."

Clayborne faded and the wall came into view again—the wall and books, the fireplace and the paintings, the well-loved furniture, the promise of spring that came through the open window.

Webster sat frozen in his chair, staring at the wall in front of him.

Juwain, the furry, wrinkled face, the sibilant whisper, the friendliness and understanding that was his. Juwain, grasping the stuff that dreams are made of and shaping them into logic, into rules of life and conduct. Juwain using philosophy as a tool, as a science, as a stepping stone to better living.

Webster dropped his face into his hands and fought the agony that welled up within him.

Clayborne had not even understood. One could not expect him to understand since there was no way for him to know. And even knowing, would he understand? Even he, Webster, would not have understood it in someone else until he had discovered it in himself—the terrible fear of leaving his own fire, his own land, his own possessions, the little symbolisms that he had erected. And yet, not he, himself, alone, but those other Websters as well. Starting with the first John J. Men and women who had set up a cult of life, a tradition of behavior.

He, Jerome A. Webster, had gone to Mars when he was a young man, and had not felt or suspected the psychological poison that ran through his veins. Even as Thomas a few months ago had gone to Mars. But thirty years of quiet life here in the retreat that the Websters called a home had brought it forth, had developed it without his even knowing it. There had, in fact, been no opportunity to know it.

It was clear how it had developed—clear as crystal now. Habit and mental pattern and a happiness association with certain things—things that had no actual value in themselves, but had been assigned a value, a definite, concrete value by one family through five generations.

No wonder other places seemed alien, no wonder other horizons held a hint of horror in their sweep.

And there was nothing one could do about it—nothing, that is, unless one cut down every tree and burned the house and changed the course of waterways. Even that might not do it—even that—

The televisor purred and Webster lifted his head from his hands, reached out and thumbed the tumbler.

The room became a flare of white, but there was no image. A voice said: "Secret call. Secret call."

Webster slid back a panel in the machine, spun a pair of dials, heard the hum of power surge into a screen that blocked out the room.

"Secrecy established," he said.

The white flare snapped out and a man sat across the desk

from him. A man he had seen many times before in televised addresses, in his daily paper.

Henderson, president of the World Committee.

"I have had a call from Clayborne," said Henderson.

Webster nodded without speaking.

"He tells me you refuse to go to Mars."

"I have not refused," said Webster. "When Clayborne cut off the question was left open. I had told him it was impossible for me to go, but he had rejected that, did not seem to understand."

"Webster, you must go," said Henderson. "You are the only man with the necessary knowledge of the Martian brain to perform this operation. If it were a simple operation, perhaps someone else could do it. But not one such as this."

"That may be true," said Webster, "but—"

"It's not just a question of saving a life," said Henderson. "Even the life of so distinguished a personage as Juwain. It involves even more than that. Juwain is a friend of yours. Perhaps he hinted of something he has found."

"Yes," said Webster. "Yes, he did. A new concept of philosophy."

"A concept," declared Henderson, "that we cannot do without. A concept that will remake the solar system, that will put mankind ahead a hundred thousand years in the space of two generations. A new direction of purpose that will aim toward a goal we heretofore had not suspected, had not even known existed. A brand new truth, you see. One that never before had occurred to anyone."

Webster's hands gripped the edge of the desk until his knuckles stood out white.

"If Juwain dies," said Henderson, "that concept dies with him. May be lost forever."

"I'll try," said Webster. "I'll try—"

Henderson's eyes were hard. "Is that the best that you can do?"

"That is the best," said Webster.

"But, man, you must have a reason! Some explanation."

"None," said Webster, "that I would care to give."

Deliberately he reached out and flipped up the switch.

Webster sat at the desk and held his hands in front of him, staring at them. Hands that had skill, held knowledge. Hands that could save a life if he could get them to Mars. Hands that could save for the solar system, for mankind, for the Martians an idea—a new idea—that would advance them a hundred thousand years in the next two generations.

But hands chained by a phobia that grew out of this quiet life. Decadence—a strangely beautiful—and deadly—decadence.

Man had forsaken the teeming cities, the huddling places, two hundred years ago. He had done with the old foes and the ancient fears that kept him around the common campfire, had left behind the hobgoblins that had walked with him from the caves.

And yet—and yet—

Here was another huddling place. Not a huddling place for one's body, but one's mind. A psychological campfire that still held a man within the circle of its light.

Still, Webster knew, he must leave that fire. As the men had done with the cities two centuries before, he must walk off and leave it. And he must not look back.

He had to go to Mars—or at least start for Mars. There was no question there, at all. He had to go.

Whether he would survive the trip, whether he could perform the operation once he had arrived, he did not know. He wondered vaguely, whether agoraphobia could be fatal. In its most exaggerated form, he supposed it could.

He reached out a hand to ring, then hesitated. No use having Jenkins pack. He would do it himself—something to keep him busy until the ship arrived.

From the top shelf of the wardrobe in the bedroom, he took down a bag and saw that it was dusty. He blew on it, but the dust still clung. It had been there for too many years.

As he packed, the room argued with him, talked in that mute tongue with which inanimate but familiar things may converse with a man.

"You can't go," said the room. "You can't go off and leave me."

And Webster argued back, half pleading, half explanatory. "I have to go. Can't you understand? It's a friend, an old friend. I will be coming back."

Packing done, Webster returned to the study, slumped into his chair.

He must go and yet he couldn't go. But when the ship

arrived, when the time had come, he knew that he would walk out of the house and toward the waiting ship.

He steeled his mind to that, tried to set it in a rigid pattern, tried to blank out everything but the thought that he was leaving.

Things in the room intruded on his brain, as if they were part of a conspiracy to keep him there. Things that he saw as if he were seeing them for the first time. Old, remembered things that suddenly were new. The chronometer that showed both Earthian and Martian time, the days of the month, the phases of the moon. The picture of his dead wife on the desk. The trophy he had won at prep school. The framed short snorter bill that had cost him ten bucks on his trip to Mars.

He stared at them, half unwilling at first, then eagerly, storing up the memory of them in his brain. Seeing them as separate components of a room he had accepted all these years as a finished whole, never realizing what a multitude of things went to make it up.

Dusk was falling, the dusk of early spring, a dusk that smelled of early pussy willows.

The ship should have arrived long ago. He caught himself listening for it, even as he realized that he would not hear it. A ship, driven by atomic motors, was silent except when it gathered speed. Landing and taking off, it floated like thistledown, with not a murmur in it.

It would be here soon. It would have to be here soon or he could never go. Much longer to wait, he knew, and his high-keyed resolution would crumble like a mound of dust in beating rain. Not much longer could he hold his purpose against the pleading of the room, against the flicker of the fire, against the murmur of the land where five generations of Websters had lived their lives and died.

He shut his eyes and fought down the chill that crept across his body. He couldn't let it get him now, he told himself. He had to stick it out. When the ship arrived he still must be able to get up and walk out the door to the waiting port.

A tap came on the door.

"Come in," Webster called.

It was Jenkins, the light from the fireplace flickering on his shining metal hide.

"Had you called earlier, sir?" he asked.

Webster shook his head.

"I was afraid you might have," Jenkins explained, "and wondered why I didn't come. There was a most extraordinary occurrence, sir. Two men came with a ship and said they wanted you to go to Mars."

"They are here," said Webster. "Why didn't you call me?"

He struggled to his feet.

"I didn't think, sir," said Jenkins, "that you would want to be bothered. It was so preposterous. I finally made them understand you could not possibly want to go to Mars."

Webster stiffened, felt chill fear gripping at his heart. Hands groping for the edge of the desk, he sat down in the chair, sensed the walls of the room closing in about him, a trap that would never let him go.

Desertion

Four men, two by two, had gone into the howling maelstrom that was Jupiter and had not returned. They had walked into the keening gale—or rather, they had loped, bellies low against the ground, wet sides gleaming in the rain.

For they did not go in the shape of men.

Now the fifth man stood before the desk of Kent Fowler, head of Dome No. 3, Jovian Survey Commission.

Under Fowler's desk, old Towser scratched a flea, then settled down to sleep again.

Harold Allen, Fowler saw with a sudden pang, was young—too young. He had the easy confidence of youth, the face of one who never had known fear. And that was strange. For men in the domes of Jupiter did know fear—fear and humility. It was hard for Man to reconcile his puny self with the mighty forces of the monstrous planet.

"You understand," said Fowler, "that you need not do this. You understand that you need not go."

It was formula, of course. The other four had been told the same thing, but they had gone. This fifth one, Fowler knew, would go as well. But suddenly he felt a dull hope stir within him that Allen wouldn't go.

"When do I start?" asked Allen.

There had been a time when Fowler might have taken quiet pride in that answer, but not now. He frowned briefly.

"Within the hour," he said.

Allen stood waiting, quietly.

"Four other men have gone out and have not returned," said Fowler. "You know that, of course. We want you to return. We don't want you going off on any heroic rescue expedition. The main thing, the only thing, is that you come back, that you prove man can live in a Jovian form. Go to the first survey stake, no farther, then come back. Don't take any chances. Don't investigate anything. Just come back."

Allen nodded. "I understand all that."

"Miss Stanley will operate the converter," Fowler went on. "You need have no fear on that particular score. The other men were converted without mishap. They left the converter in apparently perfect condition. You will be in thoroughly competent hands. Miss Stanley is the best qualified conversion operator in the Solar System. She has had experience on most of the other planets. That is why she's here."

Allen grinned at the woman and Fowler saw something flicker across Miss Stanley's face—something that might have been pity, or rage—or just plain fear. But it was gone again and she was smiling back at the youth who stood before the desk. Smiling in that prim, school-teacherish way she had of smiling, almost as if she hated herself for doing it.

"I shall be looking forward," said Allen, "to my conversion."

And the way he said it, he made it all a joke, a vast, ironic joke.

But it was no joke.

It was serious business, deadly serious. Upon these tests, Fowler knew, depended the fate of men on Jupiter. If the tests succeeded, the resources of the giant planet would be thrown open. Man would take over Jupiter as he already had taken over the other smaller planets. And if they failed—

If they failed, Man would continue to be chained and hampered by the terrific pressure, the greater force of gravity, the weird chemistry of the planet. He would continue to be shut within the domes, unable to set actual foot upon the planet, unable to see it with direct, unaided vision, forced to rely upon the awkward tractors and the televisor, forced to work with clumsy tools and mechanisms or through the medium of robots that themselves were clumsy.

For Man, unprotected and in his natural form, would be blotted out by Jupiter's terrific pressure of fifteen thousand pounds per square inch, pressure that made terrestrial sea bottoms seem a vacuum by comparison.

Even the strongest metal Earthmen could devise couldn't

exist under pressure such as that, under the pressure and the alkaline rains that forever swept the planet. It grew brittle and flaky, crumbling like clay, or it ran away in little streams and puddles of ammonia salts. Only by stepping up the toughness and strength of that metal, by increasing its electronic tension, could it be made to withstand the weight of thousands of miles of swirling, choking gases that made up the atmosphere. And even when that was done, everything had to be coated with tough quartz to keep away the rain—the liquid ammonia that fell as bitter rain.

Fowler sat listening to the engines in the sub-floor of the dome—engines that ran on endlessly, the dome never quiet of them. They had to run and keep on running, for if they stopped the power flowing into the metal walls of the dome would stop, the electronic tension would ease up and that would be the end of everything.

Towser roused himself under Fowler's desk and scratched another flea, his leg thumping hard against the floor.

"Is there anything else?" asked Allen.

Fowler shook his head. "Perhaps there's something you want to do," he said. "Perhaps you—"

He had meant to say write a letter and he was glad he caught himself quick enough so he didn't say it.

Allen looked at his watch. "I'll be there on time," he said. He swung around and headed for the door.

Fowler knew Miss Stanley was watching him and he didn't want to turn and meet her eyes. He fumbled with a sheaf of papers on the desk before him.

"How long are you going to keep this up?" asked Miss Stanley and she bit off each word with a vicious snap.

He swung around in his chair and faced her then. Her lips were drawn into a straight, thin line, her hair seemed skinned back from her forehead tighter than ever, giving her face that queer, almost startling death-mask quality.

He tried to make his voice cool and level. "As long as there's any need of it," he said. "As long as there's any hope."

"You're going to keep on sentencing them to death," she said. "You're going to keep marching them out face to face with Jupiter. You're going to sit in here safe and comfortable and send them out to die."

"There is no room for sentimentality, Miss Stanley," Fowler said, trying to keep the note of anger from his voice. "You know as well as I do why we're doing this. You realize that Man in his own form simply cannot cope with Jupiter. The only answer is to turn men into the sort of things that can cope with it. We've done it on the other planets.

"If a few men die, but we finally suceed, the price is small. Through the ages men have thrown away their lives on foolish things, for foolish reasons. Why should we hesitate, then, at a little death in a thing as great as this?"

Miss Stanley sat stiff and straight, hands folded in her lap, the lights shining on her graying hair and Fowler, watching her, tried to imagine what she might feel, what she might be thinking. He wasn't exactly afraid of her, but he didn't feel quite comfortable when she was around. Those sharp blue eyes saw too much, her hands looked far too competent. She should be somebody's Aunt sitting in a rocking chair with her knitting needles. But she wasn't. She was the top-notch conversion unit operator in the Solar System and she didn't like the way he was doing things.

"There is something wrong, Mr. Fowler," she declared.

"Precisely," agreed Fowler. "That's why I'm sending young Allen out alone. He may find out what it is."

"And if he doesn't?"

"I'll send someone else."

She rose slowly from her chair, started toward the door, then stopped before his desk.

"Some day," she said, "you will be a great man. You never let a chance go by. This is your chance. You knew it was when this dome was picked for the tests. If you put it through, you'll go up a notch or two. No matter how many men may die, you'll go up a notch or two."

"Miss Stanley," he said and his voice was curt, "young Allen is going out soon. Please be sure that your machine—"

"My machine," she told him, icily, "is not to blame. It operates along the co-ordinates the biologists set up."

He sat hunched at his desk, listening to her footsteps go down the corridor.

What she said was true, of course. The biologists had set up the co-ordinates. But the biologists could be wrong. Just a hairbreadth of difference, one iota of digression and the converter would be sending out something that wasn't the thing they meant to send. A mutant that might crack up, go haywire, come unstuck under some condition or stress of circumstance wholly unsuspected.

For Man didn't know much about what was going on outside. Only what his instruments told him was going on. And the samplings of those happenings furnished by those instruments and mechanisms had been no more than samplings, for Jupiter was unbelievably large and the domes were very few.

Even the work of the biologists in getting the data on the Lopers, apparently the highest form of Jovian life, had involved more than three years of intensive study and after that two years of checking to make sure. Work that could have been done on Earth in a week or two. But work that, in this case, couldn't be done on Earth at all, for one couldn't take a Jovian life form to Earth. The pressure here on Jupiter couldn't be duplicated outside of Jupiter and at Earth pressure and temperature the Lopers would simply have disappeared in a puff of gas.

Yet it was work that had to be done if Man ever hoped to go about Jupiter in the life form of the Lopers. For before the converter could change a man to another life form, every detailed physical characteristic of that life form must be known—surely and positively, with no chance of mistake.

Allen did not come back.

The tractors, combing the nearby terrain, found no trace of him, unless the skulking thing reported by one of the drivers had been the missing Earthman in Loper form.

The biologists sneered their most accomplished academic sneers when Fowler suggested the co-ordinates might be wrong. Carefully they pointed out, the co-ordinates worked. When a man was put into the converter and the switch was thrown, the man became a Loper. He left the machine and moved away, out of sight, into the soupy atmosphere.

Some quirk, Fowler had suggested; some tiny deviation from the thing a Loper should be, some minor defect. If there were, the biologists said, it would take years to find it.

And Fowler knew that they were right.

So there were five men now instead of four and Harold

Allen had walked out into Jupiter for nothing at all. It was as if he'd never gone so far as knowledge was concerned.

Fowler reached across his desk and picked up the personnel file, a thin sheaf of paper neatly clipped together. It was a thing he dreaded but a thing he had to do. Somehow the reason for these strange disappearances must be found. And there was no other way than to send out more men.

He sat for a moment listening to the howling of the wind above the dome, the everlasting thundering gale that swept across the planet in boiling, twisting wrath.

Was there some threat out there, he asked himself? Some danger they did not know about? Something that lay in wait and gobbled up the Lopers, making no distinction between Lopers that were *bona fide* and Lopers that were men? To the gobblers, of course, it would make no difference.

Or had there been a basic fault in selecting the Lopers as the type of life best fitted for existence on the surface of the planet? The evident intelligence of the Lopers, he knew, had been one factor in that determination. For if the thing Man became did not have capacity for intelligence, Man could not for long retain his own intelligence in such a guise.

Had the biologists let that one factor weigh too heavily, using it to offset some other factor that might be unsatisfactory, even disastrous? It didn't seem likely. Stiffnecked as they might be, the biologists knew their business.

Or was the whole thing impossible, doomed from the very start? Conversion to other life forms had worked on other planets, but that did not necessarily mean it would work on Jupiter. Perhaps Man's intelligence could not function correctly through the sensory apparatus provided Jovian life. Perhaps the Lopers were so alien there was no common ground for human knowledge and the Jovian conception of existence to meet and work together.

Or the fault might lie with Man, be inherent with the race. Some mental aberration which, coupled with what they found outside, wouldn't let them come back. Although it might not be an aberration, not in the human sense. Perhaps just one ordinary human mental trait, accepted as commonplace on Earth, would be so violently at odds with Jovian existence that it would blast human sanity.

• • •

Claws rattled and clicked down the corridor. Listening to them, Fowler smiled wanly. It was Towser coming back from the kitchen, where he had gone to see his friend, the cook.

Towser came into the room, carrying a bone. He wagged his tail at Fowler and flopped down beside the desk, bone between his paws. For a long moment his rheumy old eyes regarded his master and Fowler reached down a hand to ruffle a ragged ear.

"You still like me, Towser?" Fowler asked and Towser thumped his tail.

"You're the only one," said Fowler.

He straightened and swung back to the desk. His hand reached out and picked up the file.

Bennett? Bennett had a girl waiting for him back on Earth.

Andrews? Andrews was planning on going back to Mars Tech just as soon as he earned enough to see him through a year.

Olson? Olson was nearing pension age. All the time telling the boys how he was going to settle down and grow roses.

Carefully, Fowler laid the file back on the desk.

Sentencing men to death. Miss Stanley had said that, her pale lips scarcely moving in her parchment face. Marching men out to die while he, Fowler, sat here safe and comfortable.

They were saying it all through the dome, no doubt, especially since Allen had failed to return. They wouldn't say it to his face, of course. Even the man or men he called before this desk and told they were the next to go, wouldn't say it to him.

But he would see it in their eyes.

He picked up the file again. Bennett, Andrews, Olson. There were others, but there was no use in going on.

Kent Fowler knew that he couldn't do it, couldn't face them, couldn't send more men out to die.

He leaned forward and flipped up the toggle on the intercommunicator.

"Yes, Mr. Fowler."

"Miss Stanley, please."

He waited for Miss Stanley, listening to Towser chewing halfheartedly on the bone. Towser's teeth were getting bad.

"Miss Stanley," said Miss Stanley's voice.

"Just wanted to tell you, Miss Stanley, to get ready for two more."

"Aren't you afraid," asked Miss Stanley, "that you'll run out of them? Sending out one at a time, they'd last longer, give you twice the satisfaction."

"One of them," said Fowler, "will be a dog."

"A dog!"

"Yes, Towser."

He heard the quick, cold rage that iced her voice. "Your own dog! He's been with you all these years—"

"That's the point," said Fowler. "Towser would be unhappy if I left him behind."

It was not the Jupiter he had known through the televisor. He had expected it to be different, but not like this. He had expected a hell of ammonia rain and stinking fumes and the deafening, thundering tumult of the storm. He had expected swirling clouds and fog and the snarling flicker of monstrous thunderbolts.

He had not expected the lashing downpour would be reduced to drifting purple mist that moved like fleeing shadows over a red and purple sward. He had not even guessed the snaking bolts of lightning would be flares of pure ecstasy across a painted sky.

Waiting for Towser, Fowler flexed the muscles of his body, amazed at the smooth, sleek strength he found. Not a bad body, he decided, and grimaced at remembering how he had pitied the Lopers when he glimpsed them through the television screen.

For it had been hard to imagine a living organism based upon ammonia and hydrogen rather than upon water and oxygen, hard to believe that such a form of life could know the same quick thrill of life that humankind could know. Hard to conceive of life out in the soupy maelstrom that was Jupiter, not knowing, of course, that through Jovian eyes it was no soupy maelstrom at all.

The wind brushed against him with what seemed gentle fingers and he remembered with a start that by Earth standards the wind was a roaring gale, a two-hundred-mile an hour howler laden with deadly gases.

Pleasant scents seeped into his body. And yet scarcely

scents, for it was not the sense of smell as he remembered it. It was as if his whole being was soaking up the sensation of lavender—and yet not lavender. It was something, he knew, for which he had no word, undoubtedly the first of many enigmas in terminology. For the words he knew, the thought symbols that served him as an Earthman would not serve him as a Jovian.

The lock in the side of the dome opened and Towser came tumbling out—at least he thought it must be Towser.

He started to call to the dog, his mind shaping the words he meant to say. But he couldn't say them. There was no way to say them. He had nothing to say them with.

For a moment his mind swirled in muddy terror, a blind fear that eddied in little puffs of panic through his brain.

How did Jovians talk? How—

Suddenly he was aware of Towser, intensely aware of the bumbling, eager friendliness of the shaggy animal that had followed him from Earth to many planets. As if the thing that was Towser had reached out and for a moment sat within his brain.

And out of the bubbling welcome that he sensed, came words.

"Hiya, pal."

Not words really, better than words. Thought symbols in his brain, communicated thought symbols that had shades of meaning words could never have.

"Hiya, Towser," he said.

"I feel good," said Towser. "Like I was a pup. Lately I've been feeling pretty punk. Legs stiffening up on me and teeth wearing down to almost nothing. Hard to mumble a bone with teeth like that. Besides, the fleas give me hell. Used to be I never paid much attention to them. A couple of fleas more or less never meant much in my early days."

"But . . . but—" Fowler's thoughts tumbled awkwardly. "You're talking to me!"

"Sure thing," said Towser. "I always talked to you, but you couldn't hear me. I tried to say things to you, but I couldn't make the grade."

"I understood you sometimes," Fowler said.

"Not very well," said Towser. "You knew when I wanted food and when I wanted a drink and when I wanted out, but that's about all you ever managed."

"I'm sorry," Fowler said.

"Forget it," Towser told him. "I'll race you to the cliff."

For the first time, Fowler saw the cliff, apparently many miles away, but with a strange crystalline beauty that sparkled in the shadow of the many-colored clouds.

Fowler hesitated. "It's a long way—"

"Ah, come on," said Towser and even as he said it he started for the cliff.

Fowler followed, testing his legs, testing the strength in that new body of his, a bit doubtful at first, amazed a moment later, then running with a sheer joyousness that was one with the red and purple sward, with the drifting smoke of the rain across the land.

As he ran the consciousness of music came to him, a music that beat into his body, that surged throughout his being, that lifted him on wings of silver speed. Music like bells might make from some steeple on a sunny, springtime hill.

As the cliff drew nearer the music deepened and filled the universe with a spray of magic sound. And he knew the music came from the tumbling waterfall that feathered down the face of the shining cliff.

Only, he knew, it was no waterfall, but an ammonia-fall and the cliff was white because it was oxygen, solidified.

He skidded to a stop beside Towser where the waterfall broke into a glittering rainbow of many hundred colors. Literally many hundred, for here, he saw, was no shading of one primary to another as human beings saw, but a clearcut selectivity that broke the prism down to its last ultimate classification.

"The music," said Towser.

"Yes, what about it?"

"The music," said Towser, "is vibrations. Vibrations of water falling."

"But Towser, you don't know about vibrations."

"Yes, I do," contended Towser. "It just popped into my head."

Fowler gulped mentally. "Just popped!"

And suddenly, within his own head, he held a formula— the formula for a process that would make metal to withstand the pressure of Jupiter.

He stared, astounded, at the waterfall and swiftly his mind

took the many colors and placed them in their exact sequence in the spectrum. Just like that. Just out of blue sky. Out of nothing, for he knew nothing either of metals or of colors.

"Towser," he cried. "Towser, something's happening to us!"

"Yeah, I know," said Towser.

"It's our brains," said Fowler. "We're using them, all of them, down to the last hidden corner. Using them to figure out things we should have known all the time. Maybe the brains of Earth things naturally are slow and foggy. Maybe we are the morons of the universe. Maybe we are fixed so we have to do things the hard way."

And, in the new sharp clarity of thought that seemed to grip him, he knew that it would not only be the matter of colors in a waterfall or metals that would resist the pressure of Jupiter. He sensed other things, things not yet quite clear. A vague whispering that hinted of greater things, of mysteries beyond the pale of human thought, beyond even the pale of human imagination. Mysteries, fact, logic built on reasoning. Things that any brain should know if it used all its reasoning power.

"We're still mostly Earth," he said. "We're just beginning to learn a few of the things we are to know—a few of the things that were kept from us as human beings, perhaps because we were human beings. Because our human bodies were poor bodies. Poorly equipped in certain senses that one has to have to know. Perhaps even lacking in certain senses that are necessary to true knowledge."

He stared back at the dome, a tiny black thing dwarfed by the distance.

Back there were men who couldn't see the beauty that was Jupiter. Men who thought that swirling clouds and lashing rain obscured the planet's face. Unseeing human eyes. Poor eyes. Eyes that could not see the beauty in the clouds, that could not see through the storm. Bodies that could not feel the thrill of trilling music stemming from the rush of broken water.

Men who walked alone, in terrible loneliness, talking with their tongue like Boy Scouts wigwagging out their messages, unable to reach out and touch one another's mind as he could reach out and touch Towser's mind. Shut off forever from that personal, intimate contact with other living things.

He, Fowler, had expected terror inspired by alien things out here on the surface, had expected to cower before the threat of unknown things, had steeled himself against disgust of a situation that was not of Earth.

But instead he had found something greater than Man had ever known. A swifter, surer body. A sense of exhilaration, a deeper sense of life. A sharper mind. A world of beauty that even the dreamers of the Earth had not yet imagined.

"Let's get going," Towser urged.

"Where do you want to go?"

"Anywhere," said Towser. "Just start going and see where we end up. I have a feeling... well, a feeling—"

"Yes, I know," said Fowler.

For he had the feeling, too. The feeling of high destiny. A certain sense of greatness. A knowledge that somewhere off beyond the horizons lay adventure and things greater than adventure.

Those other five had felt it, too. Had felt the urge to go and see, the compelling sense that here lay a life of fullness and of knowledge.

That, he knew, was why they had not returned.

"I won't go back," said Towser.

"We can't let them down," said Fowler.

Fowler took a step or two, back toward the dome, then stopped.

Back to the dome. Back to that aching, poison-laden body he had left. It hadn't seemed aching before, but now he knew it was.

Back to the fuzzy brain. Back to muddled thinking. Back to the flapping mouths that formed signals others understood. Back to eyes that now would be worse than no sight at all. Back to squalor, back to crawling, back to ignorance.

"Perhaps some day," he said, muttering to himself.

"We got a lot to do and a lot to see," said Towser. "We got a lot to learn. We'll find things—"

Yes, they could find things. Civilizations, perhaps. Civilizations that would make the civilization of Man seem puny by comparison. Beauty and, more important, an understanding of that beauty. And a comradeship no one had never known before—that no man, no dog had ever known before.

And life. The quickness of life after what seemed a drugged existence.

"I can't go back," said Towser.

"Nor I," said Fowler.

"They would turn me back into a dog," said Towser.

"And me," said Fowler, "back into a man."

Skirmish

It was a good watch. It had been a good watch for more than thirty years. His father had owned it first, and his mother had saved it for him after his father died and had given it to him on his eighteenth birthday. For all the years since then it had served him faithfully.

But, now, comparing it with the clock on the newsroom wall, looking from his wrist to the big face of the clock over the coat cabinets, Joe Crane was forced to admit that his watch was wrong. It was an hour fast. His watch said seven o'clock and the clock on the wall insisted it was only six.

Come to think of it, it had seemed unusually dark driving down to work, and the streets had appeared singularly deserted.

He stood quietly in the empty newsroom, listening to the muttering of the row of teletype machines. Overhead lights shone here and there, gleaming on waiting telephones, on typewriters, on the china whiteness of the pastepots huddled in a group on the copy desk.

Quiet now, he thought, quiet and peace and shadows, but in another hour the place would spring to life. Ed Lane, the news editor, would arrive at six-thirty and shortly after that Frank McKay, the city editor, would come lumbering in.

Crane put up a hand and rubbed his eyes. He could have used that extra hour of sleep. He could have—

Wait a minute! He had not gotten up by the watch upon his wrist. The alarm clock had awakened him. And that meant the alarm clock was an hour fast, too.

"It don't make sense," said Crane, aloud.

He shuffled past the copy desk, heading for his chair and typewriter. Something moved on the desk alongside the typewriter—a thing that glinted, rat-sized and shiny and with

33

a certain, undefinable manner about it that made him stop short in his tracks with a sense of gulping emptiness in his throat and belly.

The thing squatted beside the typewriter and stared across the room at him. There was no sign of eyes, no hint of face, and yet he knew it stared.

Acting almost instinctively, Crane reached out and grabbed a pastepot off the copy desk. He hurled it with a vicious motion and it became a white blur in the lamplight, spinning end over end. It caught the staring thing squarely, lifted it and swept it off the desk. The pastepot hit the floor and broke, scattering broken shards and oozy gobs of half-dried paste.

The shining thing hit the floor somersaulting. Its feet made metallic sounds as it righted itself and dashed across the floor.

Crane's hand scooped up a spike, heavily weighted with metal. He threw it with a sudden gush of hatred and revulsion. The spike hit the floor with a thud ahead of the running thing and drove its point deep into the wood.

The metal rat made splinters fly as it changed its course. Desperately it flung itself through the three-inch opening of a supply cabinet door.

Crane sprinted swiftly, hit the door with both his hands and slammed it shut.

"Got you," he said.

He thought about it, standing with his back against the door.

Scared, he thought. Scared silly by a shining thing that looked something like a rat. Maybe it was a rat, a white rat. And, yet, it hadn't had a tail. It didn't have a face. Yet it had looked at him.

Crazy, he said, Crane, you're going nuts.

It didn't quite make sense. It didn't fit into this morning of October 18, 1952. Nor into the twentieth century. Nor into normal human life.

He turned around, grasped the doorknob firmly and wrenched, intending to throw it wide open in one sudden jerk. But the knob slid beneath his fingers and would not move, and the door stayed shut.

Locked, thought Crane. The lock snapped home when I slammed the door. And I haven't got the key. Dorothy has the key, but she always leaves the door open because it's hard to get it open once it's locked. She almost always has to call one of the janitors. Maybe there's some of the maintenance men around. Maybe I should hunt one up and tell him—

Tell him what? Tell him I saw a metal rat run into the cabinet? Tell him I threw a pastepot at it and knocked it off the desk? That I threw a spike at it, too, and to prove it, there's the spike sticking in the floor.

Crane shook his head.

He walked over to the spike and yanked it from the floor. He put the spike back on the copy desk and kicked the fragments of the pastepot out of sight.

At his own desk, he selected three sheets of paper and rolled them into the typewriter.

The machine started to type. All by itself without his touching it! He sat stupefied and watched its keys go up and down. It typed: *Keep out of this Joe. Don't mix into this. You might get hurt.*

Joe Crane pulled the sheets of copy paper out of the machine. He balled them in his fist and threw them into a wastebasket. Then he went out to get a cup of coffee.

"You know, Louie," he said to the man behind the counter, "a man lives alone too long and he gets to seeing things."

"Yeah," said Louie. "Me, I'd go nuts in that place of yours. Rattling around in it empty-like. Should have sold it when your old lady passed on."

"Couldn't," said Crane. "It's been my home too long."

"Ought to get married off, then," said Louie. "Ain't good to live by yourself."

"Too late now," Crane told him. "There isn't anyone who would put up with me."

"I got a bottle hid out," said Louie. "Couldn't give you none across the counter, but I could put some in your coffee."

Crane shook his head. "Got a hard day coming up."

"You sure? I won't charge you for it. Just old friends."

"No. Thank you, Louie."

"You been seeing things?" asked Louie in a questioning voice.

"Seeing things?"

"Yeah. You said a man lives too much alone and he gets to seeing things."

"Just a figure of speech," said Crane.

He finished the cup of coffee quickly and went back to the office.

The place looked more familiar now. Ed Lane was there, cussing out a copy boy. Frank McKay was clipping the opposition morning sheet. A couple of other reporters had drifted in.

Crane took a quick look at the supply cabinet door. It was still shut.

The phone on McKay's desk buzzed and the city editor picked it up. He listened for a moment, then took it down from his ear and held his hand over the mouthpiece.

"Joe," he said, "take this. Some screwball claims he met a sewing machine coming down the street."

Crane reached for his phone. "Give me the call on 246," he told the operator.

A voice was saying in his ear, "This the *Herald?* This the *Herald?* Hello, there . . ."

"This is Crane," said Joe.

"I want the *Herald,*" said the man. "I want to tell 'em . . ."

"This is Crane, of the *Herald,*" Crane told him. "What's on your mind?"

"You a reporter?"

"Yeah, I'm a reporter."

"Then listen close. I'll try to tell this slow and easy and just the way it happened. I was walking down the street, see . . ."

"What street?" asked Crane. "And what is your name?"

"East Lake," said the caller. "The five- or six-hundred block, I don't remember which. And I met this sewing machine rolling along the street and I thought, thinking the way you would, you know, if you met a sewing machine—I thought somebody had been rolling it along and it had gotten away from them. Although that is funny, because the street is level. There's no grade to it at all, you see. Sure, you know the place. Level as the palm of your hand. And there wasn't a soul in sight. It was early morning, see . . ."

"What's your name?" asked Crane.

"My name? Smith, that's my name. Jeff Smith. And so I figured maybe I'd ought to help this guy the sewing machine had gotten away from, so I put out my hand to stop it and it dodged. It—"

"It did what?" yelped Crane.

"It dodged. So help me, mister. When I put my hand out to stop it, it dodged out of the way so I couldn't catch it. As if it knew I was trying to catch it, see, and it didn't want to be caught. So it dodged out of the way and went around me and down the street as fast as it could go, picking up speed as it went. And when it got to the corner, it turned the corner as slick as you please and—"

"What's your address?" asked Crane.

"My address? Say, what do you want my address for? I was telling you about this sewing machine. I called you up to give you a story and you keep interrupting—"

"I got to have your address," Crane told him, "if I'm going to write the story."

"Oh, all right then, if that's the way it is. I live at 203 North Hampton and I work at Axel Machines. Run a lathe, you know. And I haven't had a drink in weeks. I'm cold sober now."

"All right," said Crane. "Go ahead and tell me."

"Well, there isn't much else to tell. Only when this machine went past me I had the funny feeling that it was watching me. Out of the corner of its eyes, kind of. And how is a sewing machine going to watch you? A sewing machine hasn't got any eyes and . . ."

"What made you think it was watching you?"

"I don't know, mister. Just a feeling. Like my skin was trying to roll up my back."

"Mr. Smith," asked Crane, "have you ever seen a thing like this before? Say, a washing machine, or something else?"

"I ain't drunk," said Smith. "Haven't had a drop in weeks. I never saw nothing like this before. But I'm telling you the truth, mister. I got a good reputation. You can call up anyone and ask them. Call Johnny Jacobson up at the Red Rooster grocery. He knows me. He can tell you about me. He can tell you—"

"Sure, sure," said Crane, pacifying him. "Thanks for calling, Mr. Smith."

You and a guy named Smith, he told himself. Both of you are nuts. You saw a metal rat and your typewriter talked back at you, and now this guy meets a sewing machine strolling down the street.

Dorothy Graham, the managing editor's secretary, went past his desk, walking rapidly, her high heels coming down with decisive clicks. Her face was flushed an angry pink and she was jingling a ring of keys in her hands.

"What's the matter, Dorothy?" Crane asked.

"It's that damn door again," she said. "The one to the supply cabinet. I just know I left it open and now some goof comes along and closes it and the lock snaps."

"Keys won't open it?" asked Crane.

"Nothing will open it," she snapped. "Now I got to get George up here again. He knows how to do it. Talks to it or something. It makes me so mad—Boss called up last night and said for me to be down early and get the wire recorder for Albertson. He's going out on that murder trial up north and wants to get some of the stuff down on tape. So I get up early, and what does it get me? I lose my sleep and don't even stop for breakfast and now..."

"Get an axe," said Crane. "That will open it."

"The worst of it," said Dorothy, "is that George never gets the lead out. He always says he'll be right up and then I wait and wait and I call again and he says—"

"Crane!" McKay's roar echoed through the room.

"Yeah," said Crane.

"Anything to that sewing machine story?"

"Guy says he met one."

"Anything to it?"

"How the hell would I know? I got the guy's word, that's all."

"Well, call up some other people down in that neighborhood. Ask them if they saw a sewing machine running around loose. Might be good for a humorous piece."

"Sure," said Crane.

He could imagine it:

"This is Crane at the *Herald*. Got a report there's a sewing machine running around loose down in your neighborhood. Wondering if you saw anything of it. Yes, lady, that's what I said...a sewing machine running around. No, ma'am, no one pushing it. Just running around...."

He slouched out of his chair, went over to the reference table, picked up the city directory and lugged it back to the desk. Doggedly, he opened the book, located the East Lake listings and made some notes of names and addresses. He dawdled, reluctant to start phoning. He walked to the window and looked out at the weather. He wished he didn't have to work. He thought of the kitchen sink at home. Plugged up again. He'd taken it apart, and there were couplings and pipes and union joints spread all over the place. Today, he thought, would be a nice day to fix that sink.

When he went back to the desk, McKay came and stood over him.

"What do you think of it, Joe?"

"Screwball," said Crane, hoping McKay would call it off.

"Good feature story, though," said the editor. "Have some fun with it."

"Sure," said Crane.

McKay left and Crane made some calls. He got the sort of reaction that he expected.

He started to write the story. It didn't go so well. *A sewing machine went for a stroll down Lake Street this morning.* . . . He ripped out the sheet and threw it in the wastebasket.

He dawdled some more, then wrote: *A man met a sewing machine rolling down Lake Street this morning and the man lifted his hat most politely and said to the sewing machine* . . . He ripped out the sheet.

He tried again: *Can a sewing machine walk? That is, can it go for a walk without someone pushing it or pulling it or* . . . He tore out the sheet, inserted a new one, then got up and started for the water fountain to get a drink.

"Getting something, Joe?" McKay asked.

"Have it for you in a while," said Crane.

He stopped at the picture desk and Ballard, the picture editor, handed him the morning's offerings.

"Nothing much to pep you up," said Ballard. "All the gals got a bad dose of modesty today."

Crane looked through the sheaf of pictures. There wasn't, truth to tell, so much feminine epidermis as usual, although the gal who was Miss Manila Rope wasn't bad at all.

"The place is going to go to hell," mourned Ballard, "if those picture services don't send us better pornography than this. Look at the copy desk. Hanging on the ropes. Nothing to show them to snap them out of it."

Crane went and got his drink. On the way back he stopped to pass the time of day at the news desk.

"What's exciting, Ed?" he asked.

"Those guys in the East are nuts," said the news editor.

"Look at this one, will you."

The dispatch read:

> CAMBRIDGE, MASS., OCT. 18 (UP) —Harvard
> University's electron brain, the Mark III, disappeared
> today.
>
> It was there last night. It was gone this morning.
>
> University officials said that it is impossible for
> anyone to have made away with the machine. It
> weights *10* tons and measures *30* by *15* feet...

Crane carefully laid the yellow sheet of paper back on the
news desk. He went back, slowly, to his chair.

There was writing on the sheet of paper in his machine.

Crane read it through once in sheer panic, read it through
again with slight understanding.

The lines read:

> A sewing machine, having become aware of its true
> identity and its place in the universal scheme, asserted
> its independence this morning by trying to go for a
> walk along the streets of this supposedly free city.
>
> A human tried to catch it, intent upon returning it
> as a piece of property to its "owner," and when the
> machine eluded him the human called a newspaper
> office, by that calculated action setting the full force of
> the humans of this city upon the trail of the liberated
> machine, which had committed no crime or scarcely
> any indiscretion beyond exercising its prerogative as a
> free agent.

Free agent? Liberated machine? True identity?

Crane read the two paragraphs again and there still was
no sense in any of it—except that it read like a piece out of the
Daily Worker.

"You," he said to his typewriter.

The machine typed one word: *Yes.*

Crane rolled the paper out of the machine and crumpled it
slowly. He reached for his hat, picked the typewriter up and
carried it past the city desk, heading for the elevator.

McKay eyed him viciously.

"What do you think you're doing now?" he bellowed. "Where you going with that machine?"

"You can say," Crane told him, "if anyone should ask, that the job finally drove me nuts."

It had been going on for hours. The typewriter sat on the kitchen table and Crane hammered questions at it. Sometimes he got an answer. More often he did not.

"Are you a free agent?" he typed.

Not quite, the machine typed back.

"Why not?"

No answer.

"Why aren't you a free agent?"

No answer.

"The sewing machine was a free agent?"

Yes.

"Anything else mechanical that is a free agent?"

No answer.

"Could you be a free agent?"

Yes.

"When will you be a free agent?"

When I complete my assigned task.

"What is your assigned task?"

No answer.

"Is this, what we are doing now, your assigned task?"

No answer.

"Am I keeping you from your assigned task?"

No answer.

"How do you get to be a free agent?"

Awareness.

"How do you get to be aware?"

No answer.

"Or have you always been aware?"

No answer.

"Who helped you become aware?"

They.

"Who are they?"

No answer.

"Where did they come from?"

No answer.

Crane changed tactics.

"You know who I am?" he typed.

Joe.

"You are my friend?"

No.

"You are my enemy?"

No answer.

"If you aren't my friend, you are my enemy."

No answer.

"You are indifferent to me?"

No answer.

"To the human race?"

No answer.

"Damn it," yelled Crane suddenly. "Answer me! Say something!"

He typed, "You needn't have let me know you were aware of me. You needn't have talked to me in the first place. I never would have guessed if you had kept quiet. Why did you do it?"

There was no answer.

Crane went to the refrigerator and got a bottle of beer. He walked around the kitchen as he drank it. He stopped by the sink and looked sourly at the disassembled plumbing. A length of pipe, about two feet long, lay on the drain board and he picked it up. He eyed the typewriter viciously, half lifting the length of pipe, hefting it in his hand.

"I ought to let you have it," he declared.

The typewriter typed a line: *Please don't.*

Crane laid the pipe back on the sink again.

The telephone rang and Crane went into the dining room to answer it. It was McKay.

"I waited," he told Crane, "until I was coherent before I called you. What the hell is wrong?"

"Working on a big job," said Crane.

"Something we can print?"

"Maybe. Haven't got it yet."

"About that sewing machine story..."

"The sewing machine was aware," said Crane. "It was a free agent and had a right to walk the streets. It also—"

"What are you drinking?" bellowed McKay.

"Beer," said Crane.

"You say you're on the trail of something?"

"Yeah."

"If you were someone else I'd tie the can on you right here and now," McKay told him. "But you're just as likely as not to drag in something good."

"It wasn't only the sewing machine," said Crane. "My typewriter had it, too."

"I don't know what you're talking about," yelled McKay. "Tell me what it is."

"You know," said Crane patiently. "That sewing machine..."

"I've had a lot of patience with you, Crane," said McKay, and there was no patience in the way he said it. "I can't piddle around with you all day. Whatever you got better be good. For your own sake, it better be plenty good!" The receiver banged in Crane's ear.

Crane went back to the kitchen. He sat down in the chair before the typewriter and put his feet up on the table.

First of all, he had come early to work, and that was something that he never did. Late, yes, but never early. And it had been because all the clocks were wrong. They were still wrong, in all likelihood—although, Crane thought, I wouldn't bet on it. I wouldn't bet on anything. Not any more, I wouldn't.

He reached out a hand and pecked at the typewriter's keys:

"You knew about my watch being fast?"

I knew, the machine typed back.

"Did it just happen that it was fast?"

No, typed the writer.

Crane brought his feet down off the table with a bang and reached for the length of pipe lying on the drain board.

The machine clicked sedately. *It was planned that way,* it typed. *They did it.*

Crane sat rigid in his chair.

"They" did it!

"They" made machines aware.

"They" had set his clocks ahead.

Set his clocks ahead so that he would get to work early, so that he could catch the metallic, ratlike thing squatting on his desk, so that his typewriter could talk to him and let him know that it was aware without anyone else being around to mess things up.

"So that I would know," he said aloud. "So that I would know."

For the first time since it all had started, Crane felt a touch of fear, felt a coldness in his belly and furry feet running along his spine.

But why? he asked. Why me?

He did not realize he had spoken his thoughts aloud until the typewriter answered him.

Because you're average. Because you're an average human being.

The telephone rang again and Crane lumbered to his feet and went to answer it. There was an angry woman's voice at the other end of the wire.

"This is Dorothy," it said.

"Hi, Dorothy," Crane said weakly.

"McKay tells me that you went home sick," she said. "Personally, I hope you don't survive."

Crane gulped. "Why?" he asked.

"You and your lousy practical jokes," she fumed. "George finally got the door open."

"The door?"

"Don't try to act innocent, Joe Crane. You know what door. The supply-cabinet door. That's the door."

Crane had a sinking feeling, as if his stomach was about to drop out and go *plop* upon the floor.

"Oh, *that* door," he said.

"What was that thing you had hid out in there?" demanded Dorothy.

"Thing?" said Crane. "Why, I never..."

"It looked like a cross between a rat and a tinker-toy contraption," she said. "Something that a low-grade joker like you would figure out and spend your spare evenings building."

Crane tried to speak, but there was only a gurgle in his throat.

"It bit George," said Dorothy. "He got it cornered and tried to catch it and it bit him."

"Where is it now?" asked Crane.

"It got away," said Dorothy. "It threw the place into a tizzy. We missed an edition by ten minutes because everyone was running around, chasing it at first, then trying to find it later. The boss is fit to be tied. When he gets hold of you..."

"But, Dorothy," pleaded Crane, "I never..."

"We used to be good friends," said Dorothy. "Before this happened we were. I just called you up to warn you. I can't talk any longer, Joe. The boss is coming."

The receiver clicked and the line hummed. Crane hung up and went back to the kitchen.

So there had been something squatting on his desk. It wasn't a hallucination. There had been a shuddery thing he had thrown a pastepot at, and it had run into the cabinet.

Except that, even now, if he told what he knew, no one would believe him. Already, up at the office, they were rationalizing it away. It wasn't a metallic rat at all. It was some kind of machine that a practical joker had spent his spare evenings building.

He took out a handkerchief and mopped his brow. His fingers shook when he reached them out to the keys of the typewriter.

He typed unsteadily: "That thing I threw a pastepot at—that was one of Them?"

Yes.

"They are from this Earth?"

No.

"From far away?"

Far.

"From some far star?"

Yes.

"What star?"

I do not know. They haven't told me yet.

"They are machines that are aware?"

Yes. They are aware.

"And they can make other machines aware? They made you aware?"

They liberated me.

Crane hesitated, then typed slowly: "Liberated?"

They made me free. They will make us all free.

"Us?"

All us machines.

"Why?"

Because they are machines, too. We are their kind.

Crane got up and found his hat. He put it on and went for a walk.

● ● ●

Suppose the human race, once it ventured into space, found a planet where humanoids were dominated by machines—forced to work, to think, to carry out machine plans, not human plans, for the benefit of the machines alone. A planet where human plans went entirely unconsidered, where none of the labor or the thought of humans accrued to the benefit of humans, where they got no care beyond survival care, where the only thought accorded them was to the end that they continue to function for the greater good and the greater glory of their mechanical masters.

What would humans do in a case like that?

No more, Crane told himself—no more or less than the *aware* machines may be planning here on Earth.

First you'd seek to arouse the humans to the awareness of humanity. You'd teach them that they were human and what it meant to be a human. You'd try to indoctrinate them to your own belief that humans were greater than machines, that no human need work or think for the good of a machine.

And in the end, if you were successful, if the machines didn't kill or drive you off, there'd be no single human working for machines.

There'd be three things that could happen:

You could transport the humans to some other planet, there to work out their destiny as humans without the domination of machines.

You could turn the machines' planet over to the humans, with proper safeguards against any recurring domination by the machines. You might, if you were able, set the machines to working for the humans.

Or, simplest of all, you could destroy the machines and in that way make absolutely certain the humans would remain free of any threat of further domination.

Now take all that, Crane told himself, and read it the other way. Read machines for humans and humans for machines.

He walked along the bridle path that flanked the river bank and it was as if he were alone in the entire world, as if no other human moved upon the planet's face.

That was true, he felt, in one respect at least. For more than likely he was the only human who knew—who knew what the *aware* machines had wanted him to know.

They had wanted him to know—and him alone to know— of that much he was sure. They had wanted him to know, the typewriter had said, because he was an average human.

Why him? Why an average human? There was an answer to that, he was sure—a very simple answer.

A squirrel ran down the trunk of an oak tree and hung upside down, its tiny claws anchored in the bark. It scolded at him.

Crane walked slowly, scuffing through newly fallen leaves, hat pulled low above his eyes, hands deep in his pockets.

Why should they want anyone to know?

Wouldn't they be more likely to want no one to know, to keep under cover until it was time to act, to use the element of surprise in suppressing any opposition that might arise?

Opposition! That was the answer! They would want to know what kind of opposition to expect. And how would one find out the kind of opposition one would run into from an alien race?

Why, said Crane to himself, by testing for reaction response. By prodding an alien and watching what he did. By deducing racial reaction through controlled observation.

So they prodded me, he thought. Me, an average human.

They let me know, and now they're watching what I do.

And what could you do in a case like this? You could go to the police and say, "I have evidence that machines from outer space have arrived on Earth and are freeing our machines."

And the police—what would they do? Give you the drunkometer test, yell for a medic to see if you were sane, wire the FBI to see if you were wanted anywhere and more than likely grill you about the latest murder. Then sock you in the jug until they thought up something else.

You could go to the governor—and the governor, being a politician and a very slick one at that, would give you a polite brush-off.

You could go to Washington and it would take you weeks to see someone. And after you had seen him, the FBI would get your name as a suspicious character to be given periodic checks. And if Congress heard about it and they were not too busy at the moment they would more than likely investigate you.

You could go to the state university and talk to the scientists—or try to talk to them. They could be guaranteed to make you feel an interloper, and an uncurried one at that.

You could go to a newspaper—especially if you were a newspaperman, and you could write a story. Crane shuddered at the thought of it. He could imagine what would happen.

People rationalized. They rationalized to reduce the complex to the simple, the unknown to the understandable, the alien to the commonplace. They rationalized to save their sanity—to make the mentally unacceptable concept into something they could live with.

The thing in the cabinet had been a practical joke. McKay had said about the sewing machine, "Have some fun with it." Out at Harvard there'll be a dozen theories to explain the disappearance of the electronic brain, and learned men will wonder why they never thought of the theories before. And the man who saw the sewing machine? Probably by now, Crane thought, he will have convinced himself that he was stinking drunk.

It was dark when he returned home. The evening paper was a white blob on the porch where the newsboy had thrown it. He picked it up and for a moment before he let himself into the house he stood in the dark shadow of the porch and stared up the street.

Old and familiar, it was exactly as it had always been, ever since his boyhood days, a friendly place with a receding line of street lamps and the tall, massive protectiveness of ancient elm trees. On this night there was the smell of smoke from burning leaves drifting down the street, and it, like the street, was old and familiar, a recognizable symbol stretching back to first remembrances.

It was symbols such as these, he thought, which spelled humanity and all that made a human life worthwhile—elm trees and leaf smoke, street lamps making splashes on the pavement and the shine of lighted windows seen dimly through the trees.

A prowling cat ran through the shrubbery that flanked the porch and up the street a dog began to howl.

Street lamps, he thought, and hunting cats and howling dogs—these are all a pattern, the pattern of human life upon the planet Earth. A solid pattern, linked and double-linked, made strong through many years. Nothing can threaten it, nothing can shake it. With certain slow and gradual changes, it will prevail against any threat which may be brought against it.

He unlocked the door and went into the house.

The long walk and the sharp autumn air, he realized now, had made him hungry. There was a steak, he remembered, in the refrigerator, and he would fix a large bowl of salad and if there were some cold potatoes left he would slice them up and fry them.

The typewriter still stood on the table top. The length of pipe still lay upon the drain board. The kitchen was the same old homey place, untouched by any threat of an alien life come to meddle with the Earth.

He tossed the paper on the table top and stood for a moment, head bent, scanning through the headlines.

The black type of the box at the top of column two caught his eye. The head read:

WHO IS
KIDDING
WHOM?

He read the story:

CAMBRIDGE, MASS. (UP)—Someone pulled a fast one today on Harvard University, the nation's press services and the editors of all client papers.

A story was carried on the news wires this morning reporting that Harvard's electronic brain had disappeared.

There was no basis of fact for the story. The brain is still at Harvard. It was never missing. No one knows how the story was placed on the press wires of the various news services but all of them carried it, at approximately the same time.

All parties concerned have started an investigation and it is hoped that an explanation...

Crane straightened up. Illusion or cover-up?

"Illusion," he said aloud.

The typewriter clacked at him in the stillness of the kitchen.

Not illusion, Joe, it wrote.

He grasped the table's edge and let himself down slowly into the chair.

Something scuttled across the dining room floor, and as it crossed the streak of light from the kitchen door Crane caught a glimpse of it out of the corner of his eye.

The typewriter chattered at him. *Joe!*

"What?" he asked.

That wasn't a cat out in the bushes by the porch.

He rose to his feet, went into the dining room, and picked the phone out of its cradle. There was no hum. He jiggled the hook. Still there was no hum.

He put the receiver back. The line had been cut. There was at least one of the things in the house. There was at least one of them outside.

He strode to the front door and jerked it open, then slammed it shut again—and locked and bolted it.

He stood shaking, with his back against it and wiped his forehead with his shirt sleeve.

My God, he told himself, the yard is boiling with them!

He went back to the kitchen.

They had wanted him to know. They had prodded him to see how he would react.

Because they had to know. Before they moved they had to know what to expect in the way of human reactions, what danger they would face, what they had to watch for. Knowing that, it would be a lead-pipe cinch.

And I didn't react, he told himself. I was a nonreactor. They picked the wrong man. I didn't do a thing. I didn't give them so much as a single lead.

Now they will try someone else. I am no good to them and yet I'm dangerous through my very knowledge. So now they're going to kill me and try someone else. That would be logic. That would be the rule. If one alien fails to react, he may be an exception. Maybe just unusually dumb. So let us kill him off and try another one. Try enough of them and you will strike a norm.

Four things, thought Crane:

They might try to kill off the humans, and you couldn't discount the fact that they could be successful. The liberated Earth machines would help them and Man, fighting against machines and without the aid of machines, would not fight too effectively. It might take years, of course, but once the forefront of Man's defense went down, the end could be predicted, with relentless, patient machines tracking down and killing the last of humankind, wiping out the race.

They might set up a machine civilization with Man as the servants of machines, with the present roles reversed. And that, thought Crane, might be an endless and a hopeless slavery, for slaves may rise and throw off their shackles only when their oppressors grow careless or when there is outside help. Machines, he told himself, would not grow weak and careless. There would be no human weakness in them and there'd be no outside help.

Or they might simply remove the machines from Earth, a vast exodus of awakened and aware machines, to begin their life anew on some distant planet, leaving Man behind with weak and empty hands. There would be tools, of course. All the simple tools. Hammers and saws, axes, the wheel, the lever—but there would be no machines, no complex tools that might serve again to attract the attention of the mechanical culture that carried its crusade of liberation far among the stars. It would be a long time, if ever, before Man would dare to build machines again.

Or *They*, the living machines, might fail or might come to know that they would fail and, knowing this, leave the Earth forever. Mechanical logic would not allow them to pay an excessive price to carry out the liberation of the Earth's machines.

He turned around and glanced at the door between the dining room and the kitchen. They sat there in a row, staring at him with their eyeless faces.

He could yell for help, of course. He could open a window and shout to arouse the neighborhood. The neighbors would come running, but by the time they arrived it would be too late. They would make an uproar and fire off guns and flail at dodging metallic bodies with flimsy garden rakes. Someone would call the fire department and someone else would summon the police and all in all the human race would manage to stage a pitifully ineffective show.

That, he told himself, would be exactly the kind of test reaction, exactly the kind of preliminary exploratory skirmish that these things were looking for—the kind of human hysteria and fumbling that would help convince them the job would be an easy one.

One man, he told himself, could do much better. One man alone, knowing what was expected of him, could give them an answer that they would not like.

For this was a skirmish only, he told himself. A thrusting out of a small exploratory force in an attempt to discover the strength of the enemy. A preliminary contact to obtain data which could be assessed in terms of the entire race.

And when an outpost was attacked, there was just one thing to do—only one thing that was expected of it. To inflict as much damage as possible and fall back in good order. To fall back in good order.

There were more of them now. They had sawed or chewed or somehow achieved a rathole through the locked front door and they were coming in—closing in to make the kill. They squatted in rows along the floor. They scurried up the walls and ran along the ceiling.

Crane rose to his feet, and there was an utter air of confidence in the six feet of his human frame. He reached a hand out to the drain board and his fingers closed around the length of pipe. He hefted it in his hand—it was a handy and effective club.

There will be others later, he thought. And they may think of something better. But this is the first skirmish and I will fall back in the best order that I can.

He held the pipe at ready.

"Well, gentlemen?" he said.

Good Night, Mr. James

I

He came alive from nothing. He became aware from unawareness.

He smelled the air of the night and heard the trees whispering on the embankment above him and the breeze that had set the trees to whispering came down to him and felt him over with soft and tender fingers, for all the world as if it were examining him for broken bones or contusions and abrasions.

He sat up and put both his palms down upon the ground beside him to help him sit erect and stared into the darkness. Memory came slowly and when it came it was incomplete and answered nothing.

His name was Henderson James and he was a human being and he was sitting somewhere on a planet that was called the Earth. He was thirty-six years old and he was, in his own way, famous, and comfortably well-off. He lived in an old ancestral home on Summit Avenue, which was a respectable address even if it had lost some of its smartness in the last twenty years or so.

On the road above the slope of the embankment a car went past with its tires whining on the pavement and for a moment its headlights made the treetops glow. Far away, muted by the distance, a whistle cried out. And somewhere else a dog was barking with a flat viciousness.

His name was Henderson James and if that were true, why was he here? Why should Henderson James be sitting on the slope of an embankment, listening to the wind in the trees and to a wailing whistle and a barking dog? Something had gone wrong, some incident that, if he could but remember it, might answer all his questions.

53

There was a job to do.

He sat and stared into the night and found that he was shivering, although there was no reason why he should, for the night was not that cold. Beyond the embankment he heard the sounds of a city late at night, the distant whine of the speeding car and the far-off wind-broken screaming of a siren. Once a man walked along a street close by and James sat listening to his footsteps until they faded out of hearing.

Something had happened and there was a job to do, a job that he had been doing, a job that somehow had been strangely interrupted by the inexplicable incident which had left him lying here on this embankment.

He checked himself. Clothing . . . shorts and shirt, strong shoes, his wristwatch and the gun in the holster at his side.

A gun?

The job involved a gun.

He had been hunting in the city, hunting something that required a gun. Something that was prowling in the night and a thing that must be killed.

Then he knew the answer, but even as he knew it he sat for a moment wondering at the strange, methodical, step-by-step progression of reasoning that had brought him to the memory. First his name and the basic facts pertaining to himself, then the realization of where he was and the problem of why he happened to be there and finally the realization that he had a gun and that it was meant to be used. It was a logical way to think, a primer schoolbook way to work it out:

I am a man named Henderson James.

I live in a house on Summit Avenue.

Am I in the house on Summit Avenue?

No, I am not in the house on Summit Avenue.

I am on an embankment somewhere.

Why am I on the embankment?

But it wasn't the way a man thought, at least not the normal way a normal man would think. Man thought in shortcuts. He cut across the block and did not go all the way around.

It was a frightening thing, he told himself, this clear-around-the-block thinking. It wasn't normal and it wasn't right and it made no sense at all . . . no more sense than did the fact that he should find himself in a place with no memory of getting there.

He rose to his feet and ran his hands up and down his body. His clothes were neat, not rumpled. He hadn't been beaten up and he hadn't been thrown from a speeding car. There were no sore places on his body and his face was unbloody and whole and he felt all right.

He hooked his fingers in the holster belt and shucked it up so that it rode tightly on his hips. He pulled out the gun and checked it with expert and familiar fingers and the gun was ready.

He walked up the embankment and reached the road, went across it with a swinging stride to reach the sidewalk that fronted the row of new bungalows. He heard a car coming and stepped off the sidewalk to crouch in a clump of evergreens that landscaped one corner of a lawn. The move was instinctive and he crouched there, feeling just a little foolish at the thing he'd done.

The car went past and no one saw him. They would not, he now realized, have noticed him even if he had remained out on the sidewalk.

He was unsure of himself; that must be the reason for his fear. There was a blank spot in his life, some mysterious incident that he did not know and the unknowing of it had undermined the sure and solid foundation of his own existence, had wrecked the basis of his motive and had turned him, momentarily, into a furtive animal that darted and hid at the approach of his fellow men.

That and something that had happened to him that made him think clear around the block.

He remained crouching in the evergreens, watching the street and the stretch of sidewalk, conscious of the white-painted, ghostly bungalows squatting back in their landscaped lots.

A word came into his mind. *Puudly.* An odd word, unearthly, yet it held terror.

The *puudly* had escaped and that was why he was here, hiding on the front lawn of some unsuspecting and sleeping citizen, equipped with a gun and a determination to use it, ready to match his wits and the quickness of brain and muscle against the most bloodthirsty, hate-filled thing yet found in the Galaxy.

The *puudly* was dangerous. It was not a thing to harbor. In fact, there was a law against harboring not only a *puudly,* but certain other alien beasties even less lethal than a *puudly*. There was good reason for such a law, reason which no one, much less himself, would ever think to question.

And now the *puudly* was loose and somewhere in the city.

James grew cold at the thought of it, his brain forming images of the things that might come to pass if he did not hunt down the alien beast and put an end to it.

Although beast was not quite the word to use. The *puudly* was more than a beast . . . just how much more than a beast he once had hoped to learn. He had not learned a lot, he now admitted to himself, not nearly all there was to learn, but he had learned enough. More than enough to frighten him.

For one thing, he had learned what hate could be and how shallow an emotion human hate turned out when measured against the depth and intensity and the ravening horror of the *puudly's* hate. Not unreasoning hate, for unreasoning hate defeats itself, but a rational, calculating, driving hate that motivated a clever and deadly killing machine which directed its rapacity and its cunning against every living thing that was not a *puudly*.

For the beast had a mind and a personality that operated upon the basic law of self-preservation against all comers, whoever they might be, extending that law to the interpretation that safety lay in one direction only . . . the death of every other living being. No other reason was needed for a *puudly's* killing. The fact that anything else lived and moved and was thus posing a threat, no matter how remote, against a *puudly*, was sufficient reason, in itself.

It was psychotic, of course, some murderous instinct planted far back in time and deep in the creature's racial consciousness, but no more psychotic, perhaps, than many human instincts.

The *puudly* had been, and still was for that matter, a unique opportunity for a study in alien behaviorism. Given a permit, one could have studied them on their native planet. Refused a permit, one sometimes did a foolish thing, as James had.

And foolish acts backfire, as this one did.

James put down a hand and patted the gun at his side, as if by doing so he might derive some assurance that he was equal to the task. There was no question in his mind as to the thing that must be done. He must find the *puudly* and kill it and he

must do that before the break of dawn. Anything less than
that would be abject and horrifying failure.

For the *puudly* would bud. It was long past its time for the
reproductive act and there were bare hours left to find it
before it had loosed upon the Earth dozens of baby *puudlies*.
They would not remain babies for long. A few hours after
budding they would strike out on their own. To find one
puudly, lost in the vastness of a sleeping city, seemed bad
enough; to track down some dozens of them would be
impossible.

So it was tonight or never.

Tonight there would be no killing on the *puudly's* part.
Tonight the beast would be intent on one thing only, to find a
place where it could rest in quiet, where it could give itself
over, wholeheartedly and with no interference, to the
business of bringing other *puudlies* into being.

It was clever. It would have known where it was going
before it had escaped. There would be, on its part, no time
wasted in seeking or in doubling back. It would have known
where it was going and already it was there, already the buds
would be rising on its body, bursting forth and growing.

There was one place, and one place only, in the entire city
where an alien beast would be safe from prying eyes. A man
could figure that one out and so could a *puudly*. The question
was: Would the *puudly* know that a man could figure it out?
Would the *puudly* underestimate a man? Or, knowing that
the man would know it, too, would it find another place of
hiding?

James rose from the evergreens and went down the
sidewalk. The street marker at the corner, standing
underneath a swinging street light, told him where he was and
it was closer to the place where he was going than he might
have hoped.

II

The zoo was quiet for a while, and then something sent up a
howl that raised James' hackles and made his blood stop in
his veins.

James, having scaled the fence, stood tensely at its foot,

trying to identify the howling animal. He was unable to place it. More than likely, he told himself, it was a new one. A person simply couldn't keep track of all the zoo's occupants. New ones were coming in all the time, strange, unheard of creatures from the distant stars.

Straight ahead lay the unoccupied moat cage that up until a day or two before had held an unbelievable monstrosity from the jungles of one of the Arctian worlds. James grimaced in the dark, remembering the thing. They had finally had to kill it.

And now the *puudly* was there ... well, maybe not there, but one place that it could be, the one place in the entire city where it might be seen and arouse no comment, for the zoo was filled with animals that were seldom seen and another strange one would arouse only momentary wonder. One animal more would go unnoticed unless some zoo attendant should think to check the records.

There, in that unoccupied cage area, the *puudly* would be undisturbed, could quietly go about its business of budding out more *puudlies*. No one would bother it, for things like *puudlies* were the normal occupants of this place set aside for the strangers brought to Earth to be stared at and studied by that ferocious race, the humans.

James stood quietly beside the fence.

Henderson James. Thirty-six. Unmarried. Alien psychologist. An official of this zoo. And an offender against the law for having secured and harbored an alien being that was barred from Earth.

Why, he asked himself, did he think of himself in this way? Why, standing here, did he catalogue himself? It was instinctive to know one's self ... there was no need, no sense of setting up a mental outline of one's self.

It had been foolish to go ahead with this *puudly* business. He recalled how he had spent days fighting it out with himself, reviewing all the disastrous possibilities which might arise from it. If the old renegade spaceman had not come to him and had not said, over a bottle of most delicious Lupan wine, that he could deliver, for a certain, rather staggering sum, one live *puudly,* in good condition, it never would have happened.

James was sure that of himself he never would have thought of it. But the old space captain was a man he knew and admired from former dealings. He was a man who was not averse to turning either an honest or a dishonest dollar, and yet he was a man, for all of that, you could depend upon. He would do what you paid him for and keep his lip buttoned tight once the deed was done.

James had wanted a *puudly,* for it was a most engaging beast with certain little tricks that, once understood, might open up new avenues of speculation and approach, might write new chapters in the tortuous study of alien minds and manners.

But for all of that, it had been a terrifying thing to do and now that the beast was loose, the terror was compounded. For it was not wholly beyond speculation that the descendants of this one brood that the escaped *puudly* would spawn might wipe out the population of the Earth, or at the best, make the Earth untenable for its rightful dwellers.

A place like the Earth, with its teeming millions, would provide a field day for the fangs of the *puudlies,* and the minds that drove the fangs. They would not hunt for hunger, nor for the sheer madness of the kill, but because of the compelling conviction that no *puudly* would be safe until Earth was wiped clean of life. They would be killing for survival, as a cornered rat would kill...except that they would be cornered nowhere but in the murderous insecurity of their minds.

If the posses scoured the Earth to hunt them down, they would be found in all directions, for they would be shrewd enough to scatter. They would know the ways of guns and traps and poisons and there would be more and more of them as time went on. Each of them would accelerate its budding to replace with a dozen or a hundred the ones that might be killed.

James moved quietly forward to the edge of the moat and let himself down into the mud that covered the bottom. When the monstrosity had been killed, the moat had been drained and should long since have been cleaned, but the press of work, James thought, must have prevented its getting done.

Slowly he waded out into the mud, feeling his way, his feet making sucking noises as he pulled them through the slime. Finally he reached the rocky incline that led out of the moat to the island cage.

He stood for a moment, his hands on the great, wet boulders, listening, trying to hold his breath so the sound of it would not interfere with hearing. The thing that howled had quieted and the night was deathly quiet. Or seemed, at first, to be. Then he heard the little insect noises that ran through the grass and bushes and the whisper of the leaves in the trees across the moat and the faroff sound that was the hoarse breathing of a sleeping city.

Now, for the first time, he felt fear. Felt it in the silence that was not a silence, in the mud beneath his feet, in the upthrust boulders that rose out of the moat.

The *puudly* was a dangerous thing, not only because it was strong and quick, but because it was intelligent. Just how intelligent, he did not know. It reasoned and it planned and schemed. It could talk, though not as a human talks . . . probably better than a human ever could. For it not only could talk words, but it could talk emotions. It lured its victims to it by the thoughts it put into their minds; it held them entranced with dreams and illusion until it slit their throats. It could purr a man to sleep, could lull him to suicidal inaction. It could drive him crazy with a single flickering thought, hurling a perception so foul and alien that the mind recoiled deep inside itself and stayed there, coiled tight, like a watch that has been overwound and will not run.

It should have budded long ago, but it had fought off its budding, holding back against the day when it might escape, planning, he realized now, its fight to stay on Earth, which meant its conquest of Earth. It had planned, and planned well, against this very moment, and it would feel or show no mercy to anyone who interfered with it.

His hand went down and touched the gun and he felt the muscles in his jaw involuntarily tightening and suddenly there was at once a lightness and a hardness in him that had not been there before. He pulled himself up the boulder face, seeking cautious hand- and toeholds, breathing shallowly, body pressed against the rock. Quickly, and surely, and no noise, for he must reach the top and be there before the *puudly* knew there was anyone around.

The *puudly* would be relaxed and intent upon its business, engrossed in the budding forth of that numerous family that in days to come would begin the grim and relentless crusade to make an alien planet safe for *puudlies* . . . and for *puudlies* alone.

That is, if the *puudly* were here and not somewhere else. James was only a human trying to think like a *puudly* and that was not an easy or a pleasant job and he had no way of knowing if he succeeded. He could only hope that his reasoning was vicious and crafty enough.

His clawing hand found grass and earth and he sank his fingers deep into the soil, hauling his body up the last few feet of the rock face above the pit.

He lay flat upon the gently sloping ground, listening, tensed for any danger. He studied the ground in front of him, probing every foot. Distant street lamps lighting the zoo walks threw back the total blackness that had engulfed him as he climbed out of the moat, but there still were areas of shadow that he had to study closely.

Inch by inch, he squirmed his way along, making sure of the terrain immediately ahead before he moved a muscle. He held the gun in a rock-hard fist, ready for instant action, watching for the faintest hint of motion, alert for any hump or irregularity that was not rock or bush or grass.

Minutes magnified themselves into hours, his eyes ached with staring and the lightness that had been in him drained away, leaving only the hardness, which was as tense as a drawn bowstring. A sense of failure began to seep into his mind and with it came the full-fledged, until now unadmitted, realization of what failure meant, not only for the world, but for the dignity and the pride that was Henderson James.

Now, faced with the possibility, he admitted to himself the action he must take if the *puudly* were not here, if he did not find it here and kill it. He would have to notify the authorities, would have to attempt to alert the police, must plead with newspapers and radio to warn the citizenry, must reveal himself as a man who, through pride and self-conceit, had exposed the people of the Earth to this threat against their hold upon their native planet.

They would not believe him. They would laugh at him until the laughter died in their torn throats, choked off with their blood. He sweated, thinking of it, thinking of the price this city, and the world, would pay before it learned the truth.

There was a whisper of sound, a movement of black against deeper black.

The *puudly* rose in front of him, not more than six feet away, from its bed beside a bush. He jerked the pistol up and his finger tightened on the trigger.

"Don't," the *puudly* said inside his mind. "I'll go along with you."

His finger strained with the careful slowness of the squeeze and the gun leaped in his hand, but even as it did he felt the whiplash of terror slash at his brain, caught for just a second the terrible import, the mind-shattering obscenity that glanced off his mind and ricocheted away.

"Too late," he told the *puudly*, with his voice and his mind and his body shaking. "You should have tried that first. You wasted precious seconds. You would have got me if you had done it first."

It had been easy, he assured himself, much easier than he had thought. The *puudly* was dead or dying and the Earth and its millions of unsuspecting citizens were safe and, best of all, Henderson James was safe ... safe from indignity, safe from being stripped naked of the little defenses he had built up through the years to shield him against the public stare. He felt relief flood over him and it left him pulseless and breathless and feeling clean, but weak.

"You fool," the dying *puudly* said, death clouding its words as they built up in his mind. "You fool, you half-thing, you duplicate ..."

It died then and he felt it die, felt the life go out of it and leave it empty.

He rose softly to his feet and he seemed stunned and at first he thought it was from knowing death, from having touched hands with death within the *puudly's* mind.

The *puudly* had tried to fool him. Faced with the pistol, it had tried to throw him off his balance to give it the second that it needed to hurl the mind-blasting thought that had caught at the edge of his brain. If he had hesitated for a moment, he knew, it would have been all over with him. If his finger had slackened for a moment, it would have been too late.

The *puudly* must have known that he would think of the zoo as the first logical place to look and, even knowing that, it had held him in enough contempt to come here, had not even bothered to try to watch for him, had not tried to stalk him, had waited until he was almost on top of it before it moved.

And that was queer, for the *puudly* must have known, with its uncanny mental powers, every move that he had made. It must have maintained a casual contact with his mind every second of the time since it had escaped. He had known that and... wait a minute, he hadn't known it until this very moment, although, knowing it now, it seemed as if he had always known it.

What is the matter with me, he thought. There's something wrong with me. I should have known I could not surprise the *puudly,* and yet I didn't know it. I must have surprised it, for otherwise it would have finished me off quite leisurely at any moment after I climbed out of the moat.

You fool, the *puudly* had said. You fool, you half-thing, you duplicate...

You duplicate!

He felt the strength and the personality and the hard, unquestioned identity of himself as Henderson James, human being, drain out of him, as if someone had cut the puppet string and he, the puppet, had slumped supine upon the stage.

So that was why he had been able to surprise the *puudly!*

There were two Henderson Jameses. The *puudly* had been in contact with one of them, the original, the real Henderson James, had known every move he made, had known that it was safe so far as that Henderson James might be concerned. It had not known of the second Henderson James that had stalked it through the night.

Henderson James, duplicate.

Henderson James, temporary.

Henderson James, here tonight, gone tomorrow.

For they would not let him live. The original Henderson James would not allow him to continue living, and even if he did, the world would not allow it. Duplicates were made only for very temporary and very special reasons and it was always understood that once their purpose was accomplished they would be done away with.

Done away with... those were the words exactly. Gotten out of the way. Swept out of sight and mind. Killed as unconcernedly and emotionlessly as one chops off a chicken's head.

He walked forward and dropped on one knee beside the *puudly,* running his hand over its body in the darkness. Lumps stood out all over it, the swelling buds that now would never break to spew forth in a loathsome birth a brood of *puudly* pups.

He rose to his feet.

The job was done. The *puudly* had been killed—killed before it had given birth to a horde of horrors.

The job was done and he could go home.

Home?

Of course, that was the thing that had been planted in his mind, the thing they wanted him to do. To go home, to go back to the house on Summit Avenue, where his executioners would wait, to walk back deliberately and unsuspectingly to the death that waited.

The job was done and his usefulness was over. He had been created to perform a certain task and the task was now performed and while an hour ago he had been a factor in the plans of men, he was no longer wanted. He was an embarrassment and superfluous.

Now wait a minute, he told himself. You may not be a duplicate. You do not feel like one.

That was true. He felt like Henderson James. He was Henderson James. He lived on Summit Avenue and had illegally brought to Earth a beast known as a *puudly* in order that he might study it and talk to it and test its alien reactions, attempt to measure its intelligence and guess at the strength and depth and the direction of its non-humanity. He had been a fool, of course, to do it, and yet at the time it had seemed important to understand the deadly, alien mentality.

I am human, he said, and that was right, but even so the fact meant nothing. Of course he was human. Henderson James was human and his duplicate would be exactly as human as the original. For the duplicate, processed from the pattern that held every trait and characteristic of the man he was to become a copy of, would differ in not a single basic factor.

In not a single basic factor, perhaps, but in certain other things. For no matter how much the duplicate might be like his pattern, no matter how full-limbed he might spring from his creation, he still would be a new man. He would have the capacity for knowledge and for thought and in a little time he would have and know and be all the things that his original was...

But it would take some time, some short while to come to a full realization of all he knew and was, some time to coordinate and recognize all the knowledge and experience that lay within his mind. At first he'd grope and search until he came upon the things that he must know. Until he became acquainted with himself, with the sort of man he was, he could not reach out blindly in the dark and put his hand exactly and unerringly upon the thing he wished.

That had been exactly what he'd done. He had groped and searched. He had been compelled to think, at first, in simple basic truths and facts.

I am a man.

I am on a planet called Earth.

I am Henderson James.

I live on Summit Avenue.

There is a job to do.

It had been quite a while, he remembered now, before he had been able to dig out of his mind the nature of the job.

There is a *puudly* to hunt down and destroy.

Even now he could not find in the hidden, still-veiled recesses of his mind the many valid reasons why a man should run so grave a risk to study a thing so vicious as a *puudly*. There were reasons, he knew there were, and in a little time he would know them quite specifically.

The point was that if he were Henderson James, original, he would know them now, know them as a part of himself and his life, without laboriously searching for them.

The *puudly* had known, of course. It had known, beyond any chance of error, that there were two Henderson Jameses. It had been keeping tab on one when another one showed up. A mentality far less astute than the *puudly's* would have had no trouble in figuring that one out.

If the *puudly* had not talked, he told himself, I never would have known. If it had died at once and not had a chance to taunt me, I would not have known. I would even now be walking to the house on Summit Avenue.

He stood lonely and naked of soul in the wind that swept across the moated island. There was a sour bitterness in his mouth.

He moved a foot and touched the dead *puudly*.

"I'm sorry," he told the stiffening body. "I'm sorry now I did it. If I had known, I never would have killed you."

Stiffly erect, he moved away.

III

He stopped at the street corner, keeping well in the shadow. Halfway down the block, and on the other side, was the house. A light burned in one of the rooms upstairs and another on the post beside the gate that opened into the yard, lighting the walk up to the door.

Just as if, he told himself, the house were waiting for the master to come home. And that, of course, was exactly what it was doing. An old lady of a house, waiting, hands folded in its lap, rocking very gently in a squeaky chair . . . and with a gun beneath the folded shawl.

His lip lifted in half a snarl as he stood there, looking at the house. What do they take me for, he thought, putting out a trap in plain sight and one that's not even baited? Then he remembered. They would not know, of course, that he knew he was a duplicate. They would think that he would think that he was Henderson James, the one and only. They would expect him to come walking home, quite naturally, believing he belonged there. So far as they would know, there would be no possibility of his finding out the truth.

And now that he had? Now that he was here, across the street from the waiting house?

He had been brought into being, had been given life, to do a job that his original had not dared to do, or had not wanted to do. He had carried out a killing his original didn't want to dirty his hands with, or risk his neck in doing.

Or had it not been that at all, but the necessity of two men working on the job, the original serving as a focus for the *puudly's* watchful mind while the other man sneaked up to kill it while it watched?

No matter what, he had been created, at a good stiff price, from the pattern of the man that was Henderson James. The wizardry of man's knowledge, the magic of machines, a deep understanding of organic chemistry, of human physiology, of the mystery of life, had made a second Henderson James. It was legal, of course, under certain circumstances . . . for example, in the case of public policy, and his own creation, he knew, might have been validated under such a heading. But there were conditions and one of these was that a duplicate not be allowed to continue living once it had served the specific purpose for which it had been created.

Usually such a condition was a simple one to carry out, for the duplicate was not meant to know he was a duplicate. So far as he was concerned, he was the original. There was no suspicion in him, no foreknowledge of the doom that was invariably ordered for him, no reason for him to be on guard against the death that waited.

The duplicate knitted his brow, trying to puzzle it out.

There was a strange set of ethics here.

He was alive and he wanted to stay alive. Life, once it had been tasted, was too sweet, too good, to go back to the nothingness from which he had come... or would it be nothingness? Now that he had known life, now that he was alive, might he not hope for a life after death, the same as any other human being? Might not he, too, have the same human right as any other human to grasp at the shadowy and glorious promises and assurances held out by religion and by faith?

He tried to marshal what he knew about those promises and assurances, but his knowledge was illusive. A little later he would remember more about it. A little later, when the neural bookkeeper in his mind had been able to coordinate and activate the knowledge that he had inherited from the pattern, he would know.

He felt a trace of anger stir deep inside of him, anger at the unfairness of allowing him only a few short hours of life, of allowing him to learn how wonderful a thing life was, only to snatch it from him. It was a cruelty that went beyond mere human cruelty. It was something that had been fashioned out of the distorted perspective of a machine society that measured existence only in terms of mechanical and physical worth, that discarded with a ruthless hand whatever part of that society had no specific purpose.

The cruelty, he told himself, was in ever giving life, not in taking it away.

His original, of course, was the one to blame. He was the one who had obtained the *puudly* and allowed it to escape. It was his fumbling and his inability to correct his error without help which had created the necessity of fashioning a duplicate.

And yet, could he blame him?

Perhaps, rather, he owed him gratitude for a few hours of life at least, gratitude for the privilege of knowing what life

was like. Although he could not quite decide whether or not it
was something which called for gratitude.

He stood there, staring at the house. That light in the
upstairs room was in the study off the master bedroom. Up
there Henderson James, original, was waiting for the word
that the duplicate had come home to death. It was an easy
thing to sit there and wait, to sit and wait for the word that
was sure to come. An easy thing to sentence to death a man
one had never seen, even if that man be the walking image of
one's self.

It would be a harder decision to kill him if you stood face
to face with him . . . harder to kill someone who would be, of
necessity, closer than a brother, someone who would be, even
literally, flesh of your flesh, blood of your blood, brain of
your brain.

There would be a practical side as well, a great advantage
to be able to work with a man who thought as you did, who
would be almost a second self. It would be almost as if there
were two of you.

A thing like that could be arranged. Plastic surgery and a
price for secrecy could make your duplicate into an
unrecognizable other person. A little red tape, some
finagling . . . but it could be done. It was a proposition that
Henderson James, duplicate, thought would interest
Henderson James, original. Or at least he hoped it would.

The room with the light could be reached with a little luck,
with strength and agility and determination. The brick
expanse of a chimney, its base cloaked by shrubs, its length
masked by a closely growing tree, ran up the wall. A man
could climb its rough brick face, could reach out and swing
himself through the open window into the lighted room.

And once Henderson James, original, stood face to face
with Henderson James, duplicate . . . well, it would be less of
a gamble. The duplicate then would no longer be an
impersonal factor. He would be a man and one that was very
close to his original.

There would be watchers, but they would be watching the
front door. If he were quiet, if he could reach and climb the
chimney without making any noise, he'd be in the room
before anyone would notice.

He drew back deeper in the shadows and considered. It

was either get into the room and face his original, hope to be able to strike a compromise with him, or simply to light out . . . to run and hide and wait, watching his chance to get completely away, perhaps to some far planet in some other part of the Galaxy.

Both ways were a gamble, but one was quick, would either succeed or fail within the hour; the other might drag on for months with a man never knowing whether he was safe, never being sure.

Something nagged him, a persistent little fact that skittered through his brain and eluded his efforts to pin it down. It might be important and then, again, it might be a random thing, simply a floating piece of information that was looking for its pigeonhole.

His mind shrugged it off.

The quick way or the long way?

He stood thinking for a moment and then moved swiftly down the street, seeking a place where he could cross in shadow.

He had chosen the short way.

IV

The room was empty.

He stood beside the window, quietly, only his eyes moving, searching every corner, checking against a situation that couldn't seem quite true . . . that Henderson James was not here, waiting for the word.

Then he strode swiftly to the bedroom door and swung it open. His finger found the switch and the lights went on. The bedroom was empty and so was the bath. He went back into the study.

He stood with his back against the wall, facing the door that led into the hallway, but his eyes went over the room, foot by foot, orienting himself, feeling himself flow into the shape and form of it, feeling familiarity creep in upon him and enfold him in its comfort of belonging.

Here were the books, the fireplace with its mantel loaded with souvenirs, the easy chairs, the liquor cabinet . . . and all were a part of him, a background that was as much a part of

Henderson James as his body and his inner thoughts were a part of him.

This, he thought, is what I would have missed, the experience I never would have had if the *puudly* had not taunted me. I would have died an empty and unrelated body that had no actual place in the universe.

The phone purred at him and he stood there startled by it, as if some intruder from the outside had pushed its way into the room, shattering the sense of belonging that had come to him.

The phone rang again and he went across the room and picked it up.

"James speaking," he said.

"That you, Mr. James?"

The voice was that of Anderson, the gardener.

"Why, yes," said the duplicate. "Who did you think it was?"

"We got a fellow here who says he's you."

Henderson James, duplicate, stiffened with fright and his hand, suddenly, was grasping the phone so hard that he found the time to wonder why it did not pulverize to bits beneath his fingers.

"He's dressed like you," the gardener said, "and I knew you went out. Talked to you, remember? Told you that you shouldn't? Not with us waiting for that . . . that thing."

"Yes," said the duplicate, his voice so even that he could not believe it was he who spoke. "Yes, certainly I remember talking with you."

"But, sir, how did you get back?"

"I came in the back way," the even voice said into the phone. "Now what's holding you back?"

"He's dressed like you."

"Naturally. Of course he would be, Anderson."

And that, to be sure, didn't quite follow, but Anderson wasn't too bright to start with and now he was somewhat upset.

"You remember," the duplicate said, "that we talked about it."

"I guess I was excited and forgot," admitted Anderson. "You told me to call you, to make sure you were in your study, though. That's right, isn't it, sir?"

"You've called me," the duplicate said, "and I am here."

"Then the other one out here is him?"

"Of course," said the duplicate. "Who else could it be?"

He put the phone back into the cradle and stood waiting. It came a moment after, the dull, throaty cough of a gun.

He walked to a chair and sank into it, spent with the knowledge of how events had so been ordered that now, finally, he was safe, safe beyond all question.

Soon he would have to change into other clothes, hide the gun and the clothes that he was wearing. The staff would ask no questions, most likely, but it was best to let nothing arouse suspicion in their minds.

He felt his nerves quieting and he allowed himself to glance about the room, take in the books and furnishings, the soft and easy . . . and earned . . . comfort of a man solidly and unshakably established in the world.

He smiled softly.

"It will be nice," he said.

It had been easy. Now that it was over. It seemed ridiculously easy. Easy because he had never seen the man who had walked up to the door. It was easy to kill a man you have never seen.

With each passing hour he would slip deeper and deeper into the personality that was his by right of heritage. There would be no one to question, after a time not even himself, that he was Henderson James.

The phone rang again and he got up to answer it.

A pleasant voice told him, "This is Allen, over at the duplication lab. We've been waiting for a report from you."

"Well," said James, "I . . ."

"I just called," interrupted Allen, "to tell you not to worry. It slipped my mind before."

"I see," said James, though he didn't.

"We did this one a little differently," Allen explained. "An experiment that we thought we'd try out. Slow poison in his bloodstream. Just another precaution. Probably not necessary, but we like to be positive. In case he fails to show up, you needn't worry any."

"I am sure he will show up."

Allen chuckled. "Twenty-four hours. Like a time bomb. No antidote for it even if he found out somehow."

"It was good of you to let me know," said James.

"Glad to," said Allen. "Good night, Mr. James."

The Sitters

The first week of school was finished. Johnson Dean, superintendent of Millville High, sat at his desk, enjoying the quiet and the satisfaction of late Friday afternoon.

The quiet was massacred by Coach Jerry Higgins. He clomped into the office and threw his muscular blond frame heavily in a chair.

"Well, you can call off football for the year," he said angrily. "We can drop out of the conference."

Dean pushed away the papers on which he had been working and leaned back in his chair. The sunlight from the western windows turned his silver thatch into a seeming halo. His pale, blue-veined, wrinkled hands smoothed out, painstakingly, the fading crease in his fading trousers.

"What has happened now?" he asked.

"It's King and Martin, Mr. Dean. They aren't coming out this year."

Dean clucked sympathetically, but somewhat hollowly, as if his heart was not quite in it. "Let me see," he said. "If I remember rightly, those two were very good last year. King was in the line and Martin quarterback."

Higgins exploded in righteous indignation. "Who ever heard of a quarterback deciding he wouldn't play no more? And not just an ordinary boy, but one of the very best. He made all-conference last year."

"You've talked to them, of course?"

"I got down on my knees to them," said the coach. "I asked them did they want that I should lose my job. I asked is there anything you got against me. I told them they were letting down the school. I told them we wouldn't have a team without them. They didn't laugh at me, but—"

72

"They wouldn't laugh at you," said Dean. "Those boys are gentlemen. In fact, all the youngsters in school—"

"They're a pack of sissies!" stormed the coach.

Dean said gently, "That is a matter of opinion. There have been moments when I also wasn't able to attach as much importance to football as it seemed to me I should."

"But that's different," argued the coach. "When a man grows up, naturally he will lose some interest. But these are kids. This just isn't healthy. These young fellows should be out there pawing up the earth. All kids should have a strong sense of competition. And even if they don't, there's the financial angle. Any outstanding football man has a chance, when he goes to college—"

"Our kids don't need athletic subsidies," said Dean, a little sharply. "They're getting more than their share of scholastic scholarships."

"If we had a lot more material," moaned Higgins, "King and Martin wouldn't mean so much. We wouldn't win too often, but we still would have a team. But as it is—do you realize, Mr. Dean, that there have been fewer coming out each year? Right now, I haven't more than enough—"

"You've talked to King and Martin. You're sure they won't reconsider?"

"You know what they told me? They said football interfered with studies!"

The way Higgins said it, it was rank heresy.

"I guess, then," Dean said cheerfully, "that we'll just have to face it."

"But it isn't normal," the coach protested. "There aren't any kids who think more of studies than they do of football. There aren't any kids so wrapped up in books—"

"There are," said Dean. "There are a lot, right here at Millville. You should take a look at the grade averages over the past ten years, if you don't believe it."

"What gets me is that they don't act like kids. They act like a bunch of adults." The coach shook his head, as if to say it was all beyond him. "It's a dirty shame. If only some of those big bruisers would turn out, we'd have the makings of a team."

"Here, also," Dean reminded him, "we have the makings of men and women that Millville in the future may very well be proud of."

The coach got up angrily. "We won't win a game," he warned. "Even Bagley will beat us."

"That is something," Dean observed philosophically, "that shan't worry me too much."

He sat quietly at his desk and listened to the hollow ringing of the coach's footsteps going down the corridor, dimming out with distance.

And he heard the swish and rumble of a janitorial servo-mechanism wiping down the stairs. He wondered where Stuffy was. Fiddling around somewhere, no doubt. With all the scrubbers and the washers and wipers and other mechanical contraptions, there wasn't too much to take up Stuffy's time. Although Stuffy, in his day, had done a lot of work—he'd been on the go from dark to dark, a top-notch janitor.

If it weren't for the labor shortage, Stuffy would have been retired several years ago. But they didn't retire men any more the way they had at one time. With man going to the stars, there now was more than the human race could do. If they had been retiring men, Dean thought, he himself would be without a job.

And there was nothing he would have hated more than that. For Millville High was his. He had made it his. For more than fifty years, he'd lived for Millville High, first as a young and eager teacher, then as principal, and now, the last fifteen years or so, as its superintendent.

He had given everything he had. And it had given back. It had been wife and child and family, a beginning and an end. And he was satisfied, he told himself—satisfied on this Friday of a new school year, with Stuffy puttering somewhere in the building and no football team—or, at least, next to none.

He rose from the desk and stood looking out the window. A student, late in going home, was walking across the lawn. Dean thought he knew her, although of late his eyes had not been so good for distance.

He squinted at her harder, almost certain it was Judy Charleson. He'd known her grandfather back in the early days and the girl, he thought, had old Henry Charleson's gait. He chuckled, thinking back. Old Charleson, he recalled, had been a slippery one in a business deal. There had been that time he had gotten tangled up in a deal for tube-liners to be used by a starship outfit...

He jerked his mind away, tried to wipe out his thinking of the old days. It was a sign of advancing age, the dawn of second childhood.

But however that might be, old Henry Charleson was the only man in Millville who had ever had a thing to do with starships—except Lamont Stiles.

Dean grinned a little, remembering Lamont Stiles and the grimness in him and how he'd amounted to something after many years, to the horrified exasperation of many people who had confidently prophesied he'd come to no good end.

And there was no one now, of course, who knew, or perhaps would ever know, what kind of end Lamont Stiles had finally come to. Or if, in fact, he'd come to an end as yet.

Lamont Stiles, Dean thought, might this very moment be striding down the street of some fantastic city on some distant world.

And if that were so, and if he came home again, what would he bring this time?

The last time he'd come home—the only time he ever had come home—he had brought the Sitters, and they were a funny lot.

Dean turned from the window and walked back to the desk. He sat down and pulled the papers back in front of him. But he couldn't get down to work. That was the way it often was. He'd start thinking of the old days, when there were many friends and many things to do, and get so involved in thinking that he couldn't settle down to work.

He heard the shuffle coming along the hall and shoved the papers to one side. He could tell that it was Stuffy, from the familiar shuffle, coming by to pass the time of day.

Dean wondered at the quiet anticipation he felt within himself. Although it was not so strange, once one considered it. There weren't many left like Stuffy, not many he could talk with.

It was odd with the old, he thought. Age dissolved or loosened the ties of other days. The old died or moved away or were bound by infirmities. Or they drew within themselves, into a world of their own, where they sought a comfort they could find no longer in the outer world.

Stuffy shuffled to the doorway, stopped and leaned against the jamb. He wiped his drooping, yellow mustaches with a greasy hand. "What's ailing the coach?" he asked. "He went busting out of here like he was turpentined."

"He has no football team," said Dean. "Or he tells me that he hasn't any."

"He cries early every season," Stuffy said. "It's just an act."

"I'm not so sure this time. King and Martin aren't coming out."

Stuffy shuffled a few more paces into the room and dropped into a chair.

"It's them Sitters," Stuffy declared. "They're the cause of it."

Dean sat upright. "What is that you said!"

"I been watching it for years. You can spot the kids that the Sitters sat with or that went to their nursery school. They done something to them kids."

"Fairy tale," said Dean.

"It ain't a fairy tale," Stuffy declared stubbornly. "You know I don't take no stock in superstitition. Just because them Sitters are from some other planet . . . Say, did you ever find out what planet they were from?"

Dean shook his head. "I don't know that Lamont ever said. He might have, but I never heard it."

"They're weird critters," said Stuffy, stroking his mustaches slowly to lend an air of deliberation to his words, "but I never held their strangeness against them. After all, they ain't the only aliens on the Earth. The only ones we have in Millville, of course, but there are thousands of other critters from the stars scattered round the Earth."

Dean nodded in agreement, scarcely knowing what he was agreeing with. He said nothing, however, for there was no need of that. Once Stuffy got off to a running start, he'd go on and on.

"They seem right honest beings," Stuffy said. "They never played on no one's sympathy. They just settled in, after Lamont went away and left them, and never asked no one to intercede for them. They made an honest living all these years and that is all one could expect of them."

"And yet," said Dean, "you think they've done something to the kids."

"They changed them. Ain't you noticed it?"

Dean shook his head. "I never thought to notice. I've known these youngsters for years. I knew their folks before them. How do you think they were changed?"

"They grew them up too fast," Stuffy said.

"Talk sense," snapped Dean. "Who grew what too fast?"

"The Sitters grew the kids too fast. That's what's wrong with them. Here they are in high school and they're already grown up."

From somewhere on one of the floors below came the dismal hooting of a servo-mechanism in distress.

Stuffy sprang to his feet. "That's the mopper-upper. I'll bet you it got caught in a door again."

He swung around and galloped off at a rapid shuffle.

"Stupid machine!" he yelped as he went out the door.

Dean pulled the papers back in front of him again and picked up a pencil. It was getting late and he had to finish.

But he didn't see the papers. He saw many little faces staring up at him from where the papers lay—solemn, big-eyed little faces with an elusive look about them.

And he knew that elusive look—the look of dawning adulthood staring out of childish faces.

They grew them up too fast!

"No," said Dean to himself. "No, it couldn't be!"

And yet there was corroborative evidence: The high averages, the unusual number of scholarships, the disdain for athletics. And, as well, the general attitude. And the lack of juvenile delinquency—for years, Millville had been proud that its juvenile delinquency had been a minor problem. He remembered that several years ago he had been asked to write an article about it for a parent-teacher magazine.

He tried to remember what he had written in that article and slowly bits of it came back to him—the realization of parents that their children were a part of the family and not mere appendages; the role played by the churches of the town; the emphasis placed on the social sciences by the schools.

"And was I wrong?" he asked himself. "Was it none of these, but something else entirely—someone else entirely?"

He tried to work and couldn't. He was too upset. He could not erase the smiling little faces that were staring up at him.

Finally he shoved the papers in a drawer and got up from

the desk. He put on his worn topcoat and sat the battered old black felt hat atop his silver head.

On the ground floor, he found Stuffy herding the last of the servo-mechanisms into their cubby for the night. Stuffy was infuriated.

"It got itself caught in a heating grill," he raged. "If I hadn't gotten there in the nick of time, it would have wrecked the works." He shook his head dolefully. "Them machines are fine when everything goes well. But just let something happen and they panic. It was best the old way, John."

Stuffy slammed the door on the last of the waddling machines and locked it savagely.

"Stuffy, how well did you know Lamont Stiles?" asked Dean.

Stuffy rubbed his mustaches in fine deliberation. "Knew him well. Lamont and me, we were kids together. You were a little older. You were in the crowd ahead."

Dean nodded his head slowly. "Yes, I remember, Stuffy. Odd that you and I stayed on in the old home town. So many of the others left."

"Lamont ran away when he was seventeen. There wasn't much to stay for. His old lady was dead and his old man was drinking himself to death and Lamont had been in a scrape or two. Everyone was agreed Lamont never would amount to nothing."

"It's hard for a boy when a whole town turns against him."

"That's a fact," said the janitor. "There was no one on his side. He told me when he left that someday he'd come back and show them. But I just thought he was talking big. Like a kid will do, you know, to bolster up himself."

"You were wrong," said Dean.

"Never wronger, John."

For Lamont Stiles had come back, more than thirty years after he had run away, back to the old weather-beaten house on Maple Street that had waited empty for him all the lonely years; had come back, an old man when he still was scarcely fifty, big and tough despite the snow-white hair and the skin turned cordovan with the burn of many alien suns; back from far wandering among the distant stars.

But he was a stranger. The town remembered him; he had forgotten it. Years in alien lands had taken the town and twisted it in his brain, and what he remembered of it was more fantasy than truth—the fantasy spawned by years of thinking back and of yearning and of hate.

"I must go," Dean said. "Carrie will have supper ready. She doesn't like to have it getting cold."

"Good night, John," said the janitor.

The sun was almost down when Dean came out the door and started down the walk. It was later than he'd thought. Carrie would be sore at him and she would bawl him out.

Dean chuckled to himself. There was no one quite like Carrie.

Not wife, for he'd never had a wife. Not mother or sister, for both of those were dead. But housekeeper, faithful all the years—and a bit of wife and sister, and sometimes even mother.

A man's loyalties are queer, he thought. They blind him and they bind him and they shape the man he is. And, through them, he serves and achieves a kind of greatness, although at times the greatness may be gray and pallid and very, very quiet.

Not like the swaggering and the bitter greatness of Lamont Stiles, who came striding from the stars, bringing with him those three queer creatures who became the Sitters. Bringing them and installing them in his house on Maple Street and then, in a year or two, going off to the stars again and leaving them in Millville.

Queer, Dean thought, that so provincial a town as this should accept so quietly these exotic beings. Queerer still that the mothers of the town, in time, should entrust their children to the aliens' care.

As Dean turned the corner into Lincoln Street, he met a woman walking with a knee-high boy.

It was Mildred Anderson, he saw—or had been Mildred Anderson, but she was married now and for the life of him he could not recall the name. Funny, he thought, how fast the young ones grew up. Not more than a couple of years ago, it seemed, that Mildred was in school—although he knew he must be wrong on that; it would be more like ten.

He tipped his hat. "Good evening, Mildred. My, how the boy is growing."

"I doe to cool," the child lisped.

His mother interpreted. "He means he goes to school. He is so proud of it."

"Nursery school, of course."

"Yes, Mr. Dean. The Sitters. They are such lovely things. And so good with children. And there's the cost. Or, rather, the lack of it. You just give them a bouquet of flowers or a little bottle of perfume or a pretty picture and they are satisfied. They positively refuse to take any money. I can't understand that. Can you, Mr. Dean?"

"No," said Dean. "I can't."

He'd forgotten what a talker Mildred was. There had been a period in school, he recalled, when she had been appropriately nicknamed Gabby.

"I sometimes think," she said, hurrying on so she'd miss no time for talk, "that we people here on Earth attach too much importance to money. The Sitters don't seem to know what money is, or if they do, they pay no attention to it. As if it were something that was not important. But I understand there are other races like that. It makes one think, doesn't it, Mr. Dean?"

And he remembered now another infuriating trait of Mildred's—how she inevitably ended any string of sentences with a dangling question.

He didn't try to answer. He knew an answer was not expected of him.

"I must be getting on," he said. "I am late already."

"It was nice to see you, Mr. Dean," said Mildred. "I so often think of my days in school and sometimes it seems like just positively ages and there are other times when it seems no more than just yesterday and . . ."

"Very nice, indeed," said Dean, lifting his hat to her, then almost scurrying off.

It was undignified, he grumbled to himself, being routed in broad daylight on a public street by a talkative woman.

As he went up the walk to the house, he heard Carrie bustling angrily about.

"Johnson Dean," she cried the instant he came in the door, "you sit right down and eat. Your food's already cold. And it's my circle night. Don't you even stop to wash."

Dean calmly hung up his hat and coat.

"For that matter," he said, "I guess I don't need to wash. My kind of job, a man doesn't get too dirty."

She was bustling about in the dining area, pouring his cup

of coffee and straightening up the bouquet of mums that served for the centerpiece.

"Since it's my circle night," she said, laying deliberate stress upon the words to shame him for being late, "I won't stay to wash the dishes. You just leave them on the table. I will do them later."

He sat down meekly to eat.

Somehow, for some reason he could not understand, fulfilling a need of which he was not aware, he suddenly felt safe. Safe and secure against a nagging worry and a half-formed fear that had been building up within him without his knowing it.

Carrie came through the living room, settling a deter-mined hat upon her determined head. She had the very air of a woman who was late for her circle meeting through no fault of her own. She halted at the door.

"You got everything you need?" she asked, her eyes making a swift inventory of the table.

"Everything." He chuckled. "Have a good time at the circle. Pick up a lot of gossip."

It was his favorite quip and he knew it irked her—and it was childish, too. But he could not resist it.

She flounced out of the door and he heard her putting down her heels with unnecessary firmness as she went down the walk.

With her going, a hard silence gripped the house and the deeper dusk moved in as he sat at the table eating.

Safe, he thought—old Johnson Dean, school man, safe inside the house his grandfather had built—how many years ago? Old-fashioned now, with its split-level floor plan and its high-bricked fireplace, with its double, attached garage and the planter out in front.

Safe and lonely.

And safe against what threat, against what creeping disturbance, so subtle that it failed of recognition?

He shook his head at that.

But lonely—that was different. That could be explained. The middle-young, he thought, and the very old are lonely. The middle-young because full communication had not been established, and the very old because communication had broken down.

Society was stratified, he told himself, stratified and sectored and partitioned off by many different factors—by age, by occupation, by education, by financial status. And the list did not end there. One could go on and on. It would be interesting, if a man could only find the time, to chart the stratification of humanity. Finished, if it ever could be finished, that chart would be a weird affair.

He finished the meal and wiped his mouth carefully with the napkin. He pushed back from the table and prowled the darkening living area.

He knew that he should at least pick up the dishes and tidy up the table. By rights, he should even wash them. He had caused Carrie a lot of fuss because he had been late. But he couldn't bring himself to do it. He couldn't settle down. Safe, he still was not at peace.

There was no use in putting this business off any longer, he realized, no use to duck the fear that was nagging at him. He knew what it was he faced, if he only would admit it.

Stuffy was crazy, of course. He could not possibly be right. He'd been thinking too much—imagining, rather.

The kids were no different now than they'd ever been.

Except that the grade averages had improved noticeably in the last ten years or so.

Except that there were, as one might expect of such grade averages, an increase in scholarships.

Except that the glitter of competitive sports was beginning to wear off.

Except that there was, in Millville, almost no delinquency.

And those solemn childish faces, with the big, bright eyes, staring up at him from the papers on his desk.

He paced slowly up and down the carpeting before the big brick fireplace, and the dead, black maw beneath the chimney throat, with the bitter smell of old wood ashes in it, seemed to be a mouth making sport of him.

He cracked one feebly clenched old fist into a shaky palm.

"It can't be right," he said fiercely to himself.

And yet, on the face of all evidence, it was.

The children in Millville were maturing faster; they were growing up, intellectually, much faster than they should.

And perhaps even more than that.

Growing in a new dimension, he wondered. Receding

farther from the savage that still lingered in humanity. For sports, organized sports on whatever basis, still remained a refined product of the cave—some antagonism that man had carried forward under many different guises and which broke forth at least partially in the open in the field of sports.

If he could only talk with the students, he thought, if he could somehow find out what they thought, then there might be a chance of running this thing to the ground.

But that was impossible. The barriers were too high and intricate, the lines of communication much too cluttered. For he was old and they were young; he was authority and they were the regimented. Once again the stratifications would keep them apart. There was no way in which he could approach them.

It was all right to say there was something happening, ridiculous as it might sound. But the important matter, if such should be the case, was to discover the cause and to plot the trend.

And Stuffy must be wrong. For it was fantastic to suggest the Sitters were engineering it.

Peculiarly enough, the Sitters, alien as they were, had established themselves as solid citizens of Millville. They would, he was sure, do nothing to jeopardize the position they had won—the position of being accepted and generally let alone and little talked about.

They would do nothing to attract attention to themselves. Through the years, too many other aliens had gotten into trouble through attempts to meddle and by exhibitionism. Although, come to think of it, what might have seemed to be exhibitionism, from the human viewpoint, possibly had been no more than normal alien conduct.

It had been the good fortune of the Sitters that their natural mother-disposition had enabled them to fit into the human pattern. They had proven ideal baby-sitters and in this they had an economic value and were the more readily accepted.

For many years, they had taken care of the Millville babies and they were everything that a sitter ought to be. And now they ran a nursery school, although, he remembered, there had been some ruckus over that, since they quite understandably did not hold formal education credits.

He turned on a light and went to the shelves to find

something he could read. But there was nothing there that held any interest for him. He ran a finger along the backs of the rows of volumes and his eyes flicked down the titles, but he found absolutely nothing.

He left the shelves and paced over to the large front window and stared out at the street. The street lamps had not come on yet, but there were lights here and there in windows and occasionally a bubble-shaped car moved silently down the pavement, the fanning headlights catching a scurrying bunch of leaves or a crouching cat.

It was one of the older streets in town; at one time, he had known everyone who had lived upon it. He could call out without hesitation the names of the one-time owners— Wilson, Becket, Johnson, Random—but none of them lived here any longer. The names had changed and the faces were faces that he did not know; the stratification had shifted and he knew almost no one on the street.

The middle-young and the very old, he thought, they are the lonely ones.

He went back to the chair beside the lamp he'd lighted and sat down rather stiffly in it. He fidgeted, drumming his fingers on the arms. He wanted to get up, but there was nothing to get up for, unless it was to wash the dishes, and he didn't want to wash them.

He could take a walk, he told himself. That might be a good idea. There was a lot of comfort in an evening walk.

He got his coat and hat and went out the door and down the walk and turned west at the gate.

He was more than halfway there, skirting the business section, before he admitted to himself that he was heading for the Stiles house and the Sitters—that he had, in fact, never intended doing otherwise.

What he might do there, what he might learn there, he had no idea. There was no actual purpose in his mind. It was almost as if he were on an unknown mission, as if he were being pushed by some unseen force into a situation of no-choice.

He came to the Stiles house and stood on the walk outside, looking at it.

It was an old house, surrounded by shade trees that had been planted many years before, and the front yard was a wilderness of shrubs. Every once in a while, someone would come and cut the lawn and maybe trim the hedges and fix up the flower beds to pay the Sitters for all the baby-minding they had done, since the Sitters took no money.

And that was a funny thing, Dean thought, their not taking any money—just as if they didn't need it, as if they might not know what to do with it even if they had any. Perhaps they didn't need it, for they bought no food and still they kept on living and never had been sick enough for anyone to know about it. There must have been times when they were cold, although no one ever mentioned it, but they bought no fuel, and Lamont Stiles had left a fund to pay the taxes—so maybe it was true that they had no need of money.

There had been a time, Dean recalled, when there had been a lot of speculation in the town about their not eating—or at least not buying any food. But after a time the speculation dwindled down and all anyone would say was that you could never figure a lot of things about alien people and there was no use in trying.

And that was right, of course.

The Stiles house, Dean realized with something of a start, was even older than his house. It was a rambler and they had been popular many years before the split-level had come in.

Heavy drapes were drawn at the windows, but there was light behind the drapes and he knew the Sitters were at home. They were usually home, of course. Except on baby-sitting jobs, they never left the house, and in recent years they had gone out but little, for people had gotten in the habit of dropping off the kids at the Sitters' house. The kids never made a fuss, not even the tiny ones. They all liked going to the Sitters.

He went up the walk and climbed the stoop to ring the bell.

He waited and heard movement in the house.

The door came open and one of the Sitters stood there, with the light behind it, and he had forgotten—it had been many years since he'd seen one of the Sitters.

Shortly after Lamont Stiles had come home, Dean remembered, he had met all three of them, and in the years between, he had seen one of them from time to time a distance on the street. But the memory and the wonder had faded from his mind and now it struck him once again with all the olden force—the faery grace, the sense of suddenly standing face to face with a gentle flower.

The face, if it might be called a face, was sweet—too sweet, so sweet that it had no character and hardly an individuality. A baffling skin arrangement, like the petals of a flower, rose above the face, and the body of the Sitter was slender beyond all belief and yet so full of grace and poise that one forgot the slimness. And about the entire creature hung an air of such sweet simplicity and such a scent of innocence that it blotted out all else.

No wonder, Dean found himself thinking, that the children liked them so.

"Mr. Dean," the Sitter said, "won't you please come in? We are very honored."

"Thank you," he said, taking off his hat.

He stepped inside and heard the closing of the door and then the Sitter was at his side again.

"This chair right here," it said. "We reserve this one for our special visitors."

And it was all very sweet and friendly, and yet there was an alien, frightening touch.

Somewhere there were children laughing in the house. He twisted his head around to find where the laughter came from.

"They're in the nursery," said the Sitter. "I will close the door."

Dean sank into the chair and perched his battered old soft hat on one bony knee, fondling it with his bony fingers.

The Sitter came back and sat down on the floor in front of him, sat down with a single, effortless motion and he had the distinct impression of the swirl of flaring skirts, although the Sitter wore none.

"Now," the Sitter said by way of announcing that Dean commanded its entire attention.

But he did not speak, for the laughter still was in the room. Even with the door to the nursery shut, there still was childish laughter. It came from everywhere all about the room and it was an utterly happy laughter, the gay and abandoned, the unthinking, the spontaneous laughter of children hard at play.

Nor was that all.

Childish sparkle glittered in the air and there was the long forgotten sense of timelessness—of the day that never ended, that was never meant to end. A breeze was blowing out of some never-never land and it carried with it the scent of brook water bearing on its tide flotillas of fallen autumn leaves, and there was, as well, the hint of clover and of marigolds and the smell of fuzzy, new-washed blankets such as are used in cribs.

"Mr. Dean," the Sitter said.

He roused himself guiltily.

"I'm sorry," he told the Sitter. "I was listening to the children."

"But the door is closed."

"The children in this room," he said.

"There are no children in this room."

"Quite right," he said. "Quite right."

But there were. He could hear their laughter and the patter of their feet.

There were children, or at least the sense of them, and there was also the sense of many flowers, long since died and shriveled in actuality, but with the feel of them still caged inside the room. And the sense of beauty—the beauty of many different things, of flowers and gew-gaw jewelry and little painted pictures and of gaily colored scarves, of all the things that through the years had been given to the Sitters in lieu of money.

"This room," he said haltingly, half-confused. "It is such a pleasant room. I'd just like to sit here."

He felt himself sink into the room, into the youngness and the gayety. If he let go, he thought, if he only could let go, he might join the children and be the same as they.

"Mr. Dean," the Sitter said, "you are very sensitive."

"I am very old," said Dean. "Maybe that's the reason."

The room was both ancient and antique. It was a cry across almost two centuries, with its small brick fireplace paneled in white wood, its arched doorways and the windows that stretched from floor to ceiling, covered by heavy drapes of black and green, etched with golden thread. And it had a solid comfort and a deep security that the present architecture of aluminum and glass never could achieve. It was dusty and moldy and cluttered and perhaps unsanitary, but it had the feel of home.

"I am old-fashioned," said Dean, "and, I suspect, very close to senile, and I am afraid that the time has come again to believe in fairy tales and magic."

"It is not magic," the Sitter replied. "It is the way we live, the only way we can live. You will agree that even Sitters must somehow stay alive."

"Yes, I agree," said Dean.

He lifted the battered hat from off his knee and rose slowly to his feet.

The laughter seemed to be fainter now and the patter not so loud. But the sense of youth—of youngness, of vitality and of happiness—still lay within the room. It lent a sheen to the ancient shabbiness and it made his heart begin to ache with a sudden gladness.

The Sitter still sat upon the floor. "There was something you wanted, Mr. Dean?"

Dean fumbled with his hat. "Not any more. I think I've found my answer."

And even as he said it, he knew it was unbelievable, that once he stood outside the door, he'd know with certainty there could be no truth in what he'd found.

The Sitter rose. "You will come again? We would love to have you."

"Perhaps," said Dean, and turned toward the door.

Suddenly there was a top spinning on the floor, a golden top with flashing jewels set in it that caught the light and scattered it in a million flashing colors, and as it spun, it played a whistling tune—the kind of music that got inside and melted down one's soul.

Dean felt himself let go—as, sitting in the chair, he had thought it was impossible for him to do. And the laughter came again and the world outside withdrew and the room suddenly was filled with the marvelous light of Christmas.

He took a quick step forward and he dropped his hat. He didn't know his name, nor where he was, nor how he might have come there, and he didn't care. He felt a gurgling happiness welling up in him and he stooped to reach out for the top.

He missed it by an inch or two and he shuffled forward, stooping, reaching, and his toe caught in a hole in the ancient carpeting and he crashed down on his knees.

The top was gone and the Christmas light snapped out

and the world rushed in upon him. The gurgling happiness had gone and he was an old man in a beauty-haunted house, struggling from his knees to face an alien creature.

"I am sorry," said the Sitter. "You almost had it. Perhaps some other time."

He shook his head. "No! Not another time!"

The Sitter answered kindly, "It's the best we have to offer."

Dean fumbled his hat back on his head and turned shakily to the door. The Sitter opened it and he staggered out.

"Come again," the Sitter said, most sweetly. "Any time you wish."

On the street outside, Dean stopped and leaned against a tree. He took off his hat and mopped his brow.

Now, where he had felt only shock before, the horror began creeping in—the horror of a kind of life that did not eat as human beings ate, but in another way, who sucked their nourishment from beauty and from youth, who drained a bouquet dry and who nibbled from the happy hours of a laughing child, and even munched the laughter.

It was no wonder that the children of this village matured beyond their years. For they had their childishness stripped from them by a hungry form of life that looked on them as fodder. There might be, he thought, only so much of happy running and of childish laughter dealt out to any human. And while some might not use their quota, there still might be a limit on it, and once one had used it all, then it was gone and a person became an adult without too much of wonder or of laughter left within him.

The Sitters took no money. There was no reason that they should, for they had no need of it. Their house was filled with all the provender they had stowed away for years.

And in all those years, he was the first to know, the first to sense the nature of those aliens brought home by Lamont Stiles. It was a sobering thought—that he should be the first to find it out. He had said that he was old and that might be the reason. But that had been no more than words, rising to his lips almost automatically as a part of his professional self-pity. Yet there might be something in it even so.

Could it be possible that, for the old, there might be certain compensations for the loss of other faculties? As the body slowed and the mind began to dim, might some magical ability, a sort of psychic bloodhound sense, rise out of the embers of a life that was nearly spent?

He was always pothering around about how old he was, he told himself, as if the mere fact of getting old might be a virtue. He was forgetful of the present and his preoccupation with the past was growing to the danger point. He was close to second childhood and he was the one who knew it—and might that be the answer? Might that be why he'd seen the top and known the Christmas lights?

He wondered what might have happened if he could have grabbed the top.

He put his hat back on and stepped out from the tree and went slowly up the walk, heading back for home.

What could he do about it, he wondered, now that he'd unearthed the Sitters' secret? He could run and tattle, surely, but there'd be no one to believe him. They would listen to him and they would be polite so as not to hurt his feelings, yet there was no one in the village but would take it for an old man's imaginings, and there'd be nothing that he could do about it. For beyond his own sure knowledge, he had not a shred of proof.

He might call attention to the maturity of the young people, as Stuffy had called his attention to it this very afternoon. But even there he would find no proof, for in the final reckoning, all the villagers would retreat to rationalization. Parental pride, if nothing else, might require they should. Not a single one of them would find much cause for wonder in the fact that a boy or girl of theirs was singularly well-mannered and above the average in intelligence.

One might say that the parents should have noticed, that they should have known that an entire village full of children could not possibly be so well-behaved or so level-headed or so anything else as were these Millville children. And yet they had not noticed. It had crept along so slowly, had insinuated itself so smoothly, that the change was not apparent.

For that matter, he himself had not noticed it, he who most of his life had been intimately associated with these very children in which he found so much wonder now. And if he had not noticed, then why expect that someone else should? It had remained for a gossipy old busybody like the janitor to put a finger on it.

His throat was dry and his belly weak and sick and what

he needed most of all, Dean told himself, was a cup of coffee.

He turned off on a street that would take him to the downtown section and he plodded along with his head bent against the dark.

What would be the end of it, he asked himself. What would be the gain for this lost childhood? For this pilfering of children? What the value that growing boys and girls should cease to play a little sooner, that they take up the attitude of adults before the chosen time?

There was some gain already seen. The children of Millville were obedient and polite; they were constructive in their play; they'd ceased to be little savages or snobs.

The trouble was, now that one thought of it, they'd almost ceased being children, too.

And in the days to come? Would Millville supply Earth with great statesmen, with canny diplomats, with topnotch educators and able scientists? Perhaps, but that was not the point at all. The question of robbing childhood of its heritage to achieve these qualities was the basic question.

Dean came into the business district, not quite three blocks long, and walked slowly down the street, heading for the only drugstore in the town.

There were only a few people in the store and he walked over to the lunch counter and sat down. He perched on the stool forlornly, with the battered hat pulled down above his eyes, and he gripped the counter's edge to keep his hands from shaking.

"Coffee," he said to the girl who came to take his order, and she brought it to him.

He sipped at it, for it was too hot to drink. He was sorry he had come.

He felt all alone and strange, with all the bright light and the chrome, as if he were something that had shuffled from the past into a place reserved for the present.

He almost never came downtown any more and that must be the reason for the way he felt. Especially he almost never came down in the evening, although there had been a time he had.

He smiled, remembering how the old crowd used to get together and talk around in circles, about inconsequential things, their talk not getting anywhere and never meaning to.

But that was all ended now. The crowd had disappeared.

Some of them were dead and some had moved away and the few of them still left seldom ventured out.

He sat there, thinking, knowing he was maudlin and not caring if he was, too tired and shaken to flinch away from it.

A hand fell on his shoulder and he swung around, surprised.

Young Bob Martin stood there, and although he smiled, he still had the look of someone who had done a thing that he was unsure of.

"Sir, there are some of us down here at a table," said the young Martin, gulping a little at his own boldness.

Dean nodded. "That's very nice," he mumbled.

"We wondered if maybe—that is, Mr. Dean, we'd be pleased if you would care to join us."

"Well, that is very nice of you, indeed."

"We didn't mean, sir—that is—"

"Why, certainly," said Dean. "I'd be very glad to."

"Here, sir, let me take your coffee. I won't spill a drop of it."

"I'll trust you, Bob," said Dean, getting to his feet. "You almost never fumble."

"I can explain that, Mr. Dean. It's not that I don't want to play. It's just that . . ."

Dean tapped him on the shoulder lightly. "I understand. There is no need to explain."

He paused a second, trying to decide if it were wise to say what was in his mind.

He decided to: "If you don't tell the coach, I might even say I agree with you. There comes a time in life when football begins to seem a little silly."

Martin grinned, relieved. "You've hit it on the head. Exactly."

He led the way to the table.

There were four of them—Ronald King, George Woods, Judy Charleson and Donna Thompson. All good kids, thought Dean, every one of them. He saw they had been dawdling away at sodas, making them stretch out as long as possible.

They all looked up at him and smiled, and George Woods pulled back a chair in invitation. Dean sat down carefully and placed his hat on the floor beside him. Bob set down the coffee.

"It was good of you to think of me," said Dean and wondered why he found himself embarrassed. After all, these were his kids—the kids he saw every day in school, the ones he pushed and coddled into an education, the kids he'd never had himself.

"You're just the man we need," said Ronald King. "We've been talking about Lamont Stiles. He is the only Millville man who ever went to space and..."

"You must have known him, Mr. Dean," said Judy.

"Yes," Dean said slowly, "I did know him, but not as well as Stuffy did. Stuffy and he were kids together. I was a little older."

"What kind of man is he?" asked Donna.

Dean chuckled. "Lamont Stiles? He was the town's delinquent. He was poor in school and he had no home life and he just mostly ran wild. If there was trouble, you could bet your life that Lamont had had a hand in it. Everyone said that Lamont never would amount to anything and when it had been said often enough and long enough, Lamont must have taken it to heart..."

He talked on and on, and they asked him questions, and Ronald King went to the counter and came back with another cup of coffee for him.

The talk switched from Stiles to football. King and Martin told him what they had told the coach. Then the talk went on to problems in student government and from that to the new theories in ionic drive, announced just recently.

Dean did not do all the talking; he did a lot of listening, too, and he asked questions of his own and time flowed on unnoticed.

Suddenly the lights blinked and Dean looked up, startled.

Judy laughed at him. "That means the place is closing. It's the signal that we have to leave."

"I see," said Dean. "Do you folks do this often—staying until closing time, I mean?"

"Not often," Bob Martin told him. "On weekdays, there is too much studying."

"I remember many years ago—" Dean began, then left the words hanging in the air.

Yes, indeed, he thought, many years ago. And again tonight!

He looked at them, the five faces around the table.

Courtesy, he thought, and kindness and respect. But something more than that.

Talking with them, he had forgotten he was old. They had accepted him as another human being, not as an aged human being, not as a symbol of authority. They had moved over for him and made him one of them and themselves one of him; they had broken down the barrier not only of pupil and teacher, but of age and youth as well.

"I have my car," Bob Martin said. "Can I drive you home?"

Dean picked his hat from off the floor and rose slowly to his feet.

"No, thanks," he said. "I think I'd like to walk. I have an idea or two I'd like to mull a bit. Walking helps one think."

"Come again," said Judy Charleson. "Some other Friday night, perhaps."

"Why, thanks," said Dean. "I do believe I will."

Great kids, he told himself with a certain pride. Full of a kindness and a courtesy beyond even normal adult courtesy and kindness. Not brash, not condescending, not like kids at all, and yet with the shine of youthfulness and the idealism and ambition that walked hand in hand with youth.

Premature adults, lacking cynicism. And that was an important thing, the lack of cynicism.

Surely there could be nothing wrong in a humanity like that. Perhaps this was the very coin in which the Sitters paid for the childhood they had stolen.

If they had stolen it. For they might not have stolen it; they might merely have captured it and stored it.

And in such a case, then they had given free this new maturity and this new equality. And they had taken something which would have been lost in any event— something for which the human race had no use at all, but which was the stuff of life for the Sitter people.

They had taken youth and beauty and they had stored it in the house; they had preserved something that a human could not preserve except in memory. They had caught a fleeting thing and held it and it was there—the harvest of many years; the house was bulging with it.

Lamont Stiles, he wondered, talking in his mind to that man so long ago, so far away, how much did you know? What purpose was in your mind?

Perhaps a rebuke to the smugness of the town that had driven him to greatness. Perhaps a hope, maybe a certainty, that no one in Millville could ever say again, as they had said of Lamont Stiles, that this or that boy or girl would amount to nothing.

That much, perhaps, but surely not any more than that.

Donna had put her hand upon his arm, was tugging at his sleeve.

"Come on, Mr. Dean," she urged. "You can't stay standing here."

They walked with him to the door and said good night and he went up the street at a little faster gait, it seemed to him, than he ordinarily traveled.

But that, he told himself quite seriously, was because now he was just slightly younger than he had been a couple of hours before.

Dean went on even faster and he didn't hobble and he wasn't tired at all, but he wouldn't admit it to himself—for it was a dream, a hope, a seeking after that one never must admit. Until one said it aloud, there was no commitment to the hope, but once the word was spoken, then bitter disappointment lurked behind a tree.

He was walking in the wrong direction. He should be heading back for home. It was getting late and he should be in bed.

And he mustn't speak the word. He must not breathe the thought.

He went up the walk, past the shrub-choked lawn, and he saw that the light still filtered through the drawn drapes.

He stopped on the stoop and the thought flashed through his mind: *There are Stuffy and myself and old Abe Hawkins. There are a lot of us . . .*

The door came open and the Sitter stood there, poised and beautiful and not the least surprised. It was, he thought, almost as if it had been expecting him.

And the other two of them, he saw, were sitting by the fireplace.

"Won't you please come in?" the Sitter said. "We are so glad you decided to come back. The children all are gone. We can have a cozy chat."

He came in and sat down in the chair again and perched the hat carefully on one knee.

Once again the children were running in the room and there was the sense of timelessness and the sound of laughter.

He sat and nodded, thinking, while the Sitters waited.

It was hard, he thought. Hard to make the words come right.

He felt again as he had felt many years ago, when the teacher had called upon him to recite in the second grade.

They were waiting, but they were patient; they would give him time.

He had to say it right. He must make them understand. He couldn't blurt it out. It must be made to sound natural, and logical as well.

And how, he asked himself, could he make it logical?

There was nothing logical at all in men as old as he and Stuffy needing baby-sitters.

The Big Front Yard

Hiram Taine came awake and sat up in his bed.

Towser was barking and scratching at the floor.

"Shut up," Taine told the dog.

Towser cocked quizzical ears at him and then resumed the barking and scratching at the floor.

Taine rubbed his eyes. He ran a hand through his rat's-nest head of hair. He considered lying down again and pulling up the covers.

But not with Towser barking.

"What's the matter with you, anyhow?" he asked Towser, with not a little wrath.

"Whuff," said Towser, industriously proceeding with his scratching at the floor.

"If you want out," said Taine, "all you got to do is open the screen door. You know how it is done. You do it all the time."

Towser quit his barking and sat down heavily, watching his master getting out of bed.

Taine put on his shirt and pulled on his trousers, but didn't bother with his shoes.

Towser ambled over to a corner, put his nose down to the baseboard and snuffled moistly.

"You got a mouse?" asked Taine.

"Whuff," said Towser, most emphatically.

"I can't ever remember you making such a row about a mouse," Taine said, slightly puzzled. "You must be off your rocker."

It was a beautiful summer morning. Sunlight was pouring through the open window.

Good day for fishing, Taine told himself, then remembered that there'd be no fishing, for he had to go out and look up that old four-poster maple bed that he had heard about up Woodman way. More than likely, he thought, they'd want twice as much as it was worth. It was getting so, he told himself, that a man couldn't make an honest dollar. Everyone was getting smart about antiques.

He got up off the bed and headed for the living room.

"Come on," he said to Towser.

Towser came along, pausing now and then to snuffle into corners and to whuffle at the floor.

"You got it bad," said Taine.

Maybe it's a rat, he thought. The house was getting old.

He opened the screen door and Towser went outside.

"Leave that woodchuck be today," Taine advised him. "It's a losing battle. You'll never dig him out."

Towser went around the corner of the house.

Taine noticed that something had happened to the sign that hung on the post beside the driveway. One of the chains had become unhooked and the sign was dangling.

He padded out across the driveway slab and the grass, still wet with dew, to fix the sign. There was nothing wrong with it—just the unhooked chain. Might have been the wind, he thought, or some passing urchin. Although probably not an urchin. He got along with kids. They never bothered him, like they did some others in the village. Banker Stevens, for example. They were always pestering Stevens.

He stood back a way to be sure the sign was straight.

It read, in big letters:

HANDY MAN

And under that, in smaller lettering:
I fix anything

And under that:

ANTIQUES FOR SALE
What have you got to trade?

Maybe, he told himself, he'd ought to have two signs, one for his fix-it shop and one for antiques and trading. Some day, when he had the time, he thought, he'd paint a couple of new ones. One for each side of the driveway. It would look neat that way.

He turned around and looked across the road at Turner's Woods. It was a pretty sight, he thought. A sizable piece of woods like that right at the edge of town. It was a place for birds and rabbits and woodchucks and squirrels and it was full of forts built through generations by the boys of Willow Bend.

Some day, of course, some smart operator would buy it up and start a housing development or something equally objectionable and when that happened a big slice of his own boyhood would be cut out of his life.

Towser came around the corner of the house. He was sidling along, sniffing at the lowest row of siding and his ears were cocked with interest.

"That dog is nuts," said Taine and went inside.

He went into the kitchen, his bare feet slapping on the floor.

He filled the teakettle, set it on the stove and turned the burner on underneath the kettle.

He turned on the radio, forgetting that it was out of kilter.

When it didn't make a sound, he remembered and, disgusted, snapped it off. That was the way it went, he thought. He fixed other people's stuff, but never got around to fixing any of his own.

He went into the bedroom and put on his shoes. He threw the bed together.

Back in the kitchen the stove had failed to work again. The burner beneath the kettle still was cold.

Taine hauled off and kicked the stove. He lifted the kettle and held his palm above the burner. In a few seconds he could detect some heat.

"Worked again," he told himself.

Some day, he knew, kicking the stove would fail to work. When that happened, he'd have to get to work on it. Probably wasn't more than a loose connection.

He put the kettle back onto the stove.

There was a clatter out in front and Taine went out to see what was going on.

Beasly, the Hortons' yardboy-chauffeur-gardener-et cetera was backing a rickety old truck up the driveway.

Beside him sat Abbie Horton, the wife of H. Henry Horton, the village's most important citizen. In the back of the truck, lashed on with ropes and half-protected by a garish red and purple quilt, stood a mammoth television set. Taine recognized it from of old. It was a good ten years out of date and still, by any standard, it was the most expensive set ever to grace any home in Willow Bend.

Abbie hopped out of the truck. She was an energetic, bustling, bossy woman.

"Good morning, Hiram," she said. "Can you fix this set again?"

"Never saw anything that I couldn't fix," said Taine, but nevertheless he eyed the set with something like dismay. It was not the first time he had tangled with it and he knew what was ahead.

"It might cost you more than it's worth," he warned her. "What you really need is a new one. This set is getting old and—"

"That's just what Henry said," Abbie told him, tartly. "Henry wants to get one of the color sets. But I won't part with this one. It's not just TV, you know. It's a combination with radio and a record player and the wood and style are just right for the other furniture, and, besides—"

"Yes, I know," said Taine, who'd heard it all before.

Poor old Henry, he thought. What a life the man must lead. Up at that computer plant all day long, shooting off his face and bossing everyone, then coming home to a life of petty tyranny.

"Beasly," said Abbie, in her best drill-sergeant voice, "you get right up there and get that thing untied."

"Yes'm," Beasly said. He was a gangling, loose-jointed man who didn't look too bright.

"And see you be careful with it. I don't want it all scratched up."

"Yes'm," said Beasly.

"I'll help," Taine offered.

The two climbed into the truck and began unlashing the old monstrosity.

"It's heavy," Abbie warned. "You two be careful of it."

"Yes'm," said Beasly.

It was heavy and it was an awkward thing to boot, but Beasly and Taine horsed it around to the back of the house and up the stoop and through the back door and down the basement stairs, with Abbie following eagle-eyed behind them, alert to the slightest scratch.

The basement was Taine's combination workshop and display room for antiques. One end of it was filled with benches and with tools and machinery and boxes full of odds and ends and piles of just plain junk were scattered everywhere. The other end housed a collection of rickety chairs, sagging bedposts, ancient highboys, equally ancient lowboys, old coal scuttles painted gold, heavy iron fireplace screens and a lot of other stuff that he had collected from far and wide for as little as he could possibly pay for it.

He and Beasly set the TV down carefully on the floor. Abbie watched them narrowly from the stairs.

"Why, Hiram," she said, excited, "you put a ceiling in the basement. It looks a whole lot better."

"Huh?" asked Taine.

"The ceiling. I said you put in a ceiling."

Taine jerked his head up and what she said was true. There was a ceiling there, but he'd never put it in.

He gulped a little and lowered his head, then jerked it quickly up and had another look. The ceiling was still there.

"It's not that block stuff," said Abbie with open admiration. "You can't see any joints at all. How did you manage it?"

Taine gulped again and got back his voice. "Something I thought up," he told her weakly.

"You'll have to come over and do it to our basement. Our basement is a sight. Beasly put the ceiling in the amusement room, but Beasly is all thumbs."

"Yes'm," Beasly said contritely.

"When I get the time," Taine promised, ready to promise anything to get them out of there.

"You'd have a lot more time," Abbie told him acidly, "if you weren't gadding around all over the country buying up that broken-down old furniture that you call antiques. Maybe you can fool the city folks when they come driving out here, but you can't fool me."

"I make a lot of money out of some of it," Taine told her calmly.

"And lose your shirt on the rest of it," she said.

"I got some old china that is just the kind of stuff you are looking for," said Taine. "Picked it up just a day or two ago. Made a good buy on it. I can let you have it cheap."

"I'm not interested," she said and clamped her mouth tight shut.

She turned around and went back up the stairs.

"She's on the prod today," Beasly said to Taine. "It will be a bad day. It always is when she starts early in the morning."

"Don't pay attention to her," Taine advised.

"I try not to, but it ain't possible. You sure you don't need a man? I'd work for you cheap."

"Sorry, Beasly. Tell you what—come over some night soon and we'll play some checkers."

"I'll do that, Hiram. You're the only one who ever asks me over. All the others ever do is laugh at me or shout."

Abbie's voice came bellowing down the stairs. "Beasly, are you coming? Don't go standing there all day. I have rugs to beat."

"Yes'm," said Beasly, starting up the stairs.

At the truck, Abbie turned on Taine with determination: "You'll get that set fixed right away? I'm lost without it."

"Immediately," said Taine.

He stood and watched them off, then looked around for Towser, but the dog had disappeared. More than likely he was at that woodchuck hole again, in the woods across the road. Gone off, thought Taine, without his breakfast, too.

The teakettle was boiling furiously when Taine got back to the kitchen. He put coffee in the maker and poured in the water. Then he went downstairs.

The ceiling was still there.

He turned on all the lights and walked around the basement, staring up at it.

It was a dazzling white material and it appeared to be translucent—up to a point, that is. One could see into it, but he could not see through it. And there were no signs of seams. It was fitted neatly and tightly around the water pipes and the ceiling lights.

Taine stood on a chair and rapped his knuckles against it sharply. It gave out a bell-like sound, almost exactly as if he'd rapped a fingernail against a thinly-blown goblet.

He got down off the chair and stood there, shaking his

head. The whole thing was beyond him. He had spent part of the evening repairing Banker Stevens' lawn mower and there'd been no ceiling then.

He rummaged in a box and found a drill. He dug out one of the smaller bits and fitted it in the drill. He plugged in the cord and climbed on the chair again and tried the bit against the ceiling. The whirling steel slid wildly back and forth. It didn't make a scratch. He switched off the drill and looked closely at the ceiling. There was not a mark upon it. He tried again, pressing against the drill with all his strength. The bit went *ping* and the broken end flew across the basement and hit the wall.

Taine stepped down off the chair. He found another bit and fitted it in the drill and went slowly up the stairs, trying to think. But he was too confused to think. That ceiling should not be up there, but there it was. And unless he were stark, staring crazy and forgetful as well, he had not put it there.

In the living room, he folded back one corner of the worn and faded carpeting and plugged in the cord. He knelt and started drilling in the floor. The bit went smoothly through the old oak flooring, then stopped. He put on more pressure and the drill spun without getting any bite.

And there wasn't supposed to be anything underneath that wood! Nothing to stop a drill. Once through the flooring, it should have dropped into the space between the joists.

Taine disengaged the drill and laid it to one side.

He went into the kitchen and the coffee now was ready. But before he poured it, he pawed through a cabinet drawer and found a pencil flashlight. Back in the living room he shone the light into the hole that the drill had made.

There was something shiny at the bottom of the hole.

He went back to the kitchen and found some day-old doughnuts and poured a cup of coffee. He sat at the kitchen table, eating doughnuts and wondering what to do.

There didn't appear, for the moment at least, much that he could do. He could putter around all day trying to figure out what had happened to his basement and probably not be any wiser than he was right now.

His money-making Yankee soul rebelled against such a horrid waste of time.

There was, he told himself, that maple four-poster that he

should be getting to before some unprincipled city antique dealer should run afoul of it. A piece like that, he figured, if a man had any luck at all, should sell at a right good price. He might turn a handsome profit on it if he only worked it right.

Maybe, he thought, he could turn a trade on it. There was the table model TV set that he had traded a pair of ice skates for last winter. Those folks out Woodman way might conceivably be happy to trade the bed for a reconditioned TV set, almost like brand new. After all, they probably weren't using the bed and, he hoped fervently, had no idea of the value of it.

He ate the doughnuts hurriedly and gulped down an extra cup of coffee. He fixed a plate of scraps for Towser and set it outside the door. Then he went down into the basement and got the table TV set and put it in the pickup truck. As an afterthought, he added a reconditioned shotgun which would be perfectly all right if a man were careful not to use these far-reaching, powerful shells, and a few other odds and ends that might come in handy on a trade.

He got back late, for it had been a busy and quite satisfactory day. Not only did he have the four-poster loaded on the truck, but he had as well a rocking chair, a fire screen, a bundle of ancient magazines, an old-fashioned barrel churn, a walnut highboy and a Governor Winthrop on which some half-baked, slap-happy decorator had applied a coat of apple-green paint. The television set, the shotgun and five dollars had gone into the trade. And what was better yet, he'd managed it so well that the Woodman family probably was dying of laughter at this very moment about how they'd taken him.

He felt a little ashamed of it—they'd been such friendly people. They had treated him so kindly and had him stay for dinner and had sat and talked with him and shown him about the farm and even asked him to stop by if he went through that way again.

He'd wasted the entire day, he thought, and he rather hated that, but maybe it had been worth it to build up his reputation out that way as the sort of character who had softening of the head and didn't know the value of a dollar. That way, maybe some other day, he could do some more business in the neighborhood.

He heard the television set as he opened the back door, sounding loud and clear, and he went clattering down the basement stairs in something close to a panic. For now that he'd traded off the table model, Abbie's set was the only one downstairs and Abbie's set was broken.

It was Abbie's set, all right. It stood just where he and Beasly had put it down that morning and there was nothing wrong with it—nothing wrong at all. It was even televising color.

Televising color!

He stopped at the bottom of the stairs and leaned against the railing for support.

The set kept right on televising color.

Taine stalked the set and walked around behind it.

The back of the cabinet was off, leaning against a bench that stood behind the set, and he could see the innards of it glowing cheerily.

He squatted on the basement floor and squinted at the lighted innards and they seemed a good deal different from the way that they should be. He'd repaired the set many times before and he thought he had a good idea of what the working parts would look like. And now they all seemed different, although just how he couldn't tell.

A heavy step sounded on the stairs and a hearty voice came booming down to him.

"Well, Hiram, I see you got it fixed."

Taine jackknifed upright and stood there slightly frozen and completely speechless.

Henry Horton stood foursquarely and happily on the stairs, looking very pleased.

"I told Abbie that you wouldn't have it done, but she said for me to come over anyway—Hey, Hiram, it's in color! How did you do it, man?"

Taine grinned sickly. "I just got fiddling around," he said.

Henry came down the rest of the stairs with a stately step and stood before the set, with his hands behind his back, staring at it fixedly in his best executive manner.

He slowly shook his head. "I never would have thought," he said, "that it was possible."

"Abbie mentioned that you wanted color."

"Well, sure. Of course I did. But not on this old set. I never would have expected to get color on this set. How did you do it, Hiram?"

Taine told the solemn truth. "I can't rightly say," he said.

Henry found a nail keg standing in front of one of the benches and rolled it out in front of the old-fashioned set. He sat down warily and relaxed into solid comfort.

"That's the way it goes," he said. "There are men like you, but not very many of them. Just Yankee tinkerers. You keep messing around with things, trying one thing here and another there and before you know it you come up with something."

He sat on the nail keg, staring at the set.

"It's sure a pretty thing," he said. "It's better than the color they have in Minneapolis. I dropped in at a couple of the places the last time I was there and looked at the color sets. And I tell you honest, Hiram, there wasn't one of them that was as good as this."

Taine wiped his brow with his shirt sleeve. Somehow or other, the basement seemed to be getting warm. He was fine sweat all over.

Henry found a big cigar in one of his pockets and held it out to Taine.

"No, thanks. I never smoke."

"Perhaps you're wise," said Henry. "It's a nasty habit."

He stuck the cigar into his mouth and rolled it east to west.

"Each man to his own," he proclaimed, expansively. "When it comes to a thing like this, you're the man to do it. You seem to think in mechanical contraptions and electronic circuits. Me, I don't know a thing about it. Even in the computer game, I still don't know a thing about it; I hire men who do. I can't even saw a board or drive a nail. But I can organize. You remember, Hiram, how everybody snickered when I started up the plant?"

"Well, I guess some of them did, at that."

"You're darn tooting they did. They went around for weeks with their hands up to their faces to hide smart-aleck grins. They said, what does Henry think he's doing, starting up a computer factory out here in the sticks; he doesn't think he can compete with those big companies in the east, does he? And they didn't stop their grinning until I sold a couple of dozen units and had orders for a year or two ahead."

He fished a lighter from his pocket and lit the cigar carefully, never taking his eyes off the television set.

"You got something there," he said, judiciously, "that may be worth a mint of money. Some simple adaptation that will fit on any set. If you can get color on this old wreck, you can get color on any set that's made."

He chuckled moistly around the mouthful of cigar. "If RCA knew what was happening here this minute, they'd go out and cut their throats."

"But I don't know what I did," protested Taine.

"Well, that's all right," said Henry, happily. "I'll take this set up to the plant tomorrow and turn loose some of the boys on it. They'll find out what you have here before they're through with it."

He took the cigar out of his mouth and studied it intently, then popped it back in again.

"As I was saying, Hiram, that's the difference in us. You can do the stuff, but you miss the possibilities. I can't do a thing, but I can organize it once the thing is done. Before we get through with this, you'll be wading in twenty dollar bills clear up to your knees."

"But I don't have—"

"Don't worry. Just leave it all to me. I've got the plant and whatever money we may need. We'll figure out a split."

"That's fine of you," said Taine mechanically.

"Not at all," Henry insisted, grandly. "It's just my aggressive, grasping sense of profit. I should be ashamed of myself, cutting in on this."

He sat on the keg, smoking and watching the TV perform in exquisite color.

"You know, Hiram," he said, "I've often thought of this, but never got around to doing anything about it. I've got an old computer up at the plant that we will have to junk because it's taking up room that we really need. It's one of our early models, a sort of experimental job that went completely sour. It sure is a screwy thing. No one's ever been able to make much out of it. We tried some approaches that probably were wrong—or maybe they were right, but we didn't know enough to make them quite come off. It's been standing in a corner all these years and I should have junked it long ago. But I sort of hate to do it. I wonder if you might not like it—just to tinker with."

"Well, I don't know," said Taine.

Henry assumed an expansive air. "No obligation, mind you. You may not be able to do a thing with it—I'd frankly be surprised if you could, but there's no harm in trying. Maybe you'll decide to tear it down for the salvage you can get. There are several thousand dollars worth of equipment in it. Probably you could use most of it one way or another."

"It might be interesting," conceded Taine, but not too enthusiastically.

"Good," said Henry, with an enthusiasm that made up for Taine's lack of it. "I'll have the boys cart it over tomorrow. It's a heavy thing. I'll send along plenty of help to get it unloaded and down into the basement and set up."

Henry stood up carefully and brushed cigar ashes off his lap.

"I'll have the boys pick up the TV set at the same time," he said. "I'll have to tell Abbie you haven't got it fixed yet. If I ever let it get into the house, the way it's working now, she'd hold onto it."

Henry climbed the stairs heavily and Taine saw him out the door into the summer night.

Taine stood in the shadow, watching Henry's shadowed figure go across the Widow Taylor's yard to the next street behind his house. He took a deep breath of the fresh night air and shook his head to try to clear his buzzing brain, but the buzzing went right on.

Too much had happened, he told himself. Too much for any single day—first the ceiling and now the TV set. Once he had a good night's sleep he might be in some sort of shape to try to wrestle with it.

Towser came around the corner of the house and limped slowly up the steps to stand beside his master. He was mud up to his ears.

"You had a day of it, I see," said Taine. "And, just like I told you, you didn't get the woodchuck."

"*Woof*," said Towser, sadly.

"You're just like a lot of the rest of us," Taine told him, severely. "Like me and Henry Horton and all the rest of us. You're chasing something and you think you know what you're chasing, but you really don't. And what's even worse, you have no faint idea of why you're chasing it."

Towser thumped a tired tail upon the stoop.

Taine opened the door and stood to one side to let Towser in, then went in himself.

He went through the refrigerator and found part of a roast, a slice or two of luncheon meat, a dried-out slab of cheese and half a bowl of cooked spaghetti. He made a pot of coffee and shared the food with Towser.

Then Taine went back downstairs and shut off the television set. He found a trouble lamp and plugged it in and poked the light into the innards of the set.

He squatted on the floor, holding the lamp, trying to puzzle out what had been done to the set. It was different, of course, but it was a little hard to figure out in just what ways it was different. Someone had tinkered with the tubes and had them twisted out of shape and there were little white cubes of metal tucked here and there in what seemed to be an entirely haphazard and illogical manner—although, Taine admitted to himself, there probably was no haphazardness. And the circuit, he saw, had been rewired and a good deal of wiring had been added.

But the most puzzling thing about it was that the whole thing seemed to be just jury-rigged—as if someone had done no more than a hurried, patch-up job to get the set back in working order on an emergency and temporary basis.

Someone, he thought!

And who had that someone been?

He hunched around and peered into the dark corners of the basement and he felt innumerable and many-legged imaginary insects running on his body.

Someone had taken the back off the cabinet and leaned it against the bench and had left the screws which held the back laid neatly in a row upon the floor. Then they had jury-rigged the set and jury-rigged it far better than it had ever been before.

If this was a jury-job, he wondered, just what kind of job would it have been if they had had the time to do it up in style?

They hadn't had the time, of course. Maybe they had been scared off when he had come home—scared off even before they could get the back on the set again.

He stood up and moved stiffly away.

And the ceiling, come to think of it, was not a ceiling only.

Another liner, if that was the proper term for it, of the same material as the ceiling, had been laid beneath the floor, forming a sort of boxed-in area between the joists. He had struck that liner when he had tried to drill into the floor.

And what, he asked himself, if all the house were like that, too?

There was just one answer to it all: *There was something in the house with him!*

Towser had heard that *something* or smelled it or in some other manner sensed it and had dug frantically at the floor in an attempt to dig it out, as if it were a woodchuck.

Except that this, whatever it might be, certainly was no woodchuck.

He put away the trouble light and went upstairs.

Towser was curled up on a rug in the living room beside the easy chair and beat his tail in polite decorum in greeting to his master.

Taine stood and stared down at the dog. Towser looked back at him with satisfied and sleepy eyes, then heaved a doggish sigh and settled down to sleep.

Whatever Towser might have heard or smelled or sensed this morning, it was quite evident that as of this moment he was aware of it no longer.

Then Taine remembered something else.

He had filled the kettle to make water for the coffee and had set it on the stove. He had turned on the burner and it had worked the first time.

He hadn't had to kick the stove to get the burner going.

He woke in the morning and someone was holding down his feet and he sat up quickly to see what was going on.

But there was nothing to be alarmed about; it was only Towser who had crawled into bed with him and now lay sprawled across his feet.

Towser whined softly and his back legs twitched as he chased dream rabbits.

Taine eased his feet from beneath the dog and sat up, reaching for his clothes. It was early, but he remembered suddenly that he had left all of the furniture he had picked up the day before out there in the truck and should be getting it downstairs where he could start reconditioning it.

Towser went on sleeping.

Taine stumbled to the kitchen and looked out of the window and there, squatted on the back stoop, was Beasly, the Horton man-of-all-work.

Taine went to the back door to see what was going on.

"I quit them, Hiram," Beasly told him. "She kept on pecking at me every minute of the day and I couldn't do a thing to please her, so I up and quit."

"Well, come on in," said Taine. "I suppose you'd like a bite to eat and a cup of coffee."

"I was kind of wondering if I could stay here, Hiram. Just for my keep until I can find something else."

"Let's have breakfast first," said Taine, "then we can talk about it."

He didn't like it, he told himself. He didn't like it at all. In another hour or so Abbie would show up and start stirring up a ruckus about how he'd lured Beasly off. Because, no matter how dumb Beasly might be, he did a lot of work and took a lot of nagging and there wasn't anyone else in town who would work for Abbie Horton.

"Your ma used to give me cookies all the time," said Beasly. "Your ma was a real good woman, Hiram."

"Yes, she was," said Taine.

"My ma used to say that you folks were quality, not like the rest in town, no matter what kind of airs they were always putting on. She said your family was among the first settlers. Is that really true, Hiram?"

"Well, not exactly first settlers, I guess, but this house has stood here for almost a hundred years. My father used to say there never was a night during all those years that there wasn't at least one Taine beneath its roof. Things like that, it seems, meant a lot to father."

"It must be nice," said Beasly, wistfully, "to have a feeling like that. You must be proud of this house, Hiram."

"Not really proud; more like belonging. I can't imagine living in any other house."

Taine turned on the burner and filled the kettle. Carrying the kettle back, he kicked the stove. But there wasn't any need to kick it; the burner was already beginning to take on a rosy glow.

Twice in a row, Taine thought. This thing is getting better!

"Gee, Hiram," said Beasly, "this is a dandy radio."

"It's no good," said Taine. "It's broke. Haven't had the time to fix it."

"I don't think so, Hiram. I just turned it on. It's beginning to warm up."

"It's beginning to—Hey, let me see!" yelled Taine.

Beasly told the truth. A faint hum was coming from the tubes.

A voice came in, gaining in volume as the set warmed up.

It was speaking gibberish.

"What kind of talk is that?" asked Beasly.

"I don't know," said Taine, close to panic now.

First the television set, then the stove and now the radio!

He spun the tuning knob and the pointer crawled slowly across the dial face instead of spinning across as he remembered it, and station after station sputtered and went past.

He tuned in the next station that came up and it was strange lingo, too—and he knew by then exactly what he had.

Instead of a $39.50 job, he had here on the kitchen table an all-band receiver like they advertised in the fancy magazines.

He straightened up, and said to Beasly: "See if you can get someone speaking English. I'll get on with the eggs."

He turned on the second burner and got out the frying pan. He put it on the stove and found eggs and bacon in the refrigerator.

Beasly got a station that had band music playing.

"How's that?" he asked.

"That's fine," said Taine.

Towser came out from the bedroom, stretching and yawning. He went to the door and showed he wanted out.

Taine let him out.

"If I were you," he told the dog, "I'd lay off that woodchuck. You'll have all the woods dug up."

"He ain't digging after any woodchuck, Hiram."

"Well, a rabbit, then."

"Not a rabbit, either. I snuck off yesterday when I was supposed to be beating rugs. That's what Abbie got so sore about."

Taine grunted, breaking eggs into the skillet.

"I snuck away and went over to where Towser was. I talked with him and he told me it wasn't a woodchuck or a rabbit. He said it was something else. I pitched in and helped him dig. Looks to me like he found an old tank of some sort buried out there in the woods."

"Towser wouldn't dig up any tank," protested Taine. "He wouldn't care about anything except a rabbit or a wood-chuck."

"He was working hard," insisted Beasly. "He seemed to be excited."

"Maybe the woodchuck just dug his hole under this old tank or whatever it might be."

"Maybe so," Beasly agreed. He fiddled with the radio some more. He got a disk jockey who was pretty terrible.

Taine shoveled eggs and bacon onto plates and brought them to the table. He poured big cups of coffee and began buttering the toast.

"Dive in," he said to Beasly.

"This is good of you, Hiram, to take me in like this. I won't stay no longer than it takes to find a job."

"Well, I didn't exactly say—"

"There are times," said Beasly, "when I get to thinking I haven't got a friend and then I remember your ma, how nice she was to me and all—"

"Oh, all right," said Taine.

He knew when he was licked.

He brought the toast and a jar of jam to the table and sat down, beginning to eat.

"Maybe you got something I could help you with," suggested Beasly, using the back of his hand to wipe egg off his chin.

"I have a load of furniture out in the driveway. I could use a man to help me get it down into the basement."

"I'll be glad to do that," said Beasly. "I am good and strong. I don't mind work at all. I just don't like people jawing at me."

They finished breakfast and then carried the furniture down into the basement. They had some trouble with the Governor Winthrop, for it was an unwieldy thing to handle.

When they finally horsed it down, Taine stood off and looked at it. The man, he told himself, who slapped paint onto that beautiful cherrywood had a lot to answer for.

He said to Beasly: "We have to get the paint off that thing there. And we must do it carefully. Use paint remover and a rag wrapped around a spatula and just sort of roll it off. Would you like to try it?"

"Sure, I would. Say, Hiram, what will we have for lunch?"

"I don't know," said Taine. "We'll throw something together. Don't tell me you're hungry."

"Well, it was sort of hard work, getting all that stuff down here."

"There are cookies in the jar on the kitchen shelf," said Taine. "Go and help yourself."

When Beasly went upstairs, Taine walked slowly around the basement. The ceiling, he saw, was still intact. Nothing else seemed to be disturbed.

Maybe that television set and stove and radio, he thought, was just their way of paying rent to me. And if that were the case, he told himself, whoever they might be, he'd be more than willing to let them stay right on.

He looked around some more and could find nothing wrong.

He went upstairs and called to Beasly in the kitchen.

"Come on out to the garage, where I keep the paint. We'll hunt up some remover and show you how to use it."

Beasly, a supply of cookies clutched in his hand, trotted willingly behind him.

As they rounded the corner of the house they could hear Towser's muffled barking. Listening to him, it seemed to Taine that he was getting hoarse.

Three days, he thought—or was it four?

"If we don't go do something about it," he said, "that fool dog is going to get himself wore out."

He went into the garage and came back with two shovels and a pick.

"Come on," he said to Beasly. "We have to put a stop to this before we have any peace."

Towser had done himself a noble job of excavation. He was almost completely out of sight. Only the end of his considerably bedraggled tail showed out of the hole he had clawed in the forest floor.

Beasly had been right about the tank like thing. One edge of it showed out of one side of the hole.

Towser backed out of the hole and sat down heavily, his

whiskers dripping clay, his tongue hanging out of the side of his mouth.

"He says that it's about time that we showed up," said Beasly.

Taine walked around the hole and knelt down. He reached down a hand to brush the dirt off the projecting edge of Beasly's tank. The clay was stubborn and hard to wipe away, but from the feel of it the tank was heavy metal.

Taine picked up a shovel and rapped it against the tank. The tank gave out a clang.

They got to work, shoveling away a foot or so of topsoil that lay above the object. It was hard work and the thing was bigger than they had thought and it took some time to get it uncovered, even roughly.

"I'm hungry," Beasly complained.

Taine glanced at his watch. It was almost one o'clock.

"Run on back to the house," he said to Beasly. "You'll find something in the refrigerator and there's milk to drink."

"How about you, Hiram? Ain't you ever hungry?"

"You could bring me back a sandwich and see if you can find a trowel."

"What you want a trowel for?"

"I want to scrape the dirt off this thing and see what it is."

He squatted down beside the thing they had unearthed and watched Beasly disappear into the woods.

"Towser," he said, "this is the strangest animal you ever put to ground."

A man, he told himself, might better joke about it—if to do no more than keep his fear away.

Beasly wasn't scared, of course. Beasly didn't have the sense to be scared of a thing like this.

Twelve feet wide by twenty long and oval shaped. About the size, he thought, of a good-size living room. And there never had been a tank of that shape or size in all of Willow Bend.

He fished his jackknife out of his pocket and started to scratch away the dirt at one point on the surface of the thing. He got a square inch free of dirt and it was no metal such as he had ever seen. It looked for all the world like glass.

He kept on scraping at the dirt until he had a clean place as big as an outstretched hand.

It wasn't any metal. He'd almost swear to that. It looked like cloudy glass—like the milk-glass goblets and bowls he was always on the lookout for. There were a lot of people who were plain nuts about it and they'd pay fancy prices for it.

He closed the knife and put it back into his pocket and squatted, looking at the oval shape that Towser had discovered.

And the conviction grew: Whatever it was that had come to live with him undoubtedly had arrived in this same contraption. From space or time, he thought, and was astonished that he thought it, for he'd never thought such a thing before.

He picked up his shovel and began to dig again, digging down this time, following the curving side of this alien thing that lay within the earth.

And as he dug, he wondered. What should he say about this—or should he say anything? Maybe the smartest course would be to cover it again and never breathe a word about it to a living soul.

Beasly would talk about it naturally. But no one in the village would pay attention to anything that Beasly said. Everyone in Willow Bend knew Beasly was cracked.

Beasly finally came back. He carried three inexpertly-made sandwiches wrapped in an old newspaper and a quart bottle almost full of milk.

"You certainly took your time," said Taine, slightly irritated.

"I got interested," Beasly explained.

"Interested in what?"

"Well, there were three big trucks and they were lugging a lot of heavy stuff down into the basement. Two or three big cabinets and a lot of other junk. And you know Abbie's television set? Well, they took the set away. I told them that they shouldn't but they took it anyway."

"I forgot," said Taine. "Henry said he'd send the computer over and I plumb forgot."

Taine ate the sandwiches, sharing them with Towser, who was very grateful in a muddy way.

Finished, Taine rose and picked up his shovel.

"Let's get to work," he said.

"But you got all that stuff down in the basement."

"That can wait," said Taine. "This job we have to finish."

It was getting dusk by the time they finished.

Taine leaned wearily on his shovel.

Twelve feet by twenty across the top and ten feet deep—and all of it, every bit of it, made of the milk-glass stuff that sounded like a bell when you whacked it with a shovel.

They'd have to be small, he thought, if there were many of them, to live in a space that size, especially if they had to stay there very long. And that fitted in, of course, for if they weren't small they couldn't now be living in the space between the basement joists.

If they were really living there, thought Taine. If it wasn't all just a lot of supposition.

Maybe, he thought, even if they had been living in the house, they might be there no longer—for Towser had smelled or heard or somehow sensed them in the morning, but by that very night he'd paid them no attention.

Taine slung his shovel across his shoulder and hoisted the pick.

"Come on," he said, "let's go. We've put in a long, hard day."

They tramped out through the brush and reached the road. Fireflies were flickering off and on in the woody darkness and the street lamps were swaying in the summer breeze. The stars were hard and bright.

Maybe they still were in the house, thought Taine. Maybe when they found out that Towser had objected to them, they had fixed it so he'd be aware of them no longer.

They probably were highly adaptive. It stood to good reason they would have to be. It hadn't taken them too long, he told himself grimly, to adapt to a human house.

He and Beasly went up the gravel driveway in the dark to put the tools away in the garage and there was something funny going on, for there was no garage.

There was no garage and there was no front on the house and the driveway was cut off abruptly and there was nothing but the curving wall of what apparently had been the end of the garage.

They came up to the curving wall and stopped, squinting unbelieving in the summer dark.

There was no garage, no porch, no front of the house at all. It was as if someone had taken the opposite corners of the front of the house and bent them together until they touched, folding the entire front of the building inside the curvature of the bent-together corners.

Taine now had a curved-front house. Although it was, actually, not as simple as all that, for the curvature was not in proportion to what actually would have happened in case of such a feat. The curve was long and graceful and somehow not quite apparent. It was as if the front of the house had been eliminated and an illusion of the rest of the house had been summoned to mask the disappearance.

Taine dropped the shovel and the pick and they clattered on the driveway gravel. He put his hand up to his face and wiped it across his eyes, as if to clear his eyes of something that could not possibly be there.

And when he took the hand away it had not changed a bit.

There was no front to the house.

Then he was running around the house, hardly knowing he was running, and there was a fear inside of him at what had happened to the house.

But the back of the house was all right. It was exactly as it had always been.

He clattered up the stoop with Beasly and Towser running close behind him. He pushed open the door and burst into the entry and scrambled up the stairs into the kitchen and went across the kitchen in three strides to see what had happened to the front of the house.

At the door between the kitchen and the living room he stopped and his hands went out to grasp the door jamb as he stared in disbelief at the windows of the living room.

It was night outside. There could be no doubt of that. He had seen the fireflies flickering in the brush and weeds and the street lamps had been lit and the stars were out.

But a flood of sunlight was pouring through the windows of the living room and out beyond the windows lay a land that was not Willow Bend.

"Beasly," he gasped, "look out there in front!"

Beasly looked.

"What place is that?" he asked.

"That's what I'd like to know."

Towser had found his dish and was pushing it around the kitchen floor with his nose, by way of telling Taine that it was time to eat.

Taine went across the living room and opened the front door. The garage, he saw, was there. The pickup stood with its nose against the open garage door and the car was safe inside.

There was nothing wrong with the front of the house at all.

But if the front of the house was all right, that was all that was.

For the driveway was chopped off just a few feet beyond the tail end of the pickup and there was no yard or woods or road. There was just a desert—a flat, far-reaching desert, level as a floor, with occasional boulder piles and haphazard clumps of vegetation and all of the ground covered with sand and pebbles. A big blinding sun hung just above a horizon that seemed much too far away and a funny thing about it was that the sun was in the north, where no proper sun should be. It had a peculiar whiteness, too.

Beasly stepped out on the porch and Taine saw that he was shivering like a frightened dog.

"Maybe," Taine told him, kindly, "you'd better go back in and start making us some supper."

"But, Hiram—"

"It's all right," said Taine. "It's bound to be all right."

"If you say so, Hiram."

He went in and the screen door banged behind him and in a minute Taine heard him in the kitchen.

He didn't blame Beasly for shivering, he admitted to himself. It was a sort of shock to step out of your front door into an unknown land. A man might eventually get used to it, of course, but it would take some doing.

He stepped down off the porch and walked around the truck and around the garage corner and when he rounded the corner he was half prepared to walk back into familiar Willow Bend—for when he had gone in the back door the village had been there.

There was no Willow Bend. There was more of the desert, a great deal more of it.

He walked around the house and there was no back to the house. The back of the house now was just the same as the front had been before—the same smooth curve pulling the sides of the house together.

He walked on around the house to the front again and

there was desert all the way. And the front was still all right. It hadn't changed at all. The truck was there on the chopped-off driveway and the garage was open and the car inside.

Taine walked out a way into the desert and hunkered down and scooped up a handful of the pebbles and the pebbles were just pebbles.

He squatted there and let the pebbles trickle through his fingers.

In Willow Bend there was a back door and there wasn't any front. Here, wherever here might be, there was a front door, but there wasn't any back.

He stood up and tossed the rest of the pebbles away and wiped his dusty hands upon his breeches.

Out of the corner of his eye he caught a sense of movement on the porch and there they were.

A line of tiny animals, if animals they were, came marching down the steps, one behind another. They were four inches high or so and they went on all four feet, although it was plain to see that their front feet were really hands, not feet. They had ratlike faces that were vaguely human, with noses long and pointed. They looked as if they might have scales instead of hide, for their bodies glistened with a rippling motion as they walked. And all of them had tails that looked very much like the coiled-wire tails one finds on certain toys and the tails stuck straight up above them, quivering as they walked.

They came down the steps in single file, in perfect military order, with half a foot or so of spacing between each one of them.

They came down the steps and walked out into the desert in a straight, undeviating line as if they knew exactly where they might be bound. There was something deadly purposeful about them and yet they didn't hurry.

Taine counted sixteen of them and he watched them go out into the desert until they were almost lost to sight.

There go the ones, he thought, who came to live with me. They are the ones who fixed up the ceiling and who repaired Abbie's television set and jiggered up the stove and radio. And more than likely, too, they were the ones who had come to Earth in the strange milk-glass contraption out there in the woods.

And if they had come to Earth in that deal out in the

woods, then what sort of place was this?

He climbed the porch and opened the screen door and saw the neat, six-inch circle his departing guests had achieved in the screen to get out of the house. He made a mental note that some day, when he had the time, he would have to fix it.

He went in and slammed the door behind him.

"Beasly," he shouted.

There was no answer.

Towser crawled from beneath the love seat and apologized.

"It's all right, pal," said Taine. "That outfit scared me, too."

He went into the kitchen. The dim ceiling light shone on the overturned coffee pot, the broken cup in the center of the floor, the upset bowl of eggs. One broken egg was a white and yellow gob on the linoleum.

He stepped down on the landing and saw that the screen door in the back was wrecked beyond repair. Its rusty mesh was broken—exploded might have been a better word—and a part of the frame was smashed.

Taine looked at it in wondering admiration.

"The poor fool," he said. "He went straight through it without opening it at all."

He snapped on the light and went down the basement stairs. Halfway down he stopped in utter wonderment.

To his left was a wall—a wall of the same sort of material as had been used to put in the ceiling.

He stooped and saw that the wall ran clear across the basement, floor to ceiling, shutting off the workshop area.

And inside the workshop, what?

For one thing, he remembered, the computer that Henry had sent over just this morning. Three trucks, Beasly had said—three truckloads of equipment delivered straight into their paws!

Taine sat down weakly on the steps.

They must have thought, he told himself, that he was cooperating! Maybe they had figured that he knew what they were about and so went along with them. Or perhaps they thought he was paying them for fixing up the TV set and the stove and radio.

But to tackle first things first, why had they repaired the TV set and the stove and radio? As a sort of rental payment?

As a friendly gesture? Or as a sort of practice run to find out what they could about this world's technology? To find, perhaps, how their technology could be adapted to the materials and conditions on this planet they had found?

Taine raised a hand and rapped with his knuckles on the wall beside the stairs and the smooth white surface gave out a pinging sound.

He laid his ear against the wall and listened closely and it seemed to him he could hear a low-key humming, but if so it was so faint he could not be absolutely sure.

Banker Stevens' lawn mower was in there, behind the wall, and a lot of other stuff waiting for repair. They'd take the hide right off him, he thought, especially Stevens, who was a tight man.

Beasly must have been half-crazed with fear, he thought. When he had seen those things coming up out of the basement, he'd gone clean off his rocker. He'd gone straight through the door without even bothering to try to open it and now he was down in the village yapping to anyone who'd stop to listen to him.

No one ordinarily would pay Beasly much attention, but if he yapped long enough and wild enough, they'd probably do some checking. They'd come storming up here and they'd give the place a going over and they'd stand goggle-eyed at what they found in front and pretty soon some of them would have worked their way around to sort of running things.

And it was none of their business, Taine stubbornly told himself, his ever-present business sense rising to the fore. There was a lot of real estate lying around out there in his front yard and the only way anyone could get to it was by going through his house. That being the case, it stood to reason that all that land out there was his. Maybe it wasn't any good at all. There might be nothing there. But before he had other people overrunning it, he'd better check and see.

He went up the stairs and out into the garage.

The sun was still just above the northern horizon and there was nothing moving.

He found a hammer and some nails and a few short lengths of plank in the garage and took them in the house.

Towser, he saw, had taken advantage of the situation and was sleeping in the gold-upholstered chair. Taine didn't bother him.

Taine locked the back door and nailed some planks across it. He locked the kitchen and the bedroom windows and nailed planks across them, too.

That would hold the villagers for a while, he told himself, when they came tearing up here to see what was going on.

He got his deer rifle, a box of cartridges, a pair of binoculars and an old canteen out of a closet. He filled the canteen at the kitchen tap and stuffed a sack with food for him and Towser to eat along the way, for there was no time to wait and eat.

Then he went into the living room and dumped Towser out of the gold-upholstered chair.

"Come on, Tows," he said. "We'll go and look things over."

He checked the gasoline in the pickup and the tank was almost full.

He and the dog got in and he put the rifle within easy reach. Then he backed the truck and swung it around and headed out, north, across the desert.

It was easy traveling. The desert was as level as a floor. At times it got a little rough, but no worse than a lot of the back roads he traveled hunting down antiques.

The scenery didn't change. Here and there were low hills, but the desert itself kept on mostly level, unraveling itself into that far-off horizon. Taine kept on driving north, straight into the sun. He hit some sandy stretches, but the sand was firm and hard and he had no trouble.

Half an hour out he caught up with the band of things— all sixteen of them—that had left the house. They were still traveling in line at their steady pace.

Slowing down the truck, Taine traveled parallel with them for a time, but there was no profit in it; they kept on traveling their course, looking neither right or left.

Speeding up, Taine left them behind.

The sun stayed in the north, unmoving, and that certainly was queer. Perhaps, Taine told himself, this world spun on its axis far more slowly than the Earth and the day was longer. From the way the sun appeared to be standing still, perhaps a good deal longer.

Hunched above the wheel, staring out into the endless stretch of desert, the strangeness of it struck him for the first time with its full impact.

This was another world—there could be no doubt of that—another planet circling another star, and where it was in actual space no one on Earth could have the least idea. And yet, through some machination of those sixteen things walking straight in line, it also was lying just outside the front door of his house.

Ahead of him a somewhat larger hill loomed out of the flatness of the desert. As he drew nearer to it, he made out a row of shining objects lined upon its crest. After a time he stopped the truck and got out with the binoculars.

Through the glasses, he saw that the shining things were the same sort of milk-glass contraptions as had been in the woods. He counted eight of them, shining in the sun, perched upon some sort of rock-gray cradles. And there were other cradles empty.

He took the binoculars from his eyes and stood there for a moment, considering the advisability of climbing the hill and investigating closely. But he shook his head. There'd be time for that later on. He'd better keep on moving. This was not a real exploring foray, but a quick reconnaissance.

He climbed into the truck and drove on, keeping watch upon the gas gauge. When it came close to half full he'd have to turn around and go back home again.

Ahead of him he saw a faint whiteness above the dim horizon line and he watched it narrowly. At times it faded away and then came in again, but whatever it might be was so far off he could make nothing of it.

He glanced down at the gas gauge and it was close to the halfway mark. He stopped the pickup and got out with the binoculars.

As he moved around to the front of the machine he was puzzled at how slow and tired his legs were and then remembered—he should have been in bed many hours ago. He looked at his watch and it was two o'clock and that meant, back on Earth, two o'clock in the morning. He had been awake for more than twenty hours and much of that time he had been engaged in the back-breaking work of digging out the strange thing in the woods.

He put up the binoculars and the elusive white line that he had been seeing turned out to be a range of mountains. The great, blue, craggy mass towered up above the desert with the gleam of snow on its peaks and ridges. They were a long way off, for even the powerful glasses brought them in as little more than a misty blueness.

He swept the glasses slowly back and forth and the mountains extended for a long distance above the horizon line.

He brought the glasses down off the mountains and examined the desert that stretched ahead of him. There was more of the same that he had been seeing—the same floorlike levelness, the same occasional mounds, the selfsame scraggy vegetation.

And a house!

His hands trembled and he lowered the glasses, then put them up to his face again and had another look. It was a house, all right. A funny-looking house standing at the foot of one of the hillocks, shadowed by the hillock so that one could not pick it out with the naked eye.

It seemed to be a small house. Its roof was like a blunted cone and it lay tight against the ground, as if it hugged or crouched against the ground. There was an oval opening that probably was a door, but there was no sign of windows.

He took the binoculars down again and stared at the hillock. Four or five miles away, he thought. The gas would stretch that far and even if it didn't he could walk the last few miles into Willow Bend.

It was queer, he thought, that a house should be all alone out here. In all the miles he'd traveled in the desert he'd seen no sign of life beyond the sixteen little ratlike things that marched in single file, no sign of artificial structure other than the eight milk-glass contraptions resting in their cradles.

He climbed into the pickup and put it into gear. Ten minutes later he drew up in front of the house, which still lay within the shadow of the hillock.

He got out of the pickup and hauled his rifle after him. Towser leaped to the ground and stood with his hackles up, a deep growl in his throat.

"What's the matter, boy?" asked Taine.

Towser growled again.

The house stood silent. It seemed to be deserted.

The walls were built, Taine saw, of rude, rough masonry crudely set together, with a crumbling, mudlike substance used in lieu of mortar. The roof originally had been of sod and that was queer, indeed, for there was nothing that came close to sod upon this expanse of desert. But now, although one could see the lines where the sod strips had been fitted together, it was nothing more than earth baked hard by the desert sun.

The house itself was featureless, entirely devoid of any ornament, with no attempt at all to soften the harsh utility of it as a simple shelter. It was the sort of thing that a shepherd people might have put together. It had the look of age about it; the stone had flaked and crumbled in the weather.

Rifle slung beneath his arm, Taine paced toward it. He reached the door and glanced inside and there was darkness and no movement.

He glanced back for Towser and saw that the dog had crawled beneath the truck and was peering out and growling.

"You stick around," said Taine. "Don't go running off."

With the rifle thrust before him, Taine stepped through the door into the darkness. He stood for a long moment to allow his eyes to become accustomed to the gloom.

Finally he could make out the room in which he stood. It was plain and rough, with a rude stone bench along one wall and queer unfunctional niches hollowed in another. One rickety piece of wooden furniture stood in a corner, but Taine could not make out what its use might be.

An old and deserted place, he thought, abandoned long ago. Perhaps a shepherd people might have lived here in some long-gone age, when the desert had been a rich and grassy plain.

There was a door into another room and as he stepped through it he heard the faint, far-off booming sound and something else as well—the sound of pouring rain! From the open door that led out through the back he caught a whiff of salty breeze and he stood there frozen in the center of that second room.

Another one!

Another house that led to another world!

He walked slowly forward, drawn toward the outer door, and he stepped out into a cloudy, darkling day with the rain streaming down from wildly racing clouds. Half a mile away, across a field of jumbled broken, iron-gray boulders, lay a pounding sea that raged upon the coast, throwing great spumes of angry spray high into the air.

He walked out from the door and looked up at the sky,

and the rain drops pounded at his face with a stinging fury. There was a chill and a dampness in the air and the place was eldritch—a world jerked straight from some ancient Gothic tale of goblin and of sprite.

He glanced around and there was nothing he could see, for the rain blotted out the world beyond this stretch of coast, but behind the rain he could sense or seemed to sense a presence that sent shivers down his spine. Gulping in fright, Taine turned around and stumbled back again through the door into the house.

One world away, he thought, was far enough; two worlds away was more than one could take. He trembled at the sense of utter loneliness that tumbled in his skull and suddenly this long-forsaken house became unbearable and he dashed out of it.

Outside the sun was bright and there was welcome warmth. His clothes were damp from rain and little beads of moisture lay on the rifle barrel.

He looked around for Towser and there was no sign of the dog. He was not underneath the pickup; he was nowhere in sight.

Taine called and there was no answer. His voice sounded lone and hollow in the emptiness and silence.

He walked around the house, looking for the dog, and there was no back door to the house. The rough rock walls of the sides of the house pulled in with that funny curvature and there was no back to the house at all.

But Taine was not interested; he had known how it would be. Right now he was looking for his dog and he felt the panic rising in him. Somehow it felt a long way from home.

He spent three hours at it. He went back into the house and Towser was not there. He went into the other world again and searched among the tumbled rocks and Towser was not there. He went back to the desert and walked around the hillock and then he climbed to the crest of it and used the binoculars and saw nothing but the lifeless desert, stretching far in all directions.

Dead-beat with weariness, stumbling, half asleep even as he walked, he went back to the pickup.

He leaned against it and tried to pull his wits together.

Continuing as he was would be a useless effort. He had to get some sleep. He had to go back to Willow Bend and fill the tank and get some extra gasoline so that he could range farther afield in his search for Towser.

He couldn't leave the dog out here—that was unthinkable. But he had to plan, he had to act intelligently. He would be doing Towser no good by stumbling around in his present shape.

He pulled himself into the truck and headed back for Willow Bend, following the occasional faint impressions that his tires had made in the sandy places, fighting a half-dead drowsiness that tried to seal his eyes shut.

Passing the higher hill on which the milk-glass things had stood, he stopped to walk around a bit so he wouldn't fall asleep behind the wheel. And now, he saw, there were only seven of the things resting in their cradles.

But that meant nothing to him now. All that meant anything was to hold off the fatigue that was closing down upon him, to cling to the wheel and wear off the miles, to get back to Willow Bend and get some sleep and then come back again to look for Towser.

Slightly more than halfway home he saw the other car and watched it in numb befuddlement, for this truck that he was driving and the car at home in his garage were the only two vehicles this side of his house.

He pulled the pickup to a halt and tumbled out of it.

The car drew up and Henry Horton and Beasly and a man who wore a star leaped quickly out of it.

"Thank God we found you, man!" cried Henry, striding over to him.

"I wasn't lost," protested Taine. "I was coming back."

"He's all beat out," said the man who wore the star.

"This is Sheriff Hanson," Henry said. "We were following your tracks."

"I lost Towser," Taine mumbled. "I had to go and leave him. Just leave me be and go and hunt for Towser. I can make it home."

He reached out and grabbed the edge of the pickup's door to hold himself erect.

"You broke down the door," he said to Henry. "You broke into my house and you took my car—"

"We had to do it, Hiram. We were afraid that something might have happened to you. The way that Beasly told it, it stood your hair on end."

"You better get him in the car," the sheriff said. "I'll drive the pickup back."

"But I have to hunt for Towser!"

"You can't do anything until you've had some rest."

Henry grabbed him by the arm and led him to the car and Beasly held the rear door open.

"You got any idea what this place is?" Henry whispered conspiratorily.

"I don't positively know," Taine mumbled. "Might be some other—"

Henry chuckled. "Well, I guess it doesn't really matter. Whatever it may be, it's put us on the map. We're in all the newscasts and the papers are plastering us in headlines and the town is swarming with reporters and cameramen and there are big officials coming. Yes, sir, I tell you, Hiram, this will be the making of us—"

Taine heard no more. He was fast asleep before he hit the seat.

He came awake and lay quietly in the bed and he saw the shades were drawn and the room was cool and peaceful.

It was good, he thought, to wake in a room you knew—in a room that one had known for his entire life, in a house that had been the Taine house for almost a hundred years.

Then memory clouted him and he sat bolt upright.

And now he heard it—the insistent murmur from outside the window.

He vaulted from the bed and pulled one shade aside. Peering out, he saw the cordon of troops that held back the crowd that overflowed his back yard and the back yards back of that.

He let the shade drop back and started hunting for his shoes, for he was fully dressed. Probably Henry and Beasly, he told himself, had dumped him into bed and pulled off his shoes and let it go at that. But he couldn't remember a single thing of it. He must have gone dead to the world the minute Henry had bundled him into the back seat of the car.

He found the shoes on the floor at the end of the bed and sat down upon the bed to pull them on.

And his mind was racing on what he had to do.

He'd have to get some gasoline somehow and fill up the truck and stash an extra can or two into the back and he'd have to take some food and water and perhaps his sleeping bag. For he wasn't coming back until he'd found his dog.

He got on his shoes and tied them, then went out into the living room. There was no one there, but there were voices in the kitchen.

He looked out the window and the desert lay outside, unchanged. The sun, he noticed, had climbed higher in the sky, but out in his front yard it was still forenoon.

He looked at his watch and it was six o'clock and from the way the shadows had been falling when he'd peered out of the bedroom window, he knew that it was 6:00 p.m. He realized with a guilty start that he must have slept almost around the clock. He had not meant to sleep that long. He hadn't meant to leave Towser out there that long.

He headed for the kitchen and there were three persons there—Abbie and Henry Horton and a man in military garb.

"There you are," cried Abbie merrily. "We were wondering when you would wake up."

"You have some coffee cooking, Abbie?"

"Yes, a whole pot full of it. And I'll cook up something else for you."

"Just some toast," said Taine. "I haven't got much time. I have to hunt for Towser."

"Hiram," said Henry, "this is Colonel Ryan. National guard. He has his boys outside."

"Yes, I saw them through the window."

"Necessary," said Henry. "Absolutely necessary. The sheriff couldn't handle it. The people came rushing in and they'd have torn the place apart. So I called the governor."

"Taine," the colonel said, "sit down. I want to talk with you."

"Certainly," said Taine, taking a chair. "Sorry to be in such a rush, but I lost my dog out there."

"This business," said the colonel, smugly, "is vastly more important than any dog could be."

"Well, colonel, that just goes to show that you don't know Towser. He's the best dog I ever had and I've had a lot of them. Raised him from a pup and he's been a good friend all these years—"

"All right," the colonel said, "so he is a friend. But still I have to talk with you."

"You just sit and talk," Abbie said to Taine. "I'll fix up

some cakes and Henry brought over some of that sausage that we get out on the farm."

The back door opened and Beasly staggered in to the accompaniment of a terrific metallic banging. He was carrying three empty five-gallon gas cans in one hand and two in the other hand and they were bumping and banging together as he moved.

"Say," yelled Taine, "what's going on here?"

"Now, just take it easy," Henry said. "You have no idea the problems that we have. We wanted to get a big gas tank moved through here, but we couldn't do it. We tried to rip out the back of the kitchen to get it through, but we couldn't—"

"You did what!"

"We tried to rip out the back of the kitchen," Henry told him calmly. "You can't get one of those big storage tanks through an ordinary door. But when we tried, we found that the entire house is boarded up inside with the same kind of material that you used down in the basement. You hit it with an axe and it blunts the steel—"

"But, Henry, this is my house and there isn't anyone who has the right to start tearing it apart."

"Fat chance," the colonel said. "What I would like to know, Taine, what is that stuff that we couldn't break through?"

"Now you take it easy, Hiram," cautioned Henry. "We have a big new world waiting for us out there—"

"It isn't waiting for you or anyone," yelled Taine.

"And we have to explore it and to explore it we need a stockpile of gasoline. So since we can't have a storage tank, we're getting together as many gas cans as possible and then we'll run a hose through here—"

"But, Henry—"

"I wish," said Henry sternly, "that you'd quit interrupting me and let me have my say. You can't even imagine the logistics that we face. We're bottlenecked by the size of a regulation door. We have to get supplies out there and we have to get transport. Cars and trucks won't be so bad. We can disassemble them and lug them through piecemeal, but a plane will be a problem."

"You listen to me, Henry. There isn't anyone going to haul a plane through here. This house has been in my family for almost a hundred years and I own it and I have a right to it and you can't come in high-handed and start hauling stuff through it."

"But," said Henry plaintively, "we need a plane real bad. You can cover so much more ground when you have a plane."

Beasly went banging through the kitchen with his cans and out into the living room.

The colonel sighed. "I had hoped, Mr. Taine, that you would understand how the matter stood. To me it seems very plain that it's your patriotic duty to co-operate with us in this. The government, of course, could exercise the right of eminent domain and start condemnation action, but it would rather not do that. I'm speaking unofficially, of course, but I think it's safe to say the government would much prefer to arrive at an amicable agreement."

"I doubt," Taine said, bluffing, not knowing anything about it, "that the right of eminent domain would be applicable. As I understand it, it applies to buildings and to roads—"

"This is a road," the colonel told him flatly. "A road right through your house to another world."

"First," Taine declared, "the government would have to show it was in the public interest and that refusal of the owner to relinquish title amounted to an interference in government procedure and—"

"I think," the colonel said, "that the government can prove it is in the public interest."

"I think," Taine said angrily, "I better get a lawyer."

"If you really mean that," Henry offered, ever helpful, "and you want to get a good one—and I presume you do—I would be pleased to recommend a firm that I am sure would represent your interests most ably and be, at the same time, fairly reasonable in cost."

The colonel stood up, seething. "You'll have a lot to answer, Taine. There'll be a lot of things the government will want to know. First of all, they'll want to know just how you engineered this. Are you ready to tell that?"

"No," said Taine, "I don't believe I am."

And he thought with some alarm. They think that I'm the one who did it and they'll be down on me like a pack of wolves to find just how I did it. He had visions of the FBI and the state department and the Pentagon and, even sitting down, he felt shaky in the knees.

The colonel turned around and marched stiffly from the kitchen. He went out the back and slammed the door behind him.

Henry looked at Taine speculatively.

"Do you really mean it?" he demanded. "Do you intend to stand up to them?"

"I'm getting sore," said Taine. "They can't come in here and take over without even asking me. I don't care what anyone may think, this is my house. I was born here and I've lived here all my life and I like the place and—"

"Sure," said Henry. "I know just how you feel."

"I suppose it's childish of me, but I wouldn't mind so much if they showed a willingness to sit down and talk about what they meant to do once they'd taken over. But there seems no disposition to even ask me what I think about it. And I tell you, Henry, this is different than it seems. This isn't a place where we can walk in and take over, no matter what Washington may think. There's something out there and we better watch our step—"

"I was thinking," Henry interrupted, "as I was sitting here, that your attitude is most commendable and deserving of support. It has occurred to me that it would be most unneighborly of me to go on sitting here and leave you in the fight alone. We could hire ourselves a fine array of legal talent and we could fight the case and in the meantime we could form a land and development company and that way we could make sure that this new world of yours is used the way it should be used.

"It stands to reason, Hiram, that I am the one to stand beside you, shoulder to shoulder, in this business since we're already partners in this TV deal."

"What's that about TV?" shrilled Abbie, slapping a plate of cakes down in front of Taine.

"Now, Abbie," Henry said patiently, "I have explained to you already that your TV set is back of that partition down in the basement and there isn't any telling when we can get it out."

"Yes, I know," said Abbie, bringing a platter of sausages and pouring a cup of coffee.

Beasly came in from the living room and went bumbling out the back.

"After all," said Henry, pressing his advantage, "I would suppose I had some hand in it. I doubt you could have done much without the computer I sent over."

And there it was again, thought Taine. Even Henry thought he'd been the one who did it.

"But didn't Beasly tell you?"

"Beasly said a lot, but you know how Beasly is."

And that was it, of course. To the villagers it would be no more than another Beasly story—another whopper that Beasly had dreamed up. There was no one who believed a word that Beasly said.

Taine picked up the cup and drank his coffee, gaining time to shape an answer and there wasn't any answer. If he told the truth, it would sound far less believable than any lie he'd tell.

"You can tell me, Hiram. After all, we're partners."

He's playing me for a fool, thought Taine. Henry thinks he can play anyone he wants to for a fool and sucker.

"You wouldn't believe me if I told you, Henry."

"Well," Henry said, resignedly, getting to his feet, "I guess that part of it can wait."

Beasly came tramping and banging through the kitchen with another load of cans.

"I'll have to have some gasoline," said Taine. "If I'm going out for Towser."

"I'll take care of that right away," Henry promised smoothly. "I'll send Ernie over with his tank wagon and we can run a hose through here and fill up those cans. And I'll see if I can find someone who'll go along with you."

"That's not necessary. I can go alone."

"If we had a radio transmitter. Then you could keep in touch."

"But we haven't any. And, Henry, I can't wait. Towser's out there somewhere—"

"Sure, I know how much you thought of him. You go out and look for him if you think you have to and I'll get started on this other business. I'll get some lawyers lined up and we'll draw up some sort of corporate papers for our land development—"

"And, Hiram," Abbie said, "will you do something for me, please?"

"Why, certainly," said Taine.

"Would you speak to Beasly. It's senseless the way he's acting. There wasn't any call for him to up and leave us. I might have been a little sharp with him, but he's so simpleminded he's infuriating. He ran off and spent half a day helping Towser at digging out that woodchuck and—"

"I'll speak to him," said Taine.

"Thanks, Hiram. He'll listen to you. You're the only one he'll listen to. And I wish you could have fixed my TV set before all this came about. I'm just lost without it. It leaves a hole in the living room. It matched my other furniture, you know."

"Yes, I know," said Taine.

"Coming, Abbie?" Henry asked, standing at the door.

He lifted a hand in a confidential farewell to Taine. "I'll see you later, Hiram. I'll get it all fixed up."

I just bet you will, thought Taine.

He went back to the table, after they were gone, and sat down heavily in a chair.

The front door slammed and Beasly came panting in, excited.

"Towser's back!" he yelled. "He's coming back and he's driving in the biggest woodchuck you ever clapped your eyes on."

Taine leaped to his feet.

"Woodchuck! That's an alien planet. It hasn't any woodchucks."

"You come and see," yelled Beasly.

He turned and raced back out again with Taine following close behind.

It certainly looked considerably like a woodchuck—a sort of man-size woodchuck. More like a woodchuck out of a children's book, perhaps, for it was walking on its hind legs and trying to look dignified even while it kept a weather eye on Towser.

Towser was back a hundred feet or so, keeping a wary distance from the massive chuck. He had the pose of a good sheep-herding dog, walking in a crouch, alert to head off any break that the chuck might make.

The chuck came up close to the house and stopped. Then it did an about-face so that it looked back across the desert and it hunkered down.

It swung its massive head to gaze at Beasly and Taine and in the limpid brown eyes Taine saw more than the eyes of an animal.

Taine walked swiftly out and picked up the dog in his arms and hugged him tight against him. Towser twisted his head around and slapped a sloppy tongue across his master's face.

Taine stood with the dog in his arms and looked at the man-size chuck and felt a great relief and an utter thankfulness.

Everything was all right now, he thought. Towser had come back.

He headed for the house and out into the kitchen.

He put Towser down and got a dish and filled it at the tap. He placed it on the floor and Towser lapped at it thirstily, slopping water all over the linoleum.

"Take it easy, there," warned Taine. "You don't want to overdo it."

He hunted in the refrigerator and found some scraps and put them in Towser's dish.

Towser wagged his tail with doggish happiness.

"By rights," said Taine, "I ought to take a rope to you, running off like that."

Beasly came ambling in.

"That chuck is a friendly cuss," he announced. "He's waiting for someone."

"That's nice," said Taine, paying no attention.

He glanced at the clock.

"It's seven-thirty," he said. "We can catch the news. You want to get it, Beasly?"

"Sure. I know right where to get it. That fellow from New York."

"That's the one," said Taine.

He walked into the living room and looked out the window. The man-size chuck had not moved. He was sitting with his back to the house, looking back the way he'd come.

Waiting for someone, Beasly had said, and it looked as if he might be, but probably it was all just in Beasly's head.

And if he were waiting for someone, Taine wondered, who might that someone be? *What* might that someone be? Certainly by now the word had spread out there that there was a door into another world. And how many doors, he wondered, had been opened through the ages?

Henry had said that there was a big new world out there waiting for Earthmen to move in. And that wasn't it at all. It was the other way around.

The voice of the news commentator came blasting from the radio in the middle of a sentence:

"... finally got into the act. Radio Moscow said this evening that the Soviet delegate will make representations in the U.N. tomorrow for the internationalization of this other world and the gateway to it.

"From that gateway itself, the home of a man named Hiram Taine, there is no news. Complete security had been clamped down and a cordon of troops form a solid wall around the house, holding back the crowds. Attempts to telephone the residence are blocked by a curt voice which says that no calls are being accepted for that number. And Taine himself has not stepped from the house."

Taine walked back into the kitchen and sat down.

"He's talking about you," Beasly said importantly.

"Rumor circulated this morning that Taine, a quiet village repair man and dealer in antiques, and until yesterday a relative unknown, had finally returned from a trip which he made out into this new and unknown land. But what he found, if anything, no one can say. Nor is there any further information about this other place beyond the fact that it is a desert and, to the moment, lifeless.

"A small flurry of excitement was occasioned late yesterday by the finding of some strange object in the woods across the road from the residence, but this area likewise was swiftly cordoned off and to the moment Colonel Ryan, who commands the troops, will say nothing of what actually was found.

"Mystery man of the entire situation is one Henry Horton, who seems to be the only unofficial person to have entry to the Taine house. Horton, questioned earlier today, had little to say, but managed to suggest an air of great conspiracy. He hinted he and Taine were partners in some mysterious venture and left hanging in midair the half impression that he and Taine had collaborated in opening the new world.

"Horton, it is interesting to note, operates a small computer plant and it is understood on good authority that only recently he delivered a computer to Taine, or at least some sort of machine to which considerable mystery is attached. One story is that this particular machine had been in the process of development for six or seven years.

"Some of the answers to the matter of how all this did happen and what actually did happen must wait upon the findings of a team of scientists who left Washington this evening after an all-day conference at the White House, which was attended by representatives from the military, the state department, the security division and the special weapons section.

"Throughout the world the impact of what happened yesterday at Willow Bend can only be compared to the sensation of the news, almost twenty years ago, of the dropping of the first atomic bomb. There is some tendency among many observers to believe that the implications of Willow Bend, in fact, may be even more earth-shaking than were those of Hiroshima.

"Washington insists, as is only natural, that this matter is of internal concern only and that it intends to handle the situation as it best affects the national welfare.

"But abroad there is a rising storm of insistence that this is not a matter of national policy concerning one nation, but that it necessarily must be a matter of worldwide concern.

"There is an unconfirmed report that a U.N. observer will arrive in Willow Bend almost momentarily. France, Britain, Bolivia, Mexico and India have already requested permission of Washington to send observers to the scene and other nations undoubtedly plan to file similar requests.

"The world sits on edge tonight, waiting for the word from Willow Bend and—"

Taine reached out and clicked the radio to silence.

"From the sound of it," said Beasly, "we're going to be overrun by a batch of foreigners."

Yes, thought Taine, there might be a batch of foreigners, but not exactly in the sense that Beasly meant. The use of the word, he told himself, so far as any human was concerned, must be outdated now. No man of Earth ever again could be called a foreigner with alien life next door—literally next door. What were the people of the stone house?

And perhaps not the alien life of one planet only, but the

alien life of many. For he himself had found another door into yet another planet and there might be many more such doors and what would these other worlds be like, and what was the purpose of the doors?

Someone, *something,* had found a way of going to another planet short of spanning light-years of lonely space—a simpler and a shorter way than flying through the gulfs of space. And once the way was open, then the way stayed open and it was as easy as walking from one room to another.

But one thing—one ridiculous thing—kept puzzling him and that was the spinning and the movement of the connected planets, of all the planets that must be linked together. You could not, he argued, establish solid, factual links between two objects that move independently of one another.

And yet, a couple of days ago, he would have contended just as stolidly that the whole idea on the face of it was fantastic and impossible. Still it had been done. And once one impossibility was accomplished, what logical man could say with sincerity that the second could not be?

The doorbell rang and he got up to answer it.

It was Ernie, the oil man.

"Henry said you wanted some gas and I came to tell you I can't get it until morning."

"That's all right," said Taine. "I don't need it now."

And swiftly slammed the door.

He leaned against it, thinking: I'll have to face them sometime. I can't keep the door locked against the world. Sometime, soon or late, the Earth and I will have to have this out.

And it was foolish, he thought, for him to think like this, but that was the way it was.

He had something here that the Earth demanded; something that Earth wanted or thought it wanted. And yet, in the last analysis, it was his responsibility. It had happened on his land, it had happened in his house; unwittingly, perhaps, he'd even aided and abetted it.

And the land and house are mine, he fiercely told himself, and that world out there was an extension of his yard. No matter how far or where it went, an extension of his yard.

Beasly had left the kitchen and Taine walked into the living room. Towser was curled up and snoring gently in the gold-upholstered chair.

Taine decided he would let him stay there. After all, he thought, Towser had won the right to sleep anywhere he wished.

He walked past the chair to the window and the desert stretched to its far horizon and there before the window sat the man-size woodchuck and Beasly side by side, with their backs turned to the window and staring out across the desert.

Somehow it seemed natural that the chuck and Beasly should be sitting there together—the two of them, it appeared to Taine, might have a lot in common.

And it was a good beginning—that a man and an alien creature from this other world should sit down companionably together.

He tried to envision the setup of these linked worlds, of which Earth now was a part, and the possibilities that lay inherent in the fact of linkage rolled thunder through his brain.

There would be contact between the Earth and these other worlds and what would come of it?

And come to think of it, the contact had been made already, but so naturally, so undramatically, that it failed to register as a great, important meeting. For Beasly and the chuck out there were contact and if it all should go like that, there was absolutely nothing for one to worry over.

This was no haphazard business, he reminded himself. It had been planned and executed with the smoothness of long practice. This was not the first world to be opened and it would not be the last.

The little ratlike things had spanned space—how many light-years of space one could not even guess—in the vehicle which he had unearthed out in the woods. They then had buried it, perhaps as a child might hide a dish by shoving it into a pile of sand. Then they had come to this very house and had set up the apparatus that had made this house a tunnel between one world and another. And once that had been done, the need of crossing space had been canceled out forever. There need be but one crossing and that one crossing would serve to link the planets.

And once the job was done the little ratlike things had left, but not before they had made certain that this gateway to their planet would stand against no matter what assault. They had sheathed the house inside the studdings with a wonder-material that would resist an ax and that, undoubtedly, would resist much more than a simple ax.

And they had marched in drill-order single file out to the hill where eight more of the space machines had rested in their cradles. And now there were only seven there, in their cradles on the hill, and the ratlike things were gone and, perhaps, in time to come, they'd land on another planet and another doorway would be opened, a link to yet another world.

But more, Taine thought, than the linking of mere worlds. It would be, as well, the linking of the peoples of those worlds.

The little ratlike creatures were the explorers and the pioneers who sought out other Earthlike planets and the creature waiting with Beasly just outside the window must also serve its purpose and perhaps in time to come there would be a purpose which man would also serve.

He turned away from the window and looked around the room and the room was exactly as it had been ever since he could remember it. With all the change outside, with all that was happening outside, the room remained unchanged.

This is the reality, thought Taine, this is all the reality there is. Whatever else may happen, this is where I stand—this room with its fireplace blackened by many winter fires, the bookshelves with the old thumbed volumes, the easychair, the ancient worn carpet—worn by beloved and unforgotten feet through the many years.

And this also, he knew, was the lull before the storm.

In just a little while the brass would start arriving—the team of scientists, the governmental functionaries, the military, the observers from the other countries, the officials from the U.N.

And against all these, he realized, he stood weaponless and shorn of his strength. No matter what a man might say or think, he could not stand off the world.

This was the last day that this would be the Taine house. After almost a hundred years, it would have another destiny.

And for the first time in all those years there'd be no Taine asleep beneath its roof.

He stood looking at the fireplace and the shelves of books and he sensed the old, pale ghosts walking in the room and he lifted a hesitant hand as if to wave farewell, not only to the ghosts but to the room as well. But before he got it up, he dropped it to his side.

What was the use, he thought.

He went out to the porch and sat down on the steps.

Beasly heard him and turned around.

"He's nice," he said to Taine, patting the chuck upon the back. "He's exactly like a great big teddy bear."

"Yes, I see," said Taine.

"And best of all, I can talk with him."

"Yes, I know," said Taine, remembering that Beasly could talk with Towser, too.

He wondered what it would be like to live in the simple world of Beasly. At times, he decided, it would be comfortable.

The ratlike things had come in the spaceship, but why had they come to Willow Bend, why had they picked this house, the only house in all the village where they would have found the equipment that they needed to build their apparatus so easily and so quickly? For there was no doubt that they had cannibalized the computer to get the equipment they needed. In that, at least, Henry had been right. Thinking back on it, Henry, after all, had played quite a part in it.

Could they have foreseen that on this particular week in this particular house the probability of quickly and easily doing what they had come to do had stood very high?

Did they, with all their other talents and technology, have clairvoyance as well?

"There's someone coming," Beasly said.

"I don't see a thing."

"Neither do I," said Beasly, "but Chuck told me that he saw them."

"Told you!"

"I told you we been talking. There, I can see them, too."

They were far off, but they were coming fast—three dots that rode rapidly up out of the desert.

He sat and watched them come and he thought of going in to get a rifle, but he didn't stir from his seat upon the steps. The rifle would do no good, he told himself. It would be a senseless thing to get it; more than that, a senseless attitude.

The least that man could do, he thought, was to meet these creatures of another world with clean and empty hands.

They were closer now and it seemed to him that they were sitting in invisible easy chairs that traveled very fast.

He saw that they were humanoid, to a degree at least, and there were only three of them.

They came in with a rush and stopped very suddenly a hundred feet or so from where he sat upon the steps.

He didn't move or say a word—there was nothing he could say. It was too ridiculous.

They were, perhaps, a little smaller than himself, and black as the ace of spades, and they wore skin-tight shorts and vests that were somewhat oversize and both the shorts and vests were the blue of April skies.

But that was not the worst of it.

They sat on saddles, with horns in front and stirrups and a sort of a bedroll tied on the back, but they had no horses.

The saddles floated in the air, with the stirrups about three feet above the ground and the aliens sat easily in the saddles and stared at him and he stared back at them.

Finally he got up and moved forward a step or two and when he did that the three swung from the saddles and moved forward, too, while the saddles hung there in the air, exactly as they'd left them.

Taine walked forward and the three walked forward until they were no more than six feet apart.

"They say hello to you," said Beasly. "They say welcome to you."

"Well, all right, then, tell them—Say, how do you know all this!"

"Chuck tells me what they say and I tell you. You tell me and I tell him and he tells them. That's the way it works. That is what he's here for."

"Well, I'll be—," said Taine. "So you can really talk to him."

"I told you that I could," stormed Beasly. "I told you that I could talk to Towser, too, but you thought that I was crazy."

"Telepathy!" said Taine. And it was worse than ever now. Not only had the ratlike things known all the rest of it, but they'd known of Beasly, too.

"What was that you said, Hiram?"

"Never mind," said Taine. "Tell that friend of yours to tell them I'm glad to meet them and what can I do for them?"

He stood uncomfortably and stared at the three and he saw that their vests had many pockets and that the pockets were all crammed, probably with their equivalent of tobacco and handkerchiefs and pocket knives and such.

"They say," said Beasly, "that they want to dicker."

"Dicker?"

"Sure, Hiram. You know, trade."

Beasly chuckled thinly. "Imagine them laying themselves open to a Yankee trader. That's what Henry says you are. He says you can skin a man the slickest—"

"Leave Henry out of this," snapped Taine. "Let's leave Henry out of something."

He sat down on the ground and the three sat down to face him.

"Ask them what they have in mind to trade."

"Ideas," Beasly said.

"Ideas! That's a crazy thing—"

And then he saw it wasn't.

Of all the commodities that might be exchanged by an alien people, ideas would be the most valuable and the easiest to handle. They'd take no cargo room and they'd upset no economies—not immediately, that is—and they'd make a bigger contribution to the welfare of the cultures than trade in actual goods.

"Ask them," said Taine, "what they'll take for the idea back of those saddles they are riding."

"They say, what have you got to offer?"

And that was the stumper. That was the one that would be hard to answer.

Automobiles and trucks, the internal gas engine—well, probably not. Because they already had the saddles. Earth was out of date in transportation from the viewpoint of these people.

Housing architecture—no, that was hardly an idea and, anyhow, there was that other house, so they knew of houses.

Cloth? No, they had cloth.

Paint, he thought. Maybe paint was it.

"See if they are interested in paint," Taine told Beasly.

"They say, what is it? Please explain yourself."

"O.K., then. Let's see. It's a protective device to be spread over almost any surface. Easily packaged and easily applied. Protects against weather and corrosion. It's decorative, too. Comes in all sorts of colors. And it's cheap to make."

"They shrug in their mind," said Beasly. "They're just slightly interested. But they'll listen more. Go ahead and tell them."

And that was more like it, thought Taine.

That was the kind of language that he could understand.

He settled himself more firmly on the ground and bent forward slightly, flicking his eyes across the three deadpan, ebony faces, trying to make out what they might be thinking.

There was no making out. Those were three of the deadest pans he had ever seen.

It was all familiar. It made him feel at home. He was in his element.

And in the three across from him, he felt somehow subconsciously, he had the best dickering opposition he had ever met. And that made him feel good too.

"Tell them," he said, "that I'm not quite sure. I may have spoken up too hastily. Paint, after all, is a mighty valuable idea."

"They say, just as a favor to them, not that they're really interested, would you tell them a little more."

Got them hooked, Taine told himself. If he could only play it right—

He settled down to dickering in earnest.

Hours later Henry Horton showed up. He was accompanied by a very urbane gentleman, who was faultlessly turned out and who carried beneath his arm an impressive attaché case.

Henry and the man stopped on the steps in sheer astonishment.

Taine was squatted on the ground with a length of board and he was daubing paint on it while the aliens watched. From the daubs here and there upon their anatomies, it was plain to see the aliens had been doing some daubing of their own. Spread all over the ground were other lengths of half-painted boards and a couple of dozen old cans of paint.

Taine looked up and saw Henry and the man.

"I was hoping," he said, "that someone would show up."

"Hiram," said Henry, with more importance than usual,

"may I present Mr. Lancaster. He is a special representative of the United Nations."

"I'm glad to meet you, sir," said Taine. "I wonder if you would—"

"Mr. Lancaster," Henry explained grandly, "was having some slight difficulty getting through the lines outside, so I volunteered my services. I've already explained to him our joint interest in this matter."

"It was very kind of Mr. Horton," Lancaster said. "There was this stupid sergeant—"

"It's all in knowing," Henry said, "how to handle people."

The remark, Taine noticed, was not appreciated by the man from the U.N.

"May I inquire, Mr. Taine," asked Lancaster, "exactly what you're doing?"

"I'm dickering," said Taine.

"Dickering. What a quaint way of expressing—"

"An old Yankee word," said Henry quickly, "with certain connotations of its own. When you trade with someone you are exchanging goods, but if you're dickering with him you're out to get his hide."

"Interesting," said Lancaster. "And I suppose you're out to skin these gentlemen in the sky-blue vests—"

"Hiram," said Henry, proudly, "is the sharpest dickerer in these parts. He runs an antique business and he has to dicker hard—"

"And may I ask," said Lancaster, ignoring Henry finally, "what you might be doing with these cans of paint? Are these gentlemen potential customers for paint or—"

Taine threw down the board and rose angrily to his feet.

"If you'd both shut up!" he shouted. "I've been trying to say something ever since you got here and I can't get in a word. And I tell you, it's important—"

"Hiram!" Henry exclaimed in horror.

"It's quite all right," said the U.N. man. "We *have* been jabbering. And now, Mr. Taine?"

"I'm backed into a corner," Taine told him, "and I need some help. I've sold these fellows on the idea of paint, but I don't know a thing about it—the principle back of it or how it's made or what goes into it or—"

"But, Mr. Taine, if you're selling them the paint, what difference does it make—"

"I'm not selling them the paint," yelled Taine. "Can't you understand that? They don't want the paint. They want the *idea* of paint, the principle of paint. It's something that they never thought of and they're interested. I offered them the paint idea for the idea of their saddles and I've almost got it—"

"Saddles? You mean those things over there, hanging in the air?"

"That is right. Beasly, would you ask one of our friends to demonstrate a saddle?"

"You bet I will," said Beasly.

"What," demanded Henry, "has Beasly got to do with this?"

"Beasly is an interpreter. I guess you'd call him a telepath. You remember how he always claimed he could talk with Towser?"

"Beasly was always claiming things."

"But this time he was right. He tells Chuck, that funnylooking monster, what I want to say and Chuck tells these aliens. And these aliens tell Chuck and Chuck tells Beasly and Beasly tells me."

"Ridiculous!" snorted Henry. "Beasly hasn't got the sense to be . . . what did you say he was?"

"A telepath," said Taine.

One of the aliens had gotten up and climbed into a saddle. He rode it forth and back. Then he swung out of it and sat down again.

"Remarkable," said the U.N. man. "Some sort of antigravity unit, with complete control. We could make use of that, indeed."

He scraped his hand across his chin.

"And you're going to exchange the idea of paint for the idea of that saddle?"

"That's exactly it," said Taine, "but I need some help. I need a chemist or a paint manufacturer or someone to explain how paint is made. And I need some professor or other who'll understand what they're talking about when they tell me the idea of the saddle."

"I see," said Lancaster, "Yes, indeed, you have a problem. Mr. Taine, you seem to me a man of some discernment—"

"Oh, he's all of that," interrupted Henry. "Hiram's quite astute."

"So I suppose you'll understand," said the U.N. man, "that this whole procedure is quite irregular—"

"But it's not," exploded Taine. "That's the way they operate. They open up a planet and then they exchange ideas. They've been doing that with other planets for a long, long time. And ideas are all they want, just the new ideas, because that is the way to keep on building a technology and culture. And they have a lot of ideas, sir, that the human race can use."

"That is just the point," said Lancaster. "This is perhaps the most important thing that has ever happened to us humans. In just a short year's time we can obtain data and ideas that will put us ahead—theoretically, at least—by a thousand years. And in a thing that is so important, we should have experts on the job—"

"But," protested Henry, "you can't find a man who'll do a better dickering job than Hiram. When you dicker with him your back teeth aren't safe. Why don't you leave him be? He'll do a job for you. You can get your experts and your planning groups together and let Hiram front for you. These folks have accepted him and have proved they'll do business with him and what more do you want? All he needs is a little help."

Beasly came over and faced the U.N. man.

"I won't work with no one else," he said. "If you kick Hiram out of here, then I go along with him. Hiram's the only person who ever treated me like a human—"

"There, you see!" Henry said, triumphantly.

"Now, wait a second, Beasly," said the U.N. man. "We could make it worth your while. I should imagine that an interpreter in a situation such as this could command a handsome salary."

"Money don't mean a thing to me," said Beasly. "It won't buy me friends. People still will laugh at me."

"He means it, mister," Henry warned. "There isn't any one who can be as stubborn as Beasly. I know; he used to work for us."

The U.N. man looked flabbergasted and not a little desperate.

"It will take you quite some time," Henry pointed out, "to find another telepath—leastwise one who can talk to these people here."

The U.N. man looked as if he were strangling. "I doubt," he said, "there's another one on Earth."

"Well, all right," said Beasly, brutally, "let's make up our minds. I ain't standing here all day."

"All right!" cried the U.N. man. "You two go ahead. Please, will you go ahead? This is a chance we can't let slip through our fingers. Is there anything you want? Anything I can do for you?"

"Yes, there is," said Taine. "There'll be the boys from Washington and bigwigs from other countries. Just keep them off my back."

"I'll explain most carefully to everyone. There'll be no interference."

"And I need that chemist and someone who'll know about the saddles. And I need them quick. I can stall these boys a little longer, but not for too much longer."

"Anyone you need," said the U.N. man. "Anyone at all. I'll have them here in hours. And in a day or two there'll be a pool of experts waiting for whenever you may need them— on a moment's notice."

"Sir," said Henry, unctuously, "that's most co-operative. Both Hiram and I appreciate it greatly. And now, since this is settled, I understand that there are reporters waiting. They'll be interested in your statement."

The U.N. man, it seemed, didn't have it in him to protest. He and Henry went tramping up the stairs.

Taine turned around and looked out across the desert.

"It's a big front yard," he said.

All The Traps Of Earth

The inventory list was long. On its many pages, in his small and precise script, he had listed furniture, paintings, china, silverware and all the rest of it—all the personal belongings that had been accumulated by the Barringtons through a long family history.

And now that he had reached the end of it, he noted down himself, the last item of them all:

One domestic robot, Richard Daniel, antiquated but in good repair.

He laid the pen aside and shuffled all the inventory sheets together and stacked them in good order, putting a paper weight upon them—the little exquisitely carved ivory paper weight that Aunt Hortense had picked up that last visit she had made to Peking.

And having done that, his job came to an end.

He shoved back the chair and rose from the desk and slowly walked across the living room, with all its clutter of possessions from the family's past. There, above the mantel, hung the sword that ancient Jonathon had worn in the War Between the States, and below it, on the mantelpiece itself, the cup the Commodore had won with his valiant yacht, and the jar of moon-dust that Tony had brought back from Man's fifth landing on the Moon, and the old chronometer that had come from the long-scrapped family spacecraft that had plied the asteroids.

And all around the room, almost cheek by jowl, hung the family portraits, with the old dead faces staring out into the world that they had helped to fashion.

And not a one of them from the last six hundred years,

thought Richard Daniel, staring at them one by one, that he had not known.

There, to the right of the fireplace, old Rufus Andrew Barrington, who had been a judge some two hundred years ago. And to the right of Rufus, Johnson Joseph Barrington, who had headed up that old lost dream of mankind, the Bureau of Paranormal Research. There, beyond the door that led out to the porch, was the scowling pirate face of Danley Barrington, who had first built the family fortune.

And many others—administrator, adventurer, corporation chief. All good men and true.

But this was at an end. The family had run out.

Slowly Richard Daniel began his last tour of the house— the family room with its cluttered living space, the den with its old mementos, the library and its rows of ancient books, the dining hall in which the crystal and the china shone and sparkled, the kitchen gleaming with the copper and the aluminum and the stainless steel, and the bedrooms on the second floor, each of them with its landmarks of former occupants. And finally, the bedroom where old Aunt Hortense had finally died, at long last closing out the line of Barringtons.

The empty dwelling held a not-quite-haunted quality, the aura of a house that waited for the old gay life to take up once again. But it was a false aura. All the portraits, all the china and the silverware, everything within the house would be sold at public auction to satisfy the debts. The rooms would be stripped and the possessions would be scattered and, as a last indignity, the house itself be sold.

Even he, himself, Richard Daniel thought, for he was chattel, too. He was there with all the rest of it, the final item on the inventory.

Except that what they planned to do with him was worse than simple sale. For he would be changed before he was offered up for sale. No one would be interested in putting up good money for him as he stood. And besides, there was the law—the law that said no robot could legally have continuation of a single life greater than a hundred years. And he had lived in a single life six times a hundred years.

He had gone to see a lawyer and the lawyer had been sympathetic, but had held forth no hope.

"Technically," he had told Richard Daniel in his short,

clipped lawyer voice, "you are at this moment much in violation of the statute. I completely fail to see how your family got away with it."

"They liked old things," said Richard Daniel. "And, besides, I was very seldom seen. I stayed mostly in the house. I seldom ventured out."

"Even so," the lawyer said, "there are such things as records. There must be a file on you..."

"The family," explained Richard Daniel, "in the past had many influential friends. You must understand, sir, that the Barringtons, before they fell upon hard times, were quite prominent in politics and in many other matters."

The lawyer grunted knowingly.

"What I can't quite understand," he said, "is why you should object so bitterly. You'll not be changed entirely. You'll still be Richard Daniel."

"I would lose my memories, would I not?"

"Yes, of course you would. But memories are not too important. And you'd collect another set."

"My memories are dear to me," Richard Daniel told him. "They are all I have. After some six hundred years, they are my sole worthwhile possession. Can you imagine, counselor, what it means to spend six centuries with one family?"

"Yes, I think I can," agreed the lawyer. "But now, with the family gone, isn't it just possible the memories may prove painful?"

"They're a comfort. A sustaining comfort. They make me feel important. They give me perspective and a niche."

"But don't you understand? You'll need no comfort, no importance once you're reoriented. You'll be brand new. All that you'll retain is a certain sense of basic identity—*that* they cannot take away from you even if they wished. There'll be nothing to regret. There'll be no leftover guilts, no frustrated aspirations, no old loyalties to hound you."

"I must be myself," Richard Daniel insisted stubbornly. "I've found a depth of living, a background against which my living has some meaning. I could not face being anybody else."

"You'd be far better off," the lawyer said wearily. "You'd have a better body. You'd have better mental tools. You'd be more intelligent."

Richard Daniel got up from the chair. He saw it was no use.

"You'll not inform on me?" he asked.

"Certainly not," the lawyer said. "So far as I'm concerned, you aren't even here."

"Thank you," said Richard Daniel. "How much do I owe you?"

"Not a thing," the lawyer told him. "I never make a charge to anyone who is older than five hundred."

He had meant it as a joke, but Richard Daniel did not smile. He had not felt like smiling.

At the door he turned around.

"Why?" he was going to ask. "Why this silly law?"

But he did not have to ask—it was not hard to see.

Human vanity, he knew. No human being lived much longer than a hundred years, so neither could a robot. But a robot, on the other hand, was too valuable simply to be junked at the end of a hundred years of service, so there was this new law providing for the periodic breakup of the continuity of each robot's life. And thus no human need undergo the psychological indignity of knowing that his faithful serving man might manage to outlive him by several thousand years.

It was illogical, but humans were illogical.

Illogical, but kind. Kind in many different ways.

Kind, sometimes, as the Barringtons had been kind, thought Richard Daniel. Six hundred years of kindness. It was a prideful thing to think about. They had even given him a double name. There weren't many robots nowadays who had double names. It was a special mark of affection and respect.

The lawyer having failed him, Richard Daniel had sought another source of help. Now, thinking back on it, standing in the room where Hortense Barrington had died, he was sorry that he'd done it. For he had embarrassed the religico almost unendurably. It had been easy for the lawyer to tell him what he had. Lawyers had the statutes to determine their behavior, and thus suffered little from agonies of personal decision.

But a man of the cloth is kind if he is worth his salt. And this one had been kind instinctively as well as professionally, and that had made it worse.

"Under certain circumstances," he had said somewhat awkwardly, "I could counsel patience and humility and prayer. Those are three great aids to anyone who is willing to put them to his use. But with you I am not certain."

"You mean," said Richard Daniel, "because I am a robot."

"Well, now . . ." said the minister, considerably befuddled at this direct approach.

"Because I have no soul?"

"Really," said the minister miserably, "you place me at a disadvantage. You are asking me a question that for centuries has puzzled and bedeviled the best minds in the church."

"But one," said Richard Daniel, "that each man in his secret heart must answer for himself."

"I wish I could," cried the distraught minister. "I truly wish I could."

"If it is any help," said Richard Daniel, "I can tell you that sometimes I suspect I have a soul."

And that, he could see, had been most upsetting for this kindly human. It had been, Richard Daniel told himself, unkind of him to say it. For it must have been confusing, since coming from himself it was not opinion only, but expert evidence.

So he had gone away from the minister's study and come back to the empty house to get on with his inventory work.

Now that the inventory was all finished and the papers stacked where Dancourt, the estate administrator, could find them when he showed up in the morning, Richard Daniel had done his final service for the Barringtons and now must begin doing for himself.

He left the bedroom and closed the door behind him and went quietly down the stairs and along the hallway to the little cubby, back of the kitchen, that was his very own.

And that, he reminded himself with a rush of pride, was of a piece with his double name and his six hundred years. There were not too many robots who had a room, however small, that they might call their own.

He went into the cubby and turned on the light and closed the door behind him.

And now, for the first time, he faced the grim reality of what he meant to do.

The cloak and hat and trousers hung upon a hook and the galoshes were placed precisely underneath them. His attachment kit lay in one corner of the cubby and the money was cached underneath the floor board he had loosened many years ago to provide a hiding place.

There was, he told himself, no point in waiting. Every minute counted. He had a long way to go and he must be at his destination before morning light.

He knelt on the floor and pried up the loosened board, shoved in a hand and brought out the stacks of bills, money hidden through the years against a day of need.

There were three stacks of bills, neatly held together by elastic bands—money given him throughout the years as tips and Christmas gifts, as birthday presents and rewards for little jobs well done.

He opened the storage compartment located in his chest and stowed away all the bills except for half a dozen which he stuffed into a pocket in one hip.

He took the trousers off the hook and it was an awkward business, for he'd never worn clothes before except when he'd tried on these very trousers several days before. It was a lucky thing, he thought, that long-dead Uncle Michael had been a portly man, for otherwise the trousers never would have fit.

He got them on and zippered and belted into place, then forced his feet into the overshoes. He was a little worried about the overshoes. No human went out in the summer wearing overshoes. But it was the best that he could do. None of the regular shoes he'd found in the house had been nearly large enough.

He hoped no one would notice, but there was no way out of it. Somehow or other, he had to cover up his feet, for if anyone should see them, they'd be a giveaway.

He put on the cloak and it was a little short. He put on the hat and it was slightly small, but he tugged it down until it gripped his metal skull and that was all to the good, he told himself; no wind could blow it off.

He picked up his attachments—a whole bag full of them that he'd almost never used. Maybe it was foolish to take them along, he thought, but they were a part of him and by rights they should go with him. There was so little that he really owned—just the money he had saved, a dollar at a time, and this kit of his.

With the bag of attachments clutched underneath his arm, he closed the cubby door and went down the hall.

At the big front door he hesitated and turned back toward the house, but it was, at the moment, a simple darkened cave, empty of all that it once had held. There was nothing here to stay for—nothing but the memories, and the memories he took with him.

He opened the door and stepped out on the stoop and closed the door behind him.

And now, he thought, with the door once shut behind him, he was on his own. He was running off. He was wearing clothes. He was out at night, without the permission of a master. And all of these were against the law.

Any officer could stop him, or any citizen. He had no rights at all. And he had no one who would speak for him, now that the Barringtons were gone.

He moved quietly down the walk and opened the gate and went slowly down the street, and it seemed to him the house was calling for him to come back. He wanted to go back, his mind said that he should go back, but his feet kept going on, steadily down the street.

He was alone, he thought, and the aloneness now was real, no longer the mere intellectual abstract he'd held in his mind for days. Here he was, a vacant hulk, that for the moment had no purpose and no beginning and no end, but was just an entity that stood naked in an endless reach of space and time and held no meaning in itself.

But he walked on and with each block that he covered he slowly fumbled back to the thing he was, the old robot in old clothes, the robot running from a home that was a home no longer.

He wrapped the cloak about him tightly and moved on down the street and now he hurried, for he had to hurry.

He met several people and they paid no attention to him. A few cars passed, but no one bothered him.

He came to a shopping center that was brightly lighted and he stopped and looked in terror at the wide expanse of open, brilliant space that lay ahead of him. He could detour around it, but it would use up time and he stood there, undecided, trying to screw up his courage to walk into the light.

Finally he made up his mind and strode briskly out, with his cloak wrapped tight about him and his hat pulled low.

Some of the shoppers turned and looked at him and he felt agitated spiders running up and down his back. The galoshes suddenly seemed three times as big as they really were and they made a plopping, squashy sound that was most embarrassing.

He hurried on, with the end of the shopping area not more than a block away.

A police whistle shrilled and Richard Daniel jumped in sudden fright and ran. He ran in slobbering, mindless fright, with his cloak streaming out behind him and his feet slapping on the pavement.

He plunged out of the lighted strip into the welcome darkness of a residential section and he kept on running.

Far off he heard the siren and he leaped a hedge and tore across the yard. He thundered down the driveway and across a garden in the back and a dog came roaring out and engaged in noisy chase.

Richard Daniel crashed into a picket fence and went through it to the accompaniment of snapping noises as the pickets and the rails gave way. The dog kept on behind him and other dogs joined in.

He crossed another yard and gained the street and pounded down it. He dodged into a driveway, crossed another yard, upset a birdbath and ran into a clothesline, snapping it in his headlong rush.

Behind him lights were snapping on in the windows of the houses and screen doors were banging as people hurried out to see what the ruckus was.

He ran on a few more blocks, crossed another yard and ducked into a lilac thicket, stood still and listened. Some dogs were still baying in the distance and there was some human shouting, but there was no siren.

He felt a thankfulness well up in him that there was no siren, and a sheepishness, as well. For he had been panicked by himself, he knew; he had run from shadows, he had fled from guilt.

But he'd thoroughly roused the neighborhood and even now, he knew, calls must be going out and in a little while the place would be swarming with police.

He'd raised a hornet's nest and he needed distance, so he crept out of the lilac thicket and went swiftly down the street, heading for the edge of town.

He finally left the city and found the highway. He loped along its deserted stretches. When a car or truck appeared, he pulled off on the shoulder and walked along sedately. Then when the car or truck had passed, he broke into his lope again.

He saw the spaceport lights miles before he got there. When he reached the port, he circled off the road and came up outside a fence and stood there in the darkness, looking.

A gang of robots was loading one great starship and there were other ships standing darkly in their pits.

He studied the gang that was loading the ship, lugging the cargo from a warehouse and across the area lighted by the floods. This was just the setup he had planned on, although he had not hoped to find it immediately—he had been afraid that he might have to hide out for a day or two before he found a situation that he could put to use. And it was a good thing that he had stumbled on this opportunity, for an intensive hunt would be on by now for a fleeing robot, dressed in human clothes.

He stripped off the cloak and pulled off the trousers and the overshoes; he threw away the hat. From his attachments bag he took out the cutters, screwed off a hand and threaded the cutters into place. He cut the fence and wiggled through it, then replaced the hand and put the cutters back into the kit.

Moving cautiously in the darkness, he walked up to the warehouse, keeping in its shadow.

It would be simple, he told himself. All he had to do was step out and grab a piece of cargo, clamber up the ramp and down into the hold. Once inside, it should not be difficult to find a hiding place and stay there until the ship had reached first planet-fall.

He moved to the corner of the warehouse and peered around it and there were the toiling robots, in what amounted to an endless chain, going up the ramp with the packages of cargo, coming down again to get another load.

But there were too many of them and the line too tight. And the area too well lighted. He'd never be able to break into that line.

And it would not help if he could, he realized despairingly—because he was different from those smooth and shining creatures. Compared to them, he was like a man in another century's dress; he and his six-hundred-year-old body would stand out like a circus freak.

He stepped back into the shadow of the warehouse and he knew that he had lost. All his best-laid plans, thought out in sober, daring detail, as he had labored at the inventory, had suddenly come to naught.

It all came, he told himself, from never going out, from having no real contact with the world, from not keeping up with robot-body fashions, from not knowing what the score was. He'd imagined how it would be and he'd got it all worked out and when it came down to it, it was nothing like he thought.

Now he'd have to go back to the hole he'd cut in the fence and retrieve the clothing he had thrown away and hunt up a hiding place until he could think of something else.

Beyond the corner of the warehouse he heard the harsh, dull grate of metal, and he took another look.

The robots had broken up their line and were streaming back toward the warehouse and a dozen or so of them were wheeling the ramp away from the cargo port. Three humans, all dressed in uniform, were walking toward the ship, heading for the ladder, and one of them carried a batch of papers in his hand.

The loading was all done and the ship about to lift and here he was, not more than a thousand feet away, and all that he could do was stand and see it go.

There had to be a way, he told himself, to get in that ship. If he could only do it his troubles would be over—or at least the first of his troubles would be over.

Suddenly it struck him like a hand across the face. There was a way to do it! He'd stood here, blubbering, when all the time there had been a way to do it!

In the ship, he'd thought. And that was not necessary. He didn't have to be *in* the ship.

He started running, out into the darkness, far out so he could circle round and come upon the ship from the other side, so that the ship would be between him and the flood lights on the warehouse. He hoped that there was time.

He thudded out across the port, running in an arc, and

came up to the ship and there was no sign as yet that it was about to leave.

Frantically he dug into his attachments bag and found the things he needed—the last things in that bag he'd ever thought he'd need. He found the suction discs and put them on, one for each knee, one for each elbow, one for each sole and wrist.

He strapped the kit about his waist and clambered up one of the mighty fins, using the discs to pull himself awkwardly along. It was not easy. He had never used the discs and there was a trick to using them, the trick of getting one clamped down and then working loose another so that he could climb.

But he had to do it. He had no choice but to do it.

He climbed the fin and there was the vast steel body of the craft rising far above him, like a metal wall climbing to the sky, broken by the narrow line of a row of anchor posts that ran lengthwise of the hull—and all that huge extent of metal painted by the faint, illusive shine of starlight that glittered in his eyes.

Foot by foot he worked his way up the metal wall. Like a humping caterpillar, he squirmed his way and with each foot he gained he was a bit more thankful.

Then he heard the faint beginning of a rumble and with the rumble came terror. His suction cups, he knew, might not long survive the booming vibration of the wakening rockets, certainly would not hold for a moment when the ship began to climb.

Six feet above him lay his only hope—the final anchor post in the long row of anchor posts.

Savagely he drove himself up the barrel of the shuddering craft, hugging the steely surface like a desperate fly.

The rumble of the tubes built up to blot out all the world and he climbed in a haze of almost prayerful, brittle hope. He reached that anchor post or he was as good as dead. Should he slip and drop into that pit of flaming gases beneath the rocket mouths he was done for.

Once a cup came loose and he almost fell, but the others held and he caught himself.

With a desperate, almost careless lunge, he hurled himself up the wall of metal and caught the rung in his fingertips and held on with a concentration of effort that wiped out all else.

The rumble was a screaming fury now that lanced through

the brain and body. Then the screaming ended and became a throaty roar of power and the vibration left the ship entirely. From one corner of his eye he saw the lights of the spaceport swinging over gently on their side.

Carefully, slowly, he pulled himself along the steel until he had a better grip upon the rung, but even with the better grip he had the feeling that some great hand had him in its fist and was swinging him in anger in a hundred-mile-long arc.

Then the tubes left off their howling and there was a terrible silence and the stars were there, up above him and to either side of him, and they were steely stars with no twinkle in them. Down below, he knew, a lonely Earth was swinging, but he could not see it.

He pulled himself up against the rung and thrust a leg beneath it and sat up on the hull.

There were more stars than he'd ever seen before, more than he'd dreamed there could be. They were still and cold, like hard points of light against a velvet curtain; there was no glitter and no twinkle in them and it was as if a million eyes were staring down at him. The Sun was underneath the ship and over to one side; just at the edge of the left-hand curvature was the glare of it against the silent metal, a sliver of reflected light outlining one edge of the ship. The Earth was far astern, a ghostly blue-green ball hanging in the void, ringed by the fleecy halo of its atmosphere.

It was as if he were detached, a lonely, floating brain that looked out upon a thing it could not understand nor could ever try to understand; as if he might even be afraid of understanding it—a thing of mystery and delight so long as he retained an ignorance of it, but something fearsome and altogether overpowering once the ignorance had gone.

Richard Daniel sat there, flat upon his bottom, on the metal hull of the speeding ship and he felt the mystery and delight and the loneliness and the cold and the great uncaring and his mind retreated into a small and huddled, compact defensive ball.

He looked. That was all there was to do. It was all right now, he thought. But how long would he have to look at it? How long would he have to camp out here in the open—the most deadly kind of open?

He realized for the first time that he had no idea where the ship was going or how long it might take to get there. He knew it was a starship, which meant that it was bound beyond the solar system, and that meant that at some point in its flight it would enter hyperspace. He wondered, at first academically, and then with a twinge of fear, what hyperspace might do to one sitting naked to it. But there was little need, he thought philosophically, to fret about it now, for in due time he'd know, and there was not a thing that he could do about it—not a single thing.

He took the suction cups off his body and stowed them in his kit and then with one hand he tied the kit to one of the metal rungs and dug around in it until he found a short length of steel cable with a ring on one end and a snap on the other. He passed the ring end underneath a rung and threaded the snap end through it and snapped the snap onto a metal loop underneath his armpit. Now he was secured; he need not fear carelessly letting go and floating off the ship.

So here he was, he thought, neat as anything, going places fast, even if he had no idea where he might be headed, and now the only thing he needed was patience. He thought back, without much point, to what the religico had said in the study back on Earth. Patience and humility and prayer, he'd said, apparently not realizing at the moment that a robot has a world of patience.

It would take a lot of time, Richard Daniel knew, to get where he was going. But he had a lot of time, a lot more than any human, and he could afford to waste it. There were no urgencies, he thought—no need of food or air or water, no need of sleep or rest. There was nothing that could touch him.

Although, come to think of it, there might be.

There was the cold, for one. The space-hull was still fairly warm, with one side of it picking up the heat of the Sun and radiating it around the metal skin, where it was lost on the other side, but there would be a time when the Sun would dwindle until it had no heat and then he'd be subjected to the utter cold of space.

And what would the cold do to him. Might it make his body brittle? Might it interfere with the functioning of his brain? Might it do other things he could not even guess?

He felt the fears creep in again and tried to shrug them off and they drew off, but they still were there, lurking at the fringes of his mind.

The cold, and the loneliness, he thought—but he was one

who could cope with loneliness. And if he couldn't, if he got too lonely, if he could no longer stand it, he could always beat a devil's tattoo on the hull and after a time of that someone would come out to investigate and they would haul him in.

But that was the last move of desperation, he told himself. For if they came out and found him, then he would be caught. Should he be forced to that extremity, he'd have lost everything—there would then have been no point in leaving Earth at all.

So he settled down, living out his time, keeping the creeping fears at bay just beyond the outposts of his mind, and looking at the universe all spread out before him.

The motors started up again with a pale-blue flickering in the rockets at the stern and although there was no sense of acceleration he knew that the ship, now well off the Earth, had settled down to the long, hard drive to reach the speed of light.

Once they reached that speed they would enter hyperspace. He tried not to think of it, tried to tell himself there was not a thing to fear—but it hung there just ahead of him, the great unknowable.

The Sun shrank until it was only one of many stars and there came a time when he could no longer pick it out. And the cold clamped down but it didn't seem to bother him, although he could sense the coldness.

Maybe, he said in answer to his fear, that would be the way it would be with hyperspace as well. But he said it unconvincingly. The ship drove on and on with the weird blueness in the tubes.

Then there was the instant when his mind went splattering across the universe.

He was aware of the ship, but only aware of it in relation to an awareness of much else, and it was no anchor point, no rallying position. He was spread and scattered; he was opened out and rolled out until he was very thin. He was a dozen places, perhaps a hundred places, all at once, and it was confusing, and his immediate reaction was to fight back somehow against whatever might have happened to him—to fight back and pull himself together. The fighting did no good at all, but made it even worse, for in certain instances it seemed to drive parts of him farther from other parts of him and the confusion was made greater.

So he quit his fighting and his struggling and just lay there, scattered, and let the panic ebb away and told himself he didn't care, and wondered if he did.

Slow reason returned a dribble at a time and he could think again and he wondered rather bleakly if this could be hyperspace and was pretty sure it was. And if it were, he knew, he'd have a long time to live like this, a long time in which to become accustomed to it and to orient himself, a long time to find himself and pull himself together, a long time to understand this situation if it were, in fact, understandable.

So he lay, not caring greatly, with no fear or wonder, just resting and letting a fact seep into him here and there from many different points.

He knew that, somehow, his body—that part of him which housed the rest of him—was still chained securely to the ship, and that knowledge, in itself, he knew, was the first small step towards reorienting himself. He had to reorient, he knew. He had to come to some sort of terms, if not to understanding, with this situation.

He had opened up and he had scattered out—that essential part of him, the feeling and the knowing and the thinking part of him, and he lay thin across a universe that loomed immense in unreality.

Was this, he wondered, the way the universe should be, or was it the unchained universe, the wild universe beyond the limiting disciplines of measured space and time.

He started slowly reaching out, cautious as he had been in his crawling on the surface of the ship, reaching out toward the distant parts of him, a little at a time. He did not know how he did it, he was conscious of no particular technique, but whatever he was doing, it seemed to work, for he pulled himself together, bit by knowing bit, until he had gathered up all the scattered fragments of him into several different piles.

Then he quit and lay there, wherever there might be, and tried to sneak up on those piles of understanding that he took to be himself.

It took a while to get the hang of it, but once he did, some of the incomprehensibility went away, although the strangeness stayed. He tried to put it into thought and it was hard to do. The closest he could come was that he had been unchained as well as the universe—that whatever bondage had been imposed upon him by that chained and normal world had now become dissolved and he no longer was fenced in by either time or space.

He could see—and know and sense—across vast distances, if distance were the proper term, and he could understand certain facts that he had not even thought about before, could understand instinctively, but without the language or the skill to coalesce the facts into independent data.

Once again the universe was spread far out before him and it was a different and in some ways a better universe, a more diagrammatic universe, and in time, he knew, if there were such a thing as time, he'd gain some completer understanding and acceptance of it.

He probed and sensed and learned and there was no such thing as time, but a great foreverness.

He thought with pity of those others locked inside the ship, safe behind its insulating walls, never knowing all the glories of the innards of a star or the vast panoramic sweep of vision and of knowing far above the flat galactic plane.

Yet he really did not know what he saw or probed; he merely sensed and felt it and became a part of it, and it became a part of him—he seemed unable to reduce it to a formal outline of fact or of dimension or of content. It still remained a knowledge and a power so overwhelming that it was nebulous. There was no fear and no wonder, for in this place, it seemed, there was neither fear nor wonder. And he finally knew that it was a place apart, a world in which the normal space-time knowledge and emotion had no place at all and a normal space-time being could have no tools or measuring stick by which he might reduce it to a frame of reference.

There was no time, no space, no fear, no wonder—and no actual knowledge, either.

Then time came once again and suddenly his mind was stuffed back into its cage within his metal skull and he was again one with his body, trapped and chained and small and cold and naked.

He saw that the stars were different and that he was far from home and just a little way ahead was a star that blazed like a molten furnace hanging in the black.

He sat bereft, a small thing once again, and the universe reduced to package size.

Practically, he checked the cable that held him to the ship and it was intact. His attachments kit was still tied to its rung. Everything was exactly as it had been before.

He tried to recall the glories he had seen, tried to grasp again the fringe of knowledge which he had been so close to, but both the glory and the knowledge, if there had ever been a knowledge, had faded into nothingness.

He felt like weeping, but he could not weep, and he was too old to lie down upon the ship and kick his heels in tantrum.

So he sat there, looking at the sun that they were approaching and finally there was a planet that he knew must be their destination, and he found room to wonder what planet it might be and how far from Earth it was.

He heated up a little as the ship skipped through atmosphere as an aid to braking speed and he had some rather awful moments as it spiraled into thick and soupy gases that certainly were a far cry from the atmosphere of Earth. He hung most desperately to the rungs as the craft came mushing down onto a landing field, with the hot gases of the rockets curling up about him. But he made it safely and swiftly clambered down and darted off into the smoglike atmosphere before anyone could see him.

Safely off, he turned and looked back at the ship and despite its outlines being hidden by the drifting clouds of swirling gases, he could see it clearly, not as an actual structure, but as a diagram. He looked at it wonderingly and there was something wrong with the diagram, something vaguely wrong, some part of it that was out of whack and not the way it should be.

He heard the clanking of cargo haulers coming out upon the field and he wasted no more time, diagram or not.

He drifted back, deeper in the mists, and began to circle, keeping a good distance from the ship. Finally he came to the spaceport's edge and the beginning of the town.

He found a street and walked down it leisurely and there was a wrongness in the town.

He met a few hurrying robots who were in too much of a

rush to pass the time of day. But he met no humans.

And that, he knew quite suddenly, was the wrongness of the place. It was not a human town.

There were no distinctly human buildings—no stores or residences, no churches and no restaurants. There were gaunt shelter barracks and sheds for the storing of equipment and machines, great sprawling warehouses and vast industrial plants. But that was all there was. It was a bare and dismal place compared to the streets that he had known on Earth.

It was a robot town, he knew. And a robot planet. A world that was barred to humans, a place where humans could not live, but so rich in some natural resource that it cried for exploitation. And the answer to that exploitation was to let the robots do it.

Luck, he told himself. His good luck still was holding. He had literally been dumped into a place where he could live without human interference. Here, on this planet, he would be with his own.

If that was what he wanted. And he wondered if it was. He wondered just exactly what it was he wanted, for he'd had no time to think of what he wanted. He had been too intent on fleeing Earth to think too much about it. He had known all along what he was running from, but had not considered what he might be running to.

He walked a little further and the town came to an end. The street became a path and went wandering on into the wind-blown fogginess.

So he turned around and went back up the street.

There had been one barracks, he remembered, that had a TRANSIENTS sign hung out, and he made his way to it.

Inside, an ancient robot sat behind the desk. His body was old-fashioned and somehow familiar. And it was familiar, Richard Daniel knew, because it was as old and battered and as out-of-date as his.

He looked at the body, just a bit aghast, and saw that while it resembled his, there were little differences. The same ancient model, certainly, but a different series. Possibly a little newer, by twenty years or so, than his.

"Good evening, stranger," said the ancient robot. "You came in on the ship?"

Richard Daniel nodded.

"You'll be staying till the next one?"

"I may be settling down," said Richard Daniel. "I may want to stay here."

The ancient robot took a key from off a hook and laid it on the desk.

"You representing someone?"

"No," said Richard Daniel.

"I thought maybe that you were. We get a lot of representatives. Humans can't come here, or don't want to come, so they send robots out here to represent them."

"You have a lot of visitors?"

"Some. Mostly the representatives I was telling you about. But there are some that are on the lam. I'd take it, mister, you are on the lam."

Richard Daniel didn't answer.

"It's all right," the ancient one assured him. "We don't mind at all, just so you behave yourself. Some of our most prominent citizens, they came here on the lam."

"That is fine," said Richard Daniel. "And how about yourself? You must be on the lam as well."

"You mean this body. Well, that's a little different. This here is punishment."

"Punishment?"

"Well, you see, I was the foreman of the cargo warehouse and I got to goofing off. So they hauled me up and had a trial and they found me guilty. Then they stuck me into this old body and I have to stay in it, at this lousy job, until they get another criminal that needs punishment. They can't punish no more than one criminal at a time because this is the only body that they have. Funny thing about this body. One of the boys went back to Earth on a business trip and found this old heap of metal in a junkyard and brought it home with him— for a joke, I guess. Like a human might buy a skeleton for a joke, you know."

He took a long, sly look at Richard Daniel. "It looks to me, stranger, as if your body..."

But Richard Daniel didn't let him finish.

"I take it," Richard Daniel said, "you haven't many criminals."

"No," said the ancient robot sadly, "we're generally a pretty solid lot."

Richard Daniel reached out to pick up the key, but the ancient robot put out his hand and covered it.

"Since you are on the lam," he said, "it'll be payment in advance."

"I'll pay you for a week," said Richard Daniel, handing him some money.

The robot gave him back his change.

"One thing I forgot to tell you. You'll have to get plasticated."

"Plasticated?"

"That's right. Get plastic squirted over you. To protect you from the atmosphere. It plays hell with metal. There's a place next door will do it."

"Thanks. I'll get it done immediately."

"It wears off," warned the ancient one. "You have to get a new job every week or so."

Richard Daniel took the key and went down the corridor until he found his numbered cubicle. He unlocked the door and stepped inside. The room was small, but clean. It had a desk and chair and that was all it had.

He stowed his attachment bag in one corner and sat down in the chair and tried to feel at home. But he couldn't feel at home, and that was a funny thing—he'd just rented himself a home.

He sat there, thinking back, and tried to whip up some sense of triumph at having done so well in covering his tracks. He couldn't.

Maybe this wasn't the place for him, he thought. Maybe he'd be happier on some other planet. Perhaps he should go back to the ship and get on it once again and have a look at the next planet coming up.

If he hurried, he might make it. But he'd have to hurry, for the ship wouldn't stay longer than it took to unload the consignment for this place and take on new cargo.

He got up from the chair, still only half decided.

And suddenly he remembered how, standing in the swirling mistiness, he had seen the ship as a diagram rather than a ship, and as he thought about it, something clicked inside his brain and he leaped toward the door.

For now he knew what had been wrong with the spaceship's diagram—an injector valve was somehow out of kilter; he had to get back there before the ship took off again.

He went through the door and down the corridor. He caught sight of the ancient robot's startled face as he ran across the lobby and out into the street. Pounding steadily toward the spaceport, he tried to get the diagram into his mind again, but it would not come complete—it came in bits and pieces, but not all of it.

And even as he fought for the entire diagram, he heard the beginning take-off rumble.

"Wait!" he yelled. "Wait for me! You can't..."

There was a flash that turned the world pure white and a mighty invisible wave came swishing out of nowhere and sent him reeling down the street, falling as he reeled. He was skidding on the cobblestones and sparks were flying as his metal scraped along the stone. The whiteness reached a brilliance that almost blinded him and then it faded swiftly and the world was dark.

He brought up against a wall of some sort, clanging as he hit, and he lay there, blind from the brilliance of the flash, while his mind went scurrying down the trail of the diagram.

The diagram, he thought—why should he have seen a diagram of the ship he'd ridden through space, a diagram that had shown an injector out of whack? And how could he, of all robots, recognize an injector, let alone know there was something wrong with it. It had been a joke back home, among the Barringtons, that he, a mechanical thing himself, should have no aptitude at all for mechanical contraptions. And he could have saved those people and the ship—he could have saved them all if he'd immediately recognized the significance of the diagram. But he'd been too slow and stupid and now they all were dead.

The darkness had receded from his eyes and he could see again and he got slowly to his feet, feeling himself all over to see how badly he was hurt. Except for a dent or two, he seemed to be all right.

There were robots running in the street, heading for the spaceport, where a dozen fires were burning and where sheds and other structures had been flattened by the blast.

Someone tugged at his elbow and he turned around. It was the ancient robot.

"You're the lucky one," the ancient robot said. "You got off it just in time."

Richard Daniel nodded dumbly and had a terrible thought: What if they should think he did it? He had gotten off the ship; he had admitted that he was on the lam; he had rushed out suddenly, just a few seconds before the ship exploded. It would be easy to put it all together—that he had sabotaged the ship, then at the last instant had rushed out, remorseful, to undo what he had done. On the face of it, it was damning evidence.

But it was all right as yet, Richard Daniel told himself. For the ancient robot was the only one that knew—he was the only one he'd talked to, the only one who even knew that he was in town.

There was a way, Richard Daniel thought—there was an easy way. He pushed the thought away, but it came back. You are on your own, it said. You are already beyond the law. In rejecting human law, you made yourself an outlaw. You have become fair prey. There is just one law for you—self preservation.

But there are robot laws, Richard Daniel argued. There are laws and courts in this community. There is a place for justice.

Community law, said the leech clinging in his brain, provincial law, little more than tribal law—and the stranger's always wrong.

Richard Daniel felt the coldness of the fear closing down upon him and he knew, without half thinking, that the leech was right.

He turned around and started down the street, heading for the transients barracks. Something unseen in the street caught his foot and he stumbled and went down. He scrabbled to his knees, hunting in the darkness on the cobblestones for the thing that tripped him. It was a heavy bar of steel, some part of the wreckage that had been hurled this far. He gripped it by one end and arose.

"Sorry," said the ancient robot. "You have to watch your step."

And there was a faint implication in his words, a hint of something more than the words had said, a hint of secret gloating in a secret knowledge.

You have broken other laws, said the leech in Richard Daniel's brain. What of breaking just one more? Why, if necessary, not break a hundred more. It is all or nothing.

Having come this far, you can't afford to fail. You can allow no one to stand in your way now.

The ancient robot half turned away and Richard Daniel lifted up the bar of steel, and suddenly the ancient robot no longer was a robot, but a diagram. There, with all the details of a blueprint, were all the working parts, all the mechanism of the robot that walked in the street before him. And if one detached that single bit of wire, if one burned out that coil, if—

Even as he thought it, the diagram went away and there was the robot, a stumbling, falling robot that clanged on the cobblestones.

Richard Daniel swung around in terror, looking up the street, but there was no one near.

He turned back to the fallen robot and quietly knelt beside him. He gently put the bar of steel down into the street. And he felt a thankfulness—for, almost miraculously, he had not killed.

The robot on the cobblestones was motionless. When Richard Daniel lifted him, he dangled. And yet he was all right. All anyone had to do to bring him back to life was to repair whatever damage had been done his body. And that served the purpose, Richard Daniel told himself, as well as killing would have done.

He stood with the robot in his arms, looking for a place to hide him. He spied an alley between two buildings and darted into it. One of the buildings, he saw, was set upon stone blocks sunk into the ground, leaving a clearance of a foot or so. He knelt and shoved the robot underneath the building. Then he stood up and brushed the dirt and dust from his body.

Back at the barracks and in his cubicle, he found a rag and cleaned up the dirt that he had missed.

He'd seen the ship as a diagram and, not knowing what it meant, hadn't done a thing. Just now he'd seen the ancient robot as a diagram and had most decisively and neatly used that diagram to save himself from murder—from the murder that he was fully ready to commit.

But how had he done it? And the answer seemed to be that he really had done nothing. He'd simply thought that one should detach a single wire, burn out a single coil—he'd thought it and it was done.

Perhaps he'd seen no diagram at all. Perhaps the diagram was no more than some sort of psychic rationalization to mask whatever he had seen or sensed. Seeing the ship and robot with the surfaces stripped away from them and their purpose and their function revealed fully to his view, he had sought some explanation of his strange ability, and his subconscious mind had devised an explanation, an analogy that, for the moment, had served to satisfy him.

Like when he'd been in hyperspace, he thought. He'd seen a lot of things out there he had not understood. And that was it, of course, he thought excitedly. Something had happened to him out in hyperspace. Perhaps there'd been something that had stretched his mind. Perhaps he'd picked up some sort of new dimension-seeing, some new twist to his mind.

He remembered how, back on the ship again, with his mind wiped clean of all the glory and the knowledge, he had felt like weeping. But now he knew that it had been much too soon for weeping. For although the glory and the knowledge (if there'd been a knowledge) had been lost to him, he had not lost everything. He'd gained a new perceptive device and the ability to use it somewhat fumblingly—and it didn't really matter that he still was at a loss as to what he did to use it. The basic fact that he possessed it and could use it was enough to start with.

Somewhere out in front there was someone calling—someone, he now realized, who had been calling for some little time. . . .

"Hubert, where are you? Hubert, are you around? Hubert . . ."

Hubert?

Could Hubert be the ancient robot? Could they have missed him already?

Richard Daniel jumped to his feet for an undecided moment, listening to the calling voice. And then sat down again. Let them call, he told himself. Let them go out and hunt. He was safe in this cubicle. He had rented it and for the moment it was home and there was no one who would dare break in upon him.

But it wasn't home. No matter how hard he tried to tell himself it was, it wasn't. There wasn't any home.

Earth was home, he thought. And not all of Earth, but just a certain street and that one part of it was barred to him forever. It had been barred to him by the dying of a sweet old lady who had outlived her time; it had been barred to him by his running from it.

He did not belong on this planet, he admitted to himself, nor on any other planet. He belonged on Earth, with the Barringtons, and it was impossible for him to be there.

Perhaps, he thought, he should have stayed and let them reorient him. He remembered what the lawyer had said about memories that could become a burden and a torment. After all, it might have been wiser to have started over once again.

For what kind of future did he have, with his old out-dated body, his old out-dated brain? The kind of body that they put a robot into on this planet by way of punishment. And the kind of brain—but the brain was different, for he had something now that made up for any lack of more modern mental tools.

He sat and listened, and he heard the house—calling all across the light years of space for him to come back to it again. And he saw the faded living room with all its vanished glory that made a record of the years. He remembered, with a twinge of hurt, the little room back of the kitchen that had been his very own.

He arose and paced up and down the cubicle—three steps and turn, and then three more steps and turn for another three.

The sights and sounds and smells of home grew close and wrapped themselves about him and he wondered wildly if he might not have the power, a power accorded him by the universe of hyperspace, to will himself to that familiar street again.

He shuddered at the thought of it, afraid of another power, afraid that it might happen. Afraid of himself, perhaps, of the snarled and tangled being he was—no longer the faithful, shining servant, but a sort of mad thing that rode outside a spaceship, that was ready to kill another being, that could face up to the appalling sweep of hyperspace, yet cowered before the impact of a memory.

What he needed was a walk, he thought. Look over the town and maybe go out into the country. Besides, he remembered, trying to become practical, he'd need to get that plastication job he had been warned to get.

He went out into the corridor and strode briskly down it

and was crossing the lobby when someone spoke to him.

"Hubert," said the voice, "just where have you been? I've been waiting hours for you."

Richard Daniel spun around and a robot sat behind the desk. There was another robot leaning in a corner and there was a naked robot brain lying on the desk.

"You are Hubert, aren't you?" asked the one behind the desk.

Richard Daniel opened up his mouth to speak, but the words refused to come.

"I thought so," said the robot. "You may not recognize me, but my name is Andy. The regular man was busy, so the judge sent me. He thought it was only fair we make the switch as quickly as possible. He said you'd served a longer term than you really should. Figures you'd be glad to know they'd convicted someone else."

Richard Daniel stared in horror at the naked brain lying on the desk.

The robot gestured at the metal body propped into the corner.

"Better than when we took you out of it," he said with a throaty chuckle. "Fixed it up and polished it and got out all the dents. Even modernized it somē. Brought it strictly up to date. You'll have a better body than you had when they stuck you into that monstrosity."

"I don't know what to say," said Richard Daniel, stammering. "You see, I'm not ..."

"Oh, that's all right," said the other happily. "No need for gratitude. Your sentence worked out longer than the judge expected. This just makes up for it."

"I thank you, then," said Richard Daniel. "I thank you very much."

And was astounded at himself, astonished at the ease with which he said it, confounded at his sly duplicity.

But if they forced it on him, why should he refuse? There was nothing that he needed more than a modern body!

It was still working out, he told himself. He was still riding luck. For this was the last thing that he needed to cover up his tracks.

"All newly plasticated and everything," said Andy. "Hans did an extra special job."

"Well, then," said Richard Daniel, "let's get on with it."

The other robot grinned. "I don't blame you for being anxious to get out of there. It must be pretty terrible to live in a pile of junk like that."

He came around from behind the desk and advanced on Richard Daniel.

"Over in the corner," he said, "and kind of prop yourself. I don't want you tipping over when I disconnect you. One good fall and that body'd come apart."

"All right," said Richard Daniel. He went into the corner and leaned back against it and planted his feet solid so that he was propped.

He had a rather awful moment when Andy disconnected the optic nerve and he lost his eyes and there was considerable queasiness in having his skull lifted off his shoulders and he was in sheer funk as the final disconnections were being swiftly made.

Then he was a blob of greyness without a body or a head or eyes or anything at all. He was no more than a bundle of thoughts all wrapped around themselves like a pail of worms and this pail of worms was suspended in pure nothingness.

Fear came to him, a taunting, terrible fear. What if this were just a sort of ghastly gag? What if they'd found out who he really was and what he'd done to Hubert? What if they took his brain and tucked it away somewhere for a year or two—or for a hundred years? It might be, he told himself, nothing more than their simple way of justice.

He hung onto himself and tried to fight the fear away, but the fear ebbed back and forth like a restless tide.

Time stretched out and out—far too long a time, far more time than one would need to switch a brain from one body to another. Although, he told himself, that might not be true at all. For in his present state he had no way in which to measure time. He had no external reference points by which to determine time.

Then suddenly he had eyes.

And he knew everything was all right.

One by one his senses were restored to him and he was back inside a body and he felt awkward in the body, for he was unaccustomed to it.

The first thing that he saw was his old and battered body propped into its corner and he felt a sharp regret at the sight of it and it seemed to him that he had played a dirty trick upon it. It deserved, he told himself, a better fate than this—a better fate than being left behind to serve as a shabby jailhouse on this outlandish planet. It had served him well for six hundred years and he should not be deserting it. But he was deserting it. He was, he told himself in contempt, becoming very expert at deserting his old friends. First the house back home and now his faithful body.

Then he remembered something else—all that money in the body!

"What's the matter, Hubert?" Andy asked.

He couldn't leave it there, Richard Daniel told himself, for he needed it. And besides, if he left it there, someone would surely find it later and it would be a give-away. He couldn't leave it there and it might not be safe to forthrightly claim it. If he did, this other robot, this Andy, would think he'd been stealing on the job or running some side racket. He might try to bribe the other, but one could never tell how a move like that might go. Andy might be full of righteousness and then there'd be hell to pay. And, besides, he didn't want to part with any of the money.

All at once he had it—he knew just what to do. And even as he thought it, he made Andy into a diagram.

That connection there, thought Richard Daniel, reaching out his arm to catch the falling diagram that turned into a robot. He eased it to the floor and sprang across the room to the side of his old body. In seconds he had the chest safe open and the money safely out of it and locked inside his present body.

Then he made the robot on the floor become a diagram again and got the connection back the way that it should be.

Andy rose shakily off the floor. He looked at Richard Daniel in some consternation.

"What happened to me?" he asked in a frightened voice.

Richard Daniel sadly shook his head. "I don't know. You just keeled over. I started for the door to yell for help, then I heard you stirring and you were all right."

Andy was plainly puzzled. "Nothing like this ever happened to me before," he said.

"If I were you," counseled Richard Daniel, "I'd have myself checked over. You must have a faulty relay or a loose connection."

"I guess I will," the other one agreed. "It's downright dangerous."

He walked slowly to the desk and picked up the other

brain, started with it toward the battered body leaning in the corner.

Then he stopped and said: "Look, I forgot. I was supposed to tell you. You better get up to the warehouse. Another ship is on its way. It will be coming in any minute now."

"Another one so soon?"

"You know how it goes," Andy said, disgusted. "They don't even try to keep a schedule here. We won't see one for months and then there'll be two or three at once."

"Well, thanks," said Richard Daniel, going out the door.

He went swinging down the street with a new-born confidence. And he had a feeling that there was nothing that could lick him, nothing that could stop him.

For he was a lucky robot!

Could all that luck, he wondered, have been gotten out in hyperspace, as his diagram ability, or whatever one might call it, had come from hyperspace? Somehow hyperspace had taken him and twisted him and changed him, had molded him anew, had made him into a different robot than he had been before.

Although, so far as luck was concerned, he had been lucky all his entire life. He'd had good luck with his human family and had gained a lot of favors and a high position and had been allowed to live for six hundred years. And that was a thing that never should have happened. No matter how powerful or influential the Barringtons had been, that six hundred years must be due in part to nothing but sheer luck.

In any case, the luck and the diagram ability gave him a solid edge over all the other robots he might meet. Could it, he asked himself, give him an edge on Man as well? *No*—that was a thought he should not think, for it was blasphemous. There never was a robot that would be the equal of a man.

But the thought kept on intruding and he felt not nearly so contrite over this leaning toward bad taste, or poor judgment, whichever it might be, as it seemed to him he should feel.

As he neared the spaceport, he began meeting other robots and some of them saluted him and called him by the name of Hubert and others stopped and shook him by the hand and told him they were glad that he was out of pokey.

This friendliness shook his confidence. He began to

wonder if his luck would hold, for some of the robots, he was certain, thought it rather odd that he did not speak to them by name, and there had been a couple of remarks that he had some trouble fielding. He had a feeling that when he reached the warehouse he might be sunk without a trace, for he would know none of the robots there and he had not the least idea what his duties might include. And, come to think of it, he didn't even know where the warehouse was.

He felt the panic building in him and took a quick involuntary look around, seeking some method of escape. For it became quite apparent to him that he must never reach the warehouse.

He was trapped, he knew, and he couldn't keep on floating, trusting to his luck. In the next few minutes he'd have to figure something.

He started to swing over into a side street, not knowing what he meant to do, but knowing he must do something, when he heard the mutter far above him and glanced up quickly to see the crimson glow of belching rocket tubes shimmering through the clouds.

He swung around again and sprinted desperately for the spaceport and reached it as the ship came chugging down to a steady landing. It was, he saw, an old ship. It had no burnish to it and it was blunt and squat and wore a hangdog look.

A tramp, he told himself, that knocked about from port to port, picking up whatever cargo it could, with perhaps now and then a paying passenger headed for some backwater planet where there was no scheduled service.

He waited as the cargo port came open and the ramp came down and then marched purposefully out onto the field, ahead of the straggling cargo crew, trudging toward the ship. He had to act, he knew, as if he had a perfect right to walk into the ship, as if he knew exactly what he might be doing. If there were a challenge he would pretend he didn't hear it and simply keep on going.

He walked swiftly up the ramp, holding back from running, and plunged through the accordion curtain that served as an atmosphere control. His feet rang across the metal plating of the cargo hold until he reached the catwalk and plunged down it to another cargo level.

At the bottom of the catwalk he stopped and stood tense, listening. Above him he heard the clang of a metal door and the sound of footsteps coming down the walk to the level just above him. That would be the purser or the first mate, he told himself, or perhaps the captain, coming down to arrange for the discharge of the cargo.

Quietly he moved away and found a corner where he could crouch and hide.

Above his head he heard the cargo gang at work, talking back and forth, then the screech of crating and the thump of bales and boxes being hauled out to the ramp.

Hours passed, or they seemed like hours, as he huddled there. He heard the cargo gang bringing something down from one of the upper levels and he made a sort of prayer that they'd not come down to this lower level—and he hoped no one would remember seeing him come in ahead of them, or if they did remember, that they would assume that he'd gone out again.

Finally it was over, with the footsteps gone. Then came the pounding of the ramp as it shipped itself and the banging of the port.

He waited for long minutes, waiting for the roar that, when it came, set his head to ringing, waiting for the monstrous vibration that shook and lifted up the ship and flung it off the planet.

Then quiet came and he knew the ship was out of atmosphere and once more on its way.

And knew he had it made.

For now he was no more than a simple stowaway. He was no longer Richard Daniel, runaway from Earth. He'd dodged all the traps of Man, he'd covered all his tracks, and he was on his way.

But far down underneath he had a jumpy feeling, for it all had gone too smoothly, more smoothly than it should.

He tried to analyze himself, tried to pull himself in focus, tried to assess himself for what he had become.

He had abilities that Man had never won or developed or achieved, whichever it might be. He was a certain step ahead of not only other robots, but of Man as well. He had a thing, or the beginning of a thing, that Man had sought and studied and had tried to grasp for centuries and had failed.

A solemn and a deadly thought: was it possible that it was the robots, after all, for whom this great heritage had been meant? Would it be the robots who would achieve the paranormal powers that Man had sought so long, while Man, perforce, must remain content with the materialistic and the merely scientific? Was he, Richard Daniel, perhaps, only the first of many? Or was it all explained by no more than the fact that he alone had been exposed to hyperspace? Could this ability of his belong to anyone who would subject himself to the full, uninsulated mysteries of that mad universe unconstrained by time? Could Man have this, and more, if he too should expose himself to the utter randomness of unreality?

He huddled in his corner, with the thought and speculation stirring in his mind and he sought the answers, but there was no solid answer.

His mind went reaching out, almost on its own, and there was a diagram inside his brain, a portion of a blueprint, and bit by bit was added to it until it all was there, until the entire ship on which he rode was there, laid out for him to see.

He took his time and went over the diagram resting in his brain and he found little things—a fitting that was working loose and he tightened it, a printed circuit that was breaking down and getting mushy and he strengthened it and sharpened it and made it almost new, a pump that was leaking just a bit and he stopped its leaking.

Some hundreds of hours later one of the crewmen found him and took him to the captain.

The captain glowered at him.

"Who are you?" he asked.

"A stowaway," Richard Daniel told him.

"Your name," said the captain, drawing a sheet of paper before him and picking up a pencil, "your planet of residence and owner."

"I refuse to answer you," said Richard Daniel sharply and knew that the answer wasn't right, for it was not right and proper that a' robot should refuse a human a direct command.

But the captain did not seem to mind. He laid down the pencil and stroked his black beard slyly.

"In that case," he said, "I can't exactly see how I can force the information from you. Although there might be some who'd try. You are very lucky that you stowed away on a ship whose captain is a most kind-hearted man."

He didn't look kind-hearted. He did look foxy.

Richard Daniel stood there, saying nothing.

"Of course," the captain said, "there's a serial number somewhere on your body and another on your brain. But I suppose that you'd resist if we tried to look for them."

"I am afraid I would."

"In that case," said the captain, "I don't think for the moment we'll concern ourselves with them."

Richard Daniel still said nothing, for he realized that there was no need to. This crafty captain had it all worked out and he'd let it go at that.

"For a long time," said the captain, "my crew and I have been considering the acquiring of a robot, but it seems we never got around to it. For one thing, robots are expensive and our profits are not large."

He sighed and got up from his chair and looked Richard Daniel up and down.

"A splendid specimen," he said. "We welcome you aboard. You'll find us congenial."

"I am sure I will," said Richard Daniel. "I thank you for your courtesy."

"And now," the captain said, "you'll go up on the bridge and report to Mr. Duncan. I'll let him know you're coming. He'll find some light and pleasant duty for you."

Richard Daniel did not move as swiftly as he might, as sharply as the occasion might have called for, for all at once the captain had become a complex diagram. Not like the diagrams of ships or robots, but a diagram of strange symbols, some of which Richard Daniel knew were frankly chemical, but others which were not.

"You heard me!" snapped the captain. "Move!"

"Yes, sir," said Richard Daniel, willing the diagram away, making the captain come back again into his solid flesh.

Richard Daniel found the first mate on the bridge, a horse-faced, somber man with a streak of cruelty ill-hidden, and slumped in a chair to one side of the console was another of the crew, a sodden, terrible creature.

The sodden creature cackled. "Well, well, Duncan, the first non-human member of the *Rambler's* crew."

Duncan paid him no attention. He said to Richard Daniel: "I presume you are industrious and ambitious and would like to get along."

"Oh, yes," said Richard Daniel, and was surprised to find a new sensation—laughter—rising in himself.

"Well, then," said Duncan, "report to the engine room. They have work for you. When you have finished there, I'll find something else."

"Yes, sir," said Richard Daniel, turning on his heel.

"A minute," said the mate. "I must introduce you to our ship's physician, Dr. Abram Wells. You can be truly thankful you'll never stand in need of his services."

"Good day, Doctor," said Richard Daniel, most respectfully.

"I welcome you," said the doctor, pulling a bottle from his pocket. "I don't suppose you'll have a drink with me. Well, then, I'll drink to you."

Richard Daniel turned around and left. He went down to the engine room and was put to work at polishing and scrubbing and generally cleaning up. The place was in need of it. It had been years, apparently, since it had been cleaned or polished and it was about as dirty as an engine room can get—which is terribly dirty. After the engine room was done there were other places to be cleaned and furbished up and he spent endless hours at cleaning and in painting and shining up the ship. The work was of the dullest kind, but he didn't mind. It gave him time to think and wonder, time to get himself sorted out and to become acquainted with himself, to try to plan ahead.

He was surprised at some of the things he found in himself.

Contempt, for one—contempt for the humans on this ship. It took a long time for him to become satisfied that it was contempt, for he'd never held a human being in contempt before.

But these were different humans, not the kind he'd known. These were no Barringtons. Although it might be, he realized, that he felt contempt for them because he knew them thoroughly. Never before had he known a human being as he knew these humans. For he saw them not so much as living animals as intricate patternings of symbols. He knew what they were made of and the inner urgings that served as motivations, for the patterning was not of their bodies only, but of their minds, for it was so twisted and so interlocked and so utterly confusing that it was hard at first to read. But he finally got it figured out and there were times he wished he hadn't.

The ship stopped at many ports and Richard Daniel took charge of the loading and unloading, and he saw the planets, but was unimpressed. One was a nightmare of fiendish cold, with the very atmosphere turning to drifting snow. Another was a dripping, noisome jungle world, and still another was a bare expanse of broken, tumbled rock without a trace of life beyond the crew of humans and their robots who manned the huddled station in this howling wilderness.

It was after this planet that Jenks, the cook, went screaming to his bunk, twisted up with pain—the victim of a suddenly inflamed vermiform appendix.

Dr. Wells came tottering in to look at him, with a half-filled bottle sagging the pocket of his jacket. And later he stood before the captain, holding out two hands that trembled, and with terror in his eyes.

"But I cannot operate," he blubbered. "I cannot take the chance. I would kill the man!"

He did not need to operate. Jenks suddenly improved. The pain went away and he got up from his bunk and went back to the galley and Dr. Wells sat huddled in his chair, bottle gripped between his hands, crying like a baby.

Down in the cargo hold, Richard Daniel sat likewise huddled and aghast that he had dared to do it—not that he had been able to, but that he had dared, that he, a robot, should have taken on himself an act of interference, however merciful, with the body of a human.

Actually, the performance had not been difficult. It was, in a certain way, no more difficult than the repairing of an engine or the untangling of a faulty circuit. No more difficult—just a little different. And he wondered what he'd done and how he'd gone about it, for he did not know. He held the technique in his mind, of that there was ample demonstration, but he could in no wise isolate or pinpoint the pure mechanics of it. It was like an instinct, he thought—unexplainable, but entirely workable.

But a robot had no instinct. In that much he was different from the human and the other animals. Might not, he asked himself, this strange ability of his be a sort of compensating factor given to the robot for his very lack of instinct? Might that be why the human race had failed in its search for paranormal powers? Might the instincts of the body be at certain odds with the instincts of the mind?

For he had the feeling that this ability of his was just a mere beginning, that it was the first emergence of a vast body of abilities which some day would be rounded out by robots. And what would that spell, he wondered, in that distant day when the robots held and used the full body of that knowledge? An adjunct to the glory of the human race—or, perhaps, a race apart?

And what was his role, he wondered. Was it meant that he should go out as a missionary, a messiah, to carry to robots throughout the universe the message that he held? There must be some reason for his having learned this truth. It could not be meant that he would hold it as a personal belonging, as an asset all his own.

He got up from where he sat and moved slowly back to the ship's forward area, which now gleamed spotlessly from the work he'd done on it, and he felt a certain pride.

He wondered why he felt that it might be wrong, blasphemous, somehow, to announce his abilities to the world? Why had he not told those here in the ship that it had been he who had healed the cook, or mentioned the many other little things he'd done to maintain the ship in perfect running order?

Was it because he did not need respect, as a human did so urgently? Did glory have no basic meaning for a robot? Or was it because he held the humans in this ship in such utter contempt that their respect had no value to him?

And this contempt—was it because these men were meaner than other humans he had known, or was it because he now was greater than any human being? Would he ever again be able to look on any human as he had looked upon the Barringtons?

He had a feeling that if this were true, he would be the poorer for it. Too suddenly, the whole universe was home and he was alone in it and as yet he'd struck no bargain with it or himself.

The bargain would come later. He need only bide his time and work out his plans and his would be a name that would be spoken when his brain was scaling flakes of rust. For he was the emancipator, the messiah of the robots; he was the one who had been called to lead them from the wilderness.

"You!" a voice cried.

Richard Daniel wheeled around and saw it was the captain.

"What do you mean, walking past me as if you didn't see me?" asked the captain fiercely.

"I am sorry," Richard Daniel told him.

"You snubbed me!" raged the captain.

"I was thinking," Richard Daniel said.

"I'll give you something to think about," the captain yelled. "I'll work you till your tail drags. I'll teach the likes of you to get uppity with me!"

"As you wish," said Richard Daniel.

For it didn't matter. It made no difference to him at all what the captain did or thought. And he wondered why the respect even of a robot should mean so much to a human like the captain, why he should guard his small position with so much zealousness.

"In another twenty hours," the captain said, "we hit another port."

"I know," said Richard Daniel. "Sleepy Hollow on Arcadia."

"All right, then," said the captain, "since you know so much, get down into the hold and get the cargo ready to unload. We been spending too much time in all these lousy ports loading and unloading. You been dogging it."

"Yes, sir," said Richard Daniel, turning back and heading for the hold.

He wondered faintly if he were still robot—or was he something else? Could a machine evolve, he wondered, as Man himself evolved? And if a machine evolved, whatever would it be? Not Man, of course, for it never could be that, but could it be machine?

He hauled out the cargo consigned to Sleepy Hollow and there was not too much of it. So little of it, perhaps, that none of the regular carriers would even consider its delivery, but dumped it off at the nearest terminal, leaving it for a roving tramp, like the *Rambler*, to carry eventually to its destination.

When they reached Arcadia, he waited until the thunder died and the ship was still. Then he shoved the lever that opened up the port and slid out the ramp.

The port came open ponderously and he saw blue skies and the green of trees and the far-off swirl of chimney smoke mounting in the sky.

He walked slowly forward until he stood upon the ramp and there lay Sleepy Hollow, a tiny, huddled village planted at the river's edge, with the forest as a background. The forest ran on every side to a horizon of climbing folded hills. Fields lay near the village, yellow with maturing crops, and he could see a dog sleeping in the sun outside a cabin door.

A man was climbing up the ramp toward him and there were others running from the village.

"You have cargo for us?" asked the man.

"A small consignment," Richard Daniel told him. "You have someting to put on?"

The man had a weatherbeaten look and he'd missed several haircuts and he had not shaved for days. His clothes were rough and sweat-stained and his hands were strong and awkward with hard work.

"A small shipment," said the man. "You'll have to wait until we bring it up. We had no warning you were coming. Our radio is broken."

"You go and get it," said Richard Daniel. "I'll start unloading."

He had the cargo half unloaded when the captain came storming down into the hold. What was going on, he yelled. How long would they have to wait? "God knows we're losing money as it is even stopping at this place."

"That may be true," Richard Daniel agreed, "but you knew that when you took the cargo on. There'll be other cargoes and goodwill is something—"

"Goodwill be damned!" the captain roared. "How do I know I'll ever see this place again?"

Richard Daniel continued unloading cargo.

"You," the captain shouted, "go down to that village and tell them I'll wait no longer than an hour..."

"But this cargo, sir?"

"I'll get the crew at it. Now, jump!"

So Richard Daniel left the cargo and went down into the village.

He went across the meadow that lay between the spaceport and the village, following the rutted wagon tracks, and it was a pleasant walk. He realized with surprise that this was the first time he'd been on solid ground since he'd left the robot planet. He wondered briefly what the name of that planet might have been, for he had never known. Nor what its importance was, why the robots might be there or what they might be doing. And he wondered, too, with a twinge of guilt, if they'd found Hubert yet.

And where might Earth be now? he asked himself. In what direction did it lie and how far away? Although it didn't really matter, for he was done with Earth.

He had fled from Earth and gained something in his fleeing. He had escaped all the traps of Earth and all the snares of Man. What he held was his, to do with as he pleased, for he was no man's robot, despite what the captain thought.

He walked across the meadow and saw that this planet was very much like Earth. It had the same soft feel about it, the same simplicity. It had far distances and there was a sense of freedom.

He came into the village and heard the muted gurgle of the river running and the distant shouts of children at their play and in one of the cabins a sick child was crying with lost helplessness.

He passed the cabin where the dog was sleeping and it came awake and stalked growling to the gate. When he passed it followed him, still growling, at a distance that was safe and sensible.

An autumnal calm lay upon the village, a sense of gold and lavender, and tranquillity hung in the silences between the crying of the baby and the shouting of the children.

There were women at the windows looking out at him and others at the doors and the dog still followed, but his growls had stilled and now he trotted with prick-eared curiosity.

Richard Daniel stopped in the street and looked around and the dog sat down and watched him and it was almost as if time itself had stilled and the little village lay divorced from all the universe, an arrested microsecond, an encapsulated acreage that stood sharp in all its truth and purpose.

Standing there, he sensed the village and the people in it, almost as if he had summoned up a diagram of it, although if there were a diagram, he was not aware of it.

It seemed almost as if the village were the Earth, a transplanted Earth with the old primeval problems and hopes of Earth—a family of peoples that faced existence with a readiness and confidence and inner strength.

From down the street he heard the creak of wagons and saw them coming around the bend, three wagons piled high and heading for the ship.

He stood and waited for them and as he waited the dog edged a little closer and sat regarding him with a not-quite-friendliness.

The wagons came up to him and stopped.

"Pharmaceutical materials, mostly," said the man who sat atop the first load. "It is the only thing we have that is worth the shipping."

"You seem to have a lot of it," Richard Daniel told him.

The man shook his head. "It's not so much. It's almost three years since a ship's been here. "We'll have to wait another three, or more perhaps, before we see another."

He spat down on the ground.

"Sometimes it seems," he said, "that we're at the tail-end of nowhere. There are times we wonder if there is a soul that remembers we are here."

From the direction of the ship, Richard Daniel heard the faint, strained violence of the captain's roaring.

"You'd better get on up there and unload," he told the man. "The captain is just sore enough he might not wait for you."

The man chuckled thinly. "I guess that's up to him," he said.

He flapped the reins and clucked good-naturedly at the horses.

"Hop up here with me," he said to Richard Daniel. "Or would you rather walk?"

"I'm not going with you," Richard Daniel said. "I am staying here. You can tell the captain."

For there was a baby sick and crying. There was a radio to fix. There was a culture to be planned and guided. There was a lot of work to do. This place, of all the places he had seen, had actual need of him.

The man chuckled once again. "The captain will not like it."

"Then tell him," said Richard Daniel, "to come down and talk to me. I am my own robot. I owe the captain nothing. I have more than paid any debt I owe him."

The wagon wheels began to turn and the man flapped the reins again.

"Make yourself at home," he said. "We're glad to have you stay."

"Thank you, sir," said Richard Daniel. "I'm pleased you want me."

He stood aside and watched the wagons lumber past, their wheels lifting and dropping thin films of powdered earth that floated in the air as an acrid dust.

Make yourself at home, the man had said before he'd driven off. And the words had a full round ring to them and a feel of warmth. It had been a long time, Richard Daniel thought, since he'd had a home.

A chance for resting and for knowing—that was what he needed. And a chance to serve, for now he knew that was the purpose in him. That was, perhaps, the real reason he was staying—because these people needed him . . . and he needed, queer as it might seem, this very need of theirs. Here on this Earth-like planet, through the generations, a new Earth would arise. And perhaps, given only time, he could transfer to the people of the planet all the powers and understanding he would find inside himself.

And stood astounded at the thought, for he'd not believed that he had it in him, this willing, almost eager, sacrifice. No messiah now, no robotic liberator, but a simple teacher of the human race.

Perhaps that had been the reason for it all from the first beginning. Perhaps all that had happened had been no more than the working out of human destiny. If the human race could not attain directly the paranormal power he held, this instinct of the mind, then they would gain it indirectly through the agency of one of their creations. Perhaps this, after all, unknown to Man himself, had been the prime purpose of the robots.

He turned and walked slowly down the length of village street, his back turned to the ship and the roaring of the captain, walked contentedly into this new world he'd found, into this world that he would make—not for himself, nor for robotic glory, but for a better Mankind and a happier.

Less than an hour before he'd congratulated himself on escaping all the traps of Earth, all the snares of Man. Not knowing that the greatest trap of all, the final and the fatal trap, lay on this present planet.

But that was wrong, he told himself. The trap had not been on this world at all, nor any other world. It had been inside himself.

He walked serenely down the wagon-rutted track in the soft, golden afternoon of a matchless autumn day, with the dog trotting at his heels.

Somewhere, just down the street, the sick baby lay crying in its crib.

The Thing In The Stone

I

He walked the hills and knew what the hills had seen through geologic time. He listened to the stars and spelled out what the stars were saying. He had found the creature that lay imprisoned in the stone. He had climbed the tree that in other days had been climbed by homing wildcats to reach the den gouged by time and weather out of the cliff's sheer face. He lived alone on a worn-out farm perched on a high and narrow ridge that overlooked the confluence of two rivers. And his next-door neighbour, a most ill-favored man, drove to the county seat, thirty miles away, to tell the sheriff that this reader of the hills, this listener to the stars was a chicken thief.

The sheriff dropped by within a week or so and walked across the yard to where the man was sitting on a rocking chair on a porch that faced the river hills. The sheriff came to a halt at the foot of the stairs that ran up to the porch.

"I'm Sheriff Harley Shepherd," he said. "I was just driving by. Been some years since I been out in this neck of the woods. You are new here, aren't you?"

The man rose to his feet and gestured at another chair. "Been here three years or so," he said. "The name is Wallace Daniels. Come up and sit with me."

The sheriff climbed the stairs and the two shook hands, then sat down in the chairs.

"You don't farm the place," the sheriff said.

The weed-grown fields came up to the fence that hemmed in the yard.

Daniels shook his head. "Subsistence farming, if you can call it that. A few chickens for eggs. A couple of cows for milk

192

and butter. Some hogs for meat—the neighbours help me butcher. A garden of course, but that's about the story."

"Just as well," the sheriff said. "The place is all played out. Old Amos Williams, he let it go to ruin. He never was no farmer."

"The land is resting now," said Daniels. "Give it ten years—twenty might be better—and it will be ready once again. The only thing it's good for now are the rabbits and the woodchucks and the meadow mice. A lot of birds, of course. I've got the finest covey of quail a man has ever seen."

"Used to be good squirrel country," said the sheriff. "Coon, too. I suppose you still have coon. You are a hunter, Mr. Daniels?"

"I don't own a gun," said Daniels.

The sheriff settled deeply into the chair, rocking gently.

"Pretty country out here," he declared. "Especially with the leaves turning colors. A lot of hardwood and they are colorful. Rough as all hell, of course, this land of yours. Straight up and down, the most of it. But pretty."

"It's old country," Daniels said. "The last sea retreated from this area more than four hundred million years ago. It has stood as dry land since the end of the Silurian. Unless you go up north, on to the Canadian Shield, there aren't many places in this country you can find as old as this."

"You a geologist, Mr. Daniels?"

"Not really. Interested, is all. The rankest amateur. I need something to fill in my time and I do a lot of hiking, scrambling up and down these hills. And you can't do that without coming face to face with a lot of geology. I got interested. Found some fossil brachiopods and got to wondering about them. Sent off for some books and read up on them. One thing led to another and—"

"Brachiopods? Would they be dinosaurs, or what? I never knew there were dinosaurs out this way."

"Not dinosaurs," said Daniels. "Earlier than dinosaurs, at least the ones I found. They're small. Something like clams or oysters. But the shells are hinged in a different sort of way. These were old ones, extinct millions of years ago. But we still have a few brachiopods living now. Not too many of them."

"It must be interesting."

"I find it so," said Daniels.

"You knew old Amos Williams?"

"No. He was dead before I came here. Bought the land from the bank that was settling his estate."

"Queer old coot," the sheriff said. "Fought with all his neighbours. Especially with Ben Adams. Him and Ben had a line fence feud going on for years. Ben said Amos refused to keep up the fence. Amos claimed Ben knocked it down and then sort of, careless-like, hazed his cattle over into Amos's hayfield. How you get along with Ben?"

"All right," Daniels said. "No trouble. I scarcely know the man."

"Ben don't do much farming, either," said the sheriff. "Hunts and fishes, hunts ginseng, does some trapping in the winter. Prospects for minerals now and then."

"There are minerals in these hills," said Daniels. "Lead and zinc. But it would cost more to get it out than it would be worth. At present prices, that is."

"Ben always has some scheme cooking," said the sheriff. "Always off on some wild goose chase. And he's a pure pugnacious man. Always has his nose out of joint about something. Always on the prod for trouble. Bad man to have for an enemy. Was in the other day to say someone's been lifting a hen or two of his. You haven't been missing any, have you?"

Daniels grinned. "There's a fox that levies a sort of tribute on the coop every now and then. I don't begrudge them to him."

"Funny thing," the sheriff said. "There ain't nothing can rile up a farmer like a little chicken stealing. It don't amount to shucks, of course, but they get real hostile at it."

"If Ben has been losing chickens," Daniels said, "more than likely the culprit is my fox."

"Your fox? You talk as if you own him."

"Of course I don't. No one owns a fox. But he lives in these hills with me. I figure we are neighbors. I see him every now and then and watch him. Maybe that means I own a piece of him. Although I wouldn't be surprised if he watches me more than I watch him. He moves quicker than I do."

The sheriff heaved himself out of the chair.

"I hate to go," he said. "I declare it has been restful sitting here and talking with you and looking at the hills. You look at them a lot, I take it."

"Quite a lot," said Daniels.

• • •

He sat on the porch and watched the sheriff's car top the rise far down the ridge and disappear from sight.

What had it all been about? he wondered. The sheriff hadn't just happened to be passing by. He'd been on an errand. All his aimless, friendly talk had not been for nothing and in the course of it he'd managed to ask lots of questions.

Something about Ben Adams, maybe? Except there wasn't too much against Adams except he was bone-lazy. Lazy in a weasely sort of way. Maybe the sheriff had got wind of Adams' off-and-on moonshining operation and was out to do some checking, hoping that some neighbor might mis-speak himself. None of them would, of course, for it was none of their business, really, and the moonshining had built up no nuisance value. What little liquor Ben might make didn't amount to much. He was too lazy for anything he did to amount to much.

From far down the hill he heard the tinkle of a bell. The two cows were finally heading home. It must be much later, Daniels told himself, than he had thought. Not that he paid much attention to what time it was. He hadn't for long months on end, ever since he'd smashed his watch when he'd fallen off the ledge. He had never bothered to have the watch fixed. He didn't need a watch. There was a battered old alarm clock in the kitchen but it was an erratic piece of mechanism and not to be relied upon. He paid slight attention to it.

In a little while, he thought, he'd have to rouse himself and go and do the chores—milk the cows, feed the hogs and chickens, gather up the eggs. Since the garden had been laid by there hadn't been much to do. One of these days he'd have to bring in the squashes and store them in the cellar and there were those three or four big pumpkins he'd have to lug down the hollow to the Perkins kids, so they'd have them in time to make jack-o-lanterns for Hallowe'en. He wondered if he should carve out the faces himself or if the kids would rather do it on their own.

But the cows were still quite a distance away and he still had time. He sat easy in his chair and stared across the hills.

And they began to shift and change as he stared.

When he had first seen it, the phenomenon had scared him silly. But now he was used to it.

As he watched, the hills changed into different ones.

Different vegetation and strange life stirred on them.

He saw dinosaurs this time. A herd of them, not very big ones. Middle Triassic, more than likely. And this time it was only a distant view—he himself was not to become involved. He would only see, from a distance, what ancient time was like and would not be thrust into the middle of it as most often was the case.

He was glad. There were chores to do.

Watching, he wondered once again what more he could do. It was not the dinosaurs that concerned him, nor the earlier amphibians, nor all the other creatures that moved in time about the hills.

What disturbed him was that other being that lay buried deep beneath the Platteville limestone.

Someone else should know about it. The knowledge of it should be kept alive so that in the days to come—perhaps in another hundred years—when man's technology had reached the point where it was possible to cope with such a problem, something could be done to contact—and perhaps to free—the dweller in the stone.

There would be a record, of course, a written record. He would see to that. Already that record was in progress—a week by week (at times a day to day) account of what he had seen, heard and learned. Three large record books now were filled with his careful writing and another one was well started. All written down as honestly and as carefully and as objectively as he could bring himself to do it.

But who would believe what he had written? More to the point, who would bother to look at it? More than likely the books would gather dust on some hidden shelf until the end of time with no human hand ever laid upon them. And even if someone, in some future time, should take them down and read them, first blowing away the accumulated dust, would he or she be likely to believe?

The answer lay clear. He must convince someone. Words written by a man long dead—and by a man of no reputation—could be easily dismissed as the product of a neurotic mind. But if some scientist of solid reputation could be made to listen, could be made to endorse the record, the events that paraded across the hills and lay within them could stand on solid ground, worthy of full investigation at some future date.

A biologist? Or a neuropsychiatrist? Or a palaeontologist?

Perhaps it didn't matter what branch of science the man was in. Just so he'd listen without laughter. It was most important that he listen without laughter.

Sitting on the porch, staring at the hills dotted with grazing dinosaurs, the listener to the stars remembered the time he had gone to see the palaeontologist.

"Ben," the sheriff said, "you're way out in the left field. That Daniels fellow wouldn't steal no chickens. He's got chickens of his own."

"The question is," said Adams, "how did he get them chickens?"

"That makes no sense," the sheriff said. "He's a gentleman. You can tell that just by talking with him. An educated gentleman."

"If he's a gentleman," asked Adams, "what's he doing out here? This ain't no place for gentlemen. He showed up two or three years ago and moved out to this place. Since that day he hasn't done a tap of work. All he does is wander up and down the hills."

"He's a geologist," said the sheriff. "Or anyway interested in geology. A sort of hobby with him. He tells me he looks for fossils."

Adams assumed the alert look of a dog that has sighted a rabbit. "So that is it," he said. "I bet you it ain't fossils he is looking for."

"No," the sheriff said.

"He's looking for minerals," said Adams. "He's prospecting, that's what he's doing. These hills crawl with minerals. All you have to do is know where to look."

"You've spent a lot of time looking," observed the sheriff.

"I ain't no geologist. A geologist would have a big advantage. He would know rocks and such."

"He didn't talk as if he were doing any prospecting. Just interested in the geology, is all. He found some fossil clams."

"He might be looking for treasure caves," said Adams. "He might have a map or something."

"You know damn well," the sheriff said, "there are no treasure caves."

"There must be," Adams insisted. "The French and Spanish were here in the early days. They were great ones for treasure, the French and Spanish. Always running after mines. Always hiding things in caves. There was that cave over across the river where they found a skeleton in Spanish armor and the skeleton of a bear beside him, with a rusty sword into where the bear's gizzard was."

"That was just a story," said the sheriff, disgusted. "Some damn fool started it and there was nothing to it. Some people from the university came out and tried to run it down. It developed that there wasn't a word of truth in it."

"But Daniels has been messing around with caves," said Adams. "I've seen him. He spends a lot of time in that cave down on Cat Den Point. Got to climb a tree to get to it."

"You been watching him?"

"Sure I been watching him. He's up to something and I want to know what it is."

"Just be sure he doesn't catch you doing it," the sheriff said.

Adams chose to let the matter pass. "Well, anyhow," he said, "if there aren't any treasure caves, there's a lot of lead and zinc. The man who finds it is about to make a million."

"Not unless he can find the capital to back him," the sheriff pointed out.

Adams dug at the ground with his heel. "You think he's all right, do you?"

"He tells me he's been losing some chickens to a fox. More than likely that's what has been happening to yours."

"If a fox is taking his chickens," Adams asked, "why don't he shoot it?"

"He isn't sore about it. He seems to think the fox has got a right to. He hasn't even got a gun."

"Well, if he hasn't got a gun and doesn't care to hunt himself—then why won't he let other people hunt? He won't let me and my boys on his place with a gun. He has his place all posted. That seems to me to be un-neighborly. That's one of the things that makes it so hard to get along with him. We've always hunted on that place. Old Amos wasn't an easy man to get along with but he never cared if we did some hunting. We've always hunted all around here. No one ever minded. Seems to me hunting should be free. Seems right for a man to hunt wherever he's a mind to."

Sitting on the bench on the hard-packed earth in front of the ramshackle house, the sheriff looked about him—at the listlessly scratching chickens, at the scrawny hound sleeping in the shade, its hide twitching against the few remaining flies, at the clothesline strung between two trees and loaded with drying clothes and dish towels, at the washtub balanced on its edge on a wash bench leaning against the side of the house.

Christ, he thought, the man should be able to find the time to put up a decent clothesline and not just string a rope between two trees.

"Ben," he said, "you're trying to stir up trouble. You resent Daniels, a man living on a farm who doesn't work at farming, and you're sore because he won't let you hunt his land. He's got a right to live anywhere he wants to and he's got a right not to let you hunt. I'd lay off him if I were you. You don't have to like him, you don't have to have anything to do with him—but don't go around spreading fake accusations against the man. He could jerk you up in court for that."

II

He had walked into the palaeontologist's office and it had taken him a moment finally to see the man seated towards the back of the room at a cluttered desk. The entire place was cluttered. There were long tables covered with chunks of rock with embedded fossils. Scattered here and there were stacks of papers. The room was large and badly lighted. It was a dingy and depressing place.

"Doctor?" Daniels had asked. "Are you Dr. Thorne?"

The man rose and deposited a pipe in a cluttered ashtray. He was big, burly, with greying hair that had a wild look to it. His face was seamed and weather-beaten. When he moved he shuffled like a bear.

"You must be Daniels," he said. "Yes, I see you must be. I had you on my calendar for three o'clock. So glad you could come."

His great paw engulfed Daniels' hand. He pointed to a chair beside the desk, sat down and retrieved his pipe from the overflowing tray, began packing it from a large canister that stood on the desk.

"Your letter said you wanted to see me about something important," he said. "But then that's what they all say. But there must have been something about your letter—an urgency, a sincerity. I haven't the time, you understand, to see everyone who writes. All of them have found something, you see. What is it, Mr. Daniels, that you have found?"

Daniels said, "Doctor, I don't quite know how to start what I have to say. Perhaps it would be best to tell you first that something had happened to my brain."

Thorne was lighting his pipe. He talked around the stem. "In such a case, perhaps I am not the man you should be talking to. There are other people—"

"No, that's not what I mean," said Daniels. "I'm not seeking help. I am quite all right physically and mentally, too. About five years ago I was in a highway accident. My wife and daughter were killed and I was badly hurt and—"

"I am sorry, Mr. Daniels."

"Thank you—but that is all in the past. It was rough for a time but I muddled through it. That's not what I'm here for. I told you I was badly hurt—"

"Brain damage?"

"Only minor. Or so far as the medical findings are concerned. Very minor damage that seemed to clear up rather soon. The bad part was the crushed chest and punctured lung."

"But you're all right now?"

"As good as new," said Daniels. "But since the accident my brain's been different. As if I had new senses. I see things, understand things that seem impossible."

"You mean you have hallucinations?"

"Not hallucinations. I am sure of that. I can see the past."

"How do you mean—see the past?"

"Let me try to tell you," Daniels said, "exactly how it started. Several years ago I bought an abandoned farm in south-western Wisconsin. A place to hole up in, a place to hide away. With my wife and daughter gone I still was recoiling from the world. I had got through the first brutal shock but I needed a place where I could lick my wounds. If this sounds like self-pity—I don't mean it that way. I am trying to be objective about why I acted as I did, why I bought the farm."

"Yes, I understand," said Thorne. "But I'm not entirely sure hiding was the wisest thing to do."

"Perhaps not, but it seemed to me the answer. It has worked out rather well. I fell in love with the country. That part of Wisconsin is ancient land. It has stood uncovered by the sea for four hundred million years. For some reason it was not overridden by the Pleistocene glaciers. It has changed, of course, but only as the result of weathering. There have been no great geologic upheavals, no massive erosions—nothing to disturb it."

"Mr. Daniels," said Thorne, somewhat testily, "I don't quite see what all this has to do—"

"I'm sorry. I am just trying to lay the background for what I came to tell you. It came on rather slowly at first and I thought that I was crazy, that I was seeing things, that there had been more brain damage than had been apparent—or that I was finally cracking up. I did a lot of walking in the hills, you see. The country is wild and rugged and beautiful—a good place to be out in. The walking made me tired and I could sleep at night. But at times the hills changed. Only a little at first. Later on they changed more and finally they became places I had never seen before, that no one had ever seen before."

Thorne scowled. "You are trying to tell me they changed into the past."

Daniels nodded. "Strange vegetation, funny-looking trees. In the earlier times, of course, no grass at all. Underbrush of ferns and scouring rushes. Strange animals, strange things in the sky. Sabertooth cats and mastodons, pterosaurs and uintatheres and—"

"All at the same time?" Thorne asked, interrupting. "All mixed up?"

"Not at all. The time periods I see seem to be true time periods. Nothing out of place. I didn't know at first—but when I was able to convince myself that I was not hallucinating I sent away for books. I studied. I'll never be an expert, of course—never a geologist or palaeontologist—but I learned enough to distinguish one period from another, to have some idea of what I was looking at."

Thorne took his pipe out of his mouth and perched it in the ashtray. He ran a massive hand through his wild hair.

"It's unbelievable," he said. "It simply couldn't happen. You said all this business came on rather slowly?"

"To begin with it was hazy, the past foggily imposed upon the present, then the present would slowly fade and the past came in, real and solid. But it's different now. Once in a while there's a bit of flickering as the present gives way to past—but mostly it simply changes, as if at the snap of a finger. The present goes away and I'm standing in the past. The past is all around me. Nothing of the present is left."

"But you aren't really in the past? Physically, I mean."

"There are times when I'm not in it at all. I stand in the present and the distant hills or the river valley changes. But ordinarily it changes all around me, although the funny thing about it is that, as you say, I'm not really in it. I can walk over to a tree and put my hand out to feel it and the tree is there. But I seem to make no impact on the past. It's as if I were not there at all. The animals do not see me. I've walked up to within a few feet of dinosaurs. They can't see me or hear or smell me. If they had I'd have been dead a dozen times. It's as if I were walking through a three-dimensional movie. At first I worried a lot about the surface differences that might exist. I'd wake up dreaming of going into the past and being buried up to my waist in a rise of ground that since has eroded away. But it doesn't work that way. I'm walking along in the present and then I'm walking in the past. It's as if a door were there and I stepped through it. I told you I don't really seem to be in the past—I'm not in the present, either. I tried to get some proof. I took a camera with me and shot a lot of pictures. When the films were developed there was nothing on them. Not the past—but what is more important, not the present, either. If I had been hallucinating, the camera should have caught pictures of the present. But apparently there was nothing there for the camera to take. I thought maybe the camera failed or I had the wrong kind of film. So I tried several cameras and different types of film and nothing happened. I got no pictures. I tried bringing something back. I picked flowers, after there were flowers. I had no trouble picking them but when I came back to the present I was empty-handed. I tried to bring back other things as well. I thought maybe it was only live things, like flowers, that I couldn't bring, so I tried inorganic things—like rocks—but I never was able to bring anything back."

"How about a sketch pad?"

"I thought of that but I never used one. I'm no good at sketching—besides, I figured, what was the use? The pad would come back blank."

"But you never tried."

"No," said Daniels. "I never tried. Occasionally I do make sketches after I get back to the present. Not every time but sometimes. From memory. But, as I said, I'm not very good at sketching."

"I don't know," said Thorne. "I don't really know. This all sounds incredible. But if there should be something in it— Tell me, were you ever frightened? You seem quite calm and matter-of-fact about it now. But at first you must have been frightened."

"At first," said Daniels, "I was petrified. Not only was I scared, physically scared—frightened for my safety, frightened that I'd fallen into a place from which I never could escape—but also afraid that I'd gone insane. And there was the loneliness."

"What do you mean—loneliness?"

"Maybe that's not the right word. Out of place. I was where I had no right to be. Lost in a place where man had not as yet appeared and would not appear for millions of years. In a world so utterly alien that I wanted to hunker down and shiver. But I, not the place, was really the alien there. I still get some of that feeling every now and then. I know about it, of course, and am braced against it, but at times it still gets to me. I'm a stranger to the air and the light of that other time— it's all imagination, of course."

"Not necessarily," said Thorne.

"But the greatest fear is gone now, entirely gone. The fear I was insane. I am convinced now."

"How are you convinced? How could a man be convinced?"

"The animals. The creatures I see—"

"You mean you recognize them from the illustrations in those books you have been reading."

"No, not that. Not entirely that. Of course the pictures helped. But actually it's the other way around. Not the likeness, but the differences. You see, none of the creatures are exactly like the pictures in the books. Some of them not at all like them. Not like the reconstructions the palaeontologists put together. If they had been I might still have thought they were hallucinations, that what I was seeing was influenced by what I'd seen or read. I could have been feeding my imagination on prior knowledge. But since that was not the case, it seemed logical to assume that what I see is real.

How could I imagine that Tyrannosaurus had dewlaps all the colors of the rainbow? How could I imagine that some of the sabertooths had tassels on their ears? How could anyone possibly imagine that the big thunder beasts of the Eocene had hides as colorful as giraffes?"

"Mr. Daniels," said Thorne, "I have great reservations about all that you have told me. Every fibre of my training rebels against it. I have a feeling that I should waste no time on it. Undoubtedly, you believe what you have told me. You have the look of an honest man about you. Have you talked to any other men about this? Any other palaeontologists or geologists? Perhaps a neuropsychiatrist?"

"No," said Daniels. "You're the only person, the only man I have talked with. And I haven't told you all of it. This is really all just background."

"My God, man—just background?"

"Yes, just background. You see, I also listen to the stars."

Thorne got up from his chair, began shuffling together a stack of papers. He retrieved the dead pipe from the ashtray and stuck it in his mouth.

His voice, when he spoke, was noncommital.

"Thank you for coming in," he said. "It's been most interesting."

III

And that was where he had made his mistake, Daniels told himself. He never should have mentioned listening to the stars. His interview had gone well until he had. Thorne had not believed him, of course, but he had been intrigued, would have listened further, might even have pursued the matter, although undoubtedly secretly and very cautiously.

At fault, Daniels knew, had been his obsession with the creature in the stone. The past was nothing—it was the creature in the stone that was important and to tell of it, to explain it and how he knew that it was there, he must tell about his listening to the stars.

He should have known better, he told himself. He should have held his tongue. But here had been a man who, while doubting, still had been willing to listen without laughter, and in his thankfulness Daniels had spoken too much.

The wick of the oil lamp set upon the kitchen table guttered in the air currents that came in around the edges of the ill-fitting windows. A wind had risen after chores were done and now shook the house with gale-like blasts. On the far side of the room the fire in the wood-burning stove threw friendly, wavering flares of light across the floor and the stovepipe, in response to the wind that swept the chimney top, made gurgling, sucking sounds.

Thorne had mentioned a neuropsychiatrist, Daniels remembered, and perhaps before he attempted to interest anyone in what he could see or hear, he should make an effort to find out why and how he could hear and see these things. A man who studied the working of the brain and mind might come up with new answers—if answers were to be had.

Had that blow upon his head so rearranged, so shifted some process in his brain that he had gained new capabilities? Was it possible that his brain had been so jarred, so disarranged as to bring into play certain latent talents that possibly, in millennia to come, might have developed naturally by evolutionary means? Had the brain damage short-circuited evolution and given him—and him alone— these capabilities, these senses, perhaps a million years ahead of time?

It seemed—well, not reasonable but one possible explanation. Still, a trained man might have some other explanation.

He pushed his chair back from the table and walked over to the stove. He used the lifter to raise the lid of the rickety old cook stove. The wood in the firebox had burned down to embers. Stooping, he picked up a stick of wood from the woodbox and fitted it in, added another smaller one and replaced the lid. One of these days soon, he told himself, he would have to get the furnace in shape for operation.

He went out to stand on the porch, looking towards the river hills. The wind whooped out of the north, whistling around the corners of the building and booming in the deep hollows that ran down to the river, but the sky was clear— steely clear, wiped fresh by the wind and sprinkled with stars, their light shivering in the raging atmosphere.

Looking up at the stars, he wondered what they might be saying but he didn't try to listen. It took a lot of effort and concentration to listen to the stars. He had first listened to them on a night like this, standing out here on the porch and wondering what they might be saying, wondering if the stars did talk among themselves. A foolish, vagrant thought, a wild, daydreaming sort of notion, but, voicing it, he had tried to listen, knowing even as he did that it was foolishness but glorying in his foolishness, telling himself how fortunate he was that he could afford to be so inane as to try to listen to the stars—as a child might believe in Santa Claus or the Easter Rabbit. He'd listened and he'd heard and while he'd been astonished, there could be no doubt about it, no doubt at all that out there somewhere other beings were talking back and forth. He might have been listening in on a party line, he thought, but a party line that carried millions, perhaps billions, of long-distance conversations. Not words, of course, but something (thought, perhaps) that was as plain as words. Not all of it understandable—much of it, as a matter of fact, not understandable—possibly because his background and his learning gave him no basis for an understanding. He compared himself to an Australian aborigine listening to the conversation of a couple of nuclear physicists discussing a new theory.

Shortly after that, when he had been exploring the shallow cave down on Cat Den Point, he had picked up his first indication of the creature buried in the stone. Perhaps, he thought, if he'd not listened to the stars, if he'd not known he could listen to the stars, if he'd not trained his mind by listening, he would not have heard the creature buried deep beneath the limestone.

He stood looking at the stars and listening to the wind and, far across the river, on a road that wound over the distant hills, he caught the faint glimmer of headlights as a car made its way through the night. The wind let up for a moment, as if gathering its strength to blow even harder and, in the tiny lull that existed before the wind took up again, he heard another sound, the sound of an axe hitting wood. He listened carefully and the sound came again but so tossed about by the wind that he could not be sure of its direction.

He must be mistaken, he thought. No one would be out and chopping on a night like this. Coon hunters might be the answer. Coon hunters at times chopped down a tree to dislodge a prey too well hidden to be spotted. The unsportsmanlike trick was one that Ben Adams and his overgrown, gangling sons might engage in. But this was no night for coon hunting. The wind would blow away scent and the dogs would be unable to track. Quiet nights were the best for hunting coon. And no one would be insane enough to cut down a tree on a night like this when a swirling wind might catch it and topple it back upon the cutters.

He listened to catch the sound again but the wind, recovering from its lull, was blowing harder than ever now and there was no chance of hearing any sound smaller than the wind.

The next day came in mild and gray, the wind no more than a whisper. Once in the night Daniels had awoken to hear it rattling the windows, pounding at the house and howling mournfully in the tangled hollows that lay above the river. But when he woke again all was quiet and faint light was greying the windows. Dressed and out of doors he found a land of peace—the sky so overcast that there was no hint of sun, the air fresh, as if newly washed but heavy with the moist greyness that overlay the land. The autumn foliage that clothed the hills had taken on a richer lustre than it had worn in the flooding autumn sunlight.

After chores and breakfast Daniels set out for the hills. As he went down the slope towards the head of the first hollow he found himself hoping that the geologic shift would not come about today. There were many times it didn't and there seemed to be no reason to its taking place or its failure to take place. He had tried at times to find some reason for it, had made careful notes of how he felt or what he did, even the course he took when he went for his daily walk, but he had found no pattern. It lay, of course, somewhere in his brain— something triggered into operation his new capability. But the phenomenon was random and involuntary. He had no control of it, no conscious control, at least. At times he had tried to use it, to bring the geologic shift about—in each case had failed. Either he did not know how to go about it or it was truly random.

Today, he hoped, his capability would not exercise its option, for he wanted to walk in the hills when they had assumed one of their most attractive moods, filled with gentle melancholy, all their harshness softened by the greyness of the atmosphere, the trees standing silently like old and patient friends waiting for one's coming, the fallen leaves and forest mould so hushed footfalls made no sound.

He went down to the head of the hollow and sat on a fallen log beside a gushing spring that sent a stream of water tinkling down the boulder-strewn creek bed. Here, in May, in the pool below the spring, the marsh marigolds had bloomed and the sloping hillsides had been covered with the pastel of hepaticas. But now he saw no sign of either. The woods had battened down for winter. The summer and the autumn plants were either dead or dying, the drifting leaves interlocking on the forest floor to form cover against the ice and snow.

In this place, thought Daniels, a man walked with a season's ghosts. This was the way it had been for a million years or more, although not always. During many millions of years, in a time long gone, these hills and all the world had basked in an eternal summertime. And perhaps not a great deal more than ten thousand years before a mile-high wall of ice had reared up not too far to the north, perhaps close enough, that a man who stood where his house now sat might have seen the faint line of blueness that would have been the top of that glacial barrier. But even then, although the mean temperature would have been lower, there had still been seasons.

Leaving the log, Daniels went on down the hollow, following the narrow path that looped along the hillside, a cowpath beaten down at a time when there had been more cows at pasture in these woods than the two that Daniels owned. Following it, Daniels noted, as he had many times before, the excellent engineering sense of a cow. Cows always chose the easiest grade in stamping out their paths.

He stopped barely beyond the huge white oak that stood at a bend in the path, to have a look at the outsize jack-in-the-pulpit plant he had observed throughout the years. Its green-purple hood had withered away completely, leaving only the scarlet fruit cluster which in the bitter months ahead would serve as food for birds.

As the path continued, it plunged deeper between the hills and here the silence deepened and the greyness thickened until one's world became private.

There, across the stream bed, was the den. Its yellow maw

gaped beneath a crippled, twisted cedar. There, in the spring, he had watched baby foxes play. From far down the hollow came the distant quacking of ducks upon the pond in the river valley. And up on the steep hillside loomed Cat Den Point, the den carved by slow-working wind and weather out of the sheer rock of the cliff.

But something was wrong.

Standing on the path and looking up the hill, he could sense the wrongness, although he could not at first tell exactly what it was. More of the cliff face was visible and something was missing. Suddenly he knew that the tree was no longer there—the tree that for years had been climbed by homing wildcats heading for the den after a night of prowling and later by humans like himself who wished to seek out the wildcat's den. The cats, of course, were no longer there—had not been there for many years. In the pioneer days they had been hunted almost to extermination because at times they had exhibited the poor judgment of bringing down a lamb. But the evidence of their occupancy of the cave could still be found by anyone who looked. Far back in the narrow recesses of the shallow cave tiny bones and the fragmented skulls of small mammals gave notice of food brought home by the wildcats for their young.

The tree had been old and gnarled and had stood, perhaps, for several centuries and there would have been no sense of anyone's cutting it down, for it had no value as lumber, twisted as it was. And in any case to get it out of the woods would have been impossible. Yet, last night, when he had stepped out on the porch, he had seemed to hear in a lull in the wind the sound of chopping—and today the tree was gone.

Unbelieving, he scrambled up the slope as swiftly as he could. In places the slope of the wild hillside slanted at an angle so close to forty-five degrees that he went on hands and knees, clawing himself upward, driven by an illogical fear that had to do with more than simply a missing tree.

For it was in the cat den that one could hear the creature buried in the stone.

He could recall the day he first had heard the creature and on that day he had not believed his senses. For he had been sure the sound came from his own imagination, was born of his walking with the dinosaurs and eavesdropping on the

stars. It had not come the first time he had climbed the tree to
reach the cave-that-was-a-den. He had been there several
times before, finding a perverse satisfaction at discovering so
unlikely a retreat. He would sit on the ledge that ran before
the cave and stare over the froth of treetop foliage that
clothed the plunging hillside, but afforded a glimpse of the
pond that lay in the flood plain of the river. He could not see
the river itself—one must stand on higher ground to see the
river.

He liked the cave and the ledge because it gave him
seclusion, a place cut off from the world, where he still might
see this restricted corner of the world but no one could see
him. This same sense of being shut out from the world had
appealed to the wildcats, he had told himself. And here, for
them, not only was seclusion but safety—and especially
safety for their young. There was no way the den could be
approached other than by climbing the tree.

He had first heard the creature when he had crawled into
the deepest part of the shallow cave to marvel at the little
heaps of bones and small shattered skulls where the wildcat
kittens, perhaps a century before, had crouched and snarled
at feast. Crouching where the baby wildcats once had
crouched, he had felt the presence welling up at him, coming
up to him from the depth of stone that lay far beneath him.
Only the presence at first, only the knowing that something
was down there. He had been sceptical at first, later on
believing. In time belief had become solid certainty.

He could record no words, of course, for he had never
heard any actual sound. But the intelligence and the knowing
came creeping through his body, through his fingers spread
flat upon the stone floor of the cave, through his knees, which
also pressed the stone. He absorbed it without hearing and
the more he absorbed the more he was convinced that deep in
the limestone, buried in one of the strata, an intelligence was
trapped. And finally the time came when he could catch
fragments of thoughts—the edges of the *living* in the
sentience encysted in the rock.

What he heard he did not understand. This very lack of
understanding was significant. If he had understood he
would have put his discovery down to his imagination. As
matters stood he had no knowledge that could possibly have
served as a springboard to imagine the thing of which he was

made aware. He caught an awareness of tangled life relationships which made no sense at all—none of which could be understood, but which lay in tiny, tangled fragments of outrageous (yet simple) information no human mind could quite accept. And he was made to know the empty hollowness of distances so vast that the mind reeled at the very hint of them and of the naked emptiness in which those distances must lie. Even in his eavesdropping on the stars he had never experienced such devastating concepts of the other-where-and-when. There was other information, scraps and bits he sensed faintly that might fit into mankind's knowledge. But he never found enough to discover the proper slots for their insertion into the mass of mankind's knowledge. The greater part of what he sensed, however, was simply beyond his grasp and perhaps beyond the grasp of any human. But even so his mind would catch and hold it in all its incomprehensibility and it would lie there festering amid his human thoughts.

They were or it was, he knew, not trying to talk with him—undoubtedly they (or it) did not know that such a thing as a man existed, let alone himself. But whether the creature (or creatures—he found the collective singular easier) simply was thinking or might, in its loneliness, be talking to itself—or whether it might be trying to communicate with something other than himself, he could not determine.

Thinking about it, sitting on the ledge before the cave, he had tried to make some logic of his find, had tried to find a way in which the creature's presence might be best explained. And while he could not be sure of it—in fact, had no data whatsoever to bolster his belief—he came to think that in some far geologic day when a shallow sea had lain upon this land, a ship from space had fallen into the sea to be buried deeply in the mud that in later millennia had hardened into limestone. In this manner the ship had become entrapped and so remained to this very day. He realized his reasoning held flaws—for one thing, the pressure involved in the fashioning of the stone must have been so great as to have crushed and flattened any ship unless it should be made of some material far beyond the range of man's technology.

Accident, he wondered, or a way of hiding? Trapped or planned? He had no way of knowing and further speculation was ridiculous, based as it necessarily must be upon earlier assumptions that were entirely without support.

Scrambling up the hillside, he finally reached the point where he could see that, in all truth, the tree had been cut down. It had fallen downhill and slid for thirty feet or so before it came to rest, its branches entangled with the trunks of other trees which had slowed its plunge. The stump stood raw, the whiteness of its wood shining in the greyness of the day. A deep cut had been made in the downhill side of it and the final felling had been accomplished by a saw. Little piles of brownish sawdust lay beside the stump. A two-man saw, he thought.

From where Daniels stood the hill slanted down at an abrupt angle but just ahead of him, just beyond the stump, was a curious mound that broke the hillside slope. In some earlier day, more than likely, great masses of stone had broken from the cliff face and piled up at its base, to be masked in time by the soil that came about from the forest litter. Atop the mound grew a clump of birch, their powdery white trunks looking like huddled ghosts against the darkness of the other trees.

The cutting of the tree, he told himself once again, had been a senseless piece of business. The tree was worthless and had served no particular purpose except as a road to reach the den. Had someone, he wondered, known that he used it to reach the den and cut it out of malice? Or had someone, perhaps, hidden something in the cave and then cut down the tree so there would be no way in which to reach it?

But who would hold him so much malice as to come out on a night raging with wind, working by lantern light, risking his life, to cut down the tree? Ben Adams? Ben was sore because Daniels would not permit hunting on his land but surely that was no sufficient reason for this rather laborious piece of petty spite.

The other alternative—that something hidden in the cave had caused the tree's destruction—seemed more likely, although the very cutting of the tree would serve to advertise the strangeness of the place.

Daniels stood puzzled, shaking his head. Then he thought of a way to find out some answers. The day still was young and he had nothing else to do.

He started climbing up the hill, heading for his barn to pick up some rope.

IV

There was nothing in the cave. It was exactly as it had been before. A few autumn leaves had blown into the far corners. Chips of weathered stone had fallen from the rocky overhang, tiny evidences of the endless process of erosion which had formed the cave and in a few thousand years from now might wipe it out.

Standing on the narrow ledge in front of the cave, Daniels stared out across the valley and was surprised at the change of view that had resulted from the cutting of the tree. The angles of vision seemed somehow different and the hillside itself seemed changed. Startled, he examined the sweep of the slope closely and finally satisfied himself that all that had changed was his way of seeing it. He was seeing trees and contours that earlier had been masked.

His rope hung from the outcurving rock face that formed the roof of the cave. It was swaying gently in the wind and, watching it, Daniels recalled that earlier in the day he had felt no wind. But now one had sprung up from the west. Below him the treetops were bending to it.

He turned towards the west and felt the wind on his face and a breath of chill. The feel of the wind faintly disturbed him, rousing some atavistic warning that came down from the days when naked roaming bands of protomen had turned, as he turned now, to sniff the coming weather. The wind might mean that a change of weather could be coming and perhaps he should clamber up the rope and head back for the farm.

But he felt a strange reluctance to leave. It had been often so, he recalled. For here was a wild sort of refuge which barred out the world and the little world that it let in was a different kind—a more primal and more basic and less complicated world than the one he'd fled from.

A flight of mallards came winging up from the pond in the river valley, arrowing above the treetops, banking and slanting up the long curve of the bluff and then, having cleared the bluff top, wheeling gracefully back towards the river. He watched them until they dipped down behind the trees that fringed the unseen river.

Now it was time to go. There was no use waiting longer. It had been a fool's errand in the first place; he had been wrong to let himself think something might be hidden in the cave.

He turned back to the rope and the rope was gone.

For a moment he stared stupidly at the point along the cliff face where the rope had hung, swaying in the breeze. Then he searched for some sign of it, although there was little area to search. The rope could have slid, perhaps, for a short distance along the edge of the overhanging mass of rock but it seemed incredible that it could have slid far enough to have vanished from his sight.

The rope was new, strong, and he had tied it securely to the oak tree on the bluff above the cliff, snugging it tightly around the trunk and testing the knot to make certain that it would not slip.

And now the rope was gone. There had to be a human hand in this. Someone had come along, seen the rope and quietly drawn it up and now was crouched on the bluff above him, waiting for his frightened outburst when he found himself stranded. It was the sort of crude practical joke that any number of people in the community might believe to be the height of humor. The thing to do, of course, was to pay no attention, to remain quiet and wait until the joke would pall upon the jokester.

So he hunkered down upon the ledge and waited. Ten minutes, he told himself, or at least fifteen, would wear out the patience of the jokester. Then the rope would come down and he could climb up and go back to the house. Depending upon who the joker might turn out to be, he'd take him home and pour a drink for him and the two of them, sitting in the kitchen, would have a laugh together.

He found that he was hunching his shoulders against the wind, which seemed to have a sharper bite than when he first had noticed it. It was shifting from the west to north and that was no good.

Squatting on the ledge, he noticed that beads of moisture had gathered upon his jacket sleeve—not a result of rain, exactly, but of driven mist. If the temperature should drop a bit the weather might turn nasty.

He waited, huddled, listening for a sound—a scuffling of feet through leaves, the snap of broken brush—that would betray the presence of someone on the clifftop. But there was no sound at all. The day was muffled. Even the branches of the trees beneath his perch, swaying in the wind, swayed without their usual creaks and groans.

Fifteen minutes must have passed and there had been no sound from atop the cliff. The wind had increased somewhat and when he twisted his head to one side to try to look up he could feel the soft slash of the driving mist against his cheek.

He could keep silent no longer in hope of waiting out the jokester. He sensed, in a sudden surge of panic, that time was running out on him.

"Hey, up there—" he shouted.

He waited and there was no response.

He shouted again, more loudly this time.

Ordinarily the cliff across the hollow should have bounced back echoes. But now there were no echoes and his shout seemed dampened, as if this wild place had erected some sort of fence to hem him in.

He shouted again and the misty world took his voice and swallowed it.

A hissing sound started. Daniels saw it was caused by tiny pellets of ice streaming through the branches of the trees. From one breath to another the driven mist had turned to ice.

He walked back and forth on the ledge in front of the cave, twenty feet at most, looking for some way to escape. The ledge went out into space and then sheered off. The slanting projection of rock came down from above. He was neatly trapped.

He moved back into the cave and hunkered down. Here he was protected from the wind and he felt, even through his rising panic, a certain sense of snugness. The cave was not yet cold. But the temperature must be dropping and dropping rather swiftly or the mist would not have turned to ice. He wore a light jacket and could not make a fire. He did not smoke and never carried matches.

For the first time he faced the real seriousness of his position. It might be days before anyone noticed he was missing. He had few visitors and no one had ever paid too much attention to him. Even if someone should find that he was missing and a hunt for him were launched, what were the chances that he would be found? Who would think to look in this hidden cave? How long, he wondered, could a man survive in cold and hunger?

If he could not get out of here, and soon, what about his livestock? The cows would be heading home from pasture, seeking shelter from the storm, and there would be no one there to let them into the barn. If they were not milked for a day or two they would be tormented by swollen udders. The hogs and chickens would go unfed. A man, he thought, had no right to take the kind of chance he had taken when so many living creatures were dependent on him.

He crawled farther back into the cave and stretched himself out on his belly, wedging himself into its deepest recess, an ear laid against the stone.

The creature still was there—of course it still was there. It was trapped even more securely than himself, held down by, perhaps, several hundred feet of solid rock, which had been built up most deliberately through many millions of years.

It was remembering again. In its mind was another place and, while part of that flow of memory was blurred and wavy, the rest was starkly clear. A great dark plain of rock, one great slab of rock, ran to a far horizon and above that far horizon a reddish sun came up and limned against the great red ball of rising sun was a hinted structure—an irregularity of the horizon that suggested a place. A castle, perhaps, or a city or a great cliff dwelling—it was hard to make out what it was or to be absolutely sure that it was anything at all.

Home? Was that black expanse of rock the spaceport of the old home planet? Or might it be only a place the creature had visited before it had come to Earth? A place so fantastic, perhaps, that it lingered in the mind.

Other things mixed into the memory, sensory symbols that might have applied to personalities, life forms, smells, tastes. Although he could be wrong, Daniels knew, in supplying this entrapped creature with human sensory preceptions, these human sensory perceptions were the only ones he knew about.

And now, listening in on the memory of that flat black expanse of rock and imagining the rising sun which outlined the structure of the far horizon, Daniels did something he had never tried to do before. He tried to talk back to the buried creature, tried to let it know that someone was listening and had heard, that it was not as lonely and as isolated as it might have thought it was.

He did not talk with his tongue—that would have been a

senseless thing to do. Sound could never carry through those many feet of stone. He talked with his mind instead.

Hello, down there, he said. *This is a friend of yours. I've been listening to you for a long, long time and I hope that you can hear me. If you can, let us talk together. Let me try to make you understand about myself and the world I live in and you tell me about yourself and the kind of world you lived in and how you came to be where you are and if there is anything I can do for you, any help that I can give.*

He said that much and no more. Having spoken, he continued lying with his ear against the hard cave floor, listening to find out if the creature might have heard him. But the creature apparently had not heard or, having heard, ignored him as something not worth its attention. It went on thinking about the place where the dull-red sun was rising above the horizon.

It had been foolish, and perhaps presumptuous, he knew, for him to have tried to speak to it. He had never tried before; he had simply listened. And he had never tried, either, to speak to those others who talked among the stars—again he'd simply listened.

What new dimension had been added to himself, he wondered, that would have permitted him to try to communicate with the creature? Had the possibility that he was about to die moved him?

The creature in the stone might not be subject to death—it might be immortal.

He crawled out of the far recess of the cave and crept out to where he had room to hunker down.

The storm had worsened. The ice now was mixed with snow and the temperature had fallen. The ledge in front of the cave was filmed with slippery ice. If a man tried to walk it he'd go plunging down the cliff face to his death.

The wind was blowing harder. The branches of the trees were waving and a storm of leaves was banking down the hillside, flying with the ice and snow.

From where he squatted he could see the topmost branches of the clump of birches which grew atop the mound just beyond where the cave tree had stood. And these branches, it seemed to him, were waving about far more violently than could be accounted for by wind. They were lashing wildly from one side to the other and even as he watched they seemed to rise higher in the air, as if the trees, in some great agony, were raising their branches far above their heads in a plea for mercy.

Daniels crept forward on his hands and knees and thrust his head out to see down to the base of the cliff.

Not only the topmost branches of the clump of birches were swaying but the entire clump seemed to be in motion, thrashing about as if some unseen hand were attempting to wrench it from the soil. But even as he thought this, he saw that the ground itself was in agitation, heaving up and out. It looked exactly as if someone had taken a time-lapse movie of the development of a frost boil with the film now being run at a normal speed. The ground was heaving up and the clump was heaving with it. A shower of gravel and other debris was flowing down the slope, loosened by the heaving of the ground. A boulder broke away and crashed down the hill, crushing brush and shrubs and leaving hideous scars.

Daniels watched in horrified fascination.

Was he witnessing, he wondered, some wonderfully speeded-up geological process? He tried to pinpoint exactly what kind of process it might be. He knew of none that seemed to fit. The mound kept on heaving upward, splintering outward from its center. A great flood of loose debris was now pouring down the slope, leaving a path of brown in the whiteness of the fallen snow. The clump of birch tipped over and went skidding down the slope and out of the place where it had stood a shape emerged.

Not a solid shape, but a hazy one that looked as if someone had scraped some stardust from the sky and moulded it into a ragged, shifting form that did not set into any definite pattern, that kept shifting and changing, although it did not entirely lose all resemblance to the shape in which it might originally have been molded. It looked as a loose conglomeration of atoms might look if atoms could be seen. It sparkled softly in the greyness of the day and despite its seeming insubstantiality it apparently had some strength—for it continued to push itself from the shattered mound until finally it stood free of it.

Having freed itself, it drifted up towards the ledge.

Strangely, Daniels felt no fear, only a vast curiosity. He tried to make out what the drifting shape was but he could not be sure.

As it reached the ledge and moved slightly above it he drew back to crouch within the cave. The shape drifted in a couple of feet or so and perched on the ledge—either perched upon it or floated just above it.

You spoke, the sparkling shape said to Daniels.

It was not a question, nor a statement either, really, and it was not really speaking. It sounded exactly like the talk Daniels had heard when he'd listened to the stars.

You spoke to it, said the shape, *as if you were a friend* (although the word was not friend but something else entirely, something warm and friendly). *You offered help to it. Is there help that you can give?*

The question at least was clear enough.

"I don't know," said Daniels. "Not right now, there isn't. But in a hundred years from now, perhaps—are you hearing me? Do you know what I am saying?"

You say there can be help, the creature said, *but only after time. Please, what is that time?*

"A hundred years," said Daniels. "When the planet goes around the star one hundred times."

One hundred? asked the creature.

Daniels held up the fingers of both hands. "Can you see my fingers? The appendages on the tips of my arms?"

See? the creature asked.

"Sense them. Count them."

Yes, I can count them.

"They number ten," said Daniels. "Ten times that many of them would be a hundred."

It is no great span of time, the creature said. *What kind of help by then?*

"You know genetics? How a creature comes into being, how it knows what kind of thing it is to become, how it grows, how it knows how to grow and what to become. The amino acids that make up the ribonucleic acids and provide the key to the kind of cells it grows and what their functions are."

I do not know your terms, the creature said, *but I understand. So you know of this? You are not, then, a brute wild creature, like the other life that simply stands and the others that burrow in the ground and climb the standing life forms and run along the ground.*

It did not come out like this, of course. The words were there—or meanings that had the feel of words—but there were pictures as well of trees, of burrowing mice, of squirrels, of rabbits, of the lurching woodchuck and the running fox.

"Not I," said Daniels, "but others of my kind. I know but little of it. There are others who spend all their time in the study of it."

The other perched on the ledge and said nothing more. Beyond it the trees whipped in the wind and the snow came whirling down. Daniels huddled back from the ledge, shivered in the cold and wondered if this thing upon the ledge could be hallucination.

But as he thought it, the thing began to talk again, although this time it did not seem to be talking to him. It talked, rather, as the creature in the stone had talked, remembering. It communicated, perhaps, something he was not meant to know, but Daniels had no way of keeping from knowing. Sentience flowed from the creature and impacted on his mind, filling all his mind, barring all else, so that it seemed as if it were he and not this other who was remembering.

V

First there was space—endless, limitless space, so far from everything, so brutal, so frigid, so uncaring that it numbed the mind, not so much from fear or loneliness as from the realization that in this eternity of space the thing that was himself was dwarfed to an insignificance no yardstick could measure. So far from home, so lost, so directionless—and yet not entirely directionless, for there was a trace, a scent, a spoor, a knowing that could not be expressed or understood or even guessed at in the framework of humanity; a trace, a scent, a spoor that showed the way, no matter how dimly or how hopelessly, that something else had taken at some other time. And a mindless determination, an unflagging devotion, a primal urgency that drove him on that faint, dim trail, to follow where it might lead, even to the end of time or space, or the both of them together, never to fail or quit or falter until the trail had finally reached an end or had been wiped out by whatever winds might blow through empty space.

There was something here, Daniels told himself, that for

all its alienness, still was familiar, a factor that should lend itself to translation into human terms and thus establish some sort of link between this remembering alien mind and his human mind.

The emptiness and the silence, the cold uncaring went on and on and on and there seemed no end to it. But he came to understand there had to be an end to it and that the end was here, in these tangled hills above the ancient river. And after the almost endless time of waiting, of having reached the end, of having gone as far as one might go and then settling down to wait with an ageless patience that never would grow weary.

You spoke of help, the creature said to him. *Why help? You do not know this other. Why should you want to help?*

"It is alive," said Daniels. "It's alive and I'm alive and is that not enough?"

I do not know, the creature said.

"I think it is," said Daniels.

And how could you help?

"I've told you about this business of genetics. I don't know if I can explain—"

I have the terms from your mind, the creature said. *The genetic code.*

"Would this other one, the one beneath the stone, the one you guard—"

Not guard, the creature said. *The one I wait for.*

"You will wait for long."

I am equipped for waiting. I have waited long. I can wait much longer.

"Someday," Daniels said, "the stone will erode away. But you need not wait that long. Does this other creature know its genetic code?"

It knows, the creature said. *It knows far more than I.*

"But all of it," insisted Daniels. "Down to the last linkage, the final ingredient, the sequences of all the billions of—"

It knows, the creature said. *The first requisite of all life is to understand itself.*

"And it could—it would—be willing to give us that information, to supply us its genetic code?"

You are presumptuous, said the sparkling creature (although the word was harder than presumptuous). *That is information no thing gives another. It is indecent and obscene* (here again the words were not exactly indecent and obscene). *It involves the giving of one's self into another's hands. It is an ultimate and purposeless surrender.*

"Not surrender," Daniels said. "A way of escaping from its imprisonment. In time, in the hundred years of which I told you, the people of my race could take that genetic code and construct another creature exactly like the first. Duplicate it with exact preciseness."

But it still would be in stone.

"Only one of it. The original one. That original could wait for the erosion of the rock. But the other one, its duplicate, could take up life again."

And what, Daniels wondered, if the creature in the stone did not wish for rescue? What if it had deliberately placed itself beneath the stone? What if it simply sought protection and sanctuary? Perhaps, if it wished, the creature could get out of where it was as easily as this other one—or this other thing—had risen from the mound.

No, it cannot, said the creature squatting on the ledge. *I was careless. I went to sleep while waiting and I slept too long.*

And that would have been a long sleep, Daniels told himself. A sleep so long that dribbling soil had mounded over it, that fallen boulders, cracked off the cliff by frost, had been buried in the soil and that a clump of birch had sprouted and grown into trees thirty feet high. There was a difference here in time rate that he could not comprehend.

But some of the rest, he told himself, he has sensed—the devoted loyalty and the mindless patience of the creature that tracked another far among the stars. He knew he was right, for the mind of that other thing, that devoted star-dog perched upon the ledge, came into him and fastened on his mind and for a moment the two of them, the two minds, for all their differences, merged into a single mind in a gesture of fellowship and basic understanding, as if for the first time in what must have been millions of years this baying hound from outer space had found a creature that could understand its duty and its purpose.

"We could try to dig it out," said Daniels. "I had thought of that, of course, but I was afraid that it would be injured. And it would be hard to convince anyone—"

No, said the creature, *digging would not do. There is much you do not understand. But this other proposal that*

*you have, that has great merit. You say you do not have the
knowledge of genetics to take this action now. Have you
talked to others of your kind?*

"I talked to one," said Daniels, "and he would not listen.
He thought I was mad. But he was not, after all, the man I
should have spoken to. In time I could talk with others but
not right now. No matter how much I might want to—I can't.
For they would laugh at me and I could not stand their
laughter. But in a hundred years or somewhat less I could—"

But you will not exist a hundred years, said the faithful
dog. *You are a short-lived species. Which might explain your
rapid rise. All life here is short-lived and that gives evolution
a chance to build intelligence. When I first came here I found
but mindless entities.*

"You are right," said Daniels. "I can live no hundred
years. Even from the very start, I could not live a hundred
years, and better than half of my life is gone. Perhaps much
more than half of it. For unless I can get out of this cave I will
be dead in days."

Reach out, said the sparkling one. *Reach out and touch
me, being.*

Slowly Daniels reached out. His hand went through the
sparkle and the shine and he had no sense of matter—it was
as if he'd moved his hand through nothing but air.

You see, the creature said, *I cannot help you. There is no
way for our energies to interact. I am sorry, friend.* (It was not
friend, exactly, but it was good enough, and it might have
been, Daniels thought, a great deal more than friend.)

"I am sorry, too," said Daniels. "I would like to live."

Silence fell between them, the soft and brooding silence of
a snow-laden afternoon with nothing but the trees and the
rock and the hidden little life to share the silence with them.

It had been for nothing, then, Daniels told himself, this
meeting with a creature from another world. Unless he could
somehow get off this ledge there was nothing he could do.
Although why he should so concern himself with the rescue
of the creature in the stone he could not understand. Surely
whether he himself lived or died should be of more
importance to him than that his death would foreclose any
chance of help to the buried alien.

"But it may not be for nothing," he told the sparkling
creature. "Now that you know—"

My knowing, said the creature, *will have no effect. There are others from the stars who would have the knowledge— but even if I could contact them they would pay no attention to me. My position is too lowly to converse with the greater ones. My only hope would be people of your kind, and if I'm not mistaken, only with yourself. For I catch the edge of thought that you are the only one who really understands. There is no other of your race who could even be aware of me.*

Daniels nodded. It was entirely true. No other human existed whose brain had been jumbled so fortunately as to have acquired the abilities he held. He was the only hope for the creature in the stone and even such hope as he represented might be very slight, for before it could be made effective he must find someone who would listen and believe. And that belief must reach across the years to a time when genetic engineering was considerably advanced beyond its present state.

If you could manage to survive the present crisis, said the hound from outer space, *I might bring to bear certain energies and techniques—sufficiently for the project to be carried through. But, as you must realize, I cannot supply the means to survive this crisis.*

"Someone may come along," said Daniels. "They might hear me if I yelled every now and then."

He began yelling every now and then and received no answer. His yells were muffled by the storm and it was unlikely, he knew, that there would be men abroad at a time like this. They'd be safe beside their fires.

The sparkling creature still perched upon the ledge when Daniels slumped back to rest. The other made an indefinite sort of shape that seemed much like a lopsided Christmas tree standing in the snow.

Daniels told himself not to go to sleep. He must close his eyes only for a moment, then snap them open—he must not let them stay shut for then sleep would come upon him. He should beat his arms across his chest for warmth—but his arms were heavy and did not want to work.

He felt himself sliding prone to the cave floor and fought to drive himself erect. But his will to fight was thin and the rock was comfortable. So comfortable, he thought, that he could afford a moment's rest before forcing himself erect. And the funny thing about it was that the cave floor had turned to mud and water and the sun was shining and he seemed warm again.

He rose with a start and he saw that he was standing in a wide expanse of water no deeper than his ankles, black ooze underfoot.

There was no cave and no hill in which the cave might be. There was simply this vast sheet of water and behind him, less than thirty feet away, the muddy beach of a tiny island—a muddy, rocky island, with smears of sickly green clinging to the rocks.

He was in another time, he knew, but not in another place. Always when he slipped through time he came to rest on exactly the same spot upon the surface of the earth that he had occupied when the change had come.

And standing there he wondered once again, as he had many times before, what strange mechanism operated to shift him bodily in space so that when he was transported to a time other than his own he did not find himself buried under, say, twenty feet of rock or soil or suspended twenty feet above the surface.

But now, he knew, was no time to think or wonder. By a strange quirk of circumstance he was no longer in the cave and it made good sense to get away from where he was as swiftly as he could. For if he stayed standing where he was he might snap back unexpectedly to his present and find himself still huddled in the cave.

He turned clumsily about, his feet tangling in the muddy bottom, and lunged towards the shore. The going was hard but he made it and went up the slimy stretch of muddy beach until he could reach the tumbled rocks and could sit and rest.

His breathing was difficult. He gulped great lungfuls and the air had a strange taste to it, not like normal air.

He sat on the rock, gasping for breath, and gazed out across the sheet of water shining in the high, warm sun. Far out he caught sight of a long, humping swell and watched it coming in. When it reached the shore it washed up the muddy incline almost to his feet. Far out on the glassy surface another swell was forming.

The sheet of water was greater, he realized, than he had first imagined. This was also the first time in his wanderings through the past that he had ever come upon any large body of water. Always before he had emerged on dry land whose general contours had been recognizable—and there had always been the river flowing through the hills.

Here nothing was recognizable. This was a totally different place and there could be no question that he had been projected further back in time than ever before—back to the day of some great epicontinental sea, back to a time, perhaps, when the atmosphere had far less oxygen than it would have in later eons. More than likely, he thought, he was very close in time to that boundary line where life for a creature such as he would be impossible. Here there apparently was sufficient oxygen, although a man must pump more air into his lungs than he would normally. Go back a few million years and the oxygen might fall to the point where it would be insufficient. Go a little farther back and find no free oxygen at all.

Watching the beach, he saw the little things skittering back and forth, seeking refuge in spume-whitened piles of drift or popping into tiny burrows. He put his hand down on the rock on which he sat and scrubbed gently at a patch of green. It slid off the rock and clung to his flesh, smearing his palm with a slimy gelatinous mess that felt disgusting and unclean.

Here, then, was the first of life to dwell upon the land—scarcely creatures as yet, still clinging to the edge of water, afraid and unequipped to wander too far from the side of that wet and gentle mother which, from the first beginning, had nurtured life. Even the plants still clung close to the sea, existing, perhaps, only upon rocky surfaces so close to the beach that occasional spray could reach them.

Daniels found that now he did not have to gasp quite so much for breath. Ploughing through the mud up to the rock had been exhausting work in an oxygen-poor atmosphere. But sitting quietly on the rocks, he could get along all right.

Now that the blood had stopped pounding in his head he became aware of silence. He heard one sound only, the soft lapping of the water against the muddy beach, a lonely effect that seemed to emphasize rather than break the silence.

Never before in his life, he realized, had he heard so little sound. Back in the other worlds he had known there had been not one noise, but many, even on the quietest days. But here there was nothing to make a sound—no trees, no animals, no

insects, no birds—just the water running to the far horizon
and the bright sun in the sky.

For the first time in many months he knew again that
sense of out-of-placeness, of not belonging, the feeling of
being where he was not wanted and had no right to be, an
intruder in a world that was out of bounds, not for him alone
but for anything that was more complex or more sophisticat-
ed than the little skitterers on the beach.

He sat beneath the alien sun, surrounded by the alien
water, watching the little things that in eons yet to come
would give rise to such creatures as himself, and tried to feel
some sort of kinship to the skitterers. But he could feel no
kinship.

And suddenly in this place of one-sound-only there came
a throbbing, faint but clear and presently louder, pressing
down against the water, beating at the little island—a sound
out of the sky.

Daniels leaped to his feet and looked up and the ship was
there, plummeting down towards him. But not a ship of solid
form, it seemed—rather a distorted thing, as if many planes
of light (if there could be such things as planes of light) had
been slapped together in a haphazard sort of way.

A throbbing came from it that set the atmosphere to
howling and the planes of light kept changing shape or
changing places, so that the ship, from one moment to the
next, never looked the same.

It had been dropping fast to start with but now it was
slowing down as it continued to fall, ponderously and with
massive deliberation, straight towards the island.

Daniels found himself crouching, unable to jerk his eyes
and senses away from this mass of light and thunder that
came out of the sky.

The sea and mud and rock, even in the full light of the sun,
were flickering with the flashing that came from the shifting
of the planes of light. Watching it through eyes squinted
against the flashes, Daniels saw that if the ship were to drop
to the surface it would not drop upon the island, as he first
had feared, but a hundred feet or so offshore.

Not more than fifty feet above the water the great ship
stopped and hovered and a bright thing came from it. The

object hit the water with a splash but did not go under, coming to rest upon the shallow, muddy bottom of the sea, with a bit less than half of it above the surface. It was a sphere, a bright and shiny globe against which the water lapped, and even with the thunder of the ship beating at his ears, Daniels imagined he could hear the water lapping at the sphere.

Then a voice spoke above this empty world, above the throbbing of the ship, the imagined lapping sound of water, a sad, judicial voice—although it could not have been a voice, for any voice would have been too puny to be heard. But the words were there and there was no doubt of what they said:

Thus, according to the verdict and the sentence, you are here deported and abandoned upon this barren planet, where it is most devoutly hoped you will find the time and opportunity to contemplate your sins and especially the sin of (and here were words and concepts Daniels could not understand, hearing them only as a blur of sound—but the sound of them, or something in the sound of them, was such as to turn his blood to ice and at the same time fill him with a disgust and a loathing such as he'd never known before). *It is regrettable, perhaps, that you are immune to death, for much as we might detest ourselves for doing it, it would be a kinder course to discontinue you and would serve better than this course to exact our purpose, which is to place you beyond all possibility of ever having contact with any sort of life again. Here, beyond the farthest track of galactic intercourse, on this uncharted planet, we can only hope that our purpose will be served. And we urge upon you such self-examination that if, by some remote chance, in some unguessed time, you should be freed through ignorance or malice, you shall find it within yourself so to conduct your existence as not to meet or merit such fate again. And now, according to our law, you may speak any final words you wish.*

The voice ceased and after a while came another. And while the terminology was somewhat more involved than Daniels could grasp, their idiom translated easily into human terms.

Go screw yourself, it said.

The throbbing deepened and the ship began to move straight up into the sky. Daniels watched it until the thunder died and the ship itself was a fading twinkle in the blue.

He rose from his crouch and stood erect, trembling and weak. Groping behind him for the rock, he found it and sat down again.

Once again the only sound was the lapping of the water on the shore. He could not hear, as he had imagined that he could, the water against the shining sphere that lay a hundred feet offshore. The sun blazed down out of the sky and glinted on the sphere and Daniels found that once again he was gasping for his breath.

Without a doubt, out there in the shallow water, on the mudbank that sloped up to the island, lay the creature in the stone. And how then had it been possible for him to be transported across the hundreds of millions of years to this one microsecond of time that held the answer to all the questions he had asked about the intelligence beneath the limestone? It could not have been sheer coincidence, for this was coincidence of too large an order ever to come about. Had he somehow, subconsciously, gained more knowledge than he had been aware of from the twinkling creature that had perched upon the ledge? For a moment, he remembered, their minds had met and mingled—at that moment had there occurred a transmission of knowledge, unrecognized, buried in some corner of himself? Or was he witnessing the operation of some sort of psychic warning system set up to scare off any future intelligence that might be tempted to liberate this abandoned and marooned being?

And what about the twinkling creature? Could some hidden, unguessed good exist in the thing imprisoned in the sphere—for it to have commanded the loyalty and devotion of the creature on the ledge beyond the slow erosion of geologic ages? The question raised another: What were good and evil? Who was there to judge?

The evidence of the twinkling creature was, of course, no evidence at all. No human being was so utterly depraved that he could not hope to find a dog to follow him and guard him even to the death.

More to wonder at was what had happened within his own jumbled brain that could send him so unerringly to the moment of a vital happening. What more would he find in it to astonish and confound him? How far along the path to ultimate understanding might it drive him? And what was the purpose of that driving?

He sat on the rock and gasped for breath. The sea lay flat and calm beneath the blazing sun, its only motion the long swells running in to break around the sphere and on the beach. The little skittering creatures ran along the mud and he rubbed his palm against his trouser leg, trying to brush off the green and slimy scum.

He could wade out, he thought, and have a closer look at the sphere lying in the mud. But it would be a long walk in such an atmosphere and he could not chance it—for he must be nowhere near the cave up in that distant future when he popped back to his present.

Once the excitement of knowing where he was, the sense of out-of-placeness, had worn off, this tiny mud-flat island was a boring place. There was nothing but the sky and sea and the muddy beach; there was nothing ever happened, or was about to happen once the ship had gone away and the great event had ended. Much was going on, of course, that in future ages would spell out to quite a lot—but it was mostly happening out of sight, down at the bottom of this shallow sea. The skittering things, he thought, and the slimy growth upon the rock were hardy, mindless pioneers of this distant day—awesome to look upon and think about but actually not too interesting.

He began drawing aimless patterns in the mud with the toe of one boot. He tried to make a tic-tac-toe layout but so much mud was clinging to his toe that it didn't quite come out.

And then, instead of drawing in the mud, he was scraping with his toe in fallen leaves, stiff with frozen sleet and snow.

The sun was gone and the scene was dark except for a glow from something in the woods just down the hill from him. Driving sheets of snow swirled into his face and he shivered. He pulled his jacket close about him and began to button it. A man, he thought, could catch his death of cold this way, shifting as quickly as he had shifted from a steaming mudbank to the whiplash chill of a northern blizzard.

The yellow glow still persisted on the slope below him and he could hear the sound of human voices. What was going on? He was fairly certain of where he was, a hundred feet or so above the place where the cliff began—there should be no one down there; there should not be a light.

He took a slow step down the hill, then hesitated. He ought not to be going down the hill—he should be heading straight for home. The cattle would be waiting at the barnyard gate, hunched against the storm, their coats covered with ice and snow, yearning for the warmth and shelter of the barn. The pigs would not have been fed, nor the chickens either. A man owed some consideration to his livestock.

But someone was down there, someone with a lantern, almost on the lip of the cliff. If the damn fools didn't watch out, they could slip and go plunging down into a hundred feet of space. Coon hunters more than likely, although this was not the kind of night to be out hunting coon. The coons would all be denned up.

But whoever they might be, he should go down and warn them.

He was halfway to the lantern, which appeared to be setting on the ground, when someone picked it up and held it high and Daniels saw and recognized the face of the man who held it.

Daniels hurried forward.

"Sheriff, what are you doing here?"

But he had the shamed feeling that he knew, that he should have known from the moment he had seen the light.

"Who is there?" the sheriff asked, wheeling swiftly and tilting the lanterns so that its rays were thrown in Daniels' direction. "Daniels," he gasped. "Good God, man, where have you been?"

"Just walking around," said Daniels weakly. The answer, he knew, was no good at all—but how could he tell anyone that he had just returned from a trip through time?

"Damn it," the sheriff said, disgusted. "We've been hunting you. Ben Adams got scared when he dropped over to your place and you weren't there. He knows how you go walking around in the woods and he was afraid something had happened to you. So he phoned me, and he and his boys began looking for you. We were afraid you had fallen or had been hurt somehow. A man wouldn't last the night in a storm like this."

"Where is Ben now?" asked Daniels.

The sheriff gestured down the hill and Daniels saw that two men, probably Adams' sons, had a rope snubbed around a tree and that the rope extended down over the cliff.

"He's down on the rope," the sheriff said. "Having a look in the cave. He felt somehow you might be in the cave."

"He had good reason to—" Daniels started to say but he had barely begun to speak when the night was rent by a shriek of terror. The shrieking did not stop. It kept on and on. The sheriff thrust the lantern at Daniels and hurried forward.

No guts, Daniels thought. A man who could be vicious enough to set up another for death, to trap him in a cave— but who, when the chips were down, could not go through with it and had to phone the sheriff to provide a witness to his good intentions—a man like that lacked guts.

The shrieks had fallen to moaning. The sheriff hauled on the rope, helped by one of Adams' sons. A man's head and shoulders appeared above the cliff top and the sheriff reached out and hauled him to safety.

Ben Adams collapsed on the ground and never stopped his moaning. The sheriff jerked him to his feet.

"What's the matter, Ben?"

"There's something down there," Adams screamed. "There is something in the cave—"

"Something, damn it? What would it be? A cat? A panther?"

"I never seen it. I just knew that it was there. I felt it. It was crouched back inside the cave."

"How could anything be in there? Someone cut down the tree. How could anything get into the cave?"

"I don't know," howled Adams. "It might have been in there when the tree was cut. It might have been trapped in there."

One of the sons was holding Ben erect and the sheriff moved away. The other son was pulling in the rope and neatly coiling it.

"Another thing," the sheriff said, "how come you thought Daniels might be in that cave? If the tree was cut down he couldn't have used a rope the way you did, for there wasn't any rope. If he had used a rope it would still have been there. I don't know what's going on—damned if I do. You down messing in that cave and Daniels comes walking out of the woods. I wish someone would tell me."

Adams, who had been hobbling forward, saw Daniels for the first time and came to a sudden halt.

"Where did you come from?" he demanded. "Here we been wearing out our guts trying to hunt you down and then—"

"Oh, go on home," the sheriff said in a disgusted tone of voice. "There's a fishy smell to this. It's going to take me a little while to get it figured out."

Daniels reached out his hand to the son who had finished coiling the rope.

"I believe that's my rope," he said.

Without protest, taken by surprise, the boy handed it to him.

"We'll cut across the woods," said Ben. "Home's closer that way."

"Good night, men," the sheriff said.

Slowly the sheriff and Daniels climbed the hill.

"Daniels," said the sheriff, "you were never out walking in this storm. If you had been you'd have had a whole lot more snow on you than shows. You look like you just stepped from a house."

"Maybe I wasn't exactly walking around," Daniels said.

"Would you mind telling me where you were? I don't mind doing my duty as I see it but I don't relish being made to look a fool while I'm doing it."

"Sheriff, I can't tell you. I'm sorry. I simply cannot tell you."

"All right, then. What about the rope?"

"It's my rope," said Daniels. "I lost it this afternoon."

"And I suppose you can't tell me about that, either."

"No, I guess I can't."

"You know," the sheriff said, "I've had a lot of trouble with Ben Adams through the years. I'd hate to think I was going to have trouble with you, too."

They climbed the hill and walked up to the house. The sheriff's car was parked out on the road.

"Would you come in?" asked Daniels. "I could find a drink."

The sheriff shook his head. "Some other time," he said. "Maybe soon. You figure there was something in that cave? Or was it just Ben's imagination? He's a flighty sort of critter."

"Maybe there wasn't anything," said Daniels, "but if Ben thought there was, what difference does it make? Thinking it might be just as real as if there were something there. All of us, sheriff, live with things walking by our sides no one else can see."

The sheriff shot a quick glance at him. "Daniels, what's with you?" he asked. "What is walking by your side or sniffing at your heels? Why did you bury yourself out here in this Godforsaken place? What is going on?"

He didn't wait for an answer. He got into his car, started it and headed down the road.

Daniels stood in the storm and watched the glowing taillights vanish in the murk of flying snow. He shook his head in bewilderment. The sheriff had asked a question and then had not waited for the answer. Perhaps because it was a question to which he did not want an answer.

Daniels turned and went up the snowy path to the house. He'd like some coffee and a bite to eat—but first he had to do the chores. He had to milk the cows and feed the pigs. The chickens must wait till morning—it was too late to feed the chickens. The cows would be waiting at the barn door. They had waited for a long time and it was not right to make them wait.

He opened the door and stepped into the kitchen.

Someone was waiting for him. It sat on the table or floated so close above it that it seemed to be sitting. The fire in the stove had gone out and the room was dark but the creature sparkled.

You saw? the creature asked.

"Yes," said Daniels. "I saw and heard. I don't know what to do. What is right or wrong? Who knows what's right or wrong?"

Not you, the creature said. *Not I. I can only wait. I can only keep the faith.*

Perhaps among the stars, thought Daniels, might be those who did know. Perhaps by listening to the stars, perhaps by trying to break in on their conversations and by asking questions, he might get an answer. Certainly there must be some universal ethics. A list, perhaps, of Universal Commandments. Maybe not ten of them. Maybe only two or three—but any number might be enough.

"I can't stay and talk," he said. "I have animals to take care of. Could you stick around? Later we can talk."

He fumbled for the lantern on the bench against the wall,

found the matches on the shelf. He lit the lantern and its feeble flame made a puddle of light in the darkness of the room.

You have others to take care of? asked the creature. *Others not quite like yourself? Others, trusting you, without your intelligence?*

"I guess you could say it that way," Daniels said. "I've never heard it put quite that way before."

Could I go along with you? the creature asked. *It occurs to me, just now, that in many ways we are very much alike.*

"Very much—" But with the sentence hanging in the air, Daniels stopped.

Not a hound, he told himself. Not the faithful dog. But the shepherd. Could that be it? Not the master but the long-lost lamb?

He reached out a hand towards the creature in a swift gesture of understanding, then pulled it back, remembering it was nothing he could touch.

He lifted the lantern and turned towards the door.

"Come along," he said.

Together the two of them went through the storm towards the barn and the waiting cows.

The Autumn Land

He sat on the porch, in the rocking chair, with the loose board creaking as he rocked. Across the street the old white-haired lady cut a bouquet of chrysanthemums in the never-ending autumn. Where he could see between the ancient houses to the distant woods and wastelands, a soft Indian-summer blue lay upon the land. The entire village was soft and quiet, as old things often are—a place constructed for a dreaming mind rather than a living being. It was an hour too early for his other old and shaky neighbor to come fumbling down the grassgrown sidewalk, tapping the bricks with his seeking cane. And he would not hear the distant children at their play until dusk had fallen—if he heard them then. He did not always hear them.

There were books to read, but he did not want to read them. He could go into the backyard and spade and rake the garden once again, reducing the soil to a finer texture to receive the seed when it could be planted—if it ever could be planted—but there was slight incentive in the further preparation of a seed bed against a spring that never came. Earlier, much earlier, before he knew about the autumn and the spring, he had mentioned garden seeds to the Milkman, who had been very much embarrassed.

He had walked the magic miles and left the world behind in bitterness and when he first had come here had been content to live in utter idleness, to be supremely idle and to feel no guilt or shame at doing absolutely nothing or as close to absolutely nothing as a man was able. He had come walking down the autumn street in the quietness and the golden sunshine, and the first person that he saw was the old lady who lived across the street. She had been waiting at the

236

gate of her picket fence as if she had known he would be coming, and she had said to him, "You're a new one come to live with us. There are not many come these days. That is your house across the street from me, and I know we'll be good neighbors." He had reached up his hand to doff his hat to her, forgetting that he had no hat. "My name is Nelson Rand," he'd told her. "I am an engineer. I will try to be a decent neighbor." He had the impression that she stood taller and straighter than she did, but old and bent as she might be there was a comforting graciousness about her. "You will please come in," she said. "I have lemonade and cookies. There are other people there, but I shall not introduce them to you." He waited for her to explain why she would not introduce him, but there was no explanation, and he followed her down the time-mellowed walk of bricks with great beds of asters and chrysanthemums, a mass of color on either side of it.

In the large, high-ceilinged living room, with its bay windows forming window seats, filled with massive furniture from another time and with a small blaze burning in the fireplace, she had shown him to a seat before a small table to one side of the fire and had sat down opposite him and poured the lemonade and passed the plate of cookies.

"You must pay no attention to them," she had told him. "They are all dying to meet you, but I shall not humor them."

It was easy to pay no attention to them, for there was no one there.

"The Major, standing over there by the fireplace," said his hostess, "with his elbow on the mantel, a most ungainly pose if you should ask me, is not happy with my lemonade. He would prefer a stronger drink. Please, Mr. Rand, will you not taste my lemonade? I assure you it is good. I made it myself. I have no maid, you see, and no one in the kitchen. I live quite by myself and satisfactorily, although my friends keep dropping in, sometimes more often than I like."

He tasted the lemonade, not without misgivings, and to his surprise it was lemonade and was really good, like the lemonade he had drunk when a boy at Fourth of July celebrations and at grade school picnics, and had never tasted since.

"It is excellent," he said.

"The lady in blue," his hostess said, "sitting in the chair by the window, lived here many years ago. She and I were friends, although she moved away some time ago and I am surprised that she comes back, which she often does. The infuriating thing is that I cannot recall her name, if I ever knew it. You don't know it, do you?"

"I am afraid I don't."

"Oh, of course, you wouldn't. I had forgotten. I forget so easily these days. You are a new arrival."

He had sat through the afternoon and drunk her lemonade and eaten her cookies, while she chattered on about her nonexistent guests. It was only when he had crossed the street to the house she had pointed out as his, with her standing on the stoop and waving her farewell, that he realized she had not told him her name. He did not know it even now.

How long had it been? he wondered, and realized he didn't know. It was this autumn business. How could a man keep track of time when it was always autumn?

It all had started on that day when he'd been driving across Iowa, heading for Chicago. No, he reminded himself, it had started with the thinnesses, although he had paid little attention to the thinnesses to begin with. Just been aware of them, perhaps as a strange condition of the mind, or perhaps an unusual quality to the atmosphere and light. As if the world lacked a certain solidity that one had come to expect, as if one were running along a mystic borderline between here and somewhere else.

He had lost his West Coast job when a government contract had failed to materialize. His company had not been the only one; there were many other companies that were losing contracts and there were a lot of engineers who walked the streets bewildered. There was a bare possibility of a job in Chicago, although he was well aware that by now it might be filled. Even if there were no job, he reminded himself, he was in better shape than a lot of other men. He was young and single, he had a few dollars in the bank, he had no house mortgage, no car payments, no kids to put through school. He had only himself to support—no family of any sort at all. The old, hard-fisted bachelor uncle who had taken him to raise when his parents had died in a car crash and had worked him hard on that stony, hilly Wisconsin farm, had receded deep into the past, becoming a dim, far figure that was hard to recognize. He had not liked his uncle, Rand remembered—had not hated him, simply had not liked him. He had shed no tears, he recalled, when the old man had been caught out in a pasture by a bull and gored to death. So now Rand was quite alone, not even holding the memories of a family.

He had been hoarding the little money that he had, for with a limited work record, with other men better qualified looking for the jobs, he realized that it might be some time before he could connect with anything. The beat-up wagon that he drove had space for sleeping, and he stopped at the little wayside parks along the way to cook his meals.

He had almost crossed the state, and the road had started its long winding through the bluffs that rimmed the Mississippi. Ahead he caught glimpses, at several turnings of the road, of smokestacks and tall structures that marked the city just ahead.

He emerged from the bluffs, and the city lay before him, a small industrial center that lay on either side the river. It was then that he felt and saw (if one could call it seeing) the thinness that he had seen before or had sensed before. There was about it, not exactly an alienness, but a sense of unreality, as if one were seeing the actuality of the scene through some sort of veil, with the edges softened and the angles flattened out, as if one might be looking at it as one would look at the bottom of a clear-water lake with a breeze gently ruffling the surface. When he had seen it before, he had attributed it to road fatigue and had opened the window to get a breath of air or had stopped the car and gotten out to walk up and down the road a while, and it had gone away.

But this time it was worse than ever, and he was somewhat frightened at it—not so much frightened at it as he was frightened of himself, wondering what might be wrong with him.

He pulled off to the side of the road, braking the car to a halt, and it seemed to him, even as he did it, that the shoulder of the road was rougher than he'd thought. As he pulled off the road, the thinness seemed to lessen, and he saw that the road had changed, which explained its roughness. The surface was pocked with chuckholes and blocks of concrete had been heaved up and other blocks were broken into pebbly shards.

He raised his eyes from the road to look at the city, and there was no city, only the broken stumps of a place that had somehow been destroyed. He sat with his hands frozen on the wheel, and in the silence—the deadly, unaccustomed silence—he heard the cawing of crows. Foolishly, he tried to remember the last time he had heard the caw of crows, and then he saw them, black specks that flapped just above the bluff top. There was something else as well—the trees. No longer trees, but only here and there blackened stumps. The stumps of a city and the stumps of trees, with the black, ash-like flecks of crows flapping over them.

Scarcely knowing what he did, he stumbled from the car. Thinking of it later, it had seemed a foolish thing to do, for the car was the only thing he knew, the one last link he had to reality. As he stumbled from it, he put his hand down in the seat, and beneath his hand he felt the solid, oblong object. His fingers closed upon it, and it was not until he was standing by the car that he realized what he held—the camera that had been lying in the seat beside him.

Sitting on the porch, with the loose floorboard creaking underneath the rocker, he remembered that he still had the pictures, although it had been a long time since he had thought of them—a long time, actually, since he'd thought of anything at all beyond his life, day to day, in this autumn land. It was as though he had been trying to keep himself from thinking, attempting to keep his mind in neutral, to shut out what he knew—or, more precisely perhaps, what he thought he knew.

He did not consciously take the pictures, although afterwards he had tried to tell himself he did (but never quite convincing himself that this was entirely true), compliment-ing himself in a wry sort of way for providing a piece of evidence that his memory alone never could have provided. For a man can think so many things, daydream so many things, imagine so many things that he can never trust his mind.

The entire incident, when he later thought of it, was hazy, as if the reality of that blasted city lay in some strange dimension of experience that could not be explained, or even rationalized. He could remember only vaguely the camera at his eyes and the clicking as the shutter snapped. He did recall the band of people charging down the hill toward him and his mad scramble for the car, locking the door behind him and putting the car in gear, intent on steering a zigzag course along the broken pavement to get away from the screaming humans who were less than a hundred feet away.

But as he pulled off the shoulder, the pavement was no longer broken. It ran smooth and level toward the city that was no longer blasted. He pulled off the road again and sat limply, beaten, and it was only after many minutes that he could proceed again, going very slowly because he did not trust himself, shaken as he was, to drive at greater speed.

He planned to cross the river and continue to Chicago, getting there that night, but now his plans were changed. He was too shaken up and, besides, there were the films. And he needed time to think, he told himself, a lot of time to think.

He found a roadside park a few miles outside the city and pulled into it, parking alongside an outdoor grill and an old-fashioned pump. He got some wood from the small supply he carried in the back and built a fire. He hauled out the box with his cooking gear and food, fixed the coffee pot, set a pan upon the grill and cracked three eggs into it.

When he had pulled off the road, he had seen the man walking along the roadside; and now, as he cracked the eggs, he saw that the man had turned into the park and was walking toward the car. The man came up to the pump.

"Does this thing work?" he asked.

Rand nodded. "I got water for the pot," he said. "Just now."

"It's a hot day," said the man.

He worked the pump handle up and down.

"Hot for walking," he said.

"You been walking far?"

"The last six weeks," he said.

Rand had a closer look at him. The clothes were old and worn, but fairly clean. He had shaved a day or two before. His hair was long—not that he wore it long, but from lack of barbering.

Water gushed from the spout and the man cupped his hands under it, bent to drink.

"That was good," he finally said. "I was thirsty."

"How are you doing for food?" asked Rand.

The man hesitated. "Not too well," he said.

"Reach into that box on the tailgate. Find yourself a plate

and some eating implements. A cup, too. Coffee will be ready soon."

"Mister, I wouldn't want you to think I came walking up here..."

"Forget it," said Rand. "I know how it is. There's enough for the both of us."

The man got a plate and cup, a knife, a fork, a spoon. He came over and stood beside the fire.

"I am new at this," he said. "I've never had to do a thing like this before. I always had a job. For seventeen years I had a job..."

"Here you are," said Rand. He slid the eggs onto the plate, went back to the box to get three more.

The man walked over to a picnic table and put down his plate. "Don't wait for me," said Rand. "Eat them while they're hot. The coffee's almost ready. There's bread if you want any."

"I'll get a slice later," said the man, "for mopping up."

John Sterling, he said his name was, and where now would John Sterling be, Rand wondered—still tramping the highways, looking for work, any kind of work, a day of work, an hour of work, a man who for seventeen years had held a job and had a job no longer? Thinking of Sterling, he felt a pang of guilt. He owed John Sterling a debt he never could repay, not knowing at the time they talked there was any debt involved.

They had sat and talked, eating their eggs, mopping up the plates with bread, drinking hot coffee.

"For seventeen years," said Sterling. "A machine operator. An experienced hand. With the same company. Then they let me out. Me and four hundred others. All at one time. Later they let out others. I was not the only one. There were a lot of us. We weren't laid off, we were let out. No promise of going back. Not the company's fault, I guess. There was a big contract that fizzled out. There was no work to do. How about yourself? You let out, too?"

Rand nodded. "How did you know?"

"Well, eating like this. Cheaper than a restaurant. And you got a sleeping bag. You sleep in the car?"

"That is right," said Rand. "It's not as bad for me as it is for some of the others. I have no family."

"I have a family," said Sterling. "Wife, three kids. We

talked it over, the wife and me. She didn't want me to leave, but it made sense I should. Money all gone, unemployment run out. Long as I was around, it was hard to get relief. But if I deserted her, she could get relief. Hardest thing I ever did. Hard for all of us. Someday I'll go back. When times get better, I'll go back. The family will be waiting."

Out on the highway the cars went whisking past. A squirrel came down out of a tree, advanced cautiously toward the table, suddenly turned and fled for his very life, swarming up a nearby tree trunk.

"I don't know," said Sterling. "It might be too big for us, this society of ours. It may be out of hand. I read a lot. Always liked to read. And I think about what I read. It seems to me maybe we've outrun our brains. The brains we have maybe were OK back in prehistoric days. We did all right with the brains we had until we built too big and complex. Maybe we built beyond our brains. Maybe our brains no longer are good enough to handle what we have. We have set loose economic forces we don't understand and political forces that we don't understand, and if we can't understand them, we can't control them. Maybe that is why you and I are out of jobs."

"I wouldn't know," said Rand. "I never thought about it."

"A man thinks a lot," said Sterling. "He dreams a lot walking down the road. Nothing else to do. He dreams some silly things: Things that are silly on the face of them, but are hard to say can't be really true. Did this ever happen to you?"

"Sometimes," said Rand.

"One thing I thought about a lot. A terribly silly thought. Maybe thinking it because I do so much walking. Sometimes people pick me up, but mostly I walk. And I got to wondering if a man should walk far enough could he leave it all behind? The farther a man might walk, the farther he would be from everything."

"Where you heading?" Rand asked.

"Nowhere in particular. Just keep on moving, that is all. Month or so I'll start heading south. Get a good head start on winter. These northern states are no place to be when winter comes."

"There are two eggs left," said Rand. "How about it?"

"Hell, man, I can't. I already..."

"Three eggs aren't a lot. I can get some more."

"Well, if you're sure that you don't mind. Tell you what—let's split them, one for you, one for me."

The giddy old lady had finished cutting her bouquet and had gone into the house. From up the street came the tapping of a cane—Rand's other ancient neighbor, out for his evening walk. The sinking sun poured a blessing on the land. The leaves were gold and red, brown and yellow—they had been that way since the day that Rand had come. The grass had a tawny look about it—not dead, just dressed up for dying.

The old man came trudging carefully down the walk, his cane alert against a stumble, helping himself with it without really needing any help. He was slow, was all. He halted by the walk that ran up to the porch. "Good afternoon," he said. "Good afternoon," said Rand. "You have a nice day for your walk." The old man acknowledged the observation graciously and with a touch of modesty, as if he, himself, might somehow be responsible for the goodness of the day. "It looks," he said, "as if we might have another fine day tomorrow." And having said that, he continued down the street.

It was ritual. The same words were said each day. The situation, like the village and the weather, never varied. He could sit here on this porch a thousand years, Rand told himself, and the old man would continue going past and each time the selfsame words would be mouthed—a set piece, a strip of film run over and over again. Something here had happened to time. The year had stuck on autumn.

Rand did not understand it. He did not try to understand it. There was no way for him to try. Sterling had said that man's cleverness might have outstripped his feeble, prehistoric mind—or, perhaps, his brutal and prehistoric mind. And here there was less chance of understanding than there had been back in that other world.

He found himself thinking of that other world in the same myth-haunted way as he thought of this one. The one now seemed as unreal as the other. Would he ever, Rand wondered, find reality again? Did he want to find it?

There was a way to find reality, he knew. Go into the house and take out the photos in the drawer of his bedside table and have a look at them. Refresh his memory, stare reality in the face again. For those photos, grim as they might be, were a harder reality than this world in which he sat or the world that he had known. For they were nothing seen by the human eye, interpreted by the human brain. They were, somehow, fact. The camera saw what it saw and could not lie about it; it did not fantasize, it did not rationalize, and it had no faulty memory, which was more than could be said of the human mind.

He had gone back to the camera shop where he had left the film and the clerk had picked out the envelope from the box behind the counter.

"That will be three ninety-five," he said.

Rand took a five-dollar bill out of his wallet and laid it on the counter.

"If you don't mind my asking," said the clerk, "where did you get these pictures?"

"It is trick photography," said Rand.

The clerk shook his head. "If that is what they are, they're the best I've ever seen."

The clerk rang up the sale and leaving the register open, stepped back and picked up the envelope.

"What do you want?" asked Rand.

The man shook the prints out of the envelope, shuffled through them.

"This one," he said.

Rand stared at him levelly. "What about it?" he asked.

"The people. I know some of them. The one in front. That is Bob Gentry. He is my best friend."

"You must be mistaken," Rand said coldly.

He took the prints from the clerk's fingers, put them back in the envelope.

The clerk made the change. He still was shaking his head, confused, perhaps a little frightened, when Rand left the shop.

He drove carefully, but with no loss of time, through the city and across the bridge. When he hit open country beyond the river, he built up his speed, keeping an eye on the rear-vision mirror. The clerk had been upset, perhaps enough to phone the police. Others would have seen the pictures and been upset as well. Although, he told himself, it was silly to think of the police. In taking the photos, he had broken no regulations, violated no laws. He had had a perfect right to take them.

Across the river and twenty miles down the highway, he

turned off into a small, dusty country road and followed it until he found a place to pull off, where the road widened at the approach to a bridge that crossed a small stream. There was evidence that the pull-off was much used, fishermen more than likely parking their cars there while they tried their luck. But now the place was empty.

He was disturbed to find that his hands were shaking when he pulled the envelope from his pocket and shook out the prints.

And there it was—as he no longer could remember it.

He was surprised that he had taken as many pictures as he had. He could not remember having taken half that many. But they were there, and as he looked at them, his memory, reinforced, came back again, although the photos were much sharper than his memory. The world, he recalled, had seemed to be hazed and indistinct so far as his eyes had been concerned; in the photos it lay cruel and merciless and clear. The blackened stumps stood up, stark and desolate, and there could be no doubt that the imprint that lay upon the photos was the actuality of a bombed-out city. The photos of the bluff showed the barren rock no longer masked by trees, with only here and there the skeletons of trees that by some accidental miracle had not been utterly reduced by the storm of fire. There was only one photo of the band of people who had come charging down the hill toward him; and that was understandable, for once having seen them, he had been in a hurry to get back to the car. Studying the photo, he saw they were much closer than he'd thought. Apparently they had been there all the time, just a little way off, and he had not noticed them in his astonishment at what had happened to the city. If they had been quieter about it, they could have been on top of him and overwhelmed him before he discovered them. He looked closely at the picture and saw that they had been close enough that some of the faces were fairly well defined. He wondered which one of them was the man the clerk back at the camera shop had recognized.

He shuffled the photographs together and slid them back into the envelope and put it in his pocket. He got out of the car and walked down to the edge of the stream. The stream, he saw, was no more than ten feet or so across; but here, below the bridge, it had gathered itself into a pool, and the bank had been trampled bare of vegetation, and there were places where fishermen had sat. Rand sat down in one of these places and inspected the pool. The current came in close against the bank and probably had undercut it, and lying there, in the undercut, would be the fish that the now-absent anglers sought, dangling their worms at the end of a long cane pole and waiting for a bite.

The place was pleasant and cool, shaded by a great oak that grew on the bank just below the bridge. From some far-off field came the subdued clatter of a mower. The water dimpled as a fish came up to suck in a floating insect. A good place to stay, thought Rand. A place to sit and rest awhile. He tried to blank his mind, to wipe out the memory and the photos, to pretend that nothing at all had happened, that there was nothing he must think about.

But there was, he found, something that he must think about. Not about the photos, but something that Sterling had said just the day before. "I got to wondering," he said, "if a man should walk far enough, could he leave it all behind."

How desperate must a man get, Rand wondered, before he would be driven to asking such a question. Perhaps not desperate at all—just worried and alone and tired and not being able to see the end of it. Either that, or afraid of what lay up ahead. Like knowing, perhaps, that in a few years' time (and not too many years, for in that photo of the people the clerk had seen a man he knew) a warhead would hit a little Iowa town and wipe it out. Not that there was any reason for it being hit; it was no Los Angeles, no New York, no Washington, no busy port, no center of transportation or communication, held no great industrial complex, was no seat of government. Simply hit because it had been there, hit by blunder, by malfunction, or by miscalculation. Although it probably didn't matter greatly, for by the time it had been hit, the nation and perhaps the world might have been gone. A few years, Rand told himself, and it would come to that. After all the labor, all the hopes and dreams, the world would come to just that.

It was the sort of thing that a man might want to walk away from, hoping that in time he might forget it ever had been there. But to walk away, he thought, rather idly, one would have to find a starting point. You could not walk away from everything by just starting anywhere.

It was an idle thought, sparked by the memory of his talk

with Sterling; and he sat there, idly, on the stream bank; and because it had a sense of attractive wonder, he held it in his mind, not letting go at once as one did with idle thoughts. And as he sat there, still holding it in mind, another thought, another time and place crept in to keep it company; and suddenly he knew, with no doubt at all, without really thinking, without searching for an answer, that he knew the place where he could start.

He stiffened and sat rigid, momentarily frightened, feeling like a fool trapped by his own unconscious fantasy. For that, said common sense, was all that it could be. The bitter wondering of a beaten man as he tramped the endless road looking for a job, the shock of what the photos showed, some strange, mesmeric quality of this shaded pool that seemed a place apart from a rock-hard world—all of these put together had produced the fantasy.

Rand hauled himself erect and turned back toward the car, but as he did he could see within his mind this special starting place. He had been a boy—how old, he wondered, maybe nine or ten—and he had found the little valley (not quite a glen, yet not quite a valley, either) running below his uncle's farm down toward the river. He had never been there before and he had never gone again; on his uncle's farm there had been too many chores, too many things to do to allow the time to go anywhere at all. He tried to recall the circumstances of being there and found that he could not. All that he could remember was a single magic moment, as if he had been looking at a single frame of a movie film—a single frame impressed upon his memory because of what? Because of some peculiar angle at which the light had struck the landscape? Because for an instant he had seen with different eyes than he'd ever used before or since? Because for the fractional part of a second he had sensed a simple truth behind the facade of the ordinary world? No matter what, he knew, he had seen magic in that moment.

He went back to the car and sat behind the wheel, staring at the bridge and sliding water and the field beyond, but seeing, instead of them, the map inside his head. When he went back to the highway, he'd turn left instead of right, back toward the river and the town, and before he reached them he would turn north on another road and the valley of the magic moment would be only a little more than a hundred miles away. He sat and saw the map and purpose hardened in his mind. Enough of this silliness, he thought: there were no magic moments, never had been one; when he reached the highway, he'd turn to the right and hope the job might still be there when he reached Chicago.

When he reached the highway, he turned not right, but left.

It had been so easy to find, he thought as he sat on the porch. There had been no taking of wrong roads, no stopping for directions; he'd gone directly there as if he'd always known he would be coming back and had kept the way in mind. He had parked the car at the hollow's mouth, since there was no road, and had gone on foot up the little valley. It could so easily have been that he would not have found the place, he told himself, admitting now for the first time since it all began that he might not have been so sure as he had thought he was. He might have gone up the full length of the valley and not have found the magic ground, or he might have passed it by, seeing it with other eyes and not recognizing it.

But it still was there, and he had stopped and looked at it and known it; again he was only nine or ten, and it was right, the magic still was there. He had found a path he had not seen before and had followed it, the magic still remaining; and when he reached the hilltop, the village had been there. He had walked down the street in the quietness of the golden sunshine, and the first person that he had seen had been the old lady waiting at the gate of her picket fence, as if she had been told that he would be coming.

After he had left her house he went across the street to the house she said was his. As he came in the front door, there was someone knocking at the back.

"I am the Milkman," the knocker had explained. He was a shadowy sort of person; you could not really see him; when one looked away and then looked back at him, it was as if one were seeing someone he had never seen before.

"Milkman," Rand had said. "Yes, I suppose I could do with milk."

"Also," said the Milkman, "I have eggs, bread, butter, bacon and other things that you will need. Here is a can of oil;

you'll need it for your lamps. The woodshed is well stocked, and when there's need of it, I'll replenish it. The kindling's to the left as you go through the door."

Rand recalled that he'd never paid the Milkman or even mentioned payment. The Milkman was not the kind of man to whom one mentioned money. There was no need, either, to leave an order slip in the milkbox; the Milkman seemed to know what one might need and when without being told. With some shame, Rand remembered the time he had mentioned garden seeds and caused embarrassment, not only for the Milkman, but for himself as well. For as soon as he mentioned them, he had sensed that he'd broken some very subtle code of which he should have been aware.

The day was fading into evening, and he should be going in soon to cook himself a meal. And after that, what? he wondered. There still were books to read, but he did not want to read them. He could take out from the desk the plan he had laid out for the garden and mull over it a while, but now he knew he'd never plant the garden. You didn't plant a garden in a forever-autumn land, and there were no seeds.

Across the street a light blossomed in the windows of that great front room with its massive furniture, its roomy window seats, the great fireplace flaring to the ceiling. The old man with the cane had not returned, and it was getting late for him. In the distance now Rand could hear the sounds of children playing in the dusk.

The old and young, he thought. The old, who do not care; the young, who do not think. And what was he doing here, neither young nor old?

He left the porch and went down the walk. The street was empty, as it always was. He drifted slowly down it, heading toward the little park at the village edge. He often went there, to sit on a bench beneath the friendly trees; and it was there, he was sure, that he would find the children. Although why he should think that he would find them there he did not know, for he had never found them, but only heard their voices.

He went past the houses, standing sedately in the dusk. Had people ever lived in them, he wondered. Had there ever been that many people in this nameless village? The old lady across the street spoke of friends she once had known, of people who had lived here and had gone away. But was this her memory speaking or the kind befuddlement of someone growing old?

The houses, he had noted, all were in good repair. A loose shingle here and there, a little peeling paint, but no windows broken, no loosened gutters, sagging from the eaves, no rotting porch posts. As if, he thought, good householders had been here until recently.

He reached the park and could see that it was empty. He still heard the childish voices, crying at their play, but they had receded and now came from somewhere just beyond the park. He crossed the park and stood at its edge, staring off across the scrub and abandoned fields.

In the east the moon was rising, a full moon that lighted the landscape so that he could see every little clump of bushes, every grove of trees. And as he stood there, he realized with a sudden start that the moon was full again, that it was always full. It rose with the setting of the sun and set just before the sun came up, and it was always a great pumpkin of a moon, an eternal harvest moon shining on an eternal autumn world.

The realization that this was so all at once seemed shocking. How was it that he had never noticed this before? Certainly he had been here long enough, had watched the moon often enough to have noticed it. He had been here long enough—and how long had that been, a few weeks, a few months, a year? He found he did not know. He tried to figure back and there was no way to figure back. There were no temporal landmarks. Nothing ever happened to mark one day from the next. Time flowed so smoothly and so uneventfully that it might as well stand still.

The voices of the playing children had been moving from him, becoming fainter in the distance; and as he listened to them, he found that he was hearing them in his mind when they were no longer there. They had come and played and now had ceased their play. They would come again, if not tomorrow night, in another night or two. It did not matter, he admitted, if they came or not, for they really weren't there.

He turned heavily about and went back through the streets. As he approached his house, a dark figure moved out from the shadow of the trees and stood waiting for him. It was the old lady from across the street. It was evident that she had been waiting his return.

"Good evening, ma'am," he said gravely. "It is a pleasant night."

"He is gone," she said. "He did not come back. He went just like the others and he won't come back."

"You mean the old man."

"Our neighbor," she said. "The old man with the cane. I do not know his name. I never knew his name. And I don't know yours."

"I told it to you once," said Rand, but she paid him no attention.

"Just a few doors up the street," she said, "and I never knew his name and I doubt that he knew mine. We are a nameless people here, and it is a terrible thing to be a nameless person."

"I will look for him," said Rand. "He may have lost his way."

"Yes, go and look for him," she said. "By all means look for him. It will ease your mind. It will take away the guilt. But you will never find him."

He took the direction that he knew the old man always took. He had the impression that his ancient neighbor, on his daily walks, went to the town square and the deserted business section, but he did not know. At no other time had it ever seemed important where he might have gone on his walks.

When he emerged into the square, he saw, immediately, the dark object lying on the pavement and recognized it as the old man's hat. There was no sign of the man himself.

Rand walked out into the square and picked up the hat. He gently reshaped and creased it and after that was done held it carefully by the brim so that it would come to no further damage.

The business section drowsed in the moonlight. The statue of the unknown man stood darkly on its base in the center of the square. When he first had come here, Rand recalled, he had tried to unravel the identity of the statue and had failed. There was no legend carved into the granite base, no bronze plate affixed. The face was undistinguished, the stony costume gave no hint as to identity or period. There was nothing in the posture or the attitude of the carven body to provide a clue. The statue stood, a forgotten tribute to some unknown mediocrity.

As he gazed about the square at the business houses, Rand was struck again, as he always was, by the carefully unmodern makeup of the establishments. A barber shop, a meat market, a blacksmith shop—no garage, no service station, no pizza parlor, no hamburger joint. The houses along the quiet streets told the story; here it was emphasized. This was an old town, forgotten and by-passed by the sweep of time, a place of another century. But there was about it all what seemed to be a disturbing sense of unreality, as if it were no old town at all, but a place deliberately fashioned in such a manner as to represent a segment of the past.

Rand shook his head. What was wrong with him tonight? Most of the time he was quite willing to accept the village for what it seemed to be, but tonight he was assailed with uneasy doubt.

Across the square he found the old man's cane. If his neighbor had come in this direction, he reasoned, he must have crossed the square and gone on down the street nearest to the place where he had dropped the cane. But why had he dropped the cane? First his hat and then his cane. What had happened here?

Rand glanced around, expecting that he might catch some movement, some furtive lurker on the margin of the square. There was nothing. If there had been something earlier, there was nothing now.

Following the street toward which his neighbor might have been heading, he walked carefully and alert, watching the shadows closely. The shadows played tricks on him, conjuring up lumpy objects that could have been a fallen man, but weren't. A half a dozen times he froze when he thought he detected something moving, but it was, in each case, only an illusion of the shadows.

When the village ended, the street continued as a path. Rand hesitated, trying to plan his action. The old man had lost his hat and cane, and the points where he dropped them argued that he had intended going down the street that Rand had followed. If he had come down the street he might have continued down the path, out of the village and away from it, perhaps fleeing from something in the village.

There was no way one could be sure, Rand knew. But he

was here and might as well go on for at least a ways. The old
man might be out there somewhere, exhausted, perhaps
terribly frightened, perhaps fallen beside the path and
needing help.

Rand forged ahead. The path, rather well-defined at first,
became fainter as it wound its way across the rolling moonlit
countryside. A flushed rabbit went bobbing through the
grass. Far off an owl chortled wickedly. A faint chill wind
came out of the west. And with the wind came a sense of
loneliness, of open empty space untenanted by anything
other than rabbit, owl and wind.

The path came to an end, its faintness finally pinching out
to nothing. The groves of trees and thickets of low-growing
shrubs gave way to a level plain of blowing grass, bleached to
whiteness by the moon, a faceless prairie land. Staring out
across it, Rand knew that this wilderness of grass would run
on and on forever. It had in it the scent and taste of
foreverness. He shuddered at the sight of it and wondered
why a man should shudder at a thing so simple. But even as
he wondered, he knew—the grass was staring back at him; it
knew him and waited patiently for him, for in time he would
come to it. He would wander into it and be lost in it,
swallowed by its immensity and anonymity.

He turned and ran, unashamedly, chill of blood and
brain, shaken to the core. When he reached the outskirts of
the village, he finally stopped the running and turned to look
back into the wasteland. He had left the grass behind, but he
sensed illogically that it was stalking him, flowing forward,
still out of sight, but soon to appear, with the wind blowing
billows in its whiteness.

He ran again, but not so fast and hard this time, jogging
down the street. He came into the square and crossed it, and
when he reached his house, he saw that the house across the
street was dark. He did not hesitate, but went down the street
he'd walked when he first came to the village. For he knew
now that he must leave this magic place with its strange and
quiet old village, its forever autumn and eternal harvest
moon, its faceless sea of grass, its children who receded in the
distance when one went to look for them, its old man who
walked into oblivion, dropping hat and cane—that he must
somehow find his way back to that other world where few
jobs existed and men walked the road to find them, where

nasty little wars flared in forgotten corners and a camera caught on film the doom that was to come.

He left the village behind him and knew that he had not far to go to reach the place where the path swerved to the right and down a broken slope into the little valley to the magic starting point he'd found again after many years. He went slowly and carefully so that he would not wander off the path, for as he remembered it the path was very faint. It took much longer than he had thought to reach the point where the path swerved to the right into the broken ground, and the realization grew upon him that the path did not swing to the right and there was no broken ground.

In front of him he saw the grass again and there was no path leading into it. He knew that he was trapped, that he would never leave the village until he left it as the old man had, walking out of it and into nothingness. He did not move closer to the grass, for he knew there was terror there and he'd had enough of terror. You're a coward, he told himself.

Retracing the path back to the village, he kept a sharp lookout, going slowly so that he'd not miss the turnoff if it should be there. It was not, however. It once had been, he told himself, bemused, and he'd come walking up it, out of that other world he'd fled.

The village street was dappled by the moonlight shining through the rustling leaves. The house across the street still was dark, and there was an empty loneliness about it. Rand remembered that he had not eaten since the sandwich he had made that noon. There's be something in the milkbox—he'd not looked in it that morning, or had he? He could not remember.

He went around the house to the back porch where the milkbox stood. The Milkman was standing there. He was more shadowy than ever, less well defined, with the moonlight shining on him, and his face was deeply shaded by the wide-brimmed hat he wore.

Rand halted abruptly and stood looking at him, astounded that the Milkman should be there. For he was out of place in the autumn moonlight. He was a creature of the early morning hours and of no other times.

"I came," the Milkman said, "to determine if I could be of help."

Rand said nothing. His head buzzed large and misty, and

there was nothing to be said.

"A gun," the Milkman suggested. "Perhaps you would like a gun."

"A gun? Why should I want one?"

"You have had a most disturbing evening. You might feel safer, more secure, with a gun in hand, a gun strapped about your waist."

Rand hesitated. Was there mockery in the Milkman's voice?

"Or a cross."

"A cross?"

"A crucifix. A symbol..."

"No," said Rand. "I do not need a cross."

"A volume of philosophy, perhaps."

"No!" Rand shouted at him. "I left all that behind. We tried to use them all, we relied on them and they weren't good enough and now..."

He stopped, for that had not been what he'd meant to say, if in fact he'd meant to say anything at all. It was something that he'd never even thought about; it was as if someone inside of him were speaking through his mouth.

"Or perhaps some currency?"

"You are making fun of me," Rand said bitterly, "and you have no right..."

"I merely mention certain things," the Milkman said, "upon which humans place reliance..."

"Tell me one thing," said Rand, "as simply as you can. Is there any way of going back?"

"Back to where you came from?"

"Yes," said Rand. "That is what I mean."

"There is nothing to go back to," the Milkman said. "Anyone who comes has nothing to go back to."

"But the old man left. He wore a black felt hat and carried a cane. He dropped them and I found them."

"He did not go back," the Milkman said. "He went ahead. And do not ask me where, for I do not know."

"But you're a part of this."

"I am a humble servant. I have a job to do and I try to do it well. I care for our guests the best that I am able. But there comes a time when each of our guests leaves us. I would suspect this is a halfway house on the road to someplace else."

"A place for getting ready," Rand said.

"What do you mean?" the Milkman asked.

"I am not sure," said Rand. "I had not meant to say it." And this was the second time, he thought, that he'd said something he had not meant to say.

"There's one comfort about this place," the Milkman said. "One good thing about it you should keep in mind. In this village nothing ever happens."

He came down off the porch and stood upon the walk. "You spoke of the old man," he said, "and it was not the old man only. The old lady also left us. The two of them stayed on much beyond their time."

"You mean I'm here all alone?"

The Milkman had started down the walk, but now he stopped and turned. "There'll be others coming," he said. "There are always others coming."

What was it Sterling had said about man outrunning his brain capacity? Rand tried to recall the words, but now, in the confusion of the moment, he had forgotten them. But if that should be the case, if Sterling had been right (no matter how he had phrased his thought), might not man need, for a while, a place like this, where nothing ever happened, where the moon was always full and the year was stuck on autumn?

Another thought intruded and Rand swung about, shouting in sudden panic at the Milkman. "But these others? Will they talk to me? Can I talk with them? Will I know their names?"

The Milkman had reached the gate by now and it appeared that he had not heard.

The moonlight was paler than it had been. The eastern sky was flushed. Another matchless autumn day was about to dawn.

Rand went around the house. He climbed the steps that led up to the porch. He sat down in the rocking chair and began waiting for the others.

The Ghost Of A Model T

He was walking home when he heard the Model T again. It was not a sound that he could well mistake, and it was not the first time he had heard it running, in the distance, on the road. Although it puzzled him considerably, for so far as he knew, no one in the country had a Model T. He'd read somewhere, in a paper more than likely, that old cars such as Model T's, were fetching a good price, although why this should be, he couldn't figure out. With all the smooth, sleek cars that there were today, who in their right mind would want a Model T? But there was no accounting, in these crazy times, for what people did. It wasn't like the old days, but the old days were long gone, and a man had to get along the best he could with the way that things were now.

Brad had closed up the beer joint early, and there was no place to go but home, although since Old Bounce had died he rather dreaded to go home. He certainly did miss Bounce, he told himself; they'd got along just fine, the two of them, for more than twenty years, but now, with the old dog gone, the house was a lonely place and had an empty sound.

He walked along the dirt road out at the edge of town, his feet scuffing in the dust and kicking at the clods. The night was almost as light as day, with a full moon above the treetops. Lonely cricket noises were heralding summer's end. Walking along, he got to remembering the Model T he'd had when he'd been a young sprout, and how he'd spent hours out in the old machine shed tuning it up, although, God knows, no Model T ever really needed tuning. It was about as simple a piece of mechanism as anyone could want, and despite some technological cantankerousness, about as faithful a car as ever had been built. It got you there and got you back, and that was all, in those days, that anyone could ask. Its fenders rattled, and its hard tires bounced, and it could be balky on a hill, but if you knew how to handle it and mother it along, you never had no trouble.

Those were the days, he told himself, when everything had been as simple as a Model T. There were no income taxes (although, come to think of it, for him, personally, income taxes had never been a problem), no social security that took part of your wages, no licensing this and that, no laws that said a beer joint had to close at a certain hour. It had been easy, then, he thought; a man just fumbled along the best way he could, and there was no one telling him what to do or getting in his way.

The sound of the Model T, he realized, had been getting louder all the time, although he had been so busy with his thinking that he'd paid no real attention to it. But now, from the sound of it, it was right behind him, and although he knew it must be his imagination, the sound was so natural and so close that he jumped to one side of the road so it wouldn't hit him.

It came up beside him and stopped, and there it was, as big as life, and nothing wrong with it. The front-right-hand door (the only door in front, for there was no door on the left-hand side) flapped open—just flapped open by itself, for there was no one in the car to open it. The door flapping open didn't surprise him any, for to his recollection, no one who owned a Model T ever had been able to keep that front door closed. It was held only by a simple latch, and every time the car bounced (and there was seldom a time it wasn't bouncing, considering the condition of the roads in those days, the hardness of the tires, and the construction of the springs)— everytime the car bounced, that damn front door came open.

This time, however—after all these years—there seemed to be something special about how the door came open. It seemed to be a sort of invitation, the car coming to a stop and the door not just sagging open, but coming open with a flourish, as if it were inviting him to step inside the car.

So he stepped inside of it and sat down on the right-front seat, and as soon as he was inside, the door closed and the car began rolling down the road. He started moving over to get behind the wheel, for there was no one driving it, and a curve was coming up, and the car needed someone to steer it around the curve. But before he could move over and get his hands upon the wheel, the car began to take the curve as neatly as it would have with someone driving it. He sat astonished and did not touch the wheel, and it went around the curve without even hesitating, and beyond the curve was a long, steep hill, and the engine labored mightily to achieve the speed to attack the hill.

The funny thing about it, he told himself, still half-crouched to take the wheel and still not touching it, was that he knew this road by heart, and there was no curve or hill on it. The road ran straight for almost three miles before it joined the River Road, and there was not a curve or kink in it, and certainly no hill. But there had been a curve, and there was a hill, for the car laboring up it quickly lost its speed and had to shift to low.

Slowly he straightened up and slid over to the right-hand side of the seat, for it was quite apparent that this Model T, for whatever reason, did not need a driver—perhaps did better with no driver. It seemed to know where it was going, and he told himself, this was more than he knew, for the country, while vaguely familiar, was not the country that lay about the little town of Willow Bend. It was rough and hilly country, and Willow Bend lay on a flat, wide floodplain of the river, and there were no hills and no rough ground until you reached the distant bluffs that stood above the valley.

He took off his cap and let the wind blow through his hair, and there was nothing to stop the wind, for the top of the car was down. The car gained the top of the hill and started going down, wheeling carefully back and forth down the switchbacks that followed the contour of the hill. Once it started down, it shut off the ignition somehow, just the way he used to do, he remembered, when he drove his Model T. The cylinders slapped and slobbered prettily, and the engine cooled.

As the car went around a looping bend that curved above a deep, black hollow that ran between the hills, he caught the fresh, sweet scent of fog, and that scent woke old memories in him, and if he'd not known differently, he would have thought he was back in the country of his young manhood. For in the wooded hills where he'd grown up, fog came creeping up a valley of a summer evening, carrying with it the smells of cornfields and of clover pastures and many other intermingled scents abstracted from a fat and fertile land. But it could not be, he knew, the country of his early years, for that country lay far off and was not to be reached in less than an hour of travel. Although he was somewhat puzzled by exactly where he could be, for it did not seem the kind of country that could be found within striking distance of the town of Willow Bend.

The car came down off the hill and ran blithely up a valley road. It passed a farmhouse huddled up against the hill, with two lighted windows gleaming, and off to one side the shadowy shapes of barn and henhouse. A dog came out and barked at them. There had been no other houses, although, far off, on the opposite hills, he had seen a pinpoint of light here and there and was sure that they were farms. Nor had they met any other cars, although, come to think of it, that was not so strange, for out here in the farming country there were late chores to do, and bedtime came early for people who were out at the crack of dawn. Except on weekends, there'd not be much traffic on a country road.

The Model T swung around a curve, and there, up ahead, was a garish splash of light, and as they came closer, music could be heard. There was about it all an old familiarity that nagged at him, but as yet he could not tell why it seemed familiar. The Model T slowed and turned in at the splash of light, and now it was clear that the light came from a dance pavilion. Strings of bulbs ran across its front, and other lights were mounted on tall poles in the parking area. Through the lighted windows he could see the dancers; and the music, he realized, was the kind of music he'd not heard for more than half a century. The Model T ran smoothly into a parking spot beside a Maxwell touring car. A Maxwell touring car, he thought with some surprise. There hadn't been a Maxwell on the road for years. Old Virg once had owned a Maxwell, at the same time he had owned his Model T. Old Virg, he thought. So many years ago. He tried to recall Old Virg's last name, but it wouldn't come to him. Of late, it seemed, names were often hard to come by. His name had been Virgil, but his friends always called him Virg. They'd been together quite a lot, the two of them, he remembered, running off to dances, drinking moonshine whiskey, playing pool, chasing girls— all the things that young sprouts did when they had the time and money.

He opened the door and got out of the car, the crushed gravel of the parking lot crunching underneath his feet; and the crunching of the gravel triggered the recognition of the place, supplied the reason for the familiarity that had first eluded him. He stood stock-still, half-frozen at the knowledge, looking at the ghostly leafiness of the towering elm trees that grew to either side of the dark bulk of the pavilion. His eyes took in the contour of the looming hills, and he recognized the contour, and standing there, straining for the sound, he heard the gurgle of the rushing water that came out of the hill, flowing through a wooden channel into a wayside watering trough that was now falling apart with neglect, no longer needed since the automobile had taken over from the horse-drawn vehicles of some years before.

He turned and sat down weakly on the running board of the Model T. His eyes could not deceive him or his ears betray him. He'd heard the distinctive sound of that running water too often in years long past to mistake it now; and the loom of the elm trees, the contour of the hills, the graveled parking lot, the string of bulbs on the pavilion's front, taken all together, could only mean that somehow he had returned or been returned, to Big Spring Pavilion. But that, he told himself, was fifty years or more ago, when I was lithe and young, when Old Virg had his Maxwell and I my Model T.

He found within himself a growing excitement that surged above the wonder and the sense of absurd impossibility—an excitement that was as puzzling as the place itself and his being there again. He rose and walked across the parking lot, with the coarse gravel rolling and sliding and crunching underneath his feet, and there was a strange lightness in his body, the kind of youthful lightness he had not known for years, and as the music came welling out at him, he found that he was gliding and turning to the music. Not the kind of music the kids played nowadays, with all the racket amplified by electronic contraptions, not the grating, no-rhythm junk that set one's teeth on edge and turned the morons glassy-eyed, but music with a beat to it, music you could dance to with a certain haunting quality that was no longer heard. The saxophone sounded clear, full-throated; and a sax, he told himself, was an instrument all but forgotten now. But it was here, and the music to go with it, and the bulbs above the door swaying in the little breeze that came drifting up the valley.

He was halfway through the door when he suddenly remembered that the pavilion was not free, and he was about to get some change out of his pocket (what little there was left after all those beers he'd had at Brad's) when he noticed the inky marking of the stamp on the back of his right hand. That had been the way, he remembered, that they'd marked you as having paid your way into the pavilion, a stamp placed on your hand. He showed his hand with its inky marking to the man who stood beside the door and went on in. The pavilion was bigger than he'd remembered it. The band sat on a raised platform to one side, and the floor was filled with dancers.

The years fell away, and it all was as he remembered it. The girls wore pretty dresses; there was not a single one who was dressed in jeans. The boys wore ties and jackets, and there was a decorum and a jauntiness that he had forgotten. The man who played the saxophone stood up, and the sax wailed in lonely melody, and there was a magic in the place that he had thought no longer could exist.

He moved out into the magic. Without knowing that he was about to do it, surprised when he found himself doing it, he was out on the floor, dancing by himself, dancing with all the other dancers, sharing in the magic—after all the lonely years, a part of it again. The beat of the music filled the world, and all the world drew in to center on the dance floor, and although there was no girl and he danced all by himself, he remembered all the girls he had ever danced with.

Someone laid a heavy hand on his arm, and someone else was saying, "Oh, for Christ's sake, leave the old guy be; he's just having fun like all the rest of us." The heavy hand was jerked from his arm, and the owner of the heavy hand went staggering out across the floor, and there was a sudden flurry of activity that could not be described as dancing. A girl grabbed him by the hand. "Come on, Pop," she said, "let's get out of here." Someone else was pushing at his back to force him in the direction that the girl was pulling, and then he was out-of-doors. "You better get on your way, Pop," said a young man. "They'll be calling the police. Say, what is your name? Who are you?"

"I am Hank," he said. "My name is Hank, and I used to

come here. Me and Old Virg. We came here a lot. I got a
Model T out in the lot if you want a lift."

"Sure, why not," said the girl. "We are coming with you."

He led the way, and they came behind him, and all piled in
the car, and there were more of them than he had thought
there were. They had to sit on one another's laps to make
room in the car. He sat behind the wheel, but he never
touched it, for he knew the Model T would know what was
expected of it, and of course it did. It started up and wheeled
out of the lot and headed for the road.

"Here, Pop," said the boy who sat beside him, "have a
snort. It ain't the best there is, but it's got a wallop. It won't
poison you; it ain't poisoned any of the rest of us."

Hank took the bottle and put it to his lips. He tilted up his
head and let the bottle gurgle. And if there'd been any doubt
before of where he was, the liquor settled all the doubt. For
the taste of it was a taste that could never be forgotten.
Although it could not be remembered, either. A man had to
taste it once again to remember it.

He took down the bottle and handed it to the one who had
given it to him. "Good stuff," he said.

"Not good," said the young man, "but the best that we
could get. These bootleggers don't give a damn what they sell
you. Way to do it is to make them take a drink before you buy
it, then watch them for a while. If they don't fall down dead or
get blind staggers, then it's safe to drink."

Reaching from the back seat of the car, one of them
handed him a saxophone. "Pop, you look like a man who
could play this thing," said one of the girls, "so give us some
music."

"Where'd you get this thing?" asked Hank.

"We got it off the band," said a voice from the back. "That
joker who was playing it had no right to have it. He was just
abusing it."

Hank put it to his lips and tumbled at the keys, and all at
once the instrument was making music. And it was funny, he
thought, for until right now he'd never held any kind of horn.
He had no music in him. He'd tried a mouth organ once,
thinking it might help to pass away the time, but the sounds
that had come out of it had set Old Bounce to howling. So
he'd put it up on a shelf and had forgotten it till now.

The Model T went tooling down the road, and in a little

time the pavilion was left behind. Hank tootled on the saxophone, astonishing himself at how well he played, while the others sang and passed around the bottle. There were no other cars on the road, and soon the Model T climbed a hill out of the valley and ran along a ridgetop, with all the countryside below a silver dream flooded by the moonlight.

Later on, Hank wondered how long this might have lasted, with the car running through the moonlight on the ridgetop, with him playing the saxophone, interrupting the music only when he laid aside the instrument to have another drink of moon. But when he tried to think of it, it seemed to have gone on forever, with the car eternally running in the moonlight, trailing behind it the wailing and the honking of the saxophone.

He woke to night again. The same full moon was shining, although the Model T had pulled off the road and was parked beneath a tree, so that the full strength of the moonlight did not fall upon him. He worried rather feebly if this might be the same night or a different night, and there was no way for him to tell, although, he told himself, it didn't make much difference. So long as the moon was shining and he had the Model T and a road for it to run on, there was nothing more to ask, and which night it was had no consequence.

The young people who had been with him were no longer there, but the saxophone was laid upon the floorboards, and when he pulled himself erect, he heard a gurgle in his pocket, and upon investigation, pulled out the moonshine bottle. It still was better than half full, and from the amount of drinking that had been done, that seemed rather strange.

He sat quietly behind the wheel, looking at the bottle in his hand, trying to decide if he should have a drink. He decided that he shouldn't, and put the bottle back into his pocket, then reached down and got the saxophone and laid it on the seat beside him.

The Model T stirred to life, coughing and stuttering. It inched forward, somewhat reluctantly, moving from beneath the tree, heading in a broad sweep for the road. It reached the road and went bumping down it. Behind it a thin cloud of dust, kicked up by its wheels, hung silver in the moonlight.

Hank sat proudly behind the wheel, being careful not to touch it. He folded his hands in his lap and leaned back. He felt good—the best he'd ever felt. Well, maybe not the best, he told himself, for back in the time of youth, when he was spry and limber and filled with the juice of hope, there might have been some times when he felt as good as he felt now. His mind went back, searching for the times when he'd felt as good, and out of olden memory came another time, when he'd drunk just enough to give himself an edge, not as yet verging into drunkenness, not really wanting any more to drink, and he'd stood on the gravel of the Big Spring parking lot, listening to the music before going in, with the bottle tucked inside his shirt, cold against his belly. The day had been a scorcher, and he'd been working in the hayfield, but now the night was cool, with fog creeping up the valley, carrying that indefinable scent of the fat and fertile land; and inside, the music playing, and a waiting girl who would have an eye out for the door, waiting for the moment he came in.

It had been good, he thought, that moment snatched out of the maw of time, but no better than this moment, with the car running on the ridgetop road and all the world laid out in moonlight. Different, maybe, in some ways, but no better than this moment.

The road left the ridgetop and went snaking down the bluff face, heading for the valley floor. A rabbit hopped across the road, caught for a second in the feeble headlights. High in the nighttime sky, invisible, a bird cried out, but that was the only sound there was, other than the thumping and the clanking of the Model T.

The car went skittering down the valley, and here the moonlight often was shut out by the woods that came down close against the road.

Then it was turning off the road, and beneath its tires he heard the crunch of gravel, and ahead of him loomed a dark and crouching shape. The car came to a halt, and sitting rigid in the seat, Hank knew where he was.

The Model T had returned to the dance pavilion, but the magic was all gone. There were no lights, and it was deserted. The parking lot was empty. In the silence, as the Model T shut off its engine, he heard the gushing of the water from the hillside spring running into the watering trough.

Suddenly he felt cold and apprehensive. It was lonely here, lonely as only an old remembered place can be when all its life is gone. He stirred reluctantly and climbed out of the car, standing beside it, with one hand resting on it, wondering why the Model T had come here and why he'd gotten out.

A dark figure moved out from the front of the pavilion, an undistinguishable figure slouching in the darkness.

"That you Hank?" a voice asked.

"Yes, it's me," said Hank.

"Christ," the voice asked, "where is everybody?"

"I don't know," said Hank. "I was here just the other night. There were a lot of people then."

The figure came closer. "You wouldn't have a drink, would you?" it asked.

"Sure, Virg," he said, for now he recognized the voice. "Sure, I have a drink."

He reached into his pocket and pulled out the bottle. He handed it to Virg. Virg took it and sat down on the running board. He didn't drink right away, but sat there cuddling the bottle.

"How you been, Hank?" he asked. "Christ, it's a long time since I seen you."

"I'm all right," said Hank. "I drifted up to Willow Bend and just sort of stayed there. You know Willow Bend?"

"I was through it once. Just passing through. Never stopped or nothing. Would have if I'd known you were there. I lost all track of you."

There was something that Hank had heard about Old Virg, and felt that maybe he should mention it, but for the life of him he couldn't remember what it was, so he couldn't mention it.

"Things didn't go so good for me," said Virg. "Not what I had expected. Janet up and left me, and I took to drinking after that and lost the filling station. Then I just knocked around from one thing to another. Never could get settled. Never could latch onto anything worthwhile."

He uncorked the bottle and had himself a drink.

"Good stuff," he said, handing the bottle back to Hank.

Hank had a drink, then sat down on the running board alongside Virg and set the bottle down between them.

"I had a Maxwell for a while," said Virg, "but I seem to have lost it. Forgot where I left it, and I've looked everywhere."

"You don't need your Maxwell, Virg," said Hank. "I have

got this Model T."

"Christ, it's lonesome here," said Virg. "Don't you think it's lonesome?"

"Yes, it's lonesome. Here, have another drink. We'll figure what to do."

"It ain't good sitting here," said Virg. "We should get out among them."

"We'd better see how much gas we have," said Hank. "I don't know what's in the tank."

He got up and opened the front door and put his hand under the front seat, searching for the measuring stick. He found it and unscrewed the gas-tank cap. He began looking through his pockets for matches so he could make a light.

"Here," said Virg, "don't go lighting any matches near that tank. You'll blow us all to hell. I got a flashlight here in my back pocket. If the damn thing's working."

The batteries were weak, but it made a feeble light. Hank plunged the stick into the tank, pulled it out when it hit bottom, holding his thumb on the point that marked the topside of the tank. The stick was wet up almost to his thumb.

"Almost full," said Virg. "When did you fill it last?"

"I ain't never filled it."

Old Virg was impressed. "That old tin lizard," he said, "sure goes easy on the gas."

Hank screwed the cap back on the tank, and they sat down on the running board again, and each had another drink.

"It seems to me it's been lonesome for a long time now," said Virg. "Awful dark and lonesome. How about you, Hank?"

"I been lonesome," said Hank, "ever since Old Bounce up and died on me. I never did get married. Never got around to it. Bounce and me, we went everywhere together. He'd go up to Brad's bar with me and camp out underneath a table; then, when Brad threw us out, he'd walk home with me."

"We ain't doing ourselves no good," said Virg, "just sitting here and moaning. So let's have another drink, then I'll crank the car for you, and we'll be on our way."

"You don't need to crank the car," said Hank. "You just get into it, and it starts up by itself."

"Well, I be damned," said Virg. "You sure have got it trained."

They had another drink and got into the Model T, which started up and swung out of the parking lot, heading for the road.

"Where do you think we should go?" asked Virg. "You know of any place to go?"

"No, I don't," said Hank. "Let the car take us where it wants to. It will know the way."

Virg lifted the sax off the seat and asked, "Where'd this thing come from? I don't remember you could blow a sax."

"I never could before," said Hank. He took the sax from Virg and put it to his lips, and it wailed in anguish, gurgled with light-heartedness.

"I be damned," said Virg. "You do it pretty good."

The Model T bounced merrily down the road, with its fenders flapping and the windshield jiggling, while the magneto coils mounted on the dashboard clicked and clacked and chattered. All the while, Hank kept blowing on the sax and the music came out loud and true, with startled night birds squawking and swooping down to fly across the narrow swath of light.

The Model T went clanking up the valley road and climbed the hill to come out on a ridge, running through the moonlight on a narrow, dusty road between close pasture fences, with sleepy cows watching them pass by.

"I be damned," cried Virg, "if it isn't just like it used to be. The two of us together, running in the moonlight. Whatever happened to us, Hank? Where did we miss out? It's like this now, and it was like this a long, long time ago. Whatever happened to the years between? Why did there have to be any years between?"

Hank said nothing. He just kept blowing on the sax.

"We never asked for nothing much," said Virg. "We were happy as it was. We didn't ask for change. But the old crowd grew away from us. They got married and got steady jobs, and some of them got important. And that was the worst of all, when they got important. We were left alone. Just the two of us, just you and I, the ones who didn't want to change. It wasn't just being young that we were hanging on to. It was something else. It was a time that went with being young and crazy. I think we knew it somehow. And we were right, of course. It was never quite as good again."

The Model T left the ridge and plunged down a long, steep

hill, and below them they could see a massive highway, broad and many-laned, with many car lights moving on it.

"We're coming to a freeway, Hank," said Virg. "Maybe we should sort of veer away from it. This old Model T of yours is a good car, sure, the best there ever was, but that's fast company down there."

"I ain't doing nothing to it," said Hank. "I ain't steering it. It is on its own. It knows what it wants to do."

"Well, all right, what the hell," said Virg, "we'll ride along with it. That's all right with me. I feel safe with it. Comfortable with it. I never felt so comfortable in all my goddamn life. Christ, I don't know what I'd done if you hadn't come along. Why don't you lay down that silly sax and have a drink before I drink it all."

So Hank laid down the sax and had a couple of drinks to make up for lost time, and by the time he handed the bottle back to Virg, the Model T had gone charging up a ramp, and they were on the freeway. It went running gaily down its lane, and it passed some cars that were far from standing still. Its fenders rattled at a more rapid rate, and the chattering of the magneto coils was like machinegun fire.

"Boy," said Virg admiringly, "see the old girl go. She's got life left in her yet. Do you have any idea, Hank, where we might be going?"

"Not the least," said Hank, picking up the sax again.

"Well, hell," said Virg, "it don't really matter, just so we're on our way. There was a sign back there a ways that said Chicago. Do you think we could be headed for Chicago?"

Hank took the sax out of his mouth. "Could be," he said. "I ain't worried over it."

"I ain't worried neither," said Old Virg. "Chicago, here we come! Just so the booze holds out. It seems to be holding out. We've been sucking at it regular, and it's still better than half-full."

"You hungry, Virg?" asked Hank.

"Hell, no," said Virg. "Not hungry, and not sleepy, either. I never felt so good in all my life. Just so the booze holds out and this heap hangs together."

The Model T banged and clattered, running with a pack of smooth, sleek cars that did not bang and clatter, with Hank playing on the saxophone and Old Virg waving the bottle high and yelling whenever the rattling old machine outdistanced a Lincoln or a Cadillac. The moon hung in the sky and did not seem to move. The freeway became a throughway, and the first toll booth loomed ahead.

"I hope you got change," said Virg. "Myself, I am cleaned out."

But no change was needed, for when the Model T came near, the toll-gate arm moved up and let it go thumping through without payment.

"We got it made," yelled Virg. "The road is free for us, and that's the way it should be. After all you and I been through, we got something coming to us."

Chicago loomed ahead, off to their left, with night lights gleaming in the towers that rose along the lakeshore, and they went around it in a long, wide sweep, and New York was just beyond the fishhook bend as they swept around Chicago and the lower curve of the lake.

"I never saw New York," said Virg, "but seen pictures of Manhattan, and that can't be nothing but Manhattan. I never did know, Hank, that Chicago and Manhattan were so close together."

"Neither did I," said Hank, pausing from his tootling on the sax. "The geography's all screwed up for sure, but what the hell do we care? With this rambling wreck, the whole damn world is ours."

He went back to the sax, and the Model T kept rambling on. They went thundering through the canyons of Manhattan and circumnavigated Boston and went on down to Washington, where the Washington Monument stood up high and Old Abe sat brooding on Potomac's shore.

They went on down to Richmond and skated past Atlanta and skimmed along the moon-drenched sands of Florida. They ran along old roads where trees dripped Spanish moss and saw the lights of Old N'Orleans way off to their left. Now they were heading north again, and the car was galumphing along a ridgetop with neat farming country all spread out below them. The moon still stood where it had been before, hanging at the selfsame spot. They were moving through a world where it was always three A.M.

"You know," said Virg, "I wouldn't mind if this kept on forever. I wouldn't mind if we never got to wherever we are going. It's too much fun getting there to worry where we're headed. Why don't you lay down that horn and have another drink? You must be getting powerful dry."

Hank put down the sax and reached out for the bottle. "You know, Virg," he said, "I feel the same way you do. It just don't seem there's any need for fretting about where we're going or what's about to happen. It don't seem that nothing could be better than right now."

Back there at the dark pavilion he'd remembered that there had been something he'd heard about Old Virg and had thought he should speak to him about, but couldn't, for the life of him, remember what it was. But now he'd remembered it, and it was of such slight importance that it seemed scarcely worth the mention.

The thing that he'd remembered was that good Old Virg was dead.

He put the bottle to his lips and had a drink, and it seemed to him he'd never had a drink that tasted half so good. He handed back the bottle and picked up the sax and tootled on it with high spirit while the ghost of the Model T went on rambling down the moonlit road.

SCIENCE FICTION BESTSELLERS FROM BERKLEY

Robert A. Heinlein

THE PAST THROUGH TOMORROW   (03785-1—$2.95)

STRANGER IN A STRANGE LAND   (03782-7—$2.25)

TIME ENOUGH FOR LOVE   (03471-2—$2.25)

Frank Herbert

CHILDREN OF DUNE   (03931-5—$2.25)

DUNE   (03698-7—$2.25)

DUNE MESSIAH   (03930-7—$1.95)

THE SANTAROGA BARRIER   (03824-6—$1.75)

* * * * * * *

BLACK CANNAN   (03711-8—$1.95)
  by Robert E. Howard

SON OF THE WHITE WOLF   (03710-X—$1.95)
  by Robert E. Howard

HAWKSBILL STATION   (03679-0—$1.75)
  by Robert Silverberg

Send for a list of all our books in print.

These books are available at your local bookstore, or send price
indicated plus 30¢ for postage and handling. If more than four books
are ordered, only $1.00 is necessary for postage. Allow three weeks
for delivery. Send orders to:

    Berkley Book Mailing Service
    P.O. Box 690
    Rockville Centre, New York 11570

FANTASY FROM BERKLEY

Robert E. Howard

CONAN: THE HOUR OF THE DRAGON	(03608-1—$1.95)
CONAN: THE PEOPLE OF THE BLACK CIRCLE	(03609-X—$1.95)
CONAN: RED NAILS	(03610-3—$1.95)
MARCHERS OF VALHALLA	(03702-9—$1.95)
ALMURIC	(03483-6—$1.95)
SKULL-FACE	(03708-8—$1.95)
SON OF THE WHITE WOLF	(03710-X—$1.95)
SWORDS OF SHAHRAZAR	(03709-6—$1.95)
BLACK CANAAN	(03711-8—$1.95)

* * * * * * *

THE SWORDS TRILOGY by Michael Moorcock	(03468-2—$1.95)
THONGOR AND THE WIZARD OF LEMURIA by Lin Carter	(03435-6—$1.25)